NO LOVE IN LA

PAGANS & POP STARS
BOOK THREE

KATTA KIS

JOIN MY NEWSLETTER

Keep up with me and my work by signing up for my newsletter! It's once a month with freebies like deleted Angie and Benji scenes from previous books, exclusive behind-the-scenes fun, and no spam. :]

PART ONE
LOS ANGELES

Omegaluvr92: Okay, so I'm new here but what's this about Benji & ANGELA ALICE??

Emoisthenewblack: That's just some old social media stuff. She screwed over our Benji's bestie, RK back in early 2020. B was defending him cuz theyre loyal & what she did was fucked.

Omegaluvr92: What'd she do???

UFObb: google is your friend, just saying. or you could search the channel…

Emoisthenewblack: Be nice, you know the real tea is here. TLDR, RK dumped AA & she IMMEDIATELY dropped a nasty break-up album, fully formed with a movie & everything. So sus.

Omegaluvr92: OMG Romance Inverted, I loved that album! That's what that was about?? WTF

Emoisthenewblack: Ya. So B put her on blast while doing promo for RK's album. We were all over her accounts after that.

UFObb: serves her right, that white trash satanic bitch

Emoisthenewblack: she also pulled her money out of the record, trying to sabotage RK & the record label he started with B.

UFObb: total psychopath behavior

Omegaluvr92: wooooow

Emoisthenewblack: there was some twitter fighting over the pandemic & i heard there some stuff went down at Endfest last summer but its been quiet since.

UFObb: too quiet

Emoisthenewblack: she's been on hiatus or whatever, maybe shes working on herself.

UFObb: no way, she's obsessed i hear she covers ufo songs all the time at shows and you should see her posts when they broke up: [links]

Omegaluvr92: Those posts! She's like one of us but…evil.

Emoisthenewblack: I still think she could retire or something, I heard she went to rehab.

UFObb: dont rag on rehab, our b went there

Emoisthenewblack: not ragging on it, just saying… maybe she's done.

Omegaluvr92: Okay, hear me out though. What if its love tho? She used to be dating all the girls, boys, & theys & now she hasnt dated anyone since RK. Maybe she's *pining* for B

Emoisthenewblack: Or maybe she'll just disappear…

UFObb: lol love yalls optimism, ask the universe to get ufo back together while your at it.

CHAPTER 1

The Bitch is Back

After an extended hiatus to focus on her mental health, the Bitch Queen is back. Infamous Satanic metal singer Angela Alice will play select dates… sometime soon. Dates aren't announced yet except for her headlining Saturday slot at October's MetalQuake 2022 in Sacramento. Rumor is she's working on a new album too. Fans know Alice loves to try her new songs out on her audience so get your tickets now if you want a sneak peek. But we want to know, will she revive her years-long feud with former singer of User-Friendly Omega, current label owner and songwriter, Benji Omega?
—Metal Music Now

Angelica "Angela" Alice paced the conference room, thrumming with energy. It buzzed in her fingertips, hummed in the soles of her feet, and vibrated in her chest. This wasn't show jitters. Performing was a high she threw herself at like a skydiver out of a plane. No, this was the anticipation of the hunt. Would Benji take the bait? Would they come?

It made her fingers curl, this wanting.

She took another lap around the conference room, resisting the urge to chew the red-black lipstick off her bottom lip. There was a view but she couldn't say what it was. No matter the angle of the smoggy LA skyline, she was in full regalia, looking good. With every step of her boots, her skirt, hair, and sleeves trailed like silver-white ghosts behind her. She was dressed for public consumption, for fear and fascination. Serving scary face, as her drummer, Dani would say.

She needed the armor. Something about the way Benji looked at her flayed her down to the girl she'd been when she'd first swooned over their voice on the radio.

She checked her custom, very stripped down, smartwatch, opening the vampire jaws covering the screen. If they were coming, they'd be here any minute. They had a reputation for being timely, early even.

Angie was careful. She pulled together her web of information in a way she would admit was obsessive, bordering on stalkerish if she'd done it intentionally.

She kept herself in check, mostly. She set limits. She didn't know where they lived. She didn't have their phone number, had no way to contact them directly. Hadn't run into them by "accident," hadn't followed them, hadn't seen them really except on social media since the Endfest tour last year.

But then the writer's block came. No words flowed, not since the call about Mama and the looming threat of her getting out. She hadn't produced an album in three years, the label was getting impatient and she just… couldn't.

Until two days ago. She'd been ruminating on the grudge Benji still held against her for certain, well, bad decisions and the way they looked at her, watching when they pretended they weren't and—suddenly—she'd gotten a spark. Benji and her. On a track together. It was all she could think about, and words flowed. Just, not for anything else.

So she'd gotten her manager, Cheryl, to call theirs. See?

Limits. Sure, her manager had been vague about which of her clients wanted to work with Benji but still, limits. Angie had talked to her therapist about those.

Cheryl was outside. Angie could barely hear her speaking to someone through the thick door. Good. No one needed to hear if Angie embarrassed herself in here.

The doorknob clicked, turning.

Angie froze, watching it like it was the end of the world. She almost smiled, because who didn't enjoy a good apocalypse?

The door opened and there they were.

Seeing them, impeccably dressed as always in a tight black suit, tailored to show off the lines of their body made her heart stutter. Benji Omega, the gorgeous singer of User-Friendly Omega she'd fangirled over years ago had been a lithe gender-bent goth with long hair and a heartbreak smile.

Benji post-UFO was even more beautiful. Their long hair was now a short, asymmetrical cut reminiscent of the floppy emo bangs popular when she was in high school. No one looked as good with it as Benji did. Their face was still a heartbreak waiting to happen with that mouth outlined in dark blue lipstick and those dark fringed deep brown eyes ringed with eyeliner, but in person they were so much more dangerous than on stage. The way they walked, somewhere between a saunter and a prowl, the way they moved, both careless and controlled...

In short, Benji "Omega" Nakamura was magnificent and not nearly as surprised as she'd thought they'd be. Had they'd hoped the mysterious artist who wanted to work with them was her?

Their gaze pinned her in place. Or at least it tried. She reminded herself she hadn't been that swooning girl in a long time. Quirking her lips up into the closest she ever got to a smile these days, she sat, gesturing for them to do the same.

Benji paused. It wasn't a hesitation. They were too much of a performer for their movements to be anything but deliberate. It was glorious, watching them sizing up the situation, parsing everything the way she did.

They strode forward but did not sit, instead leaning down and splaying their fingers on the glossy table to look at her, their long silver-tipped black acrylic nails clicking on the varnished wood. Their clothes and make-up were flawless, pitch-black armor. What a picture the two of them must make, a gothic battle scene in black and white.

She bared her teeth, wanting to lean forward to see how close she could get. To see if they'd lean away or if their eyes would dilate with want. But no, she'd barely stopped masking indoors against COVID. She wasn't about to get up in someone's face, even Benji's. Instead, she leaned back and kicked her chunky boots up on the table, letting her artfully shredded skirt fall away from her long legs.

"Oh, hello." She pitched her voice low, letting it run like dark water over the gravel of her scream-rough throat. She'd gotten nearly as many fan comments about her speaking voice as her singing. They'd been exponentially more graphic.

"What the hell, Angelica?" Their tone was flat. They weren't playing along, but damn, it was lovely all the same. A voice like that couldn't be anything but. It was smoldering silk, clear and luxe but with a faint crackle to the edges, threatening to combust at any minute. And the way they always said her full name like she was in trouble? *Mmm.*

"What the hell do you think?" She purred.

"You damn well know I'm not helping you with Rohan."

She waved the name of her ex away. "I've moved on. Ro is not my problem anymore." Rohan was irritatingly happy about it, having moved on with whiplash-inducing speed. Then again she had burned that bridge pretty spectacularly. It was a testament to his ability to forgive that the two of them were back on somewhat awkward speaking terms.

Their eyes narrowed. "Then what's with the cloak and dagger shit?"

She tipped her lips up again, dangerously close to a smile. "Would you come if I asked?"

She thought she saw their pupils flare, dilating for the briefest second before shrinking. Angie's pulse spiked.

"I have good reasons not to," Benji reminded her, their words even.

"Of course you do." She leaned back further, interlacing her fingers over her chest. "I've been an asshole. For years. I know it's cliché, but I'm working on my shit. Seeing a therapist, turning over a new leaf, making amends and reparations, all that."

"Congrats." Benji straightened, towering over her. "Is that all you wanted to tell me?"

A fizzle of anxiety hissed in her mind. Was she losing them? No. Not gonna happen. She needed their help and Mama taught her to never let go of her man. That she wasn't dealing with a man wasn't a problem. Benji was already hooked, she saw it in the way they never took their eyes off her. Like she was dangerous. Like they wanted her.

Benji stared down at her. They should've known their curiosity would get the best of them. They'd been in the industry too long to play cat and mouse games with someone who allegedly wanted to work with them.

"The client prefers to remain anonymous until your meeting," Cheryl had told them when she called. Cheryl was the kind of manager whose clients were so big she didn't bother having a website. Her client list was discrete, the stuff of rumors. People would kill to work with her and do grievous bodily harm to work with her clients.

Benji had almost hung up on her. Unfortunately, they'd been intrigued, curious as to who would try to pull that shit on them. They hadn't had many creative outlets with all the administrative duties of running a small indie label.

In hindsight, they should've known only Angelica would be that brazen, yet sneaky.

Now, they were doing their best not to be caught by the cleavage pushed up by her silver corseted bodice, emphasized by the inverted double-armed cross spanning her chest from the top of her throat to the hollow between her breasts or her endless, pale legs peeking through the shreds of her white skirt. Combined with the way she looked at them, it was dizzying. They flicked their gaze away, their attention snagging on her face, pale and framed by endless silver-white hair. Those red-black lips, those gunmetal grey eyes. She wasn't smiling. They'd never seen her wear a genuine smile, but something about her lips said she could at any minute.

Danger, danger, danger… went the alarm bells in their head. Unfortunately, the usual Klaxon cry was replaced with the purr of Angelica's voice.

They needed to get the hell out of here. So why hadn't they moved?

"I want to work with you." Her voice was an earworm all by itself. She'd sound sexy reading a fucking grocery list. It was disturbing the way everything about her was: like grasping, caressing quicksilver hooks, soft against your skin until they caught and splayed you open like a frog on a dissecting table. Benji had seen it happen many times to other people.

They gave themself a mental shake and raised an eyebrow. She notoriously worked with only the lucky (or unlucky) few artists who'd impressed her. "Who said I wanted to work with you?"

Word on the street was Angela Alice was overdue for her latest album, she hadn't toured in over a year, more than she'd ever gone before, barring the pandemic. Which meant she hadn't been out since Endfest, the last time they had to deal with her.

Her interlaced fingers tightened, already white knuckles paling, making the alchemical symbols inked on her skin stand out. Her eyes were mocking. "Oh, are you happy as a pop writer, Omega?"

The way she spun their old stage name around her tongue was aggravating no matter how many times they heard it. What was worse, she was right. They didn't need work, not with running a label on top of their songwriting gigs but ever since they'd nursed Rohan's album to life the only people calling were Disney stars who wanted to play adult. Nothing wrong with that, but... but they remembered being Benji Omega, tearing emotions from the crowd with the hooks and lines of their angst. None of the agents calling wanted to get that dark. Nobody did really, not anyone who could pay.

Except here was the so-called Bitch Queen of metal offering herself to them. In more than one way, they suspected.

Danger, danger, danger…

"Perfectly happy, Coma White," they lied, suppressing a shiver.

Why the hell had they thought giving her a nickname would give them distance? It was a *reference*, tragic yes, but obscure enough and from the same deeply problematic artist who had influenced them both, making it… well, not quite an in-joke, but something. They should leave. Why weren't they leaving?

"Liar." She stood, pulling something out of a hidden pocket in her silvery-white dress. "But I won't push. I'm playing a secret show tonight, trying out some new material. Come by, if you like." She shrugged, putting two tickets on the table. Angelica looked up at them, so close her skirts brushed their legs. Her monochrome eyes were cold, calculating. "Please."

Then she was gone, leaving Benji staring at the tickets. Something about the way she said *please*... No. No, they weren't falling for whatever scheme she was cooking up.

But they grabbed the tickets anyway. Angela Alice shows were rare these days and that made these valuable. It was a strategic move, that was all. They tucked the tickets away, their fingers buzzing with the contact.

CHAPTER 2

"There is no beginning
There is no end
We go around
Again and again
(all hail all hail)

I am nobody you know
I am everybody you think you do

There is no beginning
There is no end
We go around
Again and again
(there's nothing left)"
— "So It Begins" by User-Friendly Omega off of *Suicide King*

"I don't know what to wear." An hour after the debacle with Angelica, Benji stood in front of their bedroom closet and grimaced at the array of clothes. Their closet was a walk-in, arranged by color (black with the pop of occasional color), with a rack of breast forms and wigs.

"Should I be worried?" Their mother asked from her seat at their vanity. Hanayu "Switchblade" Nakamura was dressed like the DIY punk cult royalty she was: black skinny jeans, a blazer with a corset back Benji made for her over a plaid vest without a shirt and boots. "You always have your outfits planned." She tossed her pink-streaked ponytail and frowned at them. She looked nearly their age but for the silver laced in with the black and pink of her hair.

Benji shrugged and waded into the closet, running their fingers over their collection. Yes, they'd had an outfit picked out but now those tickets were burning a hole in their pocket. They weren't sure how much protective glamor they needed.

"Was your meeting a bust?" Hanayu's voice was somewhat muffled by the walls of clothes between them.

"It was…" Benji frowned. "Not what I expected."

"Oh?"

"It was Angela Alice."

"The Bitch Queen?" Hanayu said the title with appreciation. She would. Her band, Razor Bitches, were considered the grand dames of the Sacramento DIY punk scene. "Niiiice."

"She and I… aren't exactly on good terms." Benji grimaced, pulling out a shirt to look at it in better light.

"Old hookup?" Hanayu arched an eyebrow at them in the mirror as they stepped out of the closet.

"Mom!" She could make them feel twelve years old again at a moment's notice. "No, fucking thank you." They returned the shirt to the closet. Too casual.

"Really?" Hanayu said. "She'd have been exactly your type ten years ago."

"I'm not even five years older than her, don't make me sound like some old creep."

Hanayu laughed. "Benny-chan, you know I didn't mean it

that way." Though she occasionally reverted to calling them by their childhood nickname, complete with the endearing suffix, she barely spoke any Japanese.

Her family came back from the Manzanar concentration camp and dove headfirst into assimilation. Benji's grandmother had been considered a rebel, giving Hanayu an obviously Japanese name. When Benji'd learned that, sometime in high school, they'd felt less embarrassed by the cutesiness of the nickname.

Benji could read Japanese better than they could speak, but wasn't fluent despite years of learning. Languages just didn't stick in their brain the way music did—much to the disappointment of their paternal grandparents. Their dad's side of the family was loudly, proudly Japanese even though that got them evicted again after the war when Sacramento's Japantown was demolished to make way for the Capitol Mall.

Benji grabbed a spiky jacket, an insubstantial top, and jeans that made them look like a stick figure with an ass. They grabbed boots to match Hanayu's. "You're sure you're fine coming along to this party thing? It's probably going to be boring industry blowhards."

Hanayu waved their words away. "Boring blowhards have the best food. Who knows? Maybe a fight will break out."

Benji chuckled, emptying the pockets from the pants they were currently wearing onto the vanity. They went into the closet to change, taking the moment behind the closed door to look up at the stars they'd painted on the ceiling and breathe until they felt less scattered. When they emerged Hanayu held the tickets.

Shit.

"I was thinking about selling them," Benji said, keeping their voice calm.

"The show is tonight." Hanayu frowned. "I didn't even know she was doing shows."

"Secret shows only." Benji wished they could take the words back the moment they'd said them. Hanayu loved secret shows.

Hanayu's eyes went wide. "Benny—"

"No."

"Aw, come onnn." She whined like a teenager. Hell, she still dressed like one, even if she pulled it off. Sometimes Benji wondered if getting pregnant with them at nineteen had put her into some kind of time warp.

They rolled their eyes at her. "Go without me."

"No way, I'm here to see you." Hanayu put the tickets down. She looked her child over. "You look great by the way. Those blowhards won't know what hit them."

"Thank you." They touched up their make-up and loaded up their waist pack (leather, custom, and definitely *not* a fanny pack). They left the tickets on the vanity. They would not bend to Angelica's bait. Feeling triumphant, they offered Hanayu their arm. "Shall we?"

The party was winding down. The food had been good, the blowhards talked themselves hoarse congratulating each other on the launch of the product, whatever it was, and now Benji was standing by the edge of the roof wondering when they could convince Hanayu to slip away. Because, of course, their mother was having a blast. She'd befriended half the waitstaff and been recognized by a surprising number of execs and celebs.

"Your mom is the life of the party," remarked Rohan "RK" Kapoor, Benji's business partner and best friend. "I thought she'd be real anti-establishment about it."

He'd already worked the room twice, charming the shit out of everyone. Benji mostly lurked in the corner, talking to people they knew. There was a reason Rohan was the face of their record label. Whatever boy band boot camp he'd been put through as a teenager paid off.

Even Patrick, his barely sociable ex-bandmate could turn it on when he wanted to. Patrick didn't come out of the producer's chair these days unless coerced and he certainly did not work with Now or Never, the record label he'd helped run with Benji and Rohan anymore. Benji had burned that bridge down to the ground. Regret washed through them. They eyed the cocktail in Rohan's hand. But no, drinking never solved any of their problems.

Rohan sipped his cocktail and checked the time.

"Is your ride coming soon?" Benji asked, hugging themself as subtly as possible. They had forgotten all the parties in this building were inevitably held outside to take advantage of the dizzying view. If they'd remembered they would've worn more of a shirt because the unseasonably cold late August wind cut through this one like butter.

"She should get done with her thing soon." Rohan's smile was brief but real, lacking the strain Benji had seen when he dated Angelica. They pushed the thought of her right out of their head.

"Wedding thing or work thing?" Benji asked. They didn't always get along with his fiancé, Cazzi was a know-it-all who dished out unwarrantedly accurate psychological observations when cornered, but she and Rohan worked well together. It was enough to make Benji like her, most of the time.

"Work thing," Rohan said. "She's still trying to convince Nānī we should just elope."

Banji snorted. Rohan's grandmother was part of the reason they were getting married in the first place instead of endlessly dating. There was no way eloping was on the docket. Somehow in the compromise between big Indian wedding and pagan handfasting, Benji had been roped in as the officiant. They'd gotten ordained online and everything, but they were staying far away from the organizing.

Rohan's phone rang and he looked at the caller ID. "I'm off, she's done early." He clapped Benji on the shoulder. "Good luck getting out of here. See you tomorrow."

He stopped to say goodbye to Hanayu. Benji's mother used the conversation break to escape the execs she'd been chatting with and came to stand next to them. "Cold, Benny-chan?"

Yes, Benji was cold, but they'd hoped it wasn't *that* obvious. "You wanna get out of here?"

"How about an afterparty?" Hanayu held up the tickets Benji could've sworn were still on their vanity.

They sighed. She'd timed this carefully. They had just enough time to get across Hollywood to the venue.

"Oh my god, are you Hanayu Switchblade?" A TikTok star who looked barely into her twenties and well into her cups looked at Hanayu in awe. "I loooove *Never Bring a Knife to a Pussy Fight*! It got me through so much."

Hanayu smiled. "I'm so glad to hear people are still connecting to that album."

"Are you kidding? My comments go crazy every time I talk about you on my channel! We're, like, your fan club." The TikTok star smiled like they should know exactly who she was. Benji did but only because they'd overheard her recording a video for her account about an hour ago.

"Thank you." Hanayu clearly had no idea.

"Are you ever going to make another album?"

Hanayu's smile went flat. Benji bristled. "We're leaving. Bye now." They pushed past the TikTok star, Hanayu on their heels.

"Benji Omega? Of User-Friendly Omega?" The TikTok star screeched at their backs.

Benji sighed. It was the voice. No matter how different they looked, the voice always gave them away. They could dress like an investment banker and the minute they opened their mouth in public a fan would find them. Their mother laughed, turning back. "Kid, do you want an autograph or not?"

She did *and* she wanted to film with them but Benji put their foot down at that. They were out of the party in five minutes flat.

"Come on, Benny." Hanayu handed them the tickets in the car. "We can bitch about it over cheesecake at Canter's afterward. My treat."

They sighed and typed the venue into the GPS.

CHAPTER 3

"Through my skin you seep
I bury you with me deep

Every time you died
I was at your side
Every time I thought I was free
I carved you back into me

I am a coward behind words
I am the loser beneath chords
You broke me so I
Rebuilt me with pieces of you
Told myself it was love"
—"Coward" by User-Friendly Omega off of *Drown Them All*

etween Saturday night traffic and that TikTok star, they were late and that was before circling the venue for fifteen minutes looking for parking.

"I'm sorry," the guy at the door said, crossing his arms and making his biceps bulge in a way that didn't make him seem very sorry at all. "The doors close at eleven. It's on the ticket."

"Seriously? Is that a thing?" Hanayu asked. Benji shrugged, glancing at the ticket. Door guy wasn't wrong.

"It's a security thing," he said. "This is a secret show. It's exclusive. You should've been on time."

"My kid got these tickets from Angela Alice herself," Hanayu snapped.

Benji suppressed a grimace. People really didn't need to know that. Not with the rumors about their old social media feud.

"Show policy." Door guy settled in with the kind of weary familiarity that said he'd done this far too many times.

"Ever hear of Razor Bitches? Do you know who I am? "

Benji frowned, they'd never heard their mother invoke her fame like that.

"Don't know 'em, can't help you."

Hanayu pointed at them. "This is Benji Omega, and I guarantee you Angela Alice wants to see them."

Benji winced. They didn't have the heart to tell her that no matter their old fame way back when, they were so washed up Hot Topic wouldn't even give them VIP treatment these days. This was obviously more important to Hanayu than they'd realized. They'd get the why out of her later.

"Can you call her team for me?" They asked, regretting every word. They'd really hoped to be in and out without alerting Angelica to their presence.

Door guy's eyes widened. "Um, show policy…"

The door opened behind him. "Let them in." A person holding a clipboard and wearing an earpiece poked their head out. Door guy sidled out of their way. They gave him a nod before extending their hand to Benji. "Remy. Angela Alice's tour coordinator." They winked.

Benji noticed the they/them pin on Remy's lapel. "Benji, they/them. And my mother, Hanayu Switchblade, she/her."

Remy looked at the two of them. "Gotcha. Angie's got seats for you." They looked Benji up and down before beckoning them to follow.

Dreading every step, Benji did.

Angie listened to the crowd from behind the curtain. It was a small venue, perfect for trying new material. The show was running late, which she hated, but some fuse or something had blown. She'd been reassured several times it'd be fixed any minute.

She had no such assurances that Benji would come, but she kept listening like she could pick them out of a hundred people with her ears alone.

"What's up boss? Nervous?"

She turned to look at Dani, the drummer in her backing band, the Sirens of Scream. The woman snapped her gum at the look at Angie's face, blowing a big pink bubble. With her blonde pigtails, tiny skirt, leather crop top revealing acres of brown muscles, and drumsticks tapping against her shoulder, she looked like a six-foot-tall Harley Quinn. "Snap your gum at me one more time and I'll shove it down your damn throat," Angie said sweetly.

Dani laughed and elbowed Gemma, the guitarist. "See? I told you, she's fine."

Gemma, who had been checking her tuning, scowled. Dressed in a suit that always reminded Angie of *Three Cheers for Sweet Revenge* era My Chemical Romance, Gemma was a tiny, butch goth with a tight fade who had been dating Dani forever.

She'd been in the band the longest and recommended her girl-friend when the last drummer dropped out. Thank Lucy, because Dani and Gemma had a musical sync that was hard to find. "Don't drag me into this." She glanced up. "Besides, the Bitch Queen doesn't get nervous, right Ang?"

"Don't know how," Angie lied, like her stomach wasn't one twisted mass. What if they didn't come?

"Were you born that way or did you have it burned out, like your tear ducts?" The final member of her backing band, Marsha, grinned at Angie over her bass. In the half-light, she was a convincing living dead girl in her white make-up and torn-up clothes.

Angie rolled her eyes. That she'd burned out her tear ducts was one of the many stupid rumors about her body. She'd apparently also removed between one and three ribs for various reasons, gotten her chest tattoo as a personal brand from the devil himself, and was white-blonde because she'd died as a child and been resurrected. That didn't even touch what shitheads on the internet said about her breasts, face, ass, and pussy.

Remy materialized out of nowhere, as they often did. "They're here. Used both tickets."

Angie went still, trying to contain every emotion tumbling around inside her. "Where?"

"Exactly where you asked me to put them." Remy smiled reassuringly.

Angie resisted the urge to peer out and look at the balcony seat she'd reserved for them. "Any idea who they brought?" She asked like she didn't care.

"I dunno but the two of them look cozy." Marsha had no compunctions about peeking through the curtain. If the crowd saw Angie peeking they'd lose their mind. They were already cheering every twitch of the curtain as it was. "She's hot."

They brought *a date to her concert?* Why the fuck had she

given them two tickets? You always gave people two tickets, that was the standard but she didn't expect them to use both, let alone *bring someone.*

"Who?" Angie snarled. Everyone backstage fell silent, watching.

Remy managed to keep their smile but the expression was strained. "Their mother."

Angie closed her eyes and nodded, reeling her anger back in. She exhaled hard. "Thank you. Sorry."

Around her she could feel everyone relax, exhaling with her. Her therapist was on her to be more careful with her emotions. *Try to harness them,* she'd told Angie. *Don't just let them loose on those around you.*

Her emotions were big, extensions of her that reached far beyond her body. She'd thought she was just bad at hiding her shit until she'd gotten on stage for the first time at an open mic, depressed and desperate. She'd made an entire biker bar ugly cry. People who looked like they'd never cried a day in their lives bawled openly in front of her. She hadn't shed a tear but she'd felt lighter than clouds the minute she'd stepped off the stage into the sobbing crowd. It was her greatest asset and biggest problem.

She didn't know why it happened, how it happened, and frankly, she didn't care.

Her people could handle it. They had to or they didn't last. But they kept coming back, every tour, every show, and that made her feel like maybe she wasn't a total monster, no matter what the world kept telling her.

Tour. Fuck, she didn't want to think about touring. The grind of a tour used to be the highlight of her year, now she dreaded it. Shit, she had to tour. The fans expected it. The suits expected it. The band wouldn't get paid if she didn't. Her mutual aid projects depended on tour money. Everyone wanted the same Angela with new material but just as driven, just as relentless, grinding her brokenness to the bone for her fans—

A hand landed on her shoulder.

She looked up at Dani. "Yes?"

"Good?" The word was sharp, a little worried.

Angie trapped the automatic caustic reply behind her teeth and nodded. She wrapped the anxiety around her other emotions and buried it, humming the opening number. She focused on the vibration of her throat and the sound of her voice until her thoughts dissipated.

Dani patted her shoulder and turned away.

The venue guy hurried over. "We can start now, Ms. Alice."

Angie looked him in the eye.

He flinched.

She let it roll off her. "Thank you." She tipped her lips up in half a smile.

He flushed and smiled back before scurrying away.

Angie nodded at Remy who signaled the sound and light people that the band would be on in five. Angie turned back to her band. "Ready, ladies?"

She could do this. This was a dry run, just a show, and she still loved shows. No bus, no hotels, no sleeping in strange beds.

Her pre-show song kicked on: User-Friendly Omega's "So It Begins," the atmospheric intro song to their album *Suicide King*. Angie wondered how Benji felt hearing their voice before her show.

Marsha and Gemma put down their instruments. Dani stuck her sticks in the back pocket of her skirt. The band came together, forming a tight circle. Angie put her hands out, palms cupped together. Each woman placed her fingertips on Angie's palms. Angie concentrated on the three sets of warm callused fingers in her hands. Well, two sets.

"What the hell, Marsha, do you have icicles for fingers?" Dani mumbled.

"I had a cold water bottle, sue me," Marsha muttered back.

Angie cleared her throat.

Gemma rolled her eyes. Marsha and Dani shut up.

Angie waited a beat before saying, "Baphomet, bless this show." She closed her eyes. Tingles crawled up her back, tracing the lines of her shoulders until they relaxed. She could do this. She had a good band and her deities at her back. "Protect my people from my excess and crowd bullshit." The tingles reached out beyond her bones, spreading like wings. "Lucifer, Lightbringer, give us your spotlight. May our music sound damn good and our show be badass. Amen."

She dropped her hands. The Sirens exhaled in shaky unison and took their places. Even Gemma grinned. A mike was placed in Angie's hand. She flicked it on with her thumb.

The curtain rose, the lights went on. She opened her eyes to the crowd roaring. She picked Benji out immediately, front and center but unmoved. Next to them, the older woman who could only be their mother clapped wildly.

She opened her mouth and sang back.

Benji narrowed their eyes as "So It Begins" slid out of the speakers, stirring the crowd in only the way a song cueing the start of a show could.

"Isn't this you?" Hanayu asked.

"Yep."

"Is this girl obsessed with you?"

"Yep." They crossed their arms, leaning against the balcony railing, ready to endure this.

The music cut. The lights went out. The curtain went up.

Angelica stood center stage, eyes closed. Their seats had to be the best in the house because Benji could almost count her eyelashes. The light hit her and her eyes opened. She was looking right at them.

The bass started, the drums kicked in, the guitar wove a melody between them but it wasn't until Angelica opened her mouth that the world went electric.

Benji couldn't make it make sense, they could barely form thoughts. It was like religion but religion had never done this to them. It wasn't just her voice, though goddamn, that voice. The recordings couldn't fully capture the way she sang, howled, growled, screamed, whispered, and moaned. It was all her, no backing track. Her presence, that overwhelming feel of Angelica that they'd prided themself on resisting was perfect for the stage.

Benji found themselves leaning forward against the railing. Now, they understood why there was a line of burly security guards wrapped around the stage even at such a small venue, why they shut any latecomers out. They'd never wanted to touch someone as badly as they wanted to touch Angelica right now.

"Holy hell," Hanayu breathed as the song ended. "Holy *fucking* hell."

"Yeah," Benji said.

Angelica looked at the crowd. No, she looked right at Benji, and she *smiled*.

It was like being hit in the face with a sledgehammer. It was all they could do to not smile back. They were fucked. Absolutely fucked.

Before they could process exactly what that meant, she launched into another song. And another and another, blazing through the setlist like a forest fire. Benji couldn't look away. They were disembodied and yet every cell in their body was awake and buzzing. They'd liked her music years ago before they'd met Rohan and seen how shitty he and Angelica were together, but they'd never connected with it like this. They'd never felt it in their bones.

"This is our last song," Angelica told the crowd. Benji was relieved and horribly disappointed. "It's a cover, so sing along if you know it."

They knew it from the first three chords even though it was missing the effects they layered in painstakingly during a sleepless night. Her voice wrapped around Benji's words, husky and dangerous as every extra drink they should've turned down, every drug they regretted.

When she hit the pre-chorus she looked at them, as if checking to see if they recognized their own song on her lips.

"Every time I thought I was free," she crooned like it was just the two of them. The tilt of her lips was a fish hook, the sound of her voice was warm claws reaching around their soul. "I carved you back into me."

> "I am a coward behind words
> I am the loser beneath chords
> You broke me so I
> Rebuilt with pieces of you
> Told myself it was... friendship"

Benji met her eyes. They knew exactly how the chorus of this song built. They laid those bricks themself, building the path with sparse guitar and strategic piano, working themself up to admitting to love. They pushed away from the railing.

The curtain had barely fallen but Angie was already out the back door, her mike and battery pack shoved in some assistant's hand. They left. How could Benji have left? How dare they?

They hadn't gone far. Benji paced in front of the theater, looking dangerous. Dangerous and gorgeous. Like every parent's worst nightmare and every teenager's secret dream. The post-show high in her wanted to grab them and hold on until they realized they were hers. Someone she passed whooped ecstatically. She pulled her emotions in tightly, humming a song she half-remembered. Lucy, her therapist would be proud.

Eh, probably not.

Benji spun to face her. Their eyes were so cold she nearly stopped but inertia carried her forward.

"What the hell are you doing?" They snapped. "Your fans will go rabid if they find you out here after that."

She hesitated. Getting out of a show was always a problem. There had been close, nasty encounters with fans after shows when she wasn't careful. But it wasn't common knowledge. "Did Rohan tell you that?"

They gave her a sardonic look. "I can read a room."

"Is that why you left?" She waited for the obvious lie.

"No." Their dark eyes burned cold, focused entirely on her. It made her giddy, almost manic in a chemical way.

"Not a fan of the way I sing your song?"

They scoffed. "Don't fish. We both know you're good."

"Aw, threatened?"

"I'm not bantering with you." They looked back at the doors. Angie knew there was barely a few minutes before the crowd came pouring through. Her heart sped up. Her stolen moment was ending.

"Come on, we banter so well. Just think how good it'll

be…" She paused. Benji swiveled to look at her abruptly, the look in their eyes unreadable but so intense she nearly lost her train of thought. "When we write together."

Their shoulders relaxed slightly but the intensity remained. She was transfixed by the muscles under their jacket. Suddenly she realized their shirt was translucent. The streetlight shone right through it—

"If I tell you I'll consider it will you go back inside?"

She blinked as she wrenched her eyes away from the slender lines of their torso. She dragged her gaze up to their face. "Benji." She lingered over their name. "You sound like you care."

"Angelica," they breathed her name, holding her gaze. "You sound like you need me to."

She narrowed her eyes. "I do not."

They snorted. "You're a performer. We need everyone to care."

She rolled her eyes. "Is that why you buried yourself in that label?"

They shrugged.

She huffed. "What are you getting at?"

"You don't need me. You *want* me." The words made her whole body go hot and full of sparks. They cocked their head, studying her. "Why is that?"

She was saved from answering when someone cried. "Angelaaaa! Oh my god, it's Angelaaaa!!!"

The crowd boiled through the theater doors. With a quick prayer to Lucifer, she darted away.

Angelica disappeared like a fever dream. Reality flooded back with the crowd. Benji buttoned their jacket and leaned against a parking meter plastered with stickers, texting Hanayu to come find them. She did soon enough.

"You okay?" Hanayu leaned her head on their shoulder in greeting. Well, their arm. She barely reached their shoulder even when both of them weren't wearing boots. "That was one of your Sly songs, wasn't it?"

"The last one," Benji admitted. The hurt of their old fucked up unrequited love with thier best friend and UFO's former bassist was a wound that never quite healed. They could barely listen to a lot of UFO songs because of it.

"Did she know?"

They shook their head. "I doubt she thought that much about it."

"Singers are such narcissists," Hanayu said with wry self-awareness.

Benji chuckled and wrapped an arm around their mother's shoulders. One of their first memories was learning to sing with her at band practice.

They headed for the car.

"You think she's trying to restart that social media feud?" Hanayu asked as they walked. Under the streetlights, the dirty gum-covered sidewalk sparkled with pyrite flecks.

"She wants me to write a duet with her."

"Oh." Hanayu thought about it. "You'd sound good together. Do you want to do it?"

"After that shit she made about Rohan I don't know that I want anything to do with her." There were better ways of handling a break-up than making a whole album and film about how your ex smothered you just as he was trying to make a comeback. "Plus, I have the NoN songwriting retreat to get together for October and a house to renovate from a distance."

A knot of tension formed in their stomach at the thought of going back to Sacramento for the retreat. Though they loved their home town, Sly still lived there and it wasn't a big city. Going back these days felt like a countdown clock if they thought too much about it.

"Please, you know I'm taking care of supervising the reno. How else would I get my perfect house show venue?" Hanayu said, shaking them out of their reverie.

Benji chuckled. Hanayu was too proud to let Benji pay her for supervising the reno of their Sacramento house but she was open to very specific bribes.

"Though the ghosts have been very quiet lately," she said. "Nothing weird for weeks." She sounded disappointed.

"It's not haunted," Benji said firmly for what felt like the hundredth time. "The house's spirit just gets cranky sometimes."

"I don't see why the two have to be mutually exclusive. The house spirit could be cranky *and* there could be dead servants haunting the attic."

"*Mom*," Benji groaned. "Can we not with the servants in the attic theory?"

"I'm just saying, the people who worked in these houses, their entire lives were the house. Why wouldn't they stay—"

"*Please.*" Her theory made them feel like some shitty land-lord displacing poor hard-working ghosts instead of someone who'd bought a cool old house that turned out to be a money pit.

"Fine, fine. So this Angela chick, she's wooing you real hard right off the bat." Hanayu eyed them with concern. "Is this another one of those stalker situations?"

Benji shrugged. This was not the topic change they were

hoping for but they should've seen it coming. "That's just how she always is. Flirting to discombobulate."

"She likes you," Hanayu pronounced, like it was final.

"She's a fangirl," Benji said, remembering her watching them during the Endfest tour, or more annoyingly, giving them career advice when she was in the middle of a half-assed attempt to get Rohan back. She dropped her fully-formed break-up album days later. "She likes who she thinks I am."

"Too bad," Hanayu said. "Who you are is much cooler than that."

"That was such a mom thing to say." Benji chuckled, fishing their keys out.

"As is my right as your mother." Hanayu slid into the passenger seat. "Now, are we still on for cheesecake?"

Benji groaned, starting the car. "Can we get it to-go? I'm old and I want to be home so I can fall asleep on my cake in peace."

"Fine," Hanayu said, stretching her legs out with a groan. "But only because I have to be awake for my flight tomorrow."

CHAPTER 4

"I'm quirky, weird
Dreamy grin
With sharp teeth
Turn your life upside down?
Ha! I'll burn it to the ground

Manic pixie nightmare
Baby, you think I care? [manic laugh]
Not here for your growth
Could give a shit about your boring life
You want love, I prefer a knife"
— "Manic Pixie Nightmare" by Angela Alice off of
Murder Baby

The next morning, Hanayu woke Benji up by poking their shoulder. "I gotta ask you something."

"What?" Benji scrubbed the sleep from their eyes and squinted at her from their bed on the couch in their studio. Their LA apartment was set up for work and sleep and that was pretty much it. There was no way they were making their mother sleep on this squishy leather couch.

Benji wasn't poor by a long shot but they'd sunk a considerable amount into the label and the Sacramento house. Royalties didn't pay the way they used to. There was a reason so many heritage acts were out on the road these days.

Hanayu smoothed her hair back nervously. Benji sat up. She'd been awake for a minute, fully dressed with her minimal travel make up already in place. Ugh, they felt old. They used to be able to stay up for days straight back in their twenties. They'd had chemical help, but still.

They also hadn't sat up half the night buzzing from someone else's concert. No, that wasn't true. But it had been a long time since they hadn't been able to take their mind off of someone. *Angelica.* Their brain kept recycling images of her. Her on stage, her in the conference room, her on the dark street, pupils huge and attention only on them.

Worse, their body had not gotten the memo Benji was not into her. It had gotten embarrassingly worked up and there wasn't a damn thing they could do about it with their mother sleeping in the next room.

Genital non-concordance, Cazzi would call it. Rohan's fiancé once delivered a five-minute lecture on the subject, unprompted. Cazzi often reminded them of a walking sexology textbook, which made sense given she was a sex-ed counselor.

She explained the non-concordance thing with a metaphor involving genitalia and brains trying to agree on a restaurant or something, but all Benji remembered was it had something to do with your junk not agreeing with your brain. It didn't happen much to Benji, but then if anyone would make someone follow their pants feels instead of their brain, it'd be Angelica. She seemed to have a direct line to the lizard brain.

They shook the thoughts off. "What's up?"

Hanayu hesitated.

Benji's attention sharpened on her. "Mom?"

Hanayu shook herself. "It's about your label, Benny."

"Now or Never? What about it?" Tension spooled up their spine. There was a big ask coming, they could tell.

Hanayu sat next to them. "Do you— well, could you—" She stopped, pinched the bridge of her nose, and started again. "Benny, you know how the Razors are back together? We're looking for a label. We think Now or Never would be a good fit."

Benji's business instincts kicked in, overriding the automatic *yes* hovering in their throat. There was inherent nepotism in the question but they wanted to give her the success they'd had and she'd never achieved.

"Why not with one of the bigger labels? They'd have better reach and budgets. That's what you always wanted when I was a kid." They remembered the hope in her face every time some label looking for the next Green Day or Blink-182 breezed through town, hoping Sacramento would be the next Bay Area or San Diego. All the punks around town tore down any band who even looked like they were selling out but Hanayu shrugged that off, sure the Razors would make it big.

That is until those same A&R guys failed the band every time, disappointing her again and again.

Hanayu chuckled wryly. "I wanted a big deal back then so we wouldn't be broke anymore. But that's not a problem now. I always wanted creative control more than the money anyway and I know you'll give us that. Plus, you won't screw us. A big label happily would."

Benji blinked, realigning their memories of her disappointment in their head. They pushed away the guilt and sadness that always pricked at them whenever they thought about how they'd made it big when their mother hadn't. It seemed like she'd really been as fine about it as she'd always said.

But did she think that meant she'd get special treatment because Benji was a part owner? NoN was a co-op style label where artists kept their masters and a percentage of their earnings went into administrative costs and paying the small team that kept things afloat. There wasn't much special treatment to be had.

As if she'd heard their thoughts, Hanayu said, "If you're not comfortable having your mom on the roster, I get that too. I figured I'd try you first though. It didn't feel right to go outside the family before I talked to you. No hard feelings either way." Her hands twisted in her lap with nervous energy.

"I can't give you an answer today even if I wanted to." Benji shrugged. All new acts signed were decided on by the admin team: them and Rohan. "That said, are you thinking the Razors will be a heritage act or creating new music?"

Hanayu winced. "Heritage act? That sounds like we're some 80s MTV one-hit-wonder with hip replacements and hairpieces."

Benji didn't point out the Razors barely made the charts, let alone MTV. "Are you planning to tour?"

"Of course," Hanayu said, like it was obvious.

As far as Benji knew the band hadn't gotten together for anything more than a house show in the last decade. Hanayu was still in music through the show she hosted on one of the niche alternative punk Sirius XM channels and the small Sacramento radio station she managed part-time, but that was only because she refused to coast on Benji's money.

Benji chose their next words with care. "Are you planning to put out a new album?"

Hanayu grimaced. The pressure of trying to write a follow up to their biggest album was what broke up the band in the first place. "Maybe."

Benji didn't press it. "How many shows have you booked recently?"

"A few around town: the Torch Club, Concerts in the Park, house parties, that kinda thing." Hanayu shrugged. "We still have fans. I mean look at how many people recognized me last night!"

Benji nodded. Hanayu had cult appeal, but their business brain ran the numbers on those venues and was not impressed.

"We're not a bad investment. You know we work hard."

"I know." They hesitated, then forced the words out, spilling them over the *yes* still lurking under their tongue. "But I'm not the only one running the label. I gotta convince Rohan too. I need you to play a showcase. Somewhere bigger than the Torch Club and preferably in LA. I want to prove you have more than a local following." They braced themself for her disappointment. She'd played a million shows with A&R guys lurking in the crowd only to have them turn the band down or ask them to be tamer, sexier shadows of themselves.

"Really?"

Benji glanced up to see her grinning.

"I'll call the girls! We'll start calling in favors." She rubbed her hands together, already planning.

Benji smiled, relieved. "I have some contacts you can leverage." They texted her their list of LA venues and the people to talk to. Then, the excitement of the conversation wore off and their sleepless night crashed down on them. They leaned back and sighed, closing their eyes. "I wish I didn't have to go to this thing tonight."

"So don't," Hanayu said distractedly. "You're a busy, important person."

Benji laughed. Ten years ago when Benji had been A-list famous, Hanayu would've told them to suck it up and go for the exposure, the possibilities, the stories. A decade and their one massive breakdown later, she was much more careful about what she pressured Benji to take on. "Yeah, but it's for charity."

"One of those dinners where rich shits get together to

congratulate each other spending just enough money to write off and look good to the plebs while not actually fixing anything?"

"Yeah, but Rohan's Foundation is being honored." Rohan and his family ran a food bank and resource center in Downtown. Benji held their non-binary support group there. "I wanna support him."

"Oh." Hanayu blinked. "Well, he does good work."

"Yes, I just wish we didn't have to sit through three hours of self-congratulations to get the damn money." They lay their head back against the wall.

"Poor baby." Hanayu patted their head. "I'll text you the endless list of repairs your house needs so you have something more fun to think about."

Benji snorted, they knew construction was one of those things that never stuck to a timeline but getting this house livable was starting to feel like a lifetime project. That's what they got for buying a place that was over a hundred years old. "Way to put things in perspective." Then they had a thought. "If you're making a new album, maybe you should come to the songwriting retreat."

"If you decide to sign us," Hanayu reminded them, wryly.

Benji grimaced. "We'll burn that bridge when we get to it. I think you'll enjoy the retreat. I have some great ideas."

Hanayu squeezed their shoulder. "I'm sure it'll be amazing. You're good at that shit, Benny-chan. Now, I gotta go catch a plane so I can make the band practice tonight in your basement." She grabbed her bag and kissed the side of their head.

When Benji had been house hunting, finding a house that was old enough and high enough out of the Delta floodplain to have a basement had made Hanayu practically order them to buy it. They couldn't even hazard a guess at how many house shows she'd put on in their basement and backyard.

Benji laughed, getting up to find their keys. "Don't piss off the neighbors again."

"Are you kidding? Neighbors love me." She winked as they opened the front door for her.

Angie left the red carpet step-and-repeat slightly blind and already done with the evening. Her hair was pulled so tight she'd be lucky if she didn't get a headache and her dress wasn't as nearly as comfortable as it had been when she tried it on in the store.

She could think of about a hundred better, more pressing things to do and two hundred problems she could fix with the money wasted on putting on this glitterfest. The giant crystal chandelier overhead alone could probably cover the costs of the meal program at the Foundation for a month.

Oh fuck, there were *cameras inside the event too.*

She glanced at her manager Cheryl, her plus one. Angie thought about bringing her usual platonic date Martin Mejia, but the drama of bringing the Beatboy who broke up the band to a charity event with her ex who was also his former bandmate would've kept the cameras on the three of them all night. Boy band feuds apparently never die.

"I did tell you to be camera-ready," Cheryl said before Angie could say anything. She was rocking a power red jumpsuit that made her dark brown skin pop.

"Tell me they aren't going to film us while we're eating." Angie glanced around, clocking the exits discreetly tucked in the corners of the ballroom.

"Come on, you've been to enough of these. No one actually eats."

Unfortunately, Angie was already hungry. "No one's invited me to a charity function in a while." The only reason she'd been invited to this one was she was still half of the Foundation. They hadn't managed to kick her out completely. A thought struck her. "Did they sit me next to Rohan?"

Cheryl shook her head. "The Kapoor family nixed that."

Angie sent a silent *thank you* to Baphomet, glancing at the likeness of the goat-like androgyne tattooed on her forearm. She and Rohan were fine. They'd both moved on and she'd apologized but his family still hadn't gotten onboard the forgiveness train. Plus, his fiancé thought because she had a Ph.D. she was a fucking mind reader.

The two of them wove between the tables, stopping at every single one to make small talk with the VIPs and make empty promises to get together. She even did the awkward side hug with Rohan for a photographer before escaping the dagger eyes of his family to her table.

Good Lucy, you make one very popular break-up album and movie special while trying to torpedo your ex's comeback album and some people will never forgive you. Reasonable, but if she was bothered by everyone who hated her she might as well go back into lockdown.

She and Cheryl were seated with the interns and staff which was probably supposed to be insulting. She didn't care. Interns and staff were rising stars, ambitious and hungry. They had new ideas and unexpected artistic talent. Angie knew because she'd been one of them not so long ago. Plus, she'd found her last music video director at an event like this. She circled the table the long way, memorizing the names on the place cards. Nobody ever expected the star to know their name.

Feeling very proactive, she sat and read the name next to her.

"Aw shit," she said under her breath, suppressing a grin.

"Problem?" Cheryl asked, hand already poised over her phone.

Angie shook her head, staring at the place card.

Cheryl peered at her face. "I know it's been a day but just show a little face before you duck out, okay? You gotta remind people you do good. Especially if…" She grimaced. "Well, no use in borrowing trouble," she finished, like she didn't already have contingency plans for all that trouble.

Or at least, she hoped Cheryl did because having to face Mama still featured in Angie's night terrors. The dreams had increased since that call. The thought of Mama getting out of prison made Angie's fingers stick together with sweat and nerves and old remembered blood. She'd spent all day on the phone with her team trying to find options. There was nothing promising.

"Oh yeah." Angie tapped her fingers against her thigh. "Don't want to get bad press when the State is gonna let Mama out for good behavior." She hoped her sarcasm was sharp enough that Cheryl wouldn't notice her fingers shaking or the fear she was trying so hard to suppress.

Mama wasn't a physical threat—probably. She'd never hit Angie besides the occasional slap, it had been easier for her to cut with words, insults sugared with a smile. Daddy had the temper that made it feel like the sky was falling. Which was why that day, seeing Mama with the knife hadn't made sense at first.

Pull yourself together, Mama sneered, echoing from her memory. *You are so like your father.*

Angie clenched her fist as if she could crush the image between her fingers. Guess after Mama'd killed him, there was no point in smiling lies anymore.

Her manager gave her a look. "You know how these things work. I just don't want anything to overshadow the announcement tomorrow."

Angie nodded. She couldn't argue with that, she wanted her new project to succeed.

Cheryl's phone rang but she glanced at Angie and only picked it up when the singer gave her a thumbs up.

Ever professional, her manager left to take the call privately. Probably dealing with tour shit or, maybe even personal stuff, didn't matter to Angie.

She picked up the place card next to her again, grateful for the distraction. Baphomet knew she needed it.

Benji slid into their seat with a sigh. They managed to get through the room with as little social interaction as possible. Eventually, they'd have to track down Rohan and Cazzi but right now they just wanted to sit and brace themself for the inanity of the coming evening. They leaned back in the chair, trying to look awake when all they wanted to do was faceplant on the table.

Ugh, they were old. It was days like this they really missed cocaine. Benji would've settled for one of those terrible energy drinks they only drank while recording, but they refused to try one of the Manergy drinks that seemed to be the most caffeinated thing the bar had. The sheer number of bulging muscles and veins on the logo creeped them out.

Someone sat beside them, placing her drink on the table. "I just want you to know I didn't plan this."

Suddenly Benji was very awake. They swiveled slowly to face Angelica. "I didn't know you were into charity."

She snorted. "I *am* half of the Foundation."

Benji had forgotten. How had they forgotten *that*? "Is that why they sat you at the kiddie table?"

They both surveyed the distinctly younger population of their table. At least half of them must be assistants and interns.

"You know why I'm here," she said, like it didn't matter she was essentially a pariah at her own non-profit. "Why are you here? Piss off Ro?"

"I'm just here to support," they said, like they hadn't specifically asked to be sat somewhere where they wouldn't be in the center of attention. Wait, Rohan *had* mentioned something about Angelica being here. Very quickly and in passing when he'd told Benji about the event.

They checked their calendar app and sure enough, there was a note: *Possible A appearance—unlikely but prep.*

They'd been stuck in traffic after dropping Hanayu off and running too late to check their notes before they'd left. Of course, it was the one time they didn't already have thier notes memorized.

The lights dimmed and waitstaff appeared, setting down plates with elegantly sculpted scraps of food. Benji poked a fork at theirs. In the dark, it could've been any number of things.

Out of the corner of their eyes, they watched Angie scoop a forkful into her mouth and freeze. Her eye twitched.

"That bad?"

She visibly forced herself to swallow. "What did I just put in my mouth?" She looked shell-shocked.

Benji poked at the appetizer again. "Vegetables?"

"I'm not convinced." Angelica moved the colored strands on her plate around. "The texture…" She grimaced, leaning forward to peer down at the disaster on her plate. The movement showed off her backless dress, cut to frame the large Luciferian sigil tattooed across her back. It reminded Benji that she'd once gotten matching tattoos with Rohan, back when they were together. He'd covered his, but had she kept hers?

It didn't matter. It *shouldn't* matter.

Someone was speaking on stage, introducing the event.

Benji tried to focus on the woman at the podium rather than the one next to them.

"Are you gonna try it?"

"No," Benji said without looking at her.

"Scared?"

"What are you, twelve?"

"Try itttt." Angelica dragged out the word just like a preteen.

Benji rolled their eyes. "Peer pressurrrre."

Angelica paused and considered this. "Fine, but we try the next dish together."

"You act like I'm about to play games with you," Benji said, annoyed.

"Unbend a little, will you? We're stuck here until the giant check clears, might as well enjoy ourselves."

"I would enjoy it more if you stopped talking to me," they said, in the off-chance she'd listen.

Benji could practically hear her roll her eyes. "You're such an old grump."

For fuck's sake, they were only five years apart. "Do me a favor and take a break from living up to your reputation of being a manic pixie nightmare."

"Uh-huh, would you prefer I start badgering you about doing my duet?" She edged closer.

Benji lost the battle with themself and looked at her.

She watched them from under her red-tipped eyelashes. "Or was there something else you had in mind?"

They were having a really hard time looking away. Or forming words or…

A wave of applause crashed around them. Benji jerked their gaze to the stage as some other cause celeb congratulated themselves.

"That man spent more money on his face than he has any other cause," Angelica muttered, looking at the exec on stage. The man flashed a smile that nearly blinded the front row.

Benji frowned. "You don't know that." But, they couldn't stop themself from studying the man to see if they could tell.

"Sure do," she said. "He's one of the suits at my old label and he recommended his surgeon to me." She shrugged. "Apparently, I didn't look quite as good as his mistress."

Classic. "No one ever looks as good as a suit's side piece."

"Sad but true."

The next dish came, covering more of the plate but still hard to recognize.

"What deconstructed nonsense is this?" Angelica picked up a bite, examining it in the half-light.

"You don't have to eat it."

"I'm hungry and bored," she replied. "Try to stop me."

Benji didn't, but they watched as she popped it in her mouth. She closed her eyes but immediately opened one in a grimace.

Benji suppressed a laugh. "I hope you get caught on camera making that face. *E!* Would have a field day."

She chewed with exaggerated speed and choked down her bite. "You are a spiteful human. Here I am, putting my life on the line for your amusement and you wish the paps on me."

"What a hard life you lead." Benji poked the entree with their knife.

"I wouldn't," she said, taking another forkful.

Benji narrowed their eyes.

She winked.

"You are deeply annoying," they muttered.

"Thanks!" She said between bites. "I work at it. Just for you."

"Uh-huh." Benji stared at their forkful. Another non-profit got up, their celebrity spokesperson shedding a single tear about *how much this award means to me...*

Benji's stomach grumbled. *Fuck it,* they thought and put the food in their mouth.

A taste explosion went off in their mouth and not in a good way. It was too salty, a bit bitter, somehow flaccid and brittle at the same time. They clamped their teeth shut, forcing the bite down. Their esophagus fought them every step of the way.

"It's good to know with all the starving children around the world they didn't waste the good stuff on us rich bastards." Angelica ate another bite.

"How are you still eating that?" Benji choked out, downing half their soda. That taste would not go away.

"I've eaten worse," she said airily.

Benji had too but not recently and not voluntarily. "Are you eating that just to fuck with me?"

"I told you," she said. "I'm hungry."

Benji shuddered. "This is, by far, the scariest thing I've seen at a charity dinner."

"I aim to please."

"No, you don't."

"I aim to please myself."

Benji took another sip. "Then you must be a masochist."

"Wanna find out?" She waggled her eyebrows ridiculously. She wasn't trying to be sexy but it still made Benji's stomach curl in anticipation. Or maybe it was that food. Probably the food.

"Just don't puke on me, okay?" They smoothed their top, embroidered with black roses. "This is silk."

"Ooh fancy." Angelica rolled her eyes like she wasn't wearing a white dress that probably cost as much as a ticket to this dinner to dry clean.

She scraped her plate clean.

Benji watched in amazement. "If I cared for you at all, I'd be worried."

"You say the nicest shit, Omega."

"You bring out the worst in me."

She fanned her face sarcastically. "Oh stoppp, you're too kind!" She looked a little green.

Benji frowned. "Is the food getting to you?"

"No, just the company." But she put her fork down and pointed at Benji's drink. "Rum and coke?"

"Just coke." It'd been the most caffeinated thing at the bar after that Manergy shit.

"Perfect." She grabbed it and took a hearty sip, leaving a red-black lip print next to Benji's own silver-blue mark on the straw.

"Seriously?" Benji snatched the glass back though they didn't want it anymore. "Do you even know where I've been? *I* wouldn't share a drink with me."

"Eh, again, had worse." She winked.

"Worse than COVID?" They raised an eyebrow.

She shuddered. "No, that wasn't fun. You seem like the type to stay home if you felt sick though. All conscientious and shit."

They couldn't believe her. "I could be symptom-free."

She shrugged. "Too late now."

Benji persisted. "I could've been lying about what was in there." Her recklessness baffled them. She'd been in this industry too long to be this… this… impetuous.

"I know what alcohol tastes like and Special-K doesn't seem like your drug of choice." Angelica propped her chin on her fist, looking at them. "Besides, I know you're sober."

"Not strictly."

"You're such a worrywart." Her mouth curled into an almost smile. Benji could barely remember what they were mad about. "I never would've guessed." With deliberate slowness, she took the glass from their hand and took another sip, her lips closing over Benji's lip print on the straw. It shouldn't have been that fascinating but Benji was transfixed.

"Keep it," they said, when she tried to hand it back.

"Don't want my germs?"

"Someone has to be the sensible one in this conversation."

"Says who?"

They turned away from her, pretending to watch the stage.

"Oooh, I feel so dismissed." She sounded amused.

When they didn't respond, she leaned back in her seat, quiet.

The entree was whisked away. Something resembling dessert replaced it. Benji stared at it bleakly. They loved dessert and this looked like it could be chocolate. All they wanted was a shit ton of chocolate right now.

They touched the tines of their fork to the cake-like object and lifted up the tiniest crumb they could.

"You can do this," Angelica stage-whispered.

"Hush, creature of the night," they muttered back. They glanced around the table. Everyone else regarded their plates with the weary look that said they too tried the other dishes.

"If I do, will you touch-a touch-a-touch me?" Angelica's murmur was so quiet it was almost subsonic.

They dropped their voice to match. "If you want to be dirty I can dump this in your lap, Coma White." Great, now they were gonna have that song stuck in their head and though they loved *Rocky Horror Picture Show*, they were not in the mood for Susan Sarandon's voice.

Angelica made a low hum that sounded amused but not before Benji heard the hitch in her breath. Before they could give in to the instinct to glance over at her, they shoved the crumb of dessert in their mouth.

It was barely a morsel but it was still too sweet, wretchedly, gratingly sweet. They pushed the plate away. "I think the chef is trying to murder us."

"Then they're doing a terrible job," Angelica said. Did she

look paler? They couldn't tell in this light. "This is too obviously poisonous."

Benji noticed she hadn't touched her dessert. "Too much even for you?"

"My iron stomach is full. Thank you very much," she said primly, before taking another long pull on the soda formerly known as Benji's.

They allowed themself the barest bit of a chuckle. That was when the camera flash went off.

Angie saw Benji's slight smile in the camera flash and knew she'd see it when she closed her eyes for hours. She watched them swivel to find the camera, coming face to face with a twenty-something with the Nikon. "Who is that picture for?" Their voice was smooth and cold, edged enough everyone at the table knew thin ice was ahead. The people who hadn't already been covertly watching them certainly were now.

The kid, probably someone's intern, sputtered out the name of the charitable organization putting on this whole shit show.

"Thank you," Benji said with a smile that said *run along and don't come back.*

"We'll be seeing that in the morning." Angie chuckled.

"I hope not." Benji smashed the cake with thwarted viciousness.

Just the sight of it made her already upset stomach lurch. She took another sip of soda, the bubbles soothing her nausea. What had she been thinking, eating that disgusting attempt at food? "Afraid to be seen with me?" She posed it casually, but if the answer was yes, this, whatever it was, was over before it even started.

"Not everything is about you," they pointed out. "I hate candids."

"Don't worry, you're disturbingly photogenic, I'm sure you'll look great."

"Sure, but it still feels invasive." They frowned. "It doesn't bother you?"

She shrugged. "I get a lot of press. At least, they aren't as into upskirting as they used to be."

She'd caught the tail end of that era and at nineteen, taken it as an opportunity for performance art. Unfortunately, the press couldn't take a hint even when you wrote 'only creeps upskirt' on giant white granny panties or painted fake blood all over her crotch. It just made her an interesting headline.

For a second, their frown turned sympathetic. Angie almost physically recoiled, her insides feeling raw and shaky. She couldn't afford this, not now. Not after the threats this morning, not when Mama could be out in the world soon. She wrapped the feeling close to her ribs, concentrating on keeping it contained.

Cheryl, Baphomet bless her, chose that moment to return. "You didn't save any dinner for me."

"Trust me when I say that not saving you dinner saved you," Angie said, turning to face her manager. She lowered her voice. "Was it… ?"

"Yes, but the usual people are on it." Cheryl patted the back of Angie's hand, her touch brief and gentle. "We'll handle it." She smiled past Angie's shoulder and said, "Hi again, Mx. Nakamura."

Benji gave her a polite smile. "Ms. Danford. It's good to see you again."

"I hope you'll give the offer some thought," Cheryl said, her smile going shark-like. "The team is very excited about it."

Offer? Angie's mind went to a thousand dirty places before she remembered the duet. The melody wove its way into her thoughts and she imagined Benji's voice crooning over it. Dreamy excitement sparked over her skin.

"Right, Angela?" Cheryl nudged her hand with a finger.

Angie shook herself out of the creative daydream. Lucy, it felt good to feel excited about writing. "Of course."

She'd say yes to anything that got Benji's voice on her track. Hell, if she wasn't careful, she'd say yes to anything that'd get Benji to spend a little more time with her.

CHAPTER 5

SATANIC METAL SINGER DEBUTS BODILY AUTONOMY FUND
Angela Alice called her first album Murder Baby *and now she's putting her money where her mouth is. The controversial artist debuted her Bodily Autonomy Fund yesterday. "The fund will pay for travel for abortions, procedures, emergency contraception, and more as well as gender affirming care," according to the press release. "Basically, if you're pregnant and you don't want to be or you've got gender dysphoria and you can't access treatment, fill out an app. We got you."*

"Satanism, no matter your branch, is all about bodily autonomy," Alice said. "I'm just doing my part to protect what the American government and conservatives seem hellbent on destroying—at least for people who aren't cis men."

The backlash online was immediate and in some cases, threateningly violent. But that's not new territory for the woman who used to ragebait the Westboro Baptist Church. "If I had nickel every shithead that's threatened me, online or off, I'd be rich enough to buy my own Supreme Court judge," Alice joked.

But enough real news, check out these pictures of Alice and Benji Omega getting cozy at some bougie charity dinner. Maybe the feud is off?
—Metal Music Now

Benji left the party like a bat out of hell. Well, a bat that got stuck at the valet. They stood on the sidewalk because they couldn't stand the idea of being in the lobby and making small talk with people who figured because they donated obscene amounts of money Benji wanted to hear about their lives.

"I should've gotten drunk," Angelica said mournfully. She stood next to them, her dress and bright hair hidden by an honest to god black cloak. The giant check she and Rohan accepted earlier was nowhere to be seen.

When the hell had she shown up? How had they not noticed her arrival twice this evening? The woman was usually an electrical storm, sensed before she was seen.

They remembered her sneaking up on them at Endfest with an internal grumble. Could it be that she actually could control herself when she wanted to? Maybe she was evolving. Terrifying thought.

"You look like an elf," Benji blurted.

"You say that like it's an insult."

They hadn't meant it that way, which was somehow worse. "You definitely would've puked that food if you drank."

She shuddered. "I bet the cocktails were atrocious." She sighed. "Hey, so—fuck, that was fast. This is me."

The gothest electric car money could buy pulled up. It was matte black with a blood red interior, black hubcabs, and one of those reproduction sixties black and yellow license plates. Benji had a sudden burst of car envy. Angelica was a problem, but a problem with great taste.

Angelica tipped the driver. Just before she got in, she stopped and looked at Benji. Her gaze was open and sincere. Benji couldn't look away.

"Hey… sorry, if I came on too strong tonight. A lot's going on right now and I enjoy poking at you. But—" She pulled out a business card and a pen from the pocket of her cloak. After scribbling something on it, she held it out to them. "Here. If I haven't driven you off completely."

Benji took it, mostly because all the valets were watching them. They shoved it in their pocket without looking.

"See you around, Omega." She fluttered her fingers at them in a wave and pulled away in a smooth maneuver that had many of the valets whistling in appreciation.

"I hate her," they mumbled, mostly to convince themself.

Back home, they stripped off their party outfit, scrubbing the night off with their make up. Or they tried anyway. The business card with her number sat on their dining room table. No name with the number and it wasn't even her card, it advertised someone's styling services—probably whoever picked her dress.

They should throw it away.

They should put the number in their phone so they know if she ever—what, called them? Angelica had left that ball firmly in Benji's court, damn her. They crumpled the card but didn't throw it out, leaving it balled up on the table.

Instead they sat on the couch in their underwear, computer cooking their bare thighs and lap, wading through all the questions from the contractors Hanayu forwarded them.

They'd been renovating this house in bits and pieces since before the pandemic but now they had a deadline to make it habitable for people who hadn't grown up in various punk houses. It was surreal to think the place might be done soon.

Having answered all the questions, they flipped over to their plan for the songwriting retreat. The talent list was finalized and invites were going out soon, with a few spots left over for discretionary wiggle room. You never knew who might make a great last minute addition. Most of the NoN roster was on here—the ones that weren't on tour anyway.

As if on cue, Benji's phone rang.

They glanced at the caller ID, catching the time: 2 am. Adrenaline jolted through their system, remembering all the late night calls they'd get when Sly was back in the hospital. Those calls always came to them after User-Friendly Omega left Sacramento. Sly would put Benji as his emergency contact so they'd show up instead of his parents.

Benji had taken it as a sign of affection, maybe more, but probably Sly had just been trying to avoid another stint in the fancy private facilities his parents would send him to for his 'accidents.'

Benji shook off the memories, aching for a cigarette and pulled themself into the now. Sly didn't talk to them anymore. Benji couldn't blame him.

Now, only Leo would call them at 2 am. Benji braced themself. Leo Starr, known professionally as Steph Infection, was Rohan and Patrick's old Beatboyz bandmate and currently the only drag queen on NoN's roster. He was finishing up a summer tour of gay bars across America. He'd started on the East Coast last month which meant he was at least two hours ahead, somewhere in the middle of the country.

Benji picked up the phone, hands shaking. Nothing good ever happened at 4 am, especially on tour.

"What's wrong?" They asked.

"So, funny story," Leo replied. Benji clocked the slight slur in his words, filing it away. Leo had a strong tolerance, he was probably mostly there.

"I'm laughing already." They sank a sobering chill in their voice.

"It wasn't me, for the record."

"It's late, spare me and the bush you're about to beat around." They wished Patrick was still working with the label, then Leo could irritate him instead of Benji.

"Touchy," Leo tsked. "Fine. I think the tour's cursed."

"I swear to—" Benji took a breath. Yeah, Patrick was the one who should be dealing with this. "Elaborate. Please."

"Well, we have a flat—repair service is on the way, not the problem though I wouldn't be surprised if it was slashed after what that one guy said after the show—but that's not the—"

"Whoa, go back to the guy and the tire slashing!"

Leo sighed. "I thought you wanted me to get to the point."

"Are you and the crew in danger?"

"We're a bunch of queers in the middle of Iowa at 4 am in post-truth America. What do you think?" Leo snapped back. Then his tone softened. Benji realized he was afraid. "Beyond that, no, though the cut in our tire looks—I don't know, I'm not an expert—but it could be from a broken bottle."

Benji wasn't an expert either but they knew the specific brand of fear that came from breaking down somewhere rural when you sat visibly under a rainbow umbrella. "I see. The crew documented everything?"

"Yeah."

Benji nodded to themself, making a note to review the documentation after they got some sleep. "No one's lurking around? No slow passing vehicles or anything?"

"No."

"How long have you been stopped?"

"Um… maybe thirty minutes."

Benji grimaced. That was a long time at 4 am. "Cops?"

"Haven't called any, wasn't planning to."

"Good." Benji paused, then barrelled on. They needed to know. "How much have you had?"

"What?"

Benji kept thier tone as neutral as they could. This was not Sly, lying to them about what he'd taken. "Are you sober?"

"Yes! Mostly. Just had a little to take the edge off. And sleep, you know how it is."

They did. Unfortunately. "Good. You'll probably be fine but I'll stay on the line until the repairs are done."

"The repair truck is forty-five minutes out," Leo protested, but there was relief in his voice.

Benji rubbed their tired eyes. "I won't sleep till you're back on the road anyway."

"Aw, you're a softie. Who knew?"

"Nobody, if you keep your damn mouth shut," Benji growled, but they were too tired to put real menace in it.

Leo chuckled. "Sure, sure."

"How was the show besides that one asshole?"

"Oh, spectacular, of course. The stage was tiny but I've had worse. Those folks were dying for a Steph Infection..." Leo prattled on, falling into his usual drag bravado.

Benji let it wash over them, pacing to stay alert. Leo was a talker once you got him going. Benji fired off an email to Rohan, briefing him on the situation. Leo was also what passed for the label's financial office so he'd take care of the invoice for the repairs once it landed. Benji checked Leo's tour dates. He'd be back in LA soon to rest up.

Good. They needed to have a check-in before the retreat. Which Leo was on the list for.

When the repairs were done and Leo had talked himself out, safe on the road again, Benji fell face first into bed and passed out.

CHAPTER 6

"I met you at a show
You met me at a bar
Fucked me in a bathroom stall
You thought I looked
Like a rockstar

How sweet to be nothing but flesh
No mind, no thoughts, no fuss
How cool to be careless
Leave each other a mess
Nameless and satisfied

Together we're smooth gods
Slick and sliding, slim and slicing
Pretty, perfect, smooth gods"
—"Smooth Gods" by User-Friendly Omega off of *Suicide King*

A week later, Benji stood backstage at *The Talk Show Game*, willing their pores not to sweat and ruin their fantastic outfit. The host called out the show intro. Benji braced themself like a runner, gift bag in hand.

"Welcome to *The Talk Show Game* where we take the unspoken rules of talk shows and judge you on them. My first guest tonight is singer, songwriter, and indie record exec, Benji Nakamura. They are the founder and lead singer of the deliciously emo User-Friendly Omega, but since the band broke up they've been writing your favorite pop songs and running Now or Never Records with half of the Beatboyz. Now, they're lowering themself to our level. Please welcome Benji Nakamura!"

Benji strode on-stage, waving with determination and hitting the judges with their best stage smile. The judges, sitting at a table perpendicular to the talk show set up where the game was played, were a niche famous podcaster and a daytime famous soap actress who did their best to look stern. The crowd ate it up.

"Smiling and waving: two points," muttered the podcaster into his microphone, tallying the points as Benji made them in a notebook before him. "Cheer from the crowd: two points."

His co-host made notes on her own pad of paper.

Benji hugged the host, earning five more points, and sat in the first of three chairs, handing him a gift bag worth four points.

The three minutes allotted to bantering with the host disappeared in no time and Benji made a respectable score. The podcaster rated them: "So likable I almost forgot I've spent far too many break-ups crying to your voice."

The soap actress judged them as: "Deliciously broody and far too funny to have a face like that."

Then it was time for the next guest. Benji knew one of the

other guests on the show, comedian Matt Masters, from his stint on the Endfest tour with them. There had been a last-minute substitution for the third guest, a comedian whose wife had gone into labor. She'd run out of the studio so fast Benji thought her dressing room was on fire.

The rumor backstage was the host pulled some serious strings to replace her on such short notice.

"My next guest was supposed to be comedian Sonia Severin, but her wife rudely decided to go into labor. So, we had to get an emergency guest and I called in one of my biggest favors."

The screen behind them showed a button sitting in a glass box with a hammer next to it. A hand picked up the hammer and a voice screamed, "Emergency guest activated!" The hand smashed the hammer straight through the glass to the button.

The host chuckled. "Thanks to an extremely fortunate bet, I now present to you our emergency guest, who needs no introduction, Angela Alice. Scooch down for her, Benji. Angela Alice is a musician both famous and infamous for her confessional songs, her amazing visuals, and her open Satanism. She is also a philanthropist and activist for many causes including LGBTQIA+ rights, housing issues, and abortion rights."

Benji moved down the line of chairs on autopilot. What massive favor or bet had Angelica made with the comedian who hosted this silly show?

Whatever it was, Angelica knew the game she was playing. She charged out on stage like she was fully aware the game timer was ticking. She smiled and waved, exchanged hugs and cheek kisses with the host, and winked at Benji before sitting next to them, earning herself twelve points before she even opened her mouth. Her silvery dress was ragged in the chicest way, fluttering and flirting with her exposed skin and tattoos, her make-up was stark, shadowing her eyes and making her eyes look silver.

"Now, Angela," the host purred. "I have to thank you for coming at such short notice."

"Of course," Angelica purred back, flirting for more points. "Anything for you Brendan." "Luckily, I was going out for groceries so I was already dressed." She gestured at her outfit and the audience roared with laughter.

Benji took a sip of their very low-proof cocktail, earning themself a few more points. They'd gotten it on a whim since this was a low-stakes show and they'd had a fucking week. If they'd known they would be dealing with Angelica, they wouldn't have gotten it at all. Their tolerance was not what it used to be and they were already feeling warm.

It was weird to watch Angelica turn on this talk show-ready charm, name dropping, plugging her Bodily Autonomy Fund, and joking around. All of which earned her an ungodly number of points.

"So then Martin Mejia, half the ghouls of Ghost, Courtney Lake, and me are sitting backstage at the VMAs—"

"Oh, I'm sorry, that's time!" The host cut her off.

"That went fast!" She looked surprised but Benji could feel the exhilaration drifting off of her. It was headier than the drink in their hand. They let themself soak in it, just a little.

Benji politely clapped. She glanced at them and they realized they were smiling when her lips quirked in that almost smile of hers. "What do you think, Omega? Did I do good?"

They glanced at her score. If they were lucky, she'd barely pull ahead of them once the judges' scores came in. "We'll see if it was good enough."

"Ohhh fighting words!" The host said. "Let's see what the judges think."

The actress called her "the devil's most charming agent. I'd follow you to the nearest Hellmouth."

The podcaster said, "As a gay man I have no sexual interest

in you. That said, I could listen to you talk forever and I can't even listen to my own playbacks."

After their scores, Angelica was nearly ten points ahead of them. If they weren't careful, Benji was going to lose to her on this silly show on this tiny network they only agreed to be on because they loved the show and it looked fun as hell. Yeah, there was no fucking way.

The show cut to commercial, the lights dimmed, and everyone stood to stretch and chat now the mics were dead. The host wandered over to them. "A little bird told me Matt Masters is stoned out of his mind backstage. I doubt he'll be able to keep up with the two of you. I'd try to score as much as possible during his set." He winked and wandered off to talk to a producer.

"Aw, he wants us to fight." Angelica crinkled her eyes in amusement.

"We *are* good at that," Benji pointed out.

"Darling, I'd fight you any day." Angelica sat as an AD called for them to return to their marks.

"You wouldn't win."

"We'll see about that."

The lights came back up and they both scooted down so Matt could sit. He wandered out, grinning and waving at literally everyone. The host wasn't kidding, this guy was absolutely baked. He wandered towards the crowd and seemed to get lost there for about thirty seconds.

"Over here." Angelica knelt on her chair. "Yoo-hoo! Sailor!" The crowd laughed and all of a sudden her score was even more ahead of Benji's.

They took a very obvious sip of their drink and stood, gesturing Matt towards his chair like an air traffic controller. The crowd ate it up.

Matt squinted at them as he passed like he realized they were scoring on him.

"Good job!" Angelica reached out and ruffled his hair, hitting him with a smile. The crowd laughed.

The comedian stumbled, staring. "Whoa."

"Oh, that's cheating," Benji complained.

"You both have a yellow card for interfering with gameplay." The podcaster judge held up said card.

"Come on, it's a public service!" Angelica said as Matt finally found his seat and smiled blearily at the host. "We're helping."

"Another yellow card for disrespecting the judges."

Benji sat, chuckling into their drink and taking another ostentatious sip. They mentally pulled up the list of possible points earning actions. If they took enough drinks, did a spit take, got some laughs, and flirted with the host all while not annoying the judges they could pull ahead of Angelica.

"So Matt," the host started. "You just got back from a tour with Seth Rogan, promoting his new movie. What was that like?"

"Yes." Benji leaned forward like they cared. "Have you recovered?"

Matt laughed good-naturedly. "Not even slightly. I think I coughed up a whole bong yesterday."

"Goodness!" The host laughed. "So his reputation is well earned then?"

Matt shrugged. "I barely saw the man. But, everyone else was crazy loaded and you know I'm not one to turn down a smoke when it's offered."

"I can only imagine," the host said dryly. "Now your latest project is the new TV show

Comedysynthesis on Comedy Central."

"Yep."

"Care to tell us about it?"

"Oh man, it's fun."

The host shot Benji and Angelica a look, asking for help.

Benji propped their fist on their chin. "When you say fun, what do you *really* mean?"

"What?" Matt asked.

"Hold on," Benji held up a finger and did something they never did on TV. They pulled out their reading glasses and perched them on their nose. "Better?"

"I'll say." Angelica fanned her face with her hand. "I had no idea I had a thing for glasses."

"I have glasses." The host pushed his frames up his nose with a smoldering look.

"Yes, but darling, you're gay," Angelica pointed out, her voice light and flirty. "What would you do with me?" She waggled her eyebrows and clasped her hands, pushing up her breasts and showcasing the inverted cross descending into her cleavage. It was distracting.

"Damn," Benji said. "I should've brought some breasts too."

"They do come in handy." Angelica patted hers.

"Okay," the podcaster judge said. "You are both getting red cards for obstructing Matt's play. Off to the penalty box with you."

Benji responded with a spit take, earning themself another six points.

Angelica stuck her tongue out at him but followed Benji as they trooped over to the small PVC pipe and clear plastic chest-high box in the corner across from the judges. They opened the door and let her in first before joining her to lean against the wall across from her. It was a tight fit. They were just far enough away not to touch but only barely. They could *feel* how close she was.

To distract themself, Benji cupped their hands around their mouth to make up for their turned-off mike and yelled, "You need a bigger box."

"That's what she said!" Angelica yelled from behind them.

"Quiet or I'll extend your time in the box!" The judge yelled back with a grin. The soap actress judge smothered her laughter behind her hand.

"Seriously? A 'that's what she said' joke?" Benji turned to her, lounging with their back against the penalty box wall.

"'You need a bigger box' isn't about to win any awards, Omega." She leaned in her corner. Benji was very aware they could be *much* closer.

"Eh." Benji dismissed her insult with a wave. "I'm gonna destroy you in the final round anyway, Coma White."

She chuckled. "You're so competitive. You know the prizes on this show are literal trash, right?"

"I heard they gave out falconry lessons one time."

"Do you have a burning desire to… falcon? Is that the word?"

"I don't think that's a verb." Benji considered. "I falconed. She falconed. They were out falconing. Yeah, no."

"Thank goodness you were here to catch that or I would've embarrassed myself on live TV." Angelica rolled her eyes but her mouth lifted at the corner.

"Yeah, because neither of us has ever done *that* before."

She laughed, the sound like champagne bubbles against Benji's skin. She smelled like… cinnamon? Something spicy and sweet. Sugar and bite. Benji mentally shook themself. It didn't matter what she smelled like. It didn't.

"You're just mad cuz I'm winning," she was saying.

"Ten points is nothing." Benji crossed their arms. "I'll beat you in no time."

"Dream on, old-timer."

"Respect the five years I have on you, whippersnapper."

"Okay, boomer."

It was Benji's turn to roll their eyes. The podcaster judge was glaring at them from across the stage but they ignored him.

"So what huge favor did the host do for you that they got you to come on such short notice?"

She squinted at them, looking confused. "Favor?"

"That's the rumor backstage."

She shook her head. "I just like the show."

"That's it?"

"That and Brendan's the newest on Cheryl's roster. She said his show could use the boost." She shrugged. "I wasn't doing anything tonight, figured I'd support a fellow queer."

Benji blinked at her. Old friends couldn't drag them out of the house on this short notice and she was doing it because some stranger's show wasn't getting ratings? At least that dispelled the inane theory sitting in the back of their head that she'd done it to see them.

As if reading their mind, she purred, "But I can't say getting to beat you on TV didn't make it much more enticing. When Cheryl told me you'd be on, I knew I had to do it."

Guess, that theory wasn't so inane afterall.

"All right, you two can come out now." The host waved them out of the box and back to their seats when Matt's time expired. He barely made half Benji's score.

The judges gently roasted him. "You were so stoned you made me feel stoned," the podcaster said. "But I never turn down a free high so I enjoyed it."

"As someone who once played a mother on TV," the actress said. "I was concerned. But as a judge, I was mildly bored."

Their scores were generous but not nearly enough to get Matt anywhere close to Benji and Angelica.

"Sorry Matt," the host said. "It looks like Benji and Angela will be moving on without you. But you'll still get this fabulous third place prize! Miss Anthrope?"

An aggressively craggy-looking drag queen came out and brandished the prize at Matt like it was a weapon.

"An eggplant emoji pillow!" The host said. "That'll keep

you warm at night. I have two." He winked. "It's time for the flesh-tingling Final Round where contestants answer questions as fast as they can for as many laughs as possible!"

He gestured them over to the other half of the soundstage where two podiums with large red buttons were set up against each other, shrouded in dry ice. Once they set up, the host asked, "Are you ready?"

"Am I in an 80s music video?" Benji asked. The amount of fog swirling around the stage was only slightly concerning.

"No," the host said.

Benji pretended to be relieved. "Then I'm ready."

"Angela?"

"Dry ice is my natural element so I'm deeply ready."

"All right." The host started the timer. "Teddy Roosevelt was a colonizer with a bear named after him. How many bears are just right?"

Benji hit the button. "However many fit in my bed."

"Correct. Though I would've accepted them in my bed too."

Angelica laughed, shaking her head.

"Next question: Birds of a feather flock together. What's the best way to end a Twitter feud?"

Angelica hit the button. She leaned in towards Benji giving them an exaggeratedly seductive look. "Kiss and make up."

"No," the host said. "Benji?"

Screw it. Benji leaned in too, dropping their gaze to her lips and put on their *fuck me* voice. "Live streamed phone sex."

Angelica froze, her eyes going wide, dark, and wanting. It was only for a split second but it was a split second that drowned both of them. Then she snapped out of it, faking a laugh. "I assume by that you mean banging your phones together like I used to do with Barbies?"

Benji raised an eyebrow. "What else would it mean?"

The host fanned his face. "I'll accept that only because I'm worried about spontaneously combusting over here. Next question…"

Benji played the rest of the round on autopilot, a skill they'd perfected in their UFO years, getting through far too many important events being charming and lucid while absolutely out of their head high. They scraped out a win and ended up with an excitingly ugly grandfather clock for their trouble.

Angelica seemed to be going through the motions too. Laughing and smiling at the crowd as they all waved for the show closing, joking with the host, all the right moves with none of the investment of before. No feeling radiated off of her. The minute the lights went down, she was gone.

In the parking lot, while filming the credits sequence of trying to put their prize in their car, Benji regarded the grandfather clock on its dolly and tried to pull their thoughts away from the vulnerable wanting of Angelica's eyes. They didn't know what they'd do if she looked at them like that again without the crowd and the podiums between them.

CHAPTER 7

Angie closed her computer with a grimace. Her fancy GPS-enabled but otherwise internet-less phone sat forgotten across the room, exactly the way she liked it these days. Blessedly silent, though she wouldn't have minded if Benji had texted... No, it was probably better they hadn't.

There was no way she was going to the show. She'd been out of sorts and confused since that game show. Since Benji *flirted* with her.

Hell on wheels, that had been... been... she didn't have

words for it. It was so surreal she kept rewatching the clip to remind herself it was real. And to make sure her reaction wasn't as huge as it had felt (it wasn't). And to relive it because, *damn*.

It was heady, it was glorious, it was dangerous as fuck. She had no idea if it meant anything to them. They hadn't called the number she gave them, hadn't posted anything on social media, not even a goddamn carrier pigeon for two weeks, and now this.

Did their mother know? Was she baiting Angie? She mulled it over on the drive to her appointment.

Shaking off the paranoia, she clenched her fists as she walked down the hallway, hoping no one would come out of the other shrink offices. Sure, she was wearing a wig, not a scrap of white, and really toned down make-up, but you never knew.

Not that she was ashamed of going to therapy, but privacy was hard to come by and she'd like to keep this private as long as possible. That was the problem with playing yourself on stage, you could never go out and be you anonymously again. Especially when your music was "an overwrought diary of an oversharer" as one reviewer once put it. That article was taped on the wall in her personal studio. She threw sharp objects at it sometimes when she was pissed.

She strode into Dr. Lopez's office with a nod to the receptionist and flopped on the couch. The waiting room was gloriously empty.

Baphomet, she was tired. Tour prep was ramping up and so was her anxiety. The fund was taking off, which made her happy, though sob stories attached to the applications (where she'd very explicitly asked for only the barest bones of the applicant's story), filled her with vengeful rage.

At this rate, she'd have to tour for the rest of her life to burn off the rage. Unless one of those asshats leaving threatening comments on all her posts tried her in person. Then she'd happily curbstomp them.

It was getting to be a lot though. Even with the amount of bullshit she'd waded through over the years.

Not to mention the phone calls she'd been dealing with lately. Cheryl kept the worst from her but sometimes the most effective thing was to let Angie loose to voice her displeasure and threaten to come down to the Department of Corrections in person. The lawyers said there wasn't much she could do this time, victims' preferences weren't taken into account for release, but that was just their opinion.

Angie (and Cheryl's vast network of connections) had gotten Mama moved from Florida to California, kept her from getting parole, and kept tabs on her. But now, they were up against the statewide push to close prisons—and while Angie was fine with that in theory—in practice, her mother had thirteen years of good behavior, less than two years left on her sentence, and supposedly showed remorse, enough, apparently, to put her up for early release. What if Angie's team failed and Mama was out in the world? Would she come find Angie? Would Mama even be able to survive—

"You can go in." The receptionist smiled at her sympathetically. Angie suspected it was a practiced expression. It looked the same every time. Odds were she was an aspiring actress. It wasn't as if Angie hadn't ever faked an expression before, it just pinged her paranoia when other people did.

Dr. Lopez gave her a real smile when she entered and stood, gesturing for Angie to sit. During their first appointment, she tried to start the session by shaking Angie's hand. Angie had already been upset, anxious about being there and the other ten billion things crowding around in her head. She hadn't been thinking. She'd taken the therapist's hand.

Dr. Lopez had gone pale, her breath stuttering. Angie had been certain she'd end the session there and then. But the other woman proved stronger than Angie expected. They've lasted three months so far together.

The cynical part of Angie (the part that sounded like Mama) wondered if Dr. Lopez was writing a paper on her.

"How are you doing today, Angie?" Dr. Lopez asked. "Can you tell me your BEN?"

Angie took stock of her body, emotions, and needs. "My back aches, I'm tired from not getting enough sleep, anxious, and I need…" she considered.

This was always the hard part for her. Her needs used to be impulses, driving her without thought for herself or others. She needed to be famous. She needed to put her past to song, to put her present to song, to drain her emotions so they'd stop eating her alive. Now, she was taking apart her impulses and following them to their roots, and well, she didn't quite know what was healthy to need anymore.

"A glass of water," she said finally.

Dr. Lopez got her one from the dispenser next to her desk. "Let's talk about your anxiety. Is that what's keeping you up?"

Angie sipped the water and nodded. That and Benji, but she didn't want to talk about them. She needed this thing with Benji analyzed like she needed a hole in the head. Nothing killed the mood like psychoanalysis. "I'm worried about going back on tour."

"Is this about the incident on your last tour?"

Angie grimaced as the memory cascaded over her: the numbness that slowly consumed her after her twenty-eighth birthday in the middle of the tour last year scared her band so much that one night Gemma had shaken her just to get a reaction. The numbness had broken but Angie had also shrieked wordlessly in her face until they were both crying.

She'd dragged everyone into her emotional maelstrom until the driver of the tour bus had to pull over. Angie had limped through the last few stops of the tour, sleeping too much during the day and staring at the ceiling at night, caught in thought loops until she lost time.

She'd been going hard her entire adult life but she had never expected to live *this* long. Her band watched her like a hawk. Cheryl told her she had to start therapy or the manager would walk and the band might too.

So here she was, every week, almost twenty-nine, talking about her feelings because it helped, or whatever. She'd come to terms with the fact that she wasn't living fast and dying young. It was a good thing, a privilege. She just had to realign the entire idea of her future and that had been a struggle.

"Would you like to talk about it?" Dr. Lopez looked at her expectantly. "You seem to be feeling strongly."

Angie wrapped the emotions under her skin, humming a riff she'd been working on this morning, and examined the therapist. "I'm okay."

"Don't hold back on my account." Dr. Lopez smiled. "You seem to be getting better at controlling your feelings. This is a safe space. I want you to feel able to discuss anything."

Angie took a breath, letting it out slowly. "I'm afraid I'll go numb again. I'm afraid someone will try to fix me again and I'll break them. I'm tired of the constant grind and I'm afraid I'll lose the good habits I've built up once we're on the road. But I'm also afraid that if I don't have an outlet like touring things will get bad again."

"That's a lot to carry."

Angie shrugged. "I'll figure it out."

"I can help, if you let me."

Angie half-smiled at the floor. She knew she was supposed to be grateful but she just felt uncomfortable. People said they'd help but most of the time Angie ended up doing shit herself. It was easier not to trust anyone. Mama always said… Oh. She rarely talked about her mother here. "Mama's up for release. Early." The words came out before she could stop them.

"How do you feel about that?"

Angie thought about it, sifting through the bubbling cauldron of fucked-up-ness that was her subconscious. "I don't want her out in the world, you know? I know prison's bad and the system's shit but if she's out she could come find me…" Her knuckles tightened on the paper cup and she drained it before it spilled. "I'm not scared of her. I'm just tired of thinking about her. I'm tired of her existing." She glanced up to see if Dr. Lopez's composure would slip at that.

Nothing.

Angie chewed her lip, caught herself doing it, and stopped. Mama said it was never good to have a tell. "She wrote me some bullshit letter. The victim's board is keeping it. Supposedly it means she's sorry." Angie shook her head. "I'm not reading it."

"What I'm hearing is you think about your mother a lot but you don't want to and this letter is another reminder of her."

Angie nodded. "It's probably some guilt trip. Fuck that. I've mined a lot of that emotion right out of me, you know? I've profited off it, my pain, I mean, and I guess, hers. I've used it up. I used to cry, every night, every show when I sang—" She inhaled and crooned. "When Daddy's a corpse/And Mommy's the knife/You're raised by the radio man/Who's wrong when it's right." She paused. "Right there, that's where the tears would start. Now, the audience cries for me. I sold my pain. And frankly, I don't want it back." She looked at Dr. Lopez, daring her to try to make her feel shitty about that. "I don't want her to reopen those wounds. I don't want anyone to."

"That's understandable. Those scars feel safe to you."

"Yeah."

"Do you feel like you've resolved your issues with your mother?"

Angie let out a short *ha!* of bitter laughter. "Resolved? No, they just evolved. The void she carved in me changes shape and I just have to keep up."

"Why a void? Why that imagery?"

Angie shrugged, looking at the floor. "There's a hole where my parents once were. My dad was far from perfect, but Mama's the one who carved them out of my life. Pretty literally."

Her fingers suddenly felt warm and sticky, a faint metallic tang hanging in the air. She didn't close her eyes, she knew exactly what she'd see. Instead, she rolled her head up slowly like a ragdoll, watching Dr. Lopez struggle to keep composure.

The monster part of her was always fascinated by the way her emotions took on a life of their own outside her body. She hummed to herself, trying to latch onto a tune even as her tongue tasted like copper and her chest seized. The images kept slipping through her grip, the feelings spiraling away from her.

Mama stood in the kitchen, Daddy at her feet, washing a knife in the sink. She turned to Angie and said, *Angel, you're not supposed to be home yet.*

Angie took a deep breath and bit her lip, the pain grounding her.

Dr. Lopez's eyes were glassy but her face was blank. How much did she feel? Were her fingers tacky, sticking together? Did she see red out of the corners of her eyes? Did she taste copper? Angie's emotions were rarely so direct when they infected other people, they just snuck in and triggered whatever equivalent feelings were there. At least that's what Rohan told her, years ago.

It's overwhelming, like I can't help but feel what you do.

Dammit, why had she done that? Why had she brought up that day? Her therapist didn't deserve this.

The last time a reporter had been brave enough to raise the subject, Angie had been twenty-two and the pain was still fresh after six years. Her memories reduced him to a fetal ball on the floor as she sat in front of the camera, tears bleeding her eyeliner silently down her face.

It was one of her most watched videos to this day. Most people considered it proof she was a witch, that she'd just had the inverted cross inked down the center of her chest had only amplified her infamy. She had protesters at her shows for years, still got them from time to time when some fundamentalists were feeling frisky.

Dr. Lopez blinked rapidly. She took a deep breath and then another. It was subtle, if Angie had been distracted she would've missed it.

"Sorry." Angie sighed. Some days she felt like she couldn't go an hour without hurting someone. Sometimes that felt powerful and she hated herself later. She got up and poured a glass of water for her therapist, placing it at her elbow.

Dr. Lopez looked at the cup in surprise. "Trauma is like that. It has no sense of time and can completely shut down the decision-making part of your brain when it takes over. What I want you to do now, is to stop for a moment and listen to your body. Now that this has passed, what do you need?" She took a sip of the water.

Angie knew what she wanted: a tub of ice cream and Benji to call her so she could distract herself by baiting them. But was that what she needed?

"A hug," she whispered and her fucking voice cracked because she couldn't imagine who would give her one. Her eyes got hot and wet because she couldn't remember the last time she'd had a real hug, not some idiot trying to put their arm around her for a picture.

"And who can give you that hug?"

"N-no one." Angie stuffed her fist in her mouth and hummed around it. The song that came out of her mouth was

User-Friendly Omega's "Temptation of the King" which honestly didn't help things.

"That's not true." Dr. Lopez offered her a tissue. "You can always give yourself a hug."

"That feels ridiculous." Angie dabbed her cheeks.

"But does it help?"

Angie frowned and wrapped her arms around herself. Yeah, it was silly but it also felt nice. Comforting.

"It's not the same as a hug from someone but it helps release the same good chemicals. Humans need touch, Angie." Dr. Lopez gave her a sympathetic look. "And giving it to ourselves is the next best thing." She smiled. "Our time is up. Will you be okay to drive?"

Angie nodded.

"I want to give you some homework."

"Just what every high school dropout wants to hear," Angie joked weakly.

Dr. Lopez's smile looked fake. "Your relationship with your mother seems to be a big root of your trauma."

Angie swallowed another smart ass remark.

"I take it you never discussed that with her?"

You are so like your father, Mama hissed from Angie's memory, her skin tinged green by the shitty holding cell lights. *With your big feelings, twisting the rest of us around your fingers like puppets.*

It was one of the last times Angie had seen her. The DA wanted to trot poor little Angie out for the trial but Mama pleaded guilty and saved them all the circus.

"No," Angie said, pulling herself back to the present and Dr. Lopez's questions.

"I suggest you write her letters," the therapist said. She held up a hand as Angie tensed. "You don't need to send them and you absolutely don't have to read the letter she sent, but I think writing to her might help you work through your feelings in a way that lyrics haven't fully. If you prefer, you can write them to your younger self instead, tell her the things you wish you'd heard back then."

Angie could barely come up with lyrics these days but hell, what was another writing assignment? She nodded.

Dr. Lopez stood to show her out. Before opening the door, she hesitated. "This projecting you do, I've never come across it before. Have you ever met someone like you before?"

"Mama said all the entire Alice family was like that. She always said she was lucky to get Daddy." Angie shrugged. Daddy could talk anyone into anything and often did. How lucky either of them were to end up together was up for debate. "I never met anyone else with it. His family didn't like Mama and by the time I can remember my parents didn't really trust anyone with me."

"Why was that?"

"Too many people tried to walk off with me." She shrugged again. That was before when she was silly and innocent and not filled with spiky emotions that cut people like barbed wire. "The good news is nobody's wanted to steal me in a long time."

CHAPTER 8

"No, no I can't
I can't go out there
The hungry eyes,
The hungry mouths

Dry heaving
Expelling
I am not lonely in a crowd
I'm smothered and loud
I'm suffocating
There's nothing left

[chorus of voices]
Sad little king
We gave you our hearts
Scream us your song
Make it go down easy
To be wrong

No, no don't make me

Please, please
I'm losing myself
Piece by piece
There's nothing left"
— "Temptation of the King" by User-Friendly Omega off of
Suicide King

Benji sat in the community meeting room of the Foundation, mindlessly straightening the art supplies on the table in front of them. The heater was on blast to fight off the unseasonably cool September day but they were both too cold and too hot, their shirt sticking to their back. They ignored it. It happened every time and they always wore a jacket to cover the tell. They shouldn't be nervous, they'd done this a thousand times and it rarely went sideways. There was nothing to be reactive about here. This was safe.

Around the conference table, a ring of people sat, some of them fiddling with the crafts scattered around, some chatting. Benji picked up the beading project they'd been working on for the last few months. It was a checkerboard pattern in black and white, nothing fancy, but it soothed them to have something to do with their hands.

"Alright folks, it's six oh five so I guess we better start this thing." Jo, a tall white person with buzzed hair and fake eyelashes stood up. Benji and Jo went way back—the two of them shared a room in the same mental health treatment facility. "Welcome to Gender: Complicated. If you're here for the non-binary support and social group, you're in the right place. Otherwise, the knitting club is across the hall." Pause for laughter. "My name is Jo and my pronouns are he and they. Let's go around the room and introduce ourselves. Please remember all discussions should be respectful and kind. Everything said here stays here."

The group was small, consisting of mostly people Benji

knew. They were glad there were no newbies tonight. Inevitably, the odds were about one in four newbies would turn out to be a celebrity chaser. Gender: Complicated wasn't well advertised but Benji wasn't the only non-binary person with a bit of fame who showed up. Most of the other famous folks heard about it from Benji. Though Foundation was infamous for being run by Rohan and Angelica—and being a battle-ground during their break-up, at the moment, Benji was the biggest name in the building.

They shifted in their sea, rearranging their beads unnec-essarily.

"How did everyone's week go?" Jo asked.

A round of shrugs and smiles greeted the question.

Lena sighed, fiddling with a they/them pin Benji hadn't seen before. "Shitty. I went to visit my parents."

Sympathetic murmurs rippled around the table.

"Have they gotten any better about using your pronouns?" Jude asked, gluing a collage of sequins and magazine cutouts together.

"Yes, actually," Lena said. "Now my mother is deeply mourning the loss of her 'little girl.'"

"Are you okay?" Cam asked, er cheeks flushed. E blushed whenever e said anything to Lena.

"Yeah, probably." Lena spun their phone nervously between their fingers. "It's nothing new, you know?"

More sympathetic murmurs. Benji was reminded, as they were every meeting, that they were damn lucky to have a mom as supportive and non-judgemental as Hanayu was. Of course, given what she got up to and what Benji's dad did for a living, there really wasn't much room to judge.

"My dad thinks it's a phase," Karley said, rolling their eyes. Groans greeted their words. "I tried to explain sexuality and gender as something that can evolve over time but I could just see it go right over his head."

"Ben," Jude whispered, leaning over. Benji didn't use their full name here, pretending it gave them some semblance of anonymity. "I saw you on a *The Talk Show Game* clip last night. You killed it!"

"Thanks," Benji murmured back, hoping that would be the end of it. That episode was two weeks old already, why was it still in circulation?

"I can't believe they got Angela Alice," Jude continued. "What was she like? Was she cool? You two seemed like you knew each other...?" Jude trailed off, eyebrows up with expectation.

"Um." If this wasn't a place Benji was actively trying to make a safe space, they would've said something cutting. Instead, they caught Jo's eye, begging them for rescue.

Luckily, Jo was well used to this. "Hey," they interjected, gently. "Jude, let's pay attention to the conversation as a whole, please. Side conversations aren't respectful."

"But Ben was on *The Talk Show Game* with Angela freaking Alice!" Jude cried like this was bigger than the time Benji got a Grammy and accepted it from Dio himself. "Angela freaking Alice!"

Jo's eyebrows rose. "And how do you think Ben feels about you bringing up their business without permission?"

"Oh," Jude deflated, suddenly looking very young. "Shit. Sorry, Ben."

"Apology accepted," Benji said.

"Angela Alice is in league with the Devil," Lena said, like they were reciting something someone had once drilled into them. "She's evil."

"What, so all Satanists are evil?" Jude snapped. "Way to stereotype."

Lena looked shocked. "Are you a Satanist?" They toyed with the cross around their neck.

"No," Jude said. "But I thought we weren't supposed to

make assumptions here. Also, she, like, owns this place with RK so what are you doing here if you think she's evil, huh?"

"She *does*?" Lena said. "Ben, is Angela Alice evil?"

"No." The word came out before Benji even thought about it, cutting through the conversation like a knife. Everyone went silent, shocked. Benji was fine with that, they wanted this done.

"I'm a Satanist," Grey mumbled in the quiet, hugging their knees. They were small, usually engulfed in a faded sweatshirt. Benji and Jo worried they were homeless but Grey never stuck around to talk, so they couldn't ask.

"Why?" Lena demanded.

"Lena, is it respectful to interrogate folks about their religion?" Jo asked.

"Sorry," Lena muttered. They were so very eighteen. It was tiring sometimes.

"God never did me any good," Grey said. "Why not talk to the devil instead?"

"Because he's the incarnation of all evil!" Lena cried. "In hell, they torture you and ra—"

"Whoa! Trigger warning!" Karley said.

Tears slipped down Lena's cheeks, their knuckles white around the crucifix.

Jo offered them a tissue. "Lena, is there something you would like to talk about?"

Lena sobbed, twisting the cross back and forth anxiously. "Am I going to hell?"

"For what?" Benji asked.

Jo shot them a warning glance.

Lena waved a hand at their half-shaved head, high heels, and bound chest.

Benji cocked their head. "Is your god so closed-minded he cannot accept you for who you are? Or is it the people who claim to speak for him?"

Lena's eyes widened, fingers stilling on the cross.

"I like to think god made us just the way we are," Cam said. "And loves us flaws and all."

"Being non-binary isn't a flaw," Karley pointed out.

Lena nodded, dabbing their eyes.

"You don't have to believe anything that doesn't feel right. I think you can choose what you believe no matter what people tell you," Cam said. E offered Lena a hug and kept er arm around them.

"I prefer witchcraft," Karley said, with a smile. "I just made a dope ass altar." They whipped out their phone and showed everyone a picture.

"Religion is the opiate of the masses," Jude muttered.

"Respect, Jude." Jo's tone said they were getting real tired real fast. "Let's move on. Does anyone have any weekend plans?"

Benji let the rest of the meeting wash over them. It was fractious and funny and the only place in the whole world where they were in a room full of people who knew up close and personal exactly what it was like to be misgendered all day, to calculate the odds of assault based on how closely your outfit touched the binary, and why pronouns were so important. It wasn't exactly relaxing, but it was affirming. It made them feel less crazy, less demanding for asking people to respect their pronouns and gender fluidity.

After the meeting was over, they helped Jo clean up the craft supplies.

"You good?" Jo asked, once everyone was gone.

Benji shrugged. "It's not like this is the first time this has happened."

"I meant about them going off about your friend," Jo said.

Benji blinked. "Friend?"

"Angela Alice? Sorry, did I assume?"

"We're not friends."

"Okay." Jo paused. "Here, if you wanna talk about it."

Benji shook their head then stopped. Jo helped them through detonating their fame and leaving their old gender. Hell, they'd seen them at their lowest even before that and Benji saw Jo at theirs. Jo wouldn't judge them. "I don't know what I'm doing."

"How so?"

"I don't like her."

"Okay…"

"She's my friend's shitty ex and I'm supposed to hate her. He's moved on but he's also somehow still a teddy bear after being in the industry forever."

Jo smiled. Everyone loved Rohan. It was hard not to. "But?"

"I flirted with her, Jo. *On air*. What the hell was I thinking?" They still couldn't shake the look in her eyes, like this was everything she ever wanted.

After it aired, Rohan sent them a text that just said: *Saw the episode, be careful.*

"No one thinks what happens on TV is real." Jo patted their arm with the cheerful cynicism of an industry veteran. Then they looked at their face. "*Was* it real?"

Benji shrugged. "Have you met her?"

Jo shook their head. "I came in after the board cut her privileges, remember? I'm not sure I've ever seen her."

"She's…" Benji grimaced, looking for a word that didn't sound over the top. "When she decides you're interesting, it's like being back on stage. And she thinks I'm interesting right now."

"Okay."

"I just got caught up in the moment." That's what they kept telling themself. If they repeated it enough maybe it would come true. "I was drinking."

Jo raised their eyebrows. They were no stranger to substance abuse, though their drug of choice was coke.

Benji frowned. "I'm not backsliding." Their breakdown was years ago now. It had been a chemically enabled breakdown but dependency had never been their problem. They pushed aside memories of that night. "I just, I dunno, feel weird about it. Like I blurred a line, you know?"

"Like you opened the door to something?"

Benji grimaced. "Maybe. She ran off fast though and I feel bad? Maybe she feels more than I think she does about me."

"You are pretty great." Jo bumped their shoulder against Benji's as they passed and smiled.

Benji faked a smile. 'Great' wasn't the word they'd use. They were just trying to be better. It was really all they could aspire to.

Angie stood in front of the back door of the Foundation and took a breath. Ever since she and Rohan imploded and she'd, well, made it worse, coming to the Foundation was an act of defiance. Yes, she was still technically a co-founder and funder, but the board put their collective foot down and punished her. It didn't help that half of them were related to Rohan by blood or marriage or he was the sweeter of the two of them.

Now, she had a visitation schedule, carefully curated to keep their paths from crossing. Even though they were *fine*.

As had always been the case, nobody ever forgave her as quickly as Rohan did. It was freakishly nice and sometimes she missed it, still. Just like her to fuck up the best thing that ever happened to her.

She shook the thought off and pushed the door open. She had to do something to offset that therapy session or she was going to end up in her studio making warped things not even she could use. She strode down the hall like she owned the place because she did. It was the reason they couldn't completely shut her out. She headed for the clothing deposit, ready to sort through donations until she was too tired to think.

"Ms. A!" The receptionist stood when she entered the lobby. He was a scrawny kid but Angie was pleased to note he'd finally started filling out. She'd hired him after he did some volunteer data entry when the Foundation was still basically a soup kitchen. A few months ago, she'd helped him move from Section 8 housing into a new place by himself. His first place alone.

She half-smiled at him. "How's it going, Mac?"

"It's not your day, Ms. A."

She stopped, anger stabbing through her preoccupation. She curbed it. "It's Wednesday."

He shook his head, eyes just a bit wide. "They switched your day this week, remember? RK's fiance is doing her sex lesson thingy in half an hour. Your day is tomorrow."

"Fuck," Angie breathed. She forgot to check her calendar. Hell, she hadn't been thinking, she'd just driven here on autopilot, numb. Damn, damn, damn. The last thing she wanted after flaying herself in therapy was to run into that wannabe shrink sex educator, Cazzi.

Footsteps clattered down the stairs from the meeting rooms. Some meeting was letting out and here she was without even a wig on to disguise her.

"I won't tell," Mac said. "But you gotta get out of her. Mrs. Pandit has been arguing with Cazzi over wedding stuff again."

"Oh hell." Angie turned on her heel. Rohan's grandma was on the board and really didn't like her. "Thanks, Mac!" She hurried back the way she came, cursing herself. She was far too distracted. Now, what the hell was she going to do? Sit at home and watch TV? Write fake letters to her mother? Or, more likely, eat ice cream and rewatch that clip?

Oh Lucifer, she was pathetic.

She stomped through the parking lot, almost hoping there was a pap lurking and green enough to try and talk to her.

Dammit, all to—

"What are you doing here?"

"I'm leaving!" She snarled, whipping around before her brain recognized the voice.

Benji stood in front of her, arms crossed. "Reign in your —" They waved their fingers vaguely at the area around her. "Nonsense."

The anger spiraling around her ballooned. "Fuck off, Benji. I'm entitled to my emotions."

"Sure but—"

"No one's around!" She snarled. "And you're welcome to get the hell away from me. I am not currently hurting anyone. *I am leaving.*"

They frowned, unmoved. "Are you okay?"

"You don't care. Don't bother pretending you do because you think it makes you a good person."

"You know I don't bother pretending I'm a good person," they snapped back.

"Oh, I'm *aware*," she snarled. "I *remember*."

They narrowed their eyes. "Someone had to keep you in line."

She barked out a laugh. "So what? You're the appointed monster handler? The weapon to wield against the demon? You used to be just as bad as me, with your *Suicide King*."

"That album was never about me," Benji snapped back, so fast it sounded automatic.

"Exactly. You used someone else's pain. You caused harm," she said. "I've read your interviews."

They took a step forward. "Then you know I used to be

worse, worse than you."

She rolled her eyes. "Is this intimidation? You're off your game if you think this is scaring me. Try again."

Benji exhaled hard, aggressively.

Angie bared her teeth at them. Lucy, yes, this was what she needed. Everything was electric, focused. Nothing else mattered.

"Not here," they gritted out. "There's a bunch of paps out front, waiting for Rohan."

"Again, with the pretending you care."

Benji made a frustrated noise and grabbed her arm, towing her along with surprising strength to a nearby alley. She let them even though the smell from the nearby dumpsters was pretty awful. This was too much fun to stop.

They let her go with a flick of their wrist she supposed would've sent someone else stumbling. She just rocked back on her heels, laughing at them. "Look at you enbyhandling me into an alley. Are we gonna fight or fuck?" She shifted into a fighting stance, fists up. "I know which I'd prefer."

They leaned against the opposite wall and tried to look unimpressed but there was color staining their cheeks and their clothes were deliciously rumpled.

She raised an eyebrow. "Well? You gonna play with me?"

They shoved their hair back from their face and leaned into hers. "Not everything's a game."

"With us it is."

"Be serious."

"No."

They leaned back and groaned, the long column of their throat exposed. She wanted to sink her teeth in. Lick her way up the tendons until they forgot everything but her. "You are infuriating."

"You're fun to screw with."

"Why?" They demanded.

"Because," she surprised herself by saying. "You enjoy it."

They sputtered. "Enjoy it?"

She shrugged, suddenly uncertain but burying the feeling before it could leak out. "Why else would you keep coming back to play?" She thought back to their feud, how they baited her through subtweets and bit back every time she subtweeted them. To Endfest when she baited them in person and they snapped back every time, a gleam in their eye. The last few weeks, on the show...

They were obviously remembering the same things because they swore and scrubbed their hands over their face. "You're a goddamn menace."

Angie laughed. "You enjoy being menaced." She poked their arm, barely touching them. "Do I make you feel alive?"

"I feel perfectly alive without you," they said drily, meeting her eyes. Suddenly she realized they were close, barely a foot apart—and they were backed against the wall. She wanted to cage them in, grind herself against them, see if this was fore-play for them too.

They watched her like she was dangerous, or maybe like they wanted her, she wasn't sure. "What are you thinking, Omega?"

They glanced at her lips and licked their own. Her breath caught, her whole body going hot and still. But then they shook their head and straightened, the same height as her now that both of them were in Doc Martens. "Do you feel better, Coma White?" The question was unexpectedly tender.

She hated it. "Don't pretend you were fighting with me out of the goodness of your heart." She spun away, getting as far away as the width of the alley would allow. She should just leave, cut this cord before it tangled and tripped her. "I thought we covered that."

They moved, close enough their sleeve brushed hers as they came up behind her. Their scent surrounded her, lemon and cloves and maybe something smoky. "Yes, yes. We're both bad. But we have feelings. You, more than most people."

"Oh, am I hurting yours?" She dreaded they'd say yes.

They chuckled. "You're not trying to hurt me or I'd be hurt. I don't know what you're taking out on me and you don't have to tell me." Out of the corner of her eye she could see their mouth dip down close to her ear just before they breathed. "But are you good now, Angelica?"

She leaned back into them just enough to feel the edges of them, looking up at them through her lashes. "Call me Angie." She purred.

They met her gaze, their eyes half-lidded but intent on her alone. "No."

She suppressed a smile. "Contrary," she said it as a compliment.

"You enjoy it."

"I do." She let herself half-smile. Oh Baphomet, she revelled in it.

Their gaze darkened.

Were they going to kiss her? Should she kiss them first? Everything fell away until they were the sharpest thing in her vision. She wanted to drag them to her, to cut the tension, but she loved the way they drew it out. It had to be Benji who made the move anyway, since they were the one resisting. They had to be the one to decide.

They brushed the hair out of her face with a finger, her nerves sparkling in the wake of their touch. "Take care, Angelica," they said, their voice low and velvet.

And then they walked away.

"Oh, come on!" She yelled at their back. "Really?"

They just turned back and laughed. "I thought you liked to play."

"Jackass." But she was laughing too and they were already gone.

CHAPTER 9

Reporter: Let's talk about religion
Angela Alice: *Sure, which one?*
Reporter: Um, well the obvious choice…
AA: *Which is?*
Reporter: Yours?
AA: *Is it?*
Reporter: [clears throat] Yes, well. You are famously a Satanist.
AA: *Wow, you really did your research.*
Reporter: Thanks. What—
AA: *Then you must know my policy.*
Reporter: Um, what policy?
AA: *The one in my pinned post. I'm sure my team briefed you on it. I don't discuss Satanism if you can't name three Satanic groups and tell me the differences between them.*
Reporter: Shit, right now?
AA: [Waits]
— Real Music, Real Talk Live!

Benji lay in bed and cursed themself. All they could think about was Angelica in the alley. The barest brush of her against them and they were taut with arousal. What kind of nonsense was this? Benji met and fucked some of the sexiest, most charismatic people in the world. None of them hijacked their good sense the way Angelica could. Even with Sly, Benji had been able to control themself. But then again he had never reciprocated, never been interested.

Angelica was damn well interested. No wonder Rohan had been so hung up on her. The minute she focused all her attention on you, the minute she wanted you… it was heady. If they ever had sex—

Benji stood, cutting off the thought. They stared out at the hazy city skyline and willed themself to think about literally anything else. They would've loved to just jack it out of their head but they were afraid if they started thinking of her while playing with themself they'd never stop. They leaned their forehead against the cool glass and focused on the view they spent most of their rent paying for. Living up in the hills was a pain when it came to parking and navigating the twisting, narrow roads but when you wanted to spend the night brooding over the smoggy, sparkling sprawl of LA, there was no better place than this.

They knew exactly where she lived, not that they could see it from here. They'd been there once when she hadn't been home to help Rohan grab the last of his stuff after the break-up. It wasn't a place you forgot easily. She'd bought the biggest house on the block, a three-story faux-Victorian mansion, and painted it a violent red-purple. The inside was equally memorable with each room sporting a different goth-themed wallpaper and an altar.

Basically, it was exactly what you'd expect her house to look like. Rohan told them she'd named it the PhenoBarbie

Doll Dream House after her first platinum album but everyone who'd ever been there just called it the Castle. Probably because of the turret... and the moat, small as it was.

Benji had caught a glimpse of her room when Rohan was off getting his toothbrush or something from the ensuite bathroom. It was huge, dominated by a Cal-King four-poster bed with a ridiculous drapery ceiling and black curtains. A bed fit for the Bitch Queen and her consort.

Benji wondered if she was lying awake in that big bed thinking about them too. They shut that image down, not just because it made them feel like an angsty teenager all over again.

They grimaced at the city below them. What the hell had they gotten themself into and what did it say about them that they enjoyed it?

Angie lay in bed, curtains drawn. It was something she'd only done once or twice since she'd gotten the damn thing, thinking it was wonderfully fancy. But not being able to see the room around her made her paranoid. Especially since that fan broke into her house when she first moved in years ago.

The guy had been harmless and only wanted to wander around, touching things but it had still been disturbing as hell. She'd installed a whole new security system and for years Rohan had been there to make sure the house wasn't empty. Then the pandemic hit right after their break-up and she'd haunted the house by herself. When touring started up again she considered having a house sitter but the idea of someone being in her house for months, touching her things, wigged her out.

Instead, she'd acquired crime scene tape and sealed every door and window she could reach. She lived in a bougie area, with a house bigger than all of her apartments combined, in a neighborhood full of other celebrities. Her neighbors, half of whom actively snubbed her (or in the case of one particularly persistent country star, tried to save her soul), collectively lost their shit at the crime scene tape, even though it was barely visible. Cheryl smoothed it over but half of them still wouldn't talk to her.

Whatever. If that bothered them, it was a good thing none of them noticed the curses she'd written on the tape.

Tonight, everything was locked tight, windows, doors, skylights, and gates. These days it still took her ten minutes of telling herself she was safe and an eclectic collection of weapons hidden around her mattress to make her believe it.

She still wished she hadn't drawn the curtains, but the darkness was comforting. It didn't want anything from her. It reminded her even if someone did show up, she could probably take them. She was a scrapper, she'd faced a lot worse than the dark. She was strong. The dark was a blank canvas she could paint herself against, that she could spin her fantasies with. And oh boy, did she fantasize.

As if it heard her, the dark folded and shaped itself until Benji crouched over her, their face filling her vision.

Her breath caught, warmth pooling in her pussy with the last of the ache from the encounter in the alley. Their lips pressed against hers, completing the kiss they'd teased her with. Their lips and teeth worked their way down her throat, her breasts to the ache in her clit. Their hands tangled in her hair, on her throat, her nipples, sliding into her every way she liked. Them, in her mouth, filling her, one hole after another until she cried out, her orgasm crashing down on her until she collapsed into the mattress, spent. The fantasy broke and it was just her, fingers slick with her own juices, embraced by the dark.

The next morning she overslept because of those damn curtains. She blundered out of bed, unable to find the exit in the heavy fabric and eventually resorting to going under them in a very undignified dive and roll. She swore at the bed and flipped it off for good measure. It was unimpressed.

Her mood was a spiky cloud around her as she dressed and did her make-up.

Angie loved make-up. She could transform in a slash of lipstick or disappear under a face full of foundation. Makeup was her armor, her disguise. The defining line between her and the Bitch Queen.

Today she had a Zoom meeting with the suits from the label about her tour. She tossed her hair into a bun, put on a decent top over her pj pants and didn't even bother with eyeliner to go with the lipstick she would never go out without, even virtually. Today's shade was fuck-off black.

She paused on her way to search out her computer to pay quick respects to her living room altar, blowing a kiss to the triptych of Baphomet, Satan, and Lucifer dominating the small table.

She found her laptop wedged halfway into the couch, grabbed a breakfast bar, and dashed to the door as the doorbell rang. She hummed to herself as she did, trying to roll back her mood.

"Morning." Cheryl didn't look up from her phone as she stepped inside. "The opening act dropped out."

"Shit." Relief punched her. Oh Lucy, she really didn't want

to tour. Not that losing an opener would derail it. The machine around her was too big. Besides, she needed to tour.

Cheryl gave her an odd look.

Angie headed for the table, stuffing more of the breakfast bar in her mouth and tapping the rhythm to "PhenoBarbie Doll" on the lid of her laptop as she did. "I can't believe they're doing it *now*, we announce the tour in a month." Her gig at a festival up in Sacramento next month was already announced, set in stone. No moving that. No, wait, she wasn't moving anything.

"I'm already on it." Cheryl followed her.

"That's why I like you." And paid her very well.

"I know. You're not gonna believe why they dropped out."

"Uh-oh, why?"

"Half the band got religion." Cheryl put her laptop next to Angie's on the large farm table in the kitchen.

Angie sat down heavily. "Half of God Killing Devil Spawn got religion," she repeated blankly. "Where? How?"

"Peyote retreat over the weekend."

"God Killing Devil Spawn went to a *peyote retreat*?" Only in LA. "Which religion did they end up with?"

Cheryl shrugged. "Whatever it is, it doesn't like you."

Angie rolled her eyes. "Hot take, God Killing Devil Spawn."

"Oh, and they changed their name." Cheryl hooked up her computer to a mini-projector, projecting her screen on the one white wall in Angie's house.

Angie dragged her attention back to the conversation. "I'm almost scared to ask."

Cheryl grinned. "Manifesting Destiny."

"Don't bring up that manifesting shit. You know I can't stand the Law of Attraction."

"No, no, that's the new band name."

Angie stared at her, open mouthed. "No."

"Yes."

"Noooo."

"Not even joking." Cheryl logged them into the meeting and the virtual waiting room screen popped up.

Angie laughed. "Oh, my sweet Lucy." She was still laughing when the meeting started and a gallery of suits populated her wall.

The suits were not amused. Cheryl took control of the meeting immediately. She usually did. Angie liked it that way. She was only there to smooth the way for Cheryl.

No matter how many times she told the suits how she wanted things, no matter how many platinum albums and sold out tours she handed them, they still had to wave their dicks around and pretend they knew shit before they let her have her way. They just had trouble doing it to her face. But then, most people did, especially now she was famous. Cheryl was very effective, but it sped things up when Angie sat and glowered behind her.

The meeting was set up so the suits could try yet again to push for an expanded tour. They'd been pressuring her for months but Angie held firm on keeping West Coast only dates. She was testing material, just as she'd done on every tour, but she was also testing herself. Would she break again, the way she had on the *Romance Inverted* tour?

Fuck, she'd barely made it through that tour but she couldn't bear stopping when it would cost so many people their paychecks. Pulling herself out of that hole had been one of the hardest things she'd ever done.

Should she even tour anymore?

Listen to your body, Dr. Lopez would say if she were here.

Angie spent years ignoring the things her body screamed at her. There was no way she'd have accomplished as much as she had by doing things as trivial as eating when she was hungry, sleeping when she was tired, or stopping when she was falling apart.

Sometimes, she wondered if it was even worth it anymore. She was almost thirty and industry ageism was heading for her like an oncoming train. She was rich, she'd had a good run, better than most artists ever got. Her body was holding up relatively well. In her bleaker moments, she wondered whether it was better to just get out of the spotlight now, while her music was still good and her star was still well, not shiny, but not so tarnished she was a pariah.

Then she would do a local show and remember there was nowhere she was as good as she was on stage.

The suits discussed replacements for God Killing Devil Spawn, throwing out their pet projects and the occasional revived heritage band. None of them sounded right. Touring with Angela Alice could make a band, but only if they were right for it. You put the wrong kind of opener in front of her show and the fans rioted, demanding to see her. No, they had to have similar badass, chaotic theatrics, and music that punched you in the face and demanded you listen.

Angie floated in her mind, half paying attention. All these people whose pockets her machine lined. All these people invested in keeping her rolling until her wheels fell off.

Cheryl deflected the suit's suggestions masterfully, laying out the list of backups they'd already made. Angie and Cheryl always had a roster of backup bands under consideration. You never knew what might go wrong on a tour. The suits made some points, mostly to hear their own voices but agreed Cheryl should reach out to the bands. Angie reread the list, noting Cheryl had updated it with one new name.

Razor Bitches.

A dozen thoughts collided in her head. Scheming joy, exhaustion, knee-jerk rejection of the idea. What if they found out they were on her list and she didn't pick them? Benji would hate her. But if she picked them… they'd hate her more.

What if she didn't pick anyone?

The meeting wrapped. Cheryl turned off the projector with a sigh. "That went about as well as expected."

Angie nodded. She asked carefully, "What's up with adding Razor Bitches?"

"You boosted their show so I did some research. " Cheryl shrugged. "They fit the profile. I figured we could send someone to the show on Thursday. It doesn't hurt to cover all our bases."

"Are you stalking my social media?"

"Yep," Cheryl said unapologetically, packing her laptop away. "I like to keep ahead of the scandals."

Angie couldn't fault her. When she was younger, Angie tended to pick fights online and she still buzzed the Westboro Baptists occasionally just to rile those fuckers.

"Plus, you've been flirting like crazy with Hanayu Switchblade's kid," Cheryl said. "I wanted to see what we were working with there."

"We?"

"Who do you think is gonna pick you up the next time you decide to break your heart over someone?" Cheryl said it kindly, her smile sympathetic but Angie felt a pang of mortification.

Her manager saw more of her breakdown after Rohan than anyone else, but she only knew a sliver of the depths Angie sunk to, beating herself up for that album, that special, for fucking up the best relationship she'd had. It had been bad and then it incubated during lockdown and the pandemic with no tour and no shows to release her feelings safely. By the time she could tour again, her feelings metastasized.

She shook the memories off. "It won't be like that. Benji

doesn't like me. We're just…" She shrugged because whatever they were doing didn't make any damn sense.

"Sure about that?"

Angie nodded. "Trust me. This is safe. In a fucked up way I can't explain, it's safe. We'll play our game, at best, we'll get a duet out of it. At worst, it'll fizzle out."

Cheryl pursed her lips. "If you say so." She sighed. "I worry about you, Ang." She rested a hand on Angie's shoulder for a moment. Angie remembered Cheryl had represented a few big acts that died tragically young.

She covered Cheryl's hand with hers briefly before shrugging off her touch. "I'm too old for the White Lighter Curse and too stubborn to die for love. I think you're stuck with me and my crazy for a good long while yet." Angie didn't mention that she'd carried a white lighter around from her twenty-seventh birthday until her twenty-eighth just in case she joined Janis, Jimmi, and the others in the 27 Club. She was still surprised some days that she'd made it this long. The odds certainly hadn't been in her favor and she'd expected being a rockstar would kill her sooner than later. Not so, it seemed.

Cheryl smiled but her eyes were distant. "I like your crazy. It makes us both lots of money. How's therapy?"

Angie walked her to the door. "Still haven't scared this one off. She's hardy."

"But is she helping?"

Angie paused, opening the door. "I think so." She hugged herself, pretending it was against the chill morning air.

"Good. I'll send someone to the Razor Bitches show and get you a full report."

Angie shook her head. "I'll go." She needed the cacophonous catharsis of a show. It would realign her off-kilter brain.

"I'll send someone with you."

"No need."

"Angie…" Cheryl frowned.

"I don't know if you noticed but I get around just fine."

"I know…" Cheryl paused, choosing her words. "But I don't like you going to venues by yourself. Remember Munich?"

"That was years ago." Angie waved her words away like being cornered by a horde of fans didn't feature in some of her recurring trauma dreams.

"Minneapolis, San Jose, that one town in Idaho…"

"Again, years ago. My disguises are much better now."

Cheryl sighed. "Fine. Keep your location on and text me before and after, okay? I don't like how much those misogynist creeps have been posting about you lately."

"Yes, Mom." Cheryl might have a point, but this wasn't Angie's first rodeo with misogynist creeps. They didn't know what they were dealing with.

Cheryl shuddered. "Don't compare me to your mother."

Angie laughed but it was hollow.

CHAPTER 10

ANGELA ALICE OPENING ACT DROPS OUT OVER RELIGIOUS DIFFERENCES

Angela Alice's much awaited tour faces another setback as the band formerly known as God Killing Devil Spawn announced last night they were parting ways with the Satanic artist.

"After realigning our consciousness with the vibrations of the universe, we can no longer support the negative energy Angela puts out," said lead singer, Connor Paltro. "We urge her to realign her chakras and cleanse herself of the spiritual baggage she is allowing to weigh her down." The band, now called Manifesting Destiny, has pledged to only play with "positive people."

When asked to comment over the phone, Angela Alice laughed. "My negative energy and I love this toxic positivity journey for God Killing Devil Spawn. I do hope it pays off for them." There is no word yet on who will replace Manifesting Destiny on her tour.

Or even when the tour will be. The only confirmed date is her headlining appearance at the sold out MetalQuake Festival in Sacramento this fall.

—Metal Madness.com

"Did you see this?" Hanayu waved her phone in front of Benji's face like they could possibly read it that way.

"What?" They grabbed the phone and read the article. "So?"

"So? *So?*" Hanayu cried. "She retweeted all our show announcements. She's going to check us out, I just know it!"

"Calm down, you're making me anxious." Jean, the bassist of Razor Bitches sat in one of Benji's armchairs doing a crossword.

The Razor Bitches show was tonight. Yesterday, the band descended on Benji's apartment, filling the place with gear and Gen X punks. Both the bedroom and the studio had been taken over. The guest bathroom looked like it had been attacked by teenagers.

Besides Hanayu and Jean there was the guitarist Paulina, and a new drummer who had introduced herself just as Nancy and looked like someone's grandmother. Benji lost track of how many drummers the band had gone through.

Jean and Paulina smothered Benji with hugs and kisses the minute they arrived, forgetting their pronouns left and right until Benji corrected them as gently as they could. The two women were their aunties, having half-raised Benji along with Hanayu, and they meant well.

Hanayu had been disowned at nineteen when she refused to marry Benji's father, Kenji (and yes, Hanayu had found the name similarity hilarious in the throes of post-birth drugs), after he got her pregnant. Benji grew up surrounded by the Razor Bitches and Hanayu's chosen family of punks. Benji spent their childhood in bars, learned how to sing before they could speak, and knew some impressive but useless knife tricks. Their baby pictures sported mohawks and tiny studded bracelets an artist boyfriend of Hanayu's made custom. When they were eleven, Benji and their mom got matching lip piercings. She still had hers, Benji's had long grown closed.

Hanayu fiddled with her piercing now, sitting and fidgeting the way she did when she had nothing to fill her time before a show.

"I don't think Angelica is coming," Benji said gently.

"I thought her name was Angela." Paulina whipped out a pair of glasses and stared at her phone.

"What, you never heard of a stage name?" Jean taunted her.

"No, it's a totally foreign concept," Paulina said sarcastically.

"She's not coming," Benji repeated, trying to manage the band's expectations and silently cursing Angelica. "The crowd would tear her apart."

"Like in Munich." Nancy nodded sagely. She was knitting. Benji did a double take. Why had their mother picked this woman? She was wearing a cardigan and pearls for crying out loud. Pearls!

She caught Benji looking and winked. Benji had no idea what to do with that so they ignored it.

"Makes sense." Paulina shrugged, but she looked disappointed. "Besides," she perked up. "We sold out the show, who cares if Angela Alice is there?"

"I bet she'll be there." Hanayu wore a sly look Benji did not care for. "She has a thing for Benji. Didja see them on *The Talk Show Game*? I sent you the clip."

"I did!" Paulina said. "That's her? Good choice, Benny."

"Benny has a girlfriend?" Jean shrieked like it had never happened in Benji's thirty-odd years.

They groaned. "I don't—"

"It's about time," Paulina talked right over them. "Been too long. I was getting worried."

"Why are you worried?" Nancy asked, "Have you seen this

kid? I'm sure the girls and boys are lining up for a piece of that." She looked like she would happily pinch Benji's cheeks if they were any closer. They vowed to stay as far away from her as possible. "I hope this Angela knows exactly how lucky she is."

"She's not—" Benji didn't know why they bothered as Jean cut in.

"Aw, she's a scary bitch isn't she?" She'd Googled Angelica, scrolling through images of her. She winked at Benji. "You two will look cute together."

Benji wished fervently they could sink through the floor and disappear.

"Oh, leave the poor kid alone." Hanayu laughed. "They're not into her."

"Could you flirt with her into taking us with her?" Paulina wondered, peering over Jean's shoulder.

"No fucking way," Hanayu snapped. "We're not pimping out my kid." She smiled at Benji. "What they want to do with Angela Alice is their business."

Benji ducked into their bedroom and hid until the conversation turned elsewhere. They really hoped Angelica did not show.

Angelica stood on the sidewalk in front of the Creep Club and hugged herself, fists clenched. The place looked decrepit but had to have opened less than ten years ago. She'd played every tiny venue from San Diego to Lancaster when she started out and she'd never played here. She had some vague memory that there had been a salon here the last time she'd been in this neck of the woods.

This was a bad fucking idea. She'd argued with herself the whole drive over. Why had she told Cheryl she'd go to this? What if Benji saw her? What if she got rushed again? Was she really going to consider their mom's band for her tour?

It'll be fine, she told herself. *I'll sneak in, watch the show and no one will know I was even here.*

She'd done it before and she'd do it again, easy. Her disguise was in place and her work was good, honed over the years to give her as much freedom as possible in this life she'd made for herself. She pulled out her phone, using the reflective cover to give her face one last check. Her phone had a decent enough camera but the screen was too small to be a good mirror.

Benji might not even be here. Even if they were, they wouldn't recognize her. She touched up her baby pink eye shadow. Hell, she didn't even recognize her.

She stepped into the venue, pushing her way up the stairs through the idling people waiting for the Razors to start. The opening act was already playing, the kick of the bass drum thumping through the walls. She put in her earplugs, feeling the foam expand in her ears the way her In-Ears never did.

She showed her ticket, ID, and proof of vaccination at the door, ignoring the bouncer's raised eyebrows at the name on her vax card. (Angelica Leviathan—she'd legally changed it when it was clear minorly changing her first name didn't really hide her. At 20, it'd seemed like a badass choice.) He didn't question her though, just stamped her hand to prove she was both over 21 and vaxxed, which probably meant he'd seen weirder or they were seriously lax here. Given the Creep Club was the size of a shoe box and packed to the gills, she really hoped it wasn't the latter. She tightened the strings of her pink mask.

The place was your standard tiny venue: dark paneling, black, sticky floors, and a stage about the size of a bathtub.

Even through her mask she caught whiffs of booze, cigarettes, pot, and overzealous cologne usage, which frankly was better than the alternative.

The opening band was a group of young punks who looked about half her age and like they had just come out of someone's mom's garage. The thought made her feel old. She headed for the bar, scanning the crowd for Benji or their mother. She spotted Rohan by the far wall with Leo.

She grimaced and stuck to the opposite side of the club, putting as much of the crowd between them as possible.

She found Benji at the bar, waiting for a drink like a brooding vampire. They wore a black mask that matched thier black jumpsuit. Angie took a moment to watch them like the creeper she was, memorizing the way they looked in the shadows, the fantasy she could never have. Her inner fangirl swooned and her libido demanded she march over there and drag them even deeper into the shadows.

Instead, she found a seat across the bar from them, as close to the door as she could get while still keeping an eye on the stage, the door, and Benji. It was an occupied seat but she just pulled her mask down and smiled at the man in it before asking for it nicely, yelling over the music. He happily offered it to her. He also tried to chat her up but she just shook her head until he stopped.

He glowered, trying to loom at her. She bared her teeth and stood on the rungs of her chair, making herself taller than him. Angie let some of her anxious aggression spike out from her body and he backed away real fast. So did everyone around her.

She sat back down, tucking her feelings away, and masking up again.

Benji was looking at her. She ignored them, feigning interest in the band thrashing around on stage. The sound mix was off, too loud to make out anything but the kick drum and the muddy crunch of the guitars the singer was doing their best to yell over. Maybe in a few years the band would figure out their sound and do something interesting but right now they weren't much better than noise. She was glad for her earplugs.

Her phone buzzed. She glanced down to see a text from a number she didn't know.

> You're not coming to the Razor Bitches show, right?

Her pulse quickened. Was it…?

ANGIE
> Who is this?

> Who the fuck do you think, Angelica?

Her heart jolted and she clamped down on the impulse to look across the bar at them.

ANGIE
> Prove it.

> Is that you in the brown wig, Coma White?

ANGIE
> No. You're just missing me, Omega.

> Well, that guy who's seat you stole is coming back for round 2.

She glanced up, searching. What were they talking about? That guy was off in the mosh pit forming by the stage. Her phone buzzed again.

> Gotcha.

Benji was no longer across the bar.

Benji circled the bar, cursing her under their breath. Why had she come? If they were smart they wouldn't even be out here. Why had Hanayu chosen a place without a VIP section or even balconies? It was like being in a can of sardines that might turn into a frenzy of sharks. They'd already been clocked a few times but no one had gotten the nerve to bother them. It was only a matter of time and booze though.

They were just glad Rohan and Leo hadn't seen her yet.

They slid up to the bar next to Angelica.

"What gave me away?" She yelled over the music, sounding as calm as you could yelling but the people around them shifted nervously. It was the only reason they'd clocked her.

They nodded at the crowd around them. "That."

She swore and tapped her fingers against the bar in time with the music. The woman in front of them had Angelica's voice but nothing else. She was a brunette with rainbow eyeshadow, pink mask, a Razor Bitches long sleeve, Daisy Dukes, and Converse. Half gloves covered her finger tattoos. Freckles were scattered across her cheeks above her mask and her face was subtly contoured, giving her nose a different shape.

She flipped her braid and furrowed her brow at her phone. Wait, did she have a *flip phone*? The woman who used to be known for being glued to social media?

They looked down to see she had sent them a text.

I'm not here to bother you.

Then why are you here?

The opening band took mercy on all of them and stopped playing. Benji took out their earplugs, noting Angelica did the same.

"I'm here to see the Razor Bitches." Her Florida twang, which was normally barely there, rolled over her vowels. She crossed one leg over the other.

Benji cleared their throat, blinked and tried to ignore how *long* her legs were in those shorts. "Not Rohan?" *Not me?*

She rolled her eyes. "Lucy, no. I'd be really happy if we managed to miss each other completely tonight."

Hearing that shouldn't have made Benji as happy as it did. "Are you scouting the Razors for your tour?" They nodded at her shirt.

She leaned in. "Don't say that shit so loud," she murmured, no doubt looking like she was telling them something dirty. The thought of that voice talking dirty made them light-headed. They fought a shiver. Dammit, why her? Why now? Of all the people they didn't want to be attracted to, Angelica was right on top. "This place is one big fire code violation as it is, no need to add a crowd rush in."

Benji shuddered. "Don'teven joke about that."

The warm-up music cut off and the next band came on in a blaze of drum fills and over-loud guitars. That meant there was only one more band until the Razors came on. Benji put their earplugs in. Angelica followed suit.

Across the room, Rohan craned his neck, no doubt wondering if Benji would be back from the bar soon. Benji pretended not to notice.

But Benji did notice the bartender squinting at Angelica, trying to place her.

Their phone buzzed.

ANGELICA

I need air.

Benji looked up at her. She raised her eyebrows and seemed to come to a decision.

Wanna go with?

BENJI

I need to be here for the Razors. They might need me.

The bartender pointed at Angelica's drink, miming to ask if she wanted another. She shook her head, turning back to her phone. The guy kept watching her.

ANGELICA

When are they on?

BENJI

In 45.

The bartender looked at Benji, trying to be subtle but with the same question in his eyes.

ANGELICA

We won't go far.

Benji considered it. They'd love an excuse to get out of this crush and to keep Angelica away from Rohan. They didn't want to explain to him why they had abandoned him and Leo to hang out with his ex. They suspected she knew where he was too, she was angled away from the stretch of wall Rohan and Leo commandeered, though their disguises were nowhere near as transformative as hers.

ANGELICA

R u the roadie?

BENJI

No.

ANGELICA

Something medical going on?

BENJI

No.

She shrugged.

Your mom is a grown woman with your phone number. I think she'll be okay.

She stood and yelled, "Up to you."

She held out her hand. Behind her, the bartender's mouth opened as he visibly figured out who they were. Fuck it.

Benji took her hand.

Everything stopped. Time, the people around them, even the band massacring "Thrash Unreal" faded away. Benji stared at her, their shock mirrored in her silvery eyes.

Oh no, they thought distantly. *No, no, no, not with her.*

They couldn't tell what she was thinking or even what she was feeling, the shock was so great. She recovered first, tugging on their hand and leading them outside.

They let her lead them down the rickety stairs out into the night. The cool air hit like a slap, rebooting their brain. They pulled their hand from hers and rummaged around in their pocket, emerging with a single, battered cigarette and a Zippo. It was so rare that they smoked these days but the movements were instinctive. Ripping their mask off, they had it lit and were taking a drag in five seconds flat.

Nicotine oozed into them, dulling the shock. Their chest

warmed with the familiar feeling of fire and smoke. Damn, they missed this so much.

Angelica stepped back. "I didn't know you smoked." She popped out her earplugs.

Benji popped theirs out too. "I don't."

Anymore. Unless they were out of their depth and couldn't deal. They turned away and walked into the parking lot, far enough not to get persecuted for giving everyone second-hand cancer. They leaned their forearms on the hip-high chain link fence and stared at the street, the cars passing by, anything really to stop themselves from staring at her.

CHAPTER 11

"She walked in and saw me
Crooked her finger and had me
Strutted up, drank me down
Laughed at my frown and said:

Overthinker, overdrinker,
Can't make up your mind
Said, I know your kind,
Cute but you'll never be fine
Let me make this simpler,
And she said:

Fuck me I'm beautiful
This tie ain't suitable
This dress is removable
And you're so doable
So fuck me,
Beautiful"
— "Fuck Me I'm Beautiful" by User-Friendly Omega off
of *Grim*

ngie watched Benji smoke, irritated she found it so hot. It wasn't quite the action, though there was something compelling about the casual destruction of self. That was some sick shit conditioned into her by tobacco companies and all the apathetic small town kids she'd grown up with but that didn't make it any less sexy. Benji looked like an old time movie star, or a beautifully tormented dark angel. A thirst trap Instagram post waiting to happen in black and white.

Her fingers twitched, wanting to touch them, still tingling from that brief contact. They felt it too, she was sure. That massive slow down and fade out until it was just them, staring back at her. There was something there, a connection more than just Angie wanting there to be one. It scared her, but in the exact right way. She reached toward it before whatever was left of her fear of vulnerability could block her.

She leaned on the other side of the fence, upwind. She had a voice to protect after all. "If I asked you to sing for me, would you?"

They took a drag, exhaled. Smoke cascaded out of their nose and mouth like fog as they looked at her through the inky hair falling over their eyes. "We're back to the duet now?"

"I heard you on Rohan's album." Singing backup, what a waste. A beautiful ragged choir of Benji's voice, their darkness giving Rohan's charm depth.

They took another drag. "So?"

"I want it." She stumbled over the fuller truth. "Your voice. And your words. We'd sound so good together." The song pressed at her. She could practically hear the possibilities.

"Angelica," they sighed her name in a cloud of smoke, exhaling carefully away from her. "Even if we sounded amazing together I have to think about the implications of our collab for my label. For Rohan and our friendship. It's not as simple as a song."

They said it gently, like maybe she wouldn't understand what it was like to balance the livelihood of multiple people on her every decision. Lucy, what was she even doing here? She should—should—

"Are you happy, Omega?" She shot back. "Do you miss it? Singing, being the star, being on stage?"

They frowned. "Why do you care if I'm happy, Come White? What does my happiness have to do with your duet?"

"I—I—" This was backfiring.

They watched her, their dark eyes cool under the streetlights. "Did you assume I was suffering and only a duet with you could fix me?"

She shook her head. "It's completely selfish," she admitted. "I'm not trying to fix you. I'm trying to fix me—my song anyway. Your music was a lifeline for me during some bad times." She quelled the memories of her first years in LA, alone with no car in a tiny apartment, working every job she could get hired at and playing any club that would take her. She was supposed to be doing all that with her boyfriend but he'd dumped her the minute they'd gotten off the Greyhound downtown. In public, so she wouldn't make a scene. All she'd had back then was music. "I want that lifeline again."

"So what, you want me to save you?"

Cazzi's words rang in her head from years ago: *This is not love, Angela*. There was nothing like being haunted by the new girlfriend of your old boyfriend. She was right though and that was fine. Angie didn't want it to be love.

"No one ever saves anyone." She gave them a crooked half-smile. "The track just needs you, is that so hard to believe?"

"Yes."

"Look, if you don't want to do it, just tell me. I won't bring it up again." She'd just have to find another way to jumpstart her writing again. Fun.

"It won't affect the Razor's chance of being on your tour?"

"I've got a list of bands as long as my arm to sort through. By the time I'm done I won't remember whether my real name is Angela or Angelica, let alone how I feel about you duetting with me."

They gave her a sympathetic grimace, stubbing out the remains of their cigarette. They'd smoked it to the filter. "I'll think about it."

"Overthinker, overdrinker," she sang, taunting them. "Can't make up your mind."

They straightened, raising their eyebrows. "Really? You're gonna play this game?"

"Said, I know your kind," she continued. "Cute but you'll never be fine." She gave them the up-down look as if singing their own lyrics at them wasn't ballsy enough.

They leaned towards her over the fence, just within reach. "Angelica," their voice was low, practically a croon. "What are you asking for?"

"Sing with me," she leaned in, just a breath away.

"You're complicating this."

"Am I? Or am I making it easier?"

"What is your duet about?" Their gaze was on her lips.

"Guess."

Their gaze met hers. Their mouth opened.

A ringtone jangled from their pocket. They swore under their breath and turned away, turning it off. "They're on in five."

"You set a timer?"

They shook their head. "My mother texted me."

"Does she need you?"

"Just wondering where I was." They frowned, scrolling. "She's not the only one."

"Tell Ro I say hi."

"I absolutely will not."

She faked a pout, hiding the hurt. "Ashamed of me, Benji?"

They met her gaze. "I try not to make any choices I'd be ashamed of these days." They nodded at the club. "Come on, the show's starting."

T he sardine can was even more crowded now, Angelica's seat at the bar long gone amongst the crush. Benji edged along closer, to the stage, looking for a clear line of sight. They found it, in the dead center of the room.

"This is… cozy." Angelica looked at the crush around them, her shoulder brushing Benji's.

Too close. Benji held themself rigid. "You don't have to stay here," they said, hoping she wouldn't. Curious if she would.

"No." She spun, staring down everyone around them. The crush eased back, leaving a ring around the two of them. "It's fine. This is fine." Her shoulder stayed brushing theirs. "You really want her to know you're here, huh?"

Yes. Benji shrugged. "I like to be supportive."

She gave them an evaluating look. "You two are close."

"Yeah." Hanayu was thier rock, she'd kept them as sane as they could be during the Sly years.

Angelica nodded. They thought they caught something wistful in her expression as she turned away. "I'm glad you were able to keep that. She wasn't jealous when you got big?"

"Maybe," Benji said. That old guilt resurfaced. They squashed it. "But we always supported each other. We were each other's roadies. After my voice dropped I used to book their shows so they didn't get underpaid. I styled their clothes until Mom told me I'd made them too goth." They chuckled at the memory.

Angelica did that thing where she smiled with her eyes. "Did you do UFO's stage clothes?"

They nodded. "Sets too in the beginning."

"I did all my own stuff too at first. Did you do the thing where you decorated the mike stand?"

"Oh yeah, full goth Steven Tyler scarves."

She laughed, covering the sound with her hand. "I did bows. It was very baby's first *Nightmare Before Christmas*."

"Adorable," Benji said, deadpan. Though, it was kind of creepy cute.

"I try." She curled the end of her braid around her finger and fluttered her eyelashes at them. It was mildly disturbing.

Under their mask, they let themself smile, just a little. "Consider me suitably frightened."

The mask covered her grin but it was enough to make Benji lose all semblance of thought. Did that happen to everyone when she smiled? Was that why she rarely did it? Or was Benji especially susceptible?

What they could see of her smile wavered. Benji realized they were staring. With more effort than it should've taken, they looked away.

The lights went down and the Razor Bitches ran on stage.

Angelica raised her phone, filming the show. Did that dinky flip phone even have a decent camera? Their stomach knotted, full of nerves for the band.

Hanayu grabbed the mike aggressively. She looked ten years younger under the stage lights, back in her element. Benji smiled, feeling the tide of nostalgia pulling at them. They'd stood in the crowd of every Razor Bitches show they weren't backstage for when they were a kid.

Hanayu started the show off as she always did with the second most popular song in their catalog: "Stone Cold Killer."

The crowd wasn't there at first but by the second chorus Benji wasn't the only voice yelling the callbacks.

"You're a stone cold killer—" Hanayu would shout.

"And you like it!" The crowd shouted back.

The song ended abruptly, the way most Razor Bitches songs did. Hanayu said, "Okay, let's get this show going! We're Razor Bitches and we're here to cut the patriarchy down to size."

Benji and Angelica whooped along with a small but vocal contingent of the crowd. Benji smiled at her. That line flopped at more than a few Razor Bitches shows.

Angelica crinkled her eyes back at them. They were both relieved and disappointed not to get as close to a full smile.

The show was good, high energy. It wasn't spectacular. Benji caught a good number of clams but the band didn't let that slow them down, playing with their signature breakneck speed. They closed with the title track off their most popular album *Never Bring A Knife to a Pussy Fight!* The fans in the audience went nuts and the band left on a high note.

Benji surveyed the crowd with satisfaction. The venue was still packed at the end of the show and people buzzed with that good show excitement as they bottlenecked out the door. This had potential. Benji now had a decent business case to present to Rohan for taking on the band.

A hand clapped them on the shoulder. "I like them." Rohan grinned down at Benji. "I say let's sign 'em. Not that I was gonna say no to your mom but…" He shrugged.

"They're delightful." Leo grinned. "I still want some solid numbers though, so I can better advise on a budget for them."

"I'll get them to you," Benji said, distracted, trying to see where Angelica had disappeared to.

"If you're looking for your friend, I have no idea where they went," Leo said. "I saw you two leaving earlier though." He waggled his eyebrows.

"It was business," Benji said, dismissively.

Rohan frowned. "Do we know them? I swear I've met them before."

"Angelica put the Razors on the short list for her opening act," Benji said, before they could talk themself out of it.

Rohan froze. Benji could see him put the pieces together. He stared at the crowd by the door. "She's gotten *good*."

"At?" Leo asked.

"Disguises." Rohan shook his head. "I can't believe I didn't realize."

Benji shrugged. "The only reason I did is because she got agitated and I was nearby."

Rohan nodded. "That'll do it."

"The brown haired girl? That was her?" Leo's eyebrows shot up. "Damn. I need to know where she got that wig, it was *excellent*."

"Was she bothering you?" Rohan asked, frowning with concern.

Benji shook their head. "You guys wanna meet the band?"

The two men regarded Benji.

"That was clumsy." Leo snorted. "But sure. Why not?"

Angie stepped backstage with a smile at the venue guy who tried to stop her. "The band's expecting me."

He let her by.

It's cruel to get their hopes up, Angel, Mama whispered in her mind. It was so much worse when she was right. Angie should go home.

But if she went home, she'd have to go back to the real work of the tour, making decisions. Keeping the machine rolling forward, with her strapped to the helm, as a figurehead.

Stop being melodramatic, she scolded herself. *This is just paying your respects to another artist.*

Angie found Hanayu and the rest of the band packing their gear. "Great show," she said.

Hanayu straightened, closing her guitar case. "Thanks!" She swiped her damp hair from her face. The woman looked well-preserved for having a thirty-something year old kid. Angie was willing to bet she'd been real young when she'd had them. "It was fun." Then she grinned. "Excuse me. Benny!" She ran past Angie, reaching for her kid.

Benji grinned and raced forward, lifting their mother in the air, spinning her. It was startling to see them act so young and carefree. Were they always like this? Were they only so guarded around her?

"Put me down you little jackass!" Hanayu yelled, still laughing.

Benji did but made a point of measuring their height against their mother's. They were almost a head taller. Hanayu replied by swatting their arm. Two of her band members converged on Benji, wrapping themselves around Benji, ruffling their hair and kissing their cheeks like they were a kid again. Angie's chest ached looking at them.

Behind them, stood Leo and Rohan. Leo glared, crossing his arms so his biceps bulged menacingly. Rohan gave her an awkward wave. She waved back.

"Isn't that lovely?" Said a voice nearby, jolting her. The drummer had hung back. Angie had been too busy watching Benji to realize she'd been standing next to her.

Angie looked at her. The drummer was a Black woman of about the same age as the rest of the band but dressed like someone's grandmother. Someone's grandmother with drumsticks poking out of her giant purse.

The woman held out her hand. "Nancy."

"Angie," she replied, leaning on her accent again, and wrapping her emotions deep under her skin as she shook the other woman's hand. "Y'all had a great show."

"Thank you." Nancy peered at her. "Is Angie short for Angela by any chance?" She raised her eyebrows.

"Could be." Angie returned the look with one of her own.

"Is that so?" Nancy nodded to herself. "You really do like our boy there, don't you?"

"They're not a boy."

"Yes, yes. I'm still adjusting to that. Non-binary." She chewed on the word thoughtfully, fingering the pearls around her neck. "Not something we really knew about back in my day."

Angie said nothing. There was a rich history of non-binary folx all over the world since the dawn of civilization but she wasn't Cazzi, ready to educate at every opportunity.

Nancy didn't seem to notice her silence. "So *Angie*, do you think we made the cut?"

"Nancy," Hanayu shouted. "Get over here! Quick!"

"Forget I asked," Nancy said, heading towards Benji's mom. The excited flurry that followed told Angie the band had gotten some very good news.

Rohan broke away from the group, walking towards Angie. She wondered if he realized Benji and Leo were watching him like mother hens. Looking after him. The thought gave her a bittersweet twinge.

There hadn't been anyone looking out for her without being paid for a long time.

"Hey Angie," he said. For a moment she missed him, the feeling sharper than it'd been since their relationship was good.

"Ro." She nodded. "Here for business or support?"

"Business," he said.

"You sign 'em?"

"Yep. Where are they on your list?" Rohan knew all about her lists and how careful she was when she picked opening acts.

"You know I've got to get all my data together before I can even figure that out."

He shrugged. "Worth a shot."

"You're enjoying giving Benji and Leo an aneurysm, aren't you?" She swallowed a shit-stirring comment about his friend —were they still friends?—Rick and his falling out with the label.

"Someday we'll be able to have a conversation without everyone losing their shit."

Angie shrugged. "Once a villain, always a villain."

He bumped her shoulder with his. "Don't wallow. It's annoying."

"Yeah, yeah. How's the wedding planning?"

He grimaced. "I'm seriously thinking we should elope."

"Your Nānī would hate that." Angie chuckled. His grandmother hadn't approved of her. It hurt more than she'd let on. She'd heard through the grapevine that Cazzi was grandmother approved. She was surprised how much that stung.

Quiet descended. She wondered if they'd sent out invitations yet, if she'd hate it more if she was invited or left out. Benji watched them, their gaze unreadable.

"Wow, this is awkward," Rohan said.

"Yeah, I gotta go," Angie said. She was suddenly exhausted, her emotional resources drained. Her phone was filling up with messages, buzzing against her thigh, and she had a virtual stack of reports to review. She'd spent the afternoon rehearsing with the band and her body cried out for sleep.

"There's a door behind you to the left, goes out the back way."

She shot him a surprised look. Why hadn't she just reached out to the venue and tried to get a back way in too? Oh right, because that turned out badly for her before. You never knew who would fuck you over.

He grinned. "What? Did you come in the front?"

She gestured at herself.

He laughed, shaking his head. "Come on, Ang. You gotta be more careful. You're gonna give Cheryl a heart attack."

She rolled her eyes. "I got my panic buttons." It was true. She had three: one in her smartwatch, one on her phone, and one in the inverted cross hanging under her shirt. Sure, the suits wanted her to get full-time security to protect their investment but the idea of dealing with someone and shielding them from her emotions twenty-four/seven exhausted her. She turned for the door. "Say bye for me."

"Take care of yourself, Ang." His tone was guarded, deliberately distanced. Like he was trying to make sure she knew he wouldn't be there to worry about her. That was fine, she had long given up on expecting anyone to worry about her past the money she could bring them.

"You know I can." She slipped out the door.

CHAPTER 12

Omegaluvr92: Me again, so um, is Suicide King about Sly, UFO's old bassist?

UFObb: duh

Emoisthenewblack: I think its about both of them, there's a lot of references to singing. Feels like a blending of characters imho

Omegaluvr92: Were he and B... a thing?

Emoisthenewblack: Unclear but he left right around when that album dropped.

Omegaluvr92: shit, I would too. Great album but jeez

UFObb: not our b's best moment

Emoisthenewblack: B was HURTING, i know it didnt destroy the band then but I still think that's part of our B's breakdown and why UFO eventually broke up

Omegaluvr92: Yikes, thats messy

UFObb: wouldn't be ufo if it wasnt

ngie sat in her car, parked by a dark corner not far from the venue. She should go, she wasn't so foolish to think nothing could happen to her here.

Best not repeat past mistakes, Angel, Mama's voice goaded her.

But she didn't move. If she turned the car on, if she drove... eventually she'd get home, eventually she'd have to make a decision, eventually she'd have to feed herself back into the touring machine.

Why couldn't she just do it? She loved being on stage. She lived for it. People depended on her, the fans needed her, but, but, but—

What if she didn't? What if she just played the occasional show, when she wanted to play?

It's not like touring made people love her as a person.

Stop being selfish, Mama's voice hissed.

"Shut up," Angie hissed back. "You can't haunt me. You're not dead, you murderous bitch."

Maybe she should grab the notebook from her glove compartment and actually write a letter to Mama. Leech the poison from her mind. Maybe it would be less triggering to write to her younger self but she didn't think this anger would be healing to unleash on baby Angie.

Before her brain could serve up a reply in her mother's voice, something banged on the window.

Angie's hand fisted around the knife in her pocket, her lizard brain automatically clocking every weapon in her car before realizing she was in the driver's seat of a several ton potential murder weapon.

Think Angel! It could be a cop, Mama snapped.

Cold reason drenched her, distancing all the panic. Slowly, she turned her head, looking through the strands of her wig at the person standing at her window.

She cataloged them. The snarl. The fist, raised the bang

again against her window. The wide, bloodshot eyes. The Manergy energy drink shirt.

Oh, thank you, Lucifer. It was someone who wanted to hurt her. Relief coursed through her and she smiled. This, she could handle.

Everything receded but the red-faced man on the other side of the glass, fist banging against the window. "Get out of the car, bitch," he yelled. "I know who you are. What you *do*."

Who knew what that meant, but who cared?

Angie held up a finger and unpinned her wig slowly, dropping each bobby pin into her cup holder before laying the wig out on the passenger seat. It was a good wig and she didn't want to have to replace it.

He looked slightly perplexed, his flushed face obvious even in the low light of the distant streetlight. Then he roared and tried her door.

She took off the wig cap and unlocked the door.

He stumbled back, opening the door for her and almost falling on his ass in the process. She stepped out like he was a valet and she was on the red carpet.

Closing the door, she clocked the empty street as he scrambled upright. No, not empty. There were lit windows. No matter. An audience only fueled her creativity.

He swung at her. She caught his fist, digging her nails in. "You get two hits," she said. "Make them count."

"You're not in control here," he snarled, yanking his fist back.

She let it go, watching him aim for her face.

Good.

She let it graze her cheek, turning to protect her eye at the last moment, pain and shock blooming along the bone. It always hurt but it paid off later.

"One."

"Shut up!"

The second blow aimed for her stomach. She caught it, losing her breath but curling around his arm and yanking, tipping him off balance until he fell into her. Stepping aside, she let him fall against her car.

Then she grabbed his short hair with one hand and forced him to look at her. Her other hand pressed his chest, holding him in place. He struggled but he was too intoxicated, too off-balance. He didn't expect her to fight.

Angie took a deep, shaky breath and let herself *feel* everything. The bindings she so often struggled to keep in place fell away. The pain in her cheek, her stomach, the shaky, horrid shock of violence, her turmoil and fear and anxiety and the flickers of old bad memories of old bad days—

"You are my echo," she told him, his heart beating frantically against her palm. "You are my vessel. The pain you had no outlet for, the pain you tried to inflict on me, I give it back to you with interest. Remember this, every time you raise your fist. Remember me, every time your pain is your weapon. Remember me because I am so, so much better at this than you are." She bared her teeth, grinning. Her mouth tasted coppery. Laughter bubbled in her chest. Tears dripped off her chin.

His mouth moved soundlessly, his eyes so wide, the bloodshot whites almost glowing in the dim light.

"Every time you think you're free," she whispered, nails digging into his chest. "I'll carve myself back in, you'll see."

"Angelica!"

She jerked, almost losing her grip on her... attacker? Victim? She cocked her head, examining the way he shook under her fingers. Victim. No point in sugarcoating it.

Poor man had been hoping for an easy woman bashing, and now?

"Let him go." Benji stood next to her.

Pay attention, Angel! Mama snapped.

Reality crashed down on her. Gasping, she let go, the man sliding down her car to huddle on the ground, sobbing.

Angie stared at him, numb.

Benji could barely understand what the fuck just happened. Angelica barely seemed to realize they were here. Or that Leo and Rohan stood on the other side of her car.

"Oh shit," Leo whispered, staring over the roof of the car at the man sobbing on the asphalt.

Rohan rubbed his hands over his face, finger combing his curls. "Not again," he muttered. "Dammit, not again."

"You've seen this before?" Benji asked, keeping an eye on Angelica as she swayed gently next to them. Her cheek was red, make-up smeared down her face, but it was her expression that scared them the most. She watched the man, smiling slightly like she was stoned or fully dissociated.

Rohan sighed. "Yeah, I can't say I get it but sometimes it seems like she needs an outlet and she uh…" He frowned, waving a hand around like he was trying to pick the right word out of the air. "Finds a fight. She never starts them, she just finds someone who wants to hurt her."

"Why?" Leo asked.

Rohan snorted. "Her whole thing is she doesn't throw the first punch. Optics, you know?"

"Ohhh," said Leo, who really could stand to learn that one.

"Then what?" Benji asked, waving at her. "What is this? Is she good to drive? Does she know we're here?"

"She knows." Angelica's voice was dry, her speech slow and deliberate like each word was an effort.

Anger flared, making Benji light-headed. "So, what? You provoked some asshole who attacked you on a dark street because you figured you could take him?"

She blinked slowly, turning to face them. "I did take him."

"And now, what?" Benji demanded. "Is this your way of turning over a new leaf? Is this your doing better? You had big feelings and you decided to melt his brain because it was convenient?"

"He attacked me."

"I saw that." The only reason Benji hadn't waded in the minute they'd rounded the corner and seen the fucker's fist heading for Angelica's face was because their friends held them back. "You're telling me there was no way you could've avoided the situation? You? With all that manipulative emotional shit you've got going on?"

"Are you… blaming the victim?" She asked.

"Are you the victim?" They shot back.

She paused and considered this. The man at their feet decided this would be a great moment to let out an extra loud sob. Maybe he wasn't all gone. Angelica cocked her head at him as if studying her handiwork.

Then she grabbed his hand and hauled him up. He seemed barely functional but pliable.

"What are you doing?" Benji demanded.

"You're right," she said. "I'll fix it." She opened the back door of her car and pushed him into the seat.

"What?" Rohan practically shouted. "No! He could have a weapon. Angie!"

"Go away," Angelica said. "You have a nice girl now."

"Angie!" Rohan sputtered then threw up his hands when she closed her assailant into the car. "Where are you even taking him?"

"Nowhere bad." She opened the driver's side. That jolted

Benji out of their shock. They put their hand on hers, stopping her before she slid into the seat.

She frowned at them, the electric awareness of her touch muted but still there.

"You're not good to drive," they said.

"You don't know that."

"Doesn't matter. You're not driving. I'll make Leo carry you to the passenger seat. Don't test me." They would carry her themself if Leo didn't, this was ridiculous.

"Don't bring me into this," Leo stage-whispered.

Benji glared at them.

"Yeah, okay, fine." Leo took a step towards her.

Angelica snarled wordlessly and stalked past him to the other side of the car.

Leo shrugged, looking at Benji. "You need backup?"

Benji shook their head. They could handle her. Probably. As long as the asshole in the backseat didn't regain his senses.

"Yes, you do," Rohan said, making to get into the car.

"No," Benji and Angelica said at once.

Rohan paused, nonplussed.

"You don't need to be associated with this," Benji said before he could read too much into that. "Your reputation doesn't need any more dents."

Rohan winced. "It's fucked up that's a thing."

Benji agreed but Rohan was still the label's biggest earner. They couldn't risk it. "We'll be fine. You'd just be underfoot anyway."

Rohan grimaced but nodded. "Call me in an hour or I'll call your mom."

"Oh shit. My mom." Benji covered their eyes. Rohan knew all their buttons. "Can you guys go make sure the band is good to go?"

"We'll take care of them," Rohan said.

"Good, thank you. Now get out of here, both of you," Benji said. "Who knows who's been filming."

The two pop stars swore, glancing around, and looking generally super suspicious. Then they both produced masks from their pockets and jogged off. Benji settled into the driver's seat, adjusting the mirrors and peering at the man in the backseat.

"You gonna be a problem?" They asked him in thier hardest voice. He might be cooked but from what they saw, he deserved it.

He moaned and closed his eyes.

"He's fine," Angelica said. But she twisted her body so she could see both Benji and the man at the same time.

"You do this often? Do you have a secret clean-up crew who deal with your victims?" Benji pressed the start button. The keys must still be in the car somewhere because it turned on.

She pursed her lips. "Take the first left."

Benji growled deep in their throat but followed her directions, attention split between the road and their passengers, until they pulled up to a nondescript building downtown, not too far from the Foundation.

A shiver went down Benji's spine. It reminded them of all thc facilities they'd visited Sly in over the years, just not as nice. Not as nice as the one they'd been in either.

They tasted ash in their mouth.

Benji took a long deliberate inhale. It was shakey.

Angelica pulled out her phone and called someone. "Hey, it's me. I need a favor. No, no. Someone else." She glanced at the backseat. "Not dangerous… anymore."

The building's door opened. A tall person came out wearing scrubs and a mask. Angelica got out of the car, mask on, hair hidden under a beanie. She leaned against the roof of the car.

The person came around and peered into the backseat window. "What happened? Any drugs involved?" They asked Angelica.

She shrugged. "He attacked me. I defended myself. He was some sort of intoxicated."

Benji put on their own mask and rolled down the window. "He's worse now."

The person snorted. "Clearly." They opened the door then crouched by Angelica's victim. "Hey, buddy. You know your name?"

He moaned at them, mumbling something.

"Yeah, I don't think that's your name unless your parents really sucked." They stood. "He probably has people. I'll have to alert them or this will get out of hand real quickly. I'll keep this as quiet as I can."

Angelica shrugged again. "Do what you need to. He'll probably blab when he's able."

"Maybe lay low for a while."

"Don't worry about me, D."

D huffed. "Not likely." They leaned back into the car and unbuckled his seatbelt. "Okay, buddy, let's go. We're going to take care of you." They helped him up. He leaned hard, almost toppling them.

Benji got out to help but Angelica was faster, shoring D up.

"You really cooked this one, huh?" D said.

"I know, I know."

D sighed as the two of them guided the man into the building. At the door, Angelica jerked her head for Benji to follow them and locked the car when they slammed the door.

Steeling themself, they followed her in. *You're fine. You're not going back. He's not in there.*

The inside of the building was luxurious, a direct contrast to the nondescript exterior. Benji's skin crawled in recognition. This was definitely a private medical facility for the rich and fucked up. They felt displaced in time. Memories of multiple visits and places overlaid on each other, knocking them off balance. They rubbed their arms, reminding themself there was no blood there.

Other orderlies came and helped D put the man in a wheelchair. D quizzed Angelica on the timeline of her clash with the man.

Benji barely listened. Old lyrics, old melodies cluttered their mind. Their mouth tasted like smoke, their fingers itched for a cigarette, for a pen. Their lungs constricted against their ribs.

Any minute, Sly would be smiling at them, telling them he was all better now. Again. Any minute, they'd be back in their car, screaming at the steering wheel in a parking garage, silent like a concrete tomb as they sang…

> *There is no beginning*
> *There is no end*
> *We go around*
> *Again and again*

They'd thought they were better, dammit. Not that the wounds had healed but that the scars, keloid that they were, had numbed as the nerves around them died. Sly—or maybe the pain he'd left behind—always seemed to find a way to surprise them.

"You okay?"

They blinked. Angelica stood in front of them, eyes clear and assessing.

"I'm fine." How many times had Sly said that to Benji with a smile? Did he taste the lie on his tongue too? Or were the drugs they gave him good enough that by the time Benji visited he *was* fine?

Drugs had never made Benji feel fine. Just distant. Different. Care a little less, until they didn't.

An orderly walked by in discrete scrubs and a mask. Benji watched them go, remembering all the times they'd spent waiting in elegant lobbies like this with plants and water features and doors that only opened if you were buzzed in —or out.

Angelica's arm slipped through theirs, the touch bringing them back to the present with a jolt.

Sly survived, Benji reminded themself. *And you did too. Live in the now.*

"I don't know if you want to be touched right now," she said, propelling them towards the exit. "You probably don't but if you freak out in here, they *will* notice."

Benji nodded and sped up, the two of them barreling out the door into the cool night air. Their lungs burned and they realized they'd been holding their breath. They forced themself to take a deep inhale.

"Oh good, you're breathing." Angelica opened the passenger side door for them.

"I can drive," they protested. "You're—"

She shook her head. "You know how these things are, the more you do them, the faster they wear off."

They squinted at her. Was she really comparing melting a man's brain with her emotions to drug tolerance? (What a sentence—what portal had they fallen through for that to make sense?)

"Get in the car," she said. "You look wrecked."

"Gee, thanks."

"Beautiful, but wrecked."

They shrugged, she seemed lucid enough. Benji's hands were shaking and breathing was still a conscious effort.

"I'll take you back to your car," she said, peeling out of the parking spot into the deserted streets.

Benji gasped. "You drive like a stunt woman."

Angelica shrugged. "I live in LA."

Benji giggled, the sound a bit manic.

"Doing better?"

Better was a strong word. "I thought I had it under control," they blurted.

She glanced at them. "Been back to one of those places since…?"

"No."

"Want to uh, talk about it?" Her question was almost shy, like she wasn't sure she should be asking.

"No." They hadn't kept their breakdown a secret, but that didn't mean they wanted to discuss it. Not now. Not with her.

She nodded.

Silence spread between them, not quite comfortable, not quite not.

Benji snuck peeks at her out of the corners of their eyes. She seemed calm, fully there. No emotions radiated off of her, like she was… at peace.

What was it like, they wondered, to contain so much volatility that it had to be decanted regularly into another body?

But then again, wasn't that what they used to do with music, with performing? Was this whole incident just another performance for her?

Would it have been better if she had let herself be that guy's victim? No. Benji tried to bend towards non-violence most days but sometimes you had to defend yourself. And seeing Angelica destroy a man with nothing physical? That had been disturbingly glorious.

How fucked up was that?

Benji turned their gaze to stare out the window. They needed to get the hell out of this car.

Angie dropped off Benji at their parking spot. They leaned down to look at her before they closed their door. "You going to be okay?"

"I could ask you the same thing." The frozen look on thier face in the facility had been familiar but it had been unsettling to see them so close to what looked like a panic attack. She was glad to see more color in their cheeks.

They grimaced. "I'm fine, now that we're out of there."

She watched them breath for a second, just to be sure. Then she nodded.

"But you…" They gestured at her face, lips tight with what almost looked like fury. "That guy…"

"I'm not yours to look after," she said, impatient. They didn't really care, did they? The possibility scared her. "There are no boxes to check off here."

They grimaced. "I'm trying to be—"

"Don't try. Neither of us are nice. Now, run along. I've got some fun phone calls to make." The day was crashing down on her like a thousand pound set piece.

They sighed. "Fine. Be an asshole." They closed the door carefully and stood by their car, watching her drive away.

She ignored their figure in her rearview as she dialed Cheryl.

"What happened?" Her manager asked, sounding tired but not asleep.

"Someone tried to fight me."

Cheryl groaned. "Was it those men's rights creeps? Tell me everything."

Angie did, sparing no details. She wasn't sure it was related to the online harassment but it wasn't like she'd had a heart-to-heart with the asshole.

When she was done, Cheryl blew out a breath. "That's not as bad as I thought. Are you injured? How's your face?"

Angie touched her face and her cheek throbbed. "One second." She pulled up to a stop light and checked her reflection in the visor mirror. She lifted her shirt and poked her stomach. "Tender, might bruise. Nothing big though."

"I hate that you let them hit you, Ang," Cheryl muttered.

Angie shrugged though no one could see her. "Makes your job easier."

"Makes the lawyers' job easier," Cheryl corrected her. "It keeps *me* up at night. "

Angie swallowed the caustic words in her throat. Unloading her emotions used to make her feel better, now the best she could hope for was empty.

This is why she needed to tour. Shows were a safer outlet. She just hadn't expected to deal with this for so long. Not that she wanted to die, she'd just assumed she'd live fast and die young.

"How bad is the clean up going to be?" she asked, instead.

"Eh, depends if anyone was filming and what the quality is. Take pictures of your bruises tonight. I don't think it'll derail the tour—"

Damn.

"But maybe lay low."

"I have Martin's award thing—"

"Shit. How long do you think your attacker will be out?"

Angie hummed in thought. "He'll probably be up tomorrow. I didn't cook him too bad."

"Shame," Cheryl said. "Oh well, get those pictures. D will call me when he's up and I'll take care of it."

"Let me know how he is."

Cheryl snorted. "You're a softie, Ang." She said that every time.

Angie replied the same way she always did. She hung up.

Checking the time, she called Martin Mejia, the most famous former member of the Beatboyz, the one the rest of the band didn't talk to, and the closest thing Angie had to a friend in the industry.

"You better be dying if you're calling at this hour."

"I wanted to give you the most time to find another plus one for your award thing."

"You mean my Queer Artist of the Year Award? Why?"

"I might be entertaining a scandal soon."

Martin went silent for a second. "Murder, grevious bodily harm, sexual assault, harrassment?"

Angie knew Martin well enough not to be surprised. "No, I got into a fight."

"Did you do that freaky bruja thing you do?"

"I'm not a bruja."

"So, yes." He went quiet for another long minute.

She waited him out.

"It's fine," Martin said.

"You don't think I'll disgrace your award? Or be a bad role model for the queer community?"

"My label paid for that award fair and square and your whole brand is being a bad role model. I knew what I was getting into. Plus, it'll distract from how bad my coming out album is."

Angie winced. She'd heard *Bi-dol*. It was mediocre. He'd made much better records. "I'm too tired to lie, let's pretend I said something nice."

He sighed. "I assume you listened to it?"

"Yup."

He groaned and said through what sounded like gritted teeth. "I appreciate your honesty."

"That's why you like me," she replied breezily.

"Whatever."

"I'll see you then."

"Yeah, yeah. Make sure you use the color swatch I sent. I want us to be matching but not *matchy*."

She was about to hang up when he said, "You're not *hurt*, are you?"

"Nothing make-up can't cover."

He hissed something quiet but profane sounding in Spanish.

"Goodnight Martin." She hung up, not wanting to deal with his awkward pity. The two of them got along because they weren't particularly adept at the whole human emotion thing and it had made them plenty of enemies over the years. They weren't exactly friends but he didn't seem to mind her foibles and she'd gotten used to his.

As she drove, her mind began composing her first letter, words circling anxiously like lyrics begging to be written.

Dear Mama… no she wouldn't call her Mama in her letter. *Dear Susan…* Such a deceptively bland name. Angie's grandmother's attempt to help Mama slip under the radar, to assimilate in a town that already thought they were a little too strange. She'd been ecstatic when Susan nabbed Daddy and subsumed herself in being his housewife.

Angie had never met her grandmother. She'd disappeared soon after her parents were married. Mama never wanted to talk about it but some of Angie's relations hadn't been so reticent, repeating rumors of mobs in the middle of the night, disappearances in the swamps around their small town, accusations that Grandma Warner used old country ways and was the perfect scapegoat. For what, Angie never found out. When she pulled into her garage, Angie scribbled in her car notebook until the words in her head shut up.

Ten minutes later, she stood in her bedroom mirror, the full length one she used to post selfies. Studying her reflection, she grimaced. Her make-up was a smeared, runny mess, her hair was a frizzy and flattened, the bruise was blooming darkly around her cheekbone. She looked like a victim.

It would serve Cheryl's purpose but she hated seeing herself like this. It reminded her too much of the days after Mama's arrest when she'd bounced around relations. No one had wanted her and the ones who did well… she'd struck out on her own, bouncing around couches, taking the long hard road to LA.

She shook off the memories and posed, lifting her shirt to show off the bruise on her solar plexus and making her expression wide-eyed yet solemn.

How many of these photos had she taken over the years? She lost count, especially around 2020. It'd been so easy to find a fight then and screaming along to karaoke tracks only did so much. But she'd been better in the last year. Trying. Turning over a new leaf, like she'd told Benji. After her breakdown on tour…

She shook that off too, lowering her shirt, and putting her phone away. Angie took one more long look at her reflection. She wasn't that teenager anymore. It was more than the changes age had made to her body, it was the look in her eyes. She was the monster her teen self had needed. The scary bitch whose fear was a weapon. Everything she'd seen, everything she'd done, honed the blade. Maybe she'd write about it in her damn therapy homework.

It said more about society than her that it was safer to be a monster than a woman.

CHAPTER 13

Dear ~~Mama~~ Susan,

I'll probably never send this. It's a therapy thing. I know, therapy. You'd hate to see me in therapy but how else am I supposed to cope with what you did? I can't haul it all alone anymore. Not just you, I guess. Daddy too. I know now, he did fucked up shit. I know he was always cheating. Always lying, always twisting shit up until he had to be right cuz nothing else made sense. Maybe that's why you never left him. It took me so long to realize how much his worldview fucked up mine. But he was leaving. Wouldn't that have been better? Do you remember what you said to me when I visited that last time? (I remember everything.) You said he didn't get to do that.

I'm trying so hard not to be either of you. I'm trying so hard and I'm failing every day. I am the weapon you made me. The unkidnappable child, sharp *and scared. I'm that child every time I hear you might get out.*

Are you different now? You changed from one day to the next, I'm scared by who you might be. I'm scared you might still be the loving mother I lost thirteen years ago. I'm scared you might be the horror that still lives in my head.

I guess I could read your letter and find out, but who knows if I can even trust what you'll say there.

The next afternoon, Benji stared at their phone, still in their pjs, agonizing. Should they text Angelica? She was fine, she'd told them so. But she hadn't posted yet today. Her posting was still way down since her abrupt hiatus last year, but she was still pretty online.

But her expression last night when they'd tried to awkwardly be nice… they hadn't expected her to shut down so fast. They realized they'd gotten used to her bulletproof persona, freaky and unpredictable though it could be. They'd gotten too close to something, a real hurt. Something more painful than the bruising on her cheek, visible even in the dim lighting.

The memory of it hurt *them*. Some primal part of them railed against the fact they hadn't been able to wade into the fight and hurt that asshole too. But she'd had it handled, she'd done damage deeper than Benji ever could. She might want them on occasion, but she didn't *need* them. And that—

They shook the thoughts out of their head. It wasn't their business. They would not get entangled.

They pulled out their laptop and went over their plans for the songwriting retreat. Everything was in place for next week, planned down to the hour, provided something didn't explode, which it probably would. Even the house would be in decent-enough shape. As long as no one went into the spider-infested side of the yard. Or the attic. Or looked too hard at the paint job on the back of the house.

They'd be leaving in a few days to coordinate the finishing touches. Leo would pick up the cohort of songwriters from LA in his tour bus and drop them off before dropping off his bus at a Sacramento coach depot. Rohan would stay in the house he owned with Cazzi because their time together was apparently worth commuting over the Yolo Causeway.

Which left Benji babysitting the cohort and Leo.

Not babysitting. Everyone was an adult and as long as they didn't destroy Benji's house or each other and music was produced, Benji would count it as a win. They were trying to be less of a control freak.

All this to tell themself they didn't have time to care about Angelica. She was a big girl. She could take care of herself.

They threw down their phone, wishing they hadn't gotten so out of practice at lying to themself.

A few hours later, Benji walked into Hot Dog Marg's, dressed to the nines and still going in mental circles about last night.

Hot Dog Marg's was a small but landmarked drag bar in West Hollywood. Leo bought it years ago in what Benji assumed was a post-band break-up quarter life crisis. It was a nice enough place with a decently priced menu and drag shows every night. It was also, unfortunately, a tourist trap.

They wended their way through the scattered tables, which seemed almost equally stocked with queer folks and straight bachelorette parties to the small bar in the corner across from the stage. No one stopped them but they felt far too many gazes for their passage to have gone unnoticed. Wishing they'd done the VIP thing and gone in the back way, Benji slipped by the crowd to the employee only area.

A large drag queen dressed as Arethra Franklin stopped them. "Baby, you do not work here."

"I'm picking up Leo," Benji said. "He's expecting me."

"Oh, you're his date?" She looked them up and down. "You're a little femme for his usual."

Benji shrugged. "Maybe that's why I'm his friend. Can you let me in please?"

She snapped her fingers and pointed at them. "Benji Omega. I knew I recognized you." She stepped aside.

Benji found Leo in his dressing room, wig cap over his short blonde hair, and gown half zipped. "Don't start," he said. "I've been putting out fires all day."

"Want me to zip you up?"

"You're a doll."

Benji zipped the toxic waste green gown and straightened the straps as Leo put the finishing touches on the make-up that made him look like a glamorous swamp thing. "Your tits are lopsided."

Leo groaned, fixing them. "Why did I agree to this?"

"Because you're trying to pretend you don't want to tear Martin a new one every time you see him." Given Leo was well over six feet tall and built like a gym rat, the court of public opinion wouldn't go his way if he was pitted against his much smaller and much more famous former bandmate, Martin Mejia.

"I can't believe that twat finally tells people he's bi and gets a fucking award. I should get an award for staying in the closet with him for years." Leo grumbled. "When I came out I got community service."

"Didn't you trash a bar during your coming out party?" Benji remembered some gossip about that on the queer LA grapevine. They hadn't known any of the Beatboyz back then and had barely been out themself.

"Not the point." Leo put his green and black wig on, pinning it to his wig cap.

Benji nodded, though their knowledge of Martin and Leo was vague at best. The two of them had been in Beatboyz with Rohan and Rick. There were a lot of heavy hints they'd been a thing for a while and it ended badly. Now, they hated each other. It was really all Benji needed to know. Leo was their friend so they were on their side. Just like they'd been for Rohan against Angelica.

The parallel made them feel more twisted up than it used to.

As if sensing their line of thought, Leo, now in full Steph Infection drag, said, "Everything get dealt with last night?"

Benji nodded.

"Everyone okay?" Steph raised an eyebrow.

Benji registered how much sound leaked in from the hall and the bar, appreciating Steph's discretion. Sometimes they forgot she knew how to be.

"Seems to be."

Steph regarded them for a long moment and nodded. "Come on," she smacked Benji's ass and grabbed her purse. "Let's go survive this shitshow."

"Shoot for the stars, Stephy." Benji rolled their eyes. "And try not to moon the rest of us on the way down."

Steph laughed all the way to the black town car out back.

Angie sat in the back of the limo and drummed her fingers. The damn car didn't seem to go over forty and it couldn't even hit that with traffic tonight. "You could've just let me drive."

Martin Mejia took a long sip from his champagne flute. "I can't believe you still drive yourself. I don't even know where my driver keeps the keys."

Angie covered her grimace with a sip of gin. The idea of not having access to every possible means of escape made the instincts drilled into her as a child scream in protest. "Don't be insufferable, Marty."

He sighed, putting down his glass. "My abuela is still not talking to me. I thought since abuelo was dead, she'd come around when I came out but…" He shrugged miserably.

Angie sighed and patted his hand where it lay on the seat between them. "She'll come around. And if she doesn't? Fuck her."

Martin pulled his hand away. "You don't understand, some of us actually like our family."

She rolled her eyes. A nervous Martin was a prickly Martin.

The two of them were something between friends and conspiring agents of chaos. They were each other's default industry event dates when they were both in town or one of them needed the kind of moral support that could shut someone up with a well-placed word or a single glare, thus making the other person look like a saint in comparison. Or as close to a saint as Angie ever got.

Their pact came about during Endfest last summer when they found themselves in equally hostile territory. It turned out they were the only two big names who didn't hate Angela Alice or Martin Mejia. Since then, they had each other's backs but they didn't try to have anything deeper than that.

Angie grabbed his hand back, making Martin look at her. She gave him a small smile.

His shoulders relaxed. He exhaled, smiling back. "Thanks, Angie."

"Anytime."

This time he squeezed her hand and didn't pull away. His eyes searched her face. "Your team did a good job. I wouldn't know—" He tapped his cheek. "If I didn't know to look."

She looked away. Her event team knew better than to ask questions. She paid them well not to. Sometimes, when her make-up artist painted and powdered gently over her bruises, she wondered how much he'd covered up over the course of his career. "Thanks."

Martin squeezed her hand again and sat back.

When the limo finally pulled up to the inevitable red carpet, he helped her out and slid an arm around her waist as they posed and waved to the cameras and the crowd. She leaned into the comfort of his casual touch, ignoring the throb of pain from the bruising under her jumpsuit.

Maybe if she asked someday he'd give her a real hug. Good Lucy, that was a depressing thought. She pushed it away, doing her trademark half-smile for the cameras.

She wondered how many people would lambast him for coming to his own Queer Artist of the Year Award gala with a woman on his arm. Admittedly he was bi and she was queer but the internet wouldn't care. She asked him when he'd requested she be his date why he wasn't rolling in with six half naked models of various genders.

"Because," he'd said. "'True to Myself' and half of *Bi-dol* might be crap. Even if you agree you'll still cut down anyone who even implies that. Six half naked models will just stand there looking hot."

Though she thought that was rather harsh on models, she had to agree. The single was shit and most of the album was not up to his usual standards. She suspected label pressures and Martin's own fear of coming out. Or imposter syndrome. Fuck if she knew, she wasn't a shrink. But if anyone so much as hinted at that while she was there, they'd regret it.

They arrived at the tail end of the cocktail hour. Angie stood sipping some deliciously herby mocktail as Martin turned on the charm. She was used to this. Though Rohan spent most of their time together as her arm candy due to the break in his career, he too had the charisma to captivate a room with the most banal conversation. Angie didn't bother. She was polite, she was nice, but if she got into charming territory—well, last time she'd had to pepper spray two separate guys to get them to stop trying to come home with her.

Martin stiffened beside her. She glanced around. Leo made an entrance in full Steph Infection drag, her height and aggressively tall wig putting her hair and shoulders above the crowd. Though Steph was far from the only drag queen in attendance, she was one of the few actively in drag. Angie wondered if it felt safer than appearing as Leo Starr. She finished her drink in one large swallow and put the glass on the nearest little table.

The wig made its way towards them. She wondered if Steph was going to play nice or jump straight into backbiting comments. The crowd parted in front of the queen and Angie's heart skipped a beat as she saw who had come as Steph's plus one.

"Seven, six…" Martin counted under his breath while smiling and nodding at something the guy next to him was mansplaining.

Angie was pretty sure the mansplainer was married to a Real Housewife of Somewhere. Did that make him a Real Househusband? She pondered this longer than strictly necessary, focusing on the thought to control her swirling emotions. She hadn't expected to see Benji this soon.

The mansplainer talked louder, gesturing so hard his drink

sloshed on to his sleeve. His Real Housewife's smile got strained as she tried to look around subtly. Where were her cameras? Angie had lost track of the number of camera crews roaming about. She glanced around, noting the boom mike operator heading their way, camera on his heels. Good. Great. Just what this shitshow needed. Who let the straights into this shindig anyway?

Benji clocked her and their eyes widened briefly. They looked gorgeous in a sparkly black translucent dress with a high neck and a high slit. The fabric was opaque in strategic areas and skin tight. It matched their sparkly black smokey eye make-up and silver-black lips.

Angie couldn't take her eyes off of them. Her fingers twitched at her side, concerns about the cameras and the mikes fading. Her emotions coalesced into one clear feeling. She wanted to peel that dress off of them, run her fingers over the slender lines of their body, explore all that smooth skin…

"Four, three…" Martin glanced at her. "If you keep staring at Nakamura like that you're going to set their dress on fire and the rest of us with it."

Angie blinked and hummed Martin's latest hit under her breath, tearing her eyes away from Benji.

"Suck up," he murmured, but hummed along.

Steph arrived at their circle of Martin's sycophants just as the boom and the cameras did.

"Sorry to interrupt." Steph laid a hand on the arm of the Real Househusband who was still mansplaining. He shut up. She smiled sweetly at the group, Benji standing like an unamused shadow behind her.

"I just wanted to say congratulations on coming out and your award, Martin." Steph's voice was a softer, higher version of Leo's usual baritone, but today it verged on saccharin, pitched to be picked up by the boom mike.

"Thank you," Martin said smoothly, like she meant it sincerely.

"What a burden staying in the closet must've been," Steph said, like she'd never been in one herself. "You must feel so much freer now. I know I do."

Martin went visibly rigid besides Angie.

"How nice for you," Angie purred, stepping slightly in front of Martin. "It warms my heart to see us queer folks being happy for each other instead of backbiting for every scrap of attention we can get." She bared her teeth.

The lights flickered, indicating it was time to head to their seats for the entertainment portion of the evening. The cameraman ate it up, much to the annoyance of the Real Housecouple.

Amateurs.

"We can all learn from your good example." Benji gave her a sardonic smile that told her they didn't buy what she was selling for a second and tugged Steph's arm. "Come on Stephy, buy me a drink." But their gaze was on Angie as they turned away.

Benji settled into their seat next to Steph and took a long drink of water. Ten years ago, it would've been a bottle of vodka disguised as water but they'd long ago lost their tolerance for alcohol and the embarrassment inevitably following drinking that much at an industry event.

Steph was on her second cosmo. "I don't know why he even put me on the guest list for this."

"Probably the same reason you decided to come." *And dragged me along.*

"Ugh," she said as another performer stood on stage, singing Martin's praises. "How quickly do you think I can black out so I don't have to remember this?"

"Don't get blackout." Benji pushed Steph's water bottle towards her. "There's no way I can carry you and I absolutely will find the most embarrassing person to drag you into the towncar." They glanced around the assembled celebs and bigwigs. "Maybe that bodybuilder you were flirting with at the bar."

"Asshole," Steph grumbled, but took a drink of water.

"That's why you brought me." Benji and Leo weren't close, really. More like coworkers who spent way too much time together.

"Yeah, well, Rick's busy being happily coupled up and you're the only one who can keep up with the Bitch Queen."

It was her self-proclaimed title. Benji heard it a thousand times before, hell, they'd used it, but it was suddenly jarring. They made a non-commital noise.

"That girl has no chill. The way she was eyefucking you? I thought her eyes were going to fall out of her head." Steph said, ignoring the young up and coming artist on stage doing an altogether too earnest rendition of Martin's song "Midas Touch."

Benji lost track of whatever Steph was saying, remembering the way Angelica looked at them. It was lucky they hadn't tripped and fallen on their face.

She looked amazing in her white jumpsuit with an overlay of black lace, complemented by slender black chains draped around her wrists and fingers and throat, emphasizing the tattoos there. But it had been the intensity of her pale eyes as she stared at Benji that trapped their attention.

She was glorious.

"Are you actually watching the show or are you fantasizing

about Satan's Barbie Doll over there?" Steph whispered loudly in their ear, jerking them from their thoughts.

Benji glared at her. "Shut. Up."

Steph leaned back, wide-eyed. "I forgot how scary you get."

Benji just looked at them before turning their attention ostensibly to the show. The up and comer had finished. As the next act took the stage, Benji slipped away, telling Steph they were heading for the bathroom.

CHAPTER 14

"My unholy trinity
Lightbringer, Sabbat goat, and the rebel angel
I've fallen for you as you fell for us

Lucifer, Lucy, light in my darkness,
Show me the way
Baphomet, alchemic complexity
Mine opposites in unity
Satan, metaphor and deity
My beast of many names
Destroy my enemies
For they be legion"
— "Prayer for Mine Unholy" by Angela Alice off of *Bitch*
Queen Cometh

Angie stood in front of the mirror in the gender neutral bathroom, wishing she could splash her face with cold water. Or better yet, dump a bucketful over her head. She settled for freshening up her lipstick and fiddling with her hair, anything to delay going back out there.

You are a cool, collected, bitch queen, she told herself. A stray image of Benji flitted through her head. She was lying to herself.

"Oh, Baphomet," she murmured, bowing her head over the sink, letting the cold marble under hands cool her. "Give me strength. Give me—"

The door opened. Benji met her eyes in the mirror.

Not what I was asking for, Baphomet.

They hesitated in the doorway. She dug her fingers into the marble to keep herself from reaching for them. "Oh, hi."

Benji closed the door behind them. "Something wrong?"

"Nope." She popped the 'p' still watching them in the mirror.

They looked at her hands, white knuckled on the sink. "Are you trying to break that?"

"What do you want?"

They hesitated, as if debating something. Then they stepped forward and reached up, touching her jaw with a finger. She let them tilt her face towards the light, barely breathing at how close they were.

"How bad is it?" They asked, voice low.

"What?" She couldn't think with them so close. The lemon and cloves scent of them obscured all reason.

They brushed her cheek with the barest touch of their fingertips, tracing the edge of the bruise almost exactly, as if they had memorized its location. She barely felt the touch but Lucy, did it burn. Her breath caught.

Their touch disappeared. "That bad?"

"No." Her voice was breathy, as shaky as her knees. She swallowed her shivering anticipation. This was getting out of hand. What was the point of pining for someone unreachable when they reached back for you?

She stepped away. "Careful Omega, someone might think you're succumbing to my charms."

They tilted their head. "Does that scare you, Coma White?"

Yes. "It should scare you."

"Should it? Why?" Their eyes dipped down to her chest, lingering on the tattoos there.

She grasped for something witty to say but came up empty, all her words fleeing under their gaze. She couldn't read them. Were they fucking with her?

Baphomet, it would hurt so much if they were. The revelation hit her between the eyes. She was in too deep, vulnerable.

"Because I'll just hurt you," she said, hoping the truth would protect her where wit failed.

They took this in with a slow blink. "I'm not changing our relationship status, I'm just pausing the game to see if you need a break."

"Then believe me when I tell you I'm fine," she snarled.

"Only if you stop lying to me."

"Why do you care?"

"Because I do." Their equilibrium was infuriating. How dare they be so calm?

This time she stepped forward, getting in their space until the two of them were nearly nose to nose. They didn't back away but their hands hovered around her hips as if afraid to touch her.

Good, they should be afraid. She leaned close, almost brushing the piercings on the shell of their ear with her lips. Her palms brushed their collarbones. She resisted the urge to circle them around their pretty neck, to play rough. "Run, Omega. Run while you still can."

Their hands landed, thumbs notching into the curve of her hips. They held her, again barely touching, an easily broken cage. "Angelica—"

The door opened.

Benji turned to face the door, ready to snarl.

Steph stood in the doorway. Her mouth opened in shock. Then she shut the door behind her, leaning against it. She grinned. "Are you two killing each other in here or have there been some new developments?"

Angelica broke out of Benji's grip, crossing her arms. "Here to watch?"

Benji sighed, leaning back against the wall. The moment, whatever it was, was gone. Perhaps for the best.

"No, I'm here to talk to Benji, but if you're offering…" Steph raised her glued down eyebrows.

Benji thought Angelica would take the bait and parry with something witty but she just said, "Not tonight." And headed for the door, not looking at either of them.

Steph opened it for her, looking shocked.

"What the hell is going on?" Steph hissed when the door closed behind Angelica.

"I'm not sure I have words for it," Benji said. The image of her, clutching that sink was burned in their brain. They couldn't stop thinking about the black rose inked over her heart, covering the spot where she and Rohan famously got matching tattoos. Of course she'd covered it. But the satisfaction they got seeing the rose was practically primal.

"Words are literally your job," Steph replied, breaking them out of their reverie. "Are you two into each other or what?"

"It's complicated." They couldn't, didn't want to explain it because then they'd have to stop lying to themself.

"Is it? It's a yes or no question."

"Oh, like you've never been in a complicated situation with

someone." Benji made a gesture encompassing the entire event.

"You don't know the half of it." Steph sighed. She leaned against the wall next to them. "I thought I could handle this. It's been years! Why aren't I over it? It's not like we were good together."

They nodded, the words confirming what they'd suspected about Martin and Leo's time in the Beatboyz. "Maybe it's a closure thing."

Steph waved this away. "I'm tangenting. This is about you. You and the devil's best girl. Want to talk about it?"

"Not here," Benji said. "Maybe at the retreat next week. I'll have my head together more then." Hopefully.

"If you say so." Steph pushed off the wall. "I'm going to bury my troubles in a very hot body builder. You'll be okay?"

Benji nodded. Okay was way out of reach but a person could dream. They followed Steph out into the party, pasting a neutral expression over their unease.

CHAPTER 15

— "Hate Crush" by Angela Alice off of *Murder Baby*

Angie sat in the limo, half-listening as Martin bitched about Leo.

"I mean, come on, how tacky can you be?" he

was saying. "The poor asshole Leo was slobbering all over looked like his lips were molding by the time he escaped."

Given the bodybuilder who made out with Leo quite happily went home with the drag queen directly after the show, Angie didn't think he was too worried about the ring of green lipstick around his mouth. "Uh-huh, gross."

Martin paused his diatribe and actually looked at her. "Don't think I didn't notice who was also gone while you had your extended potty break."

"Potty break?" Angie's brain came back online. "I'm not ten and neither are you."

Martin leaned in. "Benji Omega."

Angie blinked, mentally scrambling. "What about them?"

"I knew it! I *knew* it!" Martin crowed.

"How much did you have to drink and how much of it was white powder?"

"You like Benji, you like Benji," Martin sang.

"Remember that thing where we established neither of us were ten years old?"

"Benji and Angie K-I-S-S-I-N-G..."

"What the hell were you and Leo doing way back when?" Angie snapped before she could stop herself. "You think that shit's not obvious?"

Martin stared at her, open-mouthed.

Angie realized she'd gone too far. "Sorry," she said. "But did you really think nobody was going to clock that?"

"I-I—" Martin slumped, putting his head in his hands. "I don't know."

Angie hesitated, debating. "Do you... want to talk about... it?"

"God, no."

Angie blew out a breath. "You maybe should, you know, with someone."

Martin laughed bitterly. "Who? You're the closest thing I have to a friend."

"Ouch," Angie said. "But also, ditto."

They sat in silence.

"Wow, that's depressing," Martin said, after a moment.

"You're telling me." Angie sighed, dropping her head back against the seat. "I have a therapist. It… helps. I could give you her number?" Was that a thing you did? Would it be weird to offer that? Whatever, she'd said it.

"Are we trying to be friends?" Martin sounded suspicious.

Angie raised her head, squinting at him. "Look, we may be lonely, pathetic, hugely successful celebrities but at least we can be lonely, pathetic, hugely successful celebrities together."

"Thank goodness you managed to subtly shoehorn in our success," Martin said drily.

"I may be friendless but my ego sure isn't dead."

"I'll drink to that." Martin poured them both drinks. "To two egos attempting friendship."

Angie clinked her glass against his. "If we fail, at least we're still hot."

Martin laughed and kissed her cheek. "As long as our priorities are in order."

After Martin and his driver dropped her off, Angie stood in her front hall. The house was empty but her, the prep team, long gone. It was 10:30 pm on a Saturday night and she was too wired to be here alone.

She put her hand on her first tattoo, inked along her ribs and hidden under her outfit, still one of her most painful pieces, though it was hard to top the thick line of the inverted cross running down her throat and the underside of her jaw. She'd gotten her first tatt cheap from a cute apprentice she'd dated during her brief stint in NYC when she was eighteen.

"Don't dream it, be it," she murmured, reciting from memory.

She did a quick search on her computer and yes—the Nuart Theater had a showing tonight. It used to be a given that the *Rocky Horror Picture Show*, complete with shadow cast, happened every Saturday at midnight, but the pandemic changed that.

She smiled. It'd been too long.

An hour later she sat in a classic red velvet movie theater chair, dressed in her Transylvanian partygoer best, staring up at the blank screen through her sunglasses. Her chest loosened as the lights went down and the MC went through the usual "do's and don'ts" speech. The Rocky Horror virgins were sacrificed to the screams and cheers of the crowd. Angie savored the joyous queer energy, though the sacrifices had gotten significantly tamer since she'd popped her show cherry a decade or so ago.

Then the stage lights contracted to a single spotlight and the famous red lips started singing "Science Fiction/Double Feature" as a pretty curvy woman stripped on stage.

Angie sang the words, losing herself in the crowd of voices. This is what she'd needed.

A latecomer shuffled into the end of her row just as the woman on stage traipsed away. Angie sat in the back left close to the door for an easy exit, so this wasn't really a surprise. Probably just a member of the shadowcast or security crew. She'd been coming to enough midnight showings over the years that she knew the regular audience members and volunteers by sight. They didn't know her but it was safer that way.

She peered at the figure at the end of the row. Another Transylvanian partygoer by their black suit, pointy paper hat, and sunglasses. They were hard to make out in the muted light of the wedding scene. But they looked familiar. Angie missed a few callbacks, trying to place them. They didn't yell much until

Brad and Janet introduced themselves and the person in her row yelled the classic "Asshole!" and "Slut!" callbacks after their names.

She could just barely hear their voice under everyone else's, but when she isolated it, she knew exactly who it was.

enji loved a full-on *Rocky Horror Picture Show* showing and few shadow casts were as good as the Nuart's Sins O' the Flesh. It felt as revitalizing and centering as they imagined worship services must feel for the religiously inclined. Hanayu took them to their first show at fourteen and staring up at Dr. Frank 'N Furter in his genderbending glory had been a revelation. Tonight, it had been their reward for being Leo's platonic arm candy. And damn, they needed it. That moment with Angelica—

No, they weren't here to sort out their feelings. They were here to release them. They yelled the callbacks, sang along as Brad and Janet duetted about "a light over at the Frankenstein place" then they were up and dancing, doing the Time Warp again.

Jump to the left... they kept an eye on the person down the row from them. They'd clocked the other party outfit when they'd come in but the two of them weren't close enough to bump into each other.

They stepped to the right, did the pelvic thrust with their hands on their hips while several people yelled, "Group sex, group sex!"

Benji spun in a circle with their hands in the air. They saw the person down the row do the same, seeming to really go for it. Their movements were sinuous, adding extra flare and emphasis to the simple moves. So much so that they knocked their hat off. It hit the ground and despite the angle of the floor, it rolled towards Benji. They grabbed it before it made a break for the next row and offered it to its owner.

The other Transylvanian stood stock still, staring at them. "Shit."

Then, despite the curly black wig, the suit, the sunglasses, the make up, Benji knew.

Of all the Rocky Horror showings in Los Angeles, Benji had walked into hers. They dropped the hat.

The two of them stared at each other for a long moment, the only people standing who weren't in the shadow cast acting out Frank's famous exit to his laboratory.

She started to say something but glanced at the smartwatch on her wrist, swore again and took off, pushing past Benji, anxious energy radiating off of her.

Without thinking, they dashed after her through the tiny lobby into cold night air. She whipped around when the door slammed behind them.

"Oh," she said. Her smartwatch pinged again. She wrestled her phone out of her slacks pocket. "I'm moving, Cheryl. What? Fuck. Okay, no, it's fine I'll find a place. I'll call you back."

She hung up and exhaled audibly, the air scraping out of her in almost a growl.

"Everything okay?" Benji asked.

"I don't have time to deal with whatever the hell we have going," Angelica said. "I have to—" She stalked off towards the tiny lot by the theater.

Benji kept pace. "You need somewhere to go," they guessed, possible scenarios scrolling through their mind.

"I—I" She turned the corner and stopped abruptly. Two paps were camped out by her car. Her fists knotted. "Oh shit—"

Benji didn't think. They grabbed her arm and towed her in the opposite direction to the lot where they parked. She mumbled a steady stream of curses but let them. She even got in the car when they opened the passenger door for her.

"Tell me," they said, fastening their seatbelt and starting the car.

Her nostrils flared. "I have to leave town."

"Cops, paps, mobs? What are we talking about here?" The spicy-sweet smell they were coming to associate with her filled the car, making it hard to think.

"Just the last two if I'm lucky." She rubbed her temples.

"What'd they dig up on you?" Benji pulled out of the lot, heading down Santa Monica Boulevard.

"Take a wild guess."

Benji sucked in a breath, brain spinning through possibilities. "That fucker talked?"

"Not just him."

Benji glanced at her but she was facing the window.

"How many?"

She sighed. "People love to hate me. It's easy to find someone who wants to take a swing."

"And what, they all came out of the woodwork at once?"

"Some internet sleuth has been digging up receipts. I guess the asshole I fought with is a men's rights 'activist.' It was a set up. There was a video."

"Shit. Were we—?"

"No, the camera guy ran when he saw other people coming. Cheryl says it ends right after I take him down. Apparently, it was enough though. I've got conspiracy nuts and misogynists live streaming from both my house and my vacation place." She glanced at her texts and gave a wry laugh. "The hashtag is pretty great though."

"Do I want to know?"

"#Bitchhunt."

"Jesus." Benji felt sick.

"I know, that might have to be my next album name." Her tone was flippant but the air in the car felt heavy. "I hope this gives my Bodily Autonomy Fund some extra exposure. All press being good press."

Given her fund was already being talked about in Benji's social media circles, they didn't think Angelica's team was falling down on the PR campaign. It was vaguely annoying that the more they saw it, the less grudging their respect for her became. Not that they'd ever found much fault with her philanthropic efforts. She wasn't afraid to put her money into concrete solutions like the Fund and the Foundation, much less get her hands dirty.

"Where can you go?" Benji realized they'd been driving home on autopilot. They stayed the course. It seemed like the best plan right now.

"I'll figure something out."

"Maybe Martin—"

"No."

"Your other friends—"

"You can't solve this. I'll just rent something somewhere. It'll blow over. It always does."

Benji went silent, reading between the lines. Did Angelica really not have any friends? No one she could trust? Damn, that was depressing. The fix-it side of their brain whirred, whispering, *What if you—*

They cut it off. They couldn't offer that.

Just for a few days. Just until this blew over. You were going to go up there tomorrow anyway.

No. They were already too tangled up in her as it was.

It would be a distraction from your Sly anxiety. You wouldn't be thinking about him the whole time you're driving up, not this time.

"You can drop me at the nearest hotel. Cheryl's going to bring my go bag so I can bug out as soon as I can get a car."

Her chuckle was not convincing. "I haven't been on the road by myself since the last time I ran away from home. Maybe I can make a vacation out of it."

Benji's hands tightened on the steering wheel. They glanced over at her. She looked defiant but tired, her make-up wearing away to show the shadows under her eyes, the outline of the bruise on her cheek. She looked... she looked human. Vulnerable.

It made Benji want to reach out and hold her, touch her, something to melt the rigid tension in her body.

Fuck it.

"You're coming home with me."

"Oh, am I?" She turned to face them for the first time since the theater.

"Yes. Tomorrow morning we're driving to my house upstate." They pulled up to a stop light. "I'm still doing renovations and it's got some personality but you'll be safe there."

Personality? They sounded like a realtor trying to talk around a murder house. Though, given how old the house was, the odds were somebody died there. But it *wasn't* haunted, no matter what Hanayu said.

"You've got this all decided, have you?" She sounded amused.

They turned to meet her gaze. "Do you have a better plan?"

She glared at them. "I will. Give me a couple hours."

They shrugged. "I'll be waiting."

PART TWO
SACRAMENTO

"Pink paint
Sharp picket fence
Two and a half bath
Winding little path
To the front door

(Come in, come in
Welcome home pretty thing)

IKEA catalog of dreams
Perfectly placed,
Smoothed at the seams
Splatter under ultraviolet
The envy of the neighborhood

(Come in, come in
Welcome home sweet thing)

Take off your shoes, stay awhile
Rum? Punch? I wanna see that smile
Tea with sugar, so sweet you can't taste
Mixed it in so good, you can't find a trace
Mama's secret recipe

Come in, come in my dear
My house is yours
Cut in half and open to all
Tell them what you saw
They'll never believe it

Plastic and nice
All sugar, no spice
My dreamhouse is a work of art
Ready to tear you apart
Stitched up tight

Come in, come in my dear
My house is a sore
Cut in half and open to all
You never knew what was in store

Harmless and neat
Crown jewel of the street
The puddle, the lake
The blood, it caked
But we always wiped our shoes clean."
— "Dreamhouse of Horrors" by Angela Alice off of
PhenoBarbie Doll

CHAPTER 16

DANI

Yeah, we're laying low just in case.

GEMMA

In Santa Barbara.

DANI

No one says you can't lay low in style.

MARSHA

I'm hiding in the library.

What are we hiding from?

DANI IS TYPING...
GEMMA IS TYPING...
MARSHA

Oh wait. Men.

*Men's rights losers.

I think I'm safe here.

Angie was out of good ideas. Which is how she found herself back in Benji's passenger seat, hair stuffed back in her wig from last night and wearing the generic clothes she'd packed in the go-bag years ago when this last happened.

Cheryl brought the bag by at an ungodly hour last night. Her manager listened to Benji's plan and agreed it was probably the best option too, the traitor. The legal team didn't think there would be any charges pressed by the people who'd come out of the woodwork—mostly because they'd all thrown the first punch and didn't have a scratch on them while Angie had well-documented injuries. It appeared the group riling them up was more concerned with social media frenzy and intimidation at this point. Which was not exactly comforting.

After that, Angie slept on Benji's couch because she refused to sleep in their bed and they apparently didn't believe in using their spare bedroom as a bedroom. Not that she could talk, none of her spare bedrooms were used for guests either.

Unfortunately, the couch still smelled intoxicatingly like them, lemon and cloves wrapping around her, exactly why she'd been avoiding taking their bed. She'd slept restlessly, Benji stalking through her incoherent dreams.

Their LA place was nice enough from what she'd seen. Practical, with much less attention to design than they put into their own appearance. Their car was similar: electric and expensive but not ostentatiously so, like they had picked it for its ability to fly under the radar. It fit this trip perfectly.

Benji was dressed to match: black jeans and tight black long sleeve shirt that covered their famous User-Friendly Omega tattoo, sunglasses shielding their eyes, hair brushed but unstyled. They drove with confidence Angie found way too hot, looking like a model in a road trip themed music video.

The image worked with the Palaye Royale album playing through the speakers.

She looked at the notebook in her lap. She used to get carsick writing but years of living on tour had inured her to it. And yes, she had a notebook and pen in her go-bag.

Dear Susan,

I'm on the run again. We're probably passing by your prison right now. I know you're somewhere out here. I can feel you. Can you feel me? Do you miss me?

Pathetic. She shut the notebook and shoved it in her bag.

"I can drive if you want a break," she said, ready to get out of her head. They'd been on the road for three hours, almost halfway to Sacramento by the road signs, and it was still morning. Getting up that early should be illegal but she couldn't argue with the logic. Sticking around LA any longer felt like a gamble.

They shrugged. "It's fine. I do this drive all the time."

"Yeah, but not with a fugitive in tow. At least let me give you a break."

They glanced at her. "Are you going to drive like we're in the *Fast & Furious* franchise?"

"Please," she said. "No one shifts that much."

"Not reassuring."

She huffed. "I'll be good, I swear."

They snorted. "That, I'll never believe. But." They tapped the battery gauge. "We could use a stop and I could use some food. You can drive the second leg."

They stopped at a tourist trap ranch with overpriced food but fast charging for the car and a gender neutral bathroom.

Angie sat across from Benji in the booth with their plastic menus and wondered if anyone mistook the two of them for a normal couple. She snorted. Even with most of her tattoos covered, normal was the last thing she looked like.

The waiter was far too enamored of Benji to notice the occult symbols peeking through the ends of her half-fingered gloves anyway. Angie hadn't been overshadowed like that in a while and it entertained the hell out of her to watch Benji deftly handle the waiter's flirting. He didn't seem to recognize he was hitting on a celebrity.

She pressed her lips together on her smile as one of the other booths burst into giggles. She glanced back to see two older men looking surprised at themselves. *Whoops.*

Benji caught her eye as the waiter drifted away. "Enjoying yourself?"

"If a girl can't enjoy herself on the lam, when can she?"

They raised thier eyebrows. "Do you go on the lam often?"

She grimaced, her good humor punctured. "I'm usually already moving, so not exactly."

Benji nodded. "Ah the endless touring."

"Tell me about it."

"Is that why you haven't been out in a while?"

"What is this, twenty questions?"

Benji gave her a look.

"Ooh so *stern*," she cooed with an exaggerated pout.

She expected them to be exasperated but they just chuckled. "Chaos brat."

She waggled her eyebrows. "What are you gonna do, punish me?"

They rested their chin on their interlaced fingers, elbows on the table in an insolent manner Mama would deeply disapprove of. They looked up at her through their subtly mascaraed lashes and said, in a voice dipped in sin, "You'd enjoy it too much."

Heat flared in her face and her thighs clenched involuntarily. "You're mean," she said hoarsely.

They smiled. "You like it."

She bit her lip, then caught herself. This was a bad idea. "Maybe."

The waiter bustled up with their brunch, breaking the moment. Thank Lucy, the last thing she needed was to throw sex on top of the garbage fire that was her life right now. Benji seemed to agree because there was no more innuendo even in the car as she ran her hands over the leather interior, adjusting everything minutely even though the two of them were basically the same height.

She couldn't help but hum in appreciation as she did, enjoying the sleek lines and supple leather. She even appreciated they had found a model that still had buttons, not just everything on a touch screen. "You're a tactile person, huh?" She pressed the power button then the climate controls and music. Oops, there she went again. They were just too fun to tease.

Benji raised an eyebrow at her. "Are you done pushing my buttons?"

"Never." She pushed the cigarette lighter just for the hell of it.

They rolled their eyes, turning away but not before she caught a hint of a smile on their lips.

It's for the best, she told herself. Maybe she'd get them to do a song with her instead of doing her. It'd last longer, anyway.

She was mustering her arguments for why they should reconsider doing the duet as she pulled up to the garage of the house Benji directed her to. They got out and raised the manual garage door, ushering her in.

The house was a massive Victorian dollhouse painted in shades of blue. Gorgeous and ornate with a slightly eerie air. Suddenly, she remembered Benji had said the house had 'personality.'

It reminded her of when she was looking for houses. The

realtor learned real fast he didn't have to sugarcoat the number of mansions in LA that had people die violently in them. The PhenoBarbie Doll Dreamhouse had been a stop on true crime star tours long before Angie bought it. It turned out to be dreadfully unhaunted.

This place, though, had haunting potential.

The garage was a newer addition, maybe converted from a stable but by someone without a lick of style. It was utilitarian, full of tools and random bits of wood from what she assumed were renovations.

Benji grimaced at the mess as she grabbed her stuff from the trunk. "This is a liability issue," they muttered.

Angie glanced at the biggest pile. "I'm not planning on suing you if I trip in your garage. Give me some credit."

"Not you," they said. "I'm having a label songwriting retreat next week. Musicians get into everything."

Angie nodded. "Like termites." So, she had to be out by the time the retreat rolled around. No problem, this would probably blow over by then.

They chuckled as they opened the door to the main house.

Angie smiled to herself. Benji was allowing themselves to actually laugh at her jokes more and it felt like a victory. To what end, she wasn't sure. It's not like they wanted to be friends or—

She shook the thought out of her head, following them into the house. Evidence of the renovations continued, from the ungrouted kitchen missing several cabinet doors to the entryway with wires hanging down from the ceiling.

Benji rubbed their temples as they led her to the partially furnished living room. "Fucking hell," they said. "Um, just put your stuff down on the couch."

They walked over to an alcove by the front door. A little offering bowl full of salt and a glass of water sat in it. Benji quickly dumped and refilled the water and the salt. Then they laid their hand on the wall and inclined their head, murmuring something.

"Ancestor altar?" She asked when they were done, perplexed by the lack of photos and decor. This had to be the plainest altar she'd seen.

Benji shook their head. "Paying my respects to the house. It's an elder in its own right." They patted the wall and smiled at it.

Oh yeah, this house was totally haunted.

There was a crash upstairs. Benji's smile dropped. "I have to find Mom."

Angie perked up. "Your mom's here?" Sense kicked in. "Should I pretend to be someone else? Or hide?" She glanced around. "Maybe in the backyard."

"No!" Benji held up a staying hand. "The patio stairs are going to be fixed tomorrow. They are *not* safe right now. Just, stay. Okay?"

"If you insist," she said. "But I am going to snoop."

"Fine, just be careful."

"Aw you *do* care."

"I can't with you right now." They shook their head and dashed up the stairs with what seemed like reckless speed, given the state of the house. She could hear them yelling for Hanayu as they went.

With a shrug, Angie poked around the downstairs. The kitchen had last been updated sometime in the seventies judging by popcorn ceiling and muddy colors. The backsplash looked recently tiled. The pantry contained the kind of ramen she'd eaten when she was broke, the kind of boxed mac she'd eaten as a kid when there was no one to cook for her, and some teas with handwritten labels that contained herbs Angie had mostly encountered in grimores. *Interesting.*

The bathroom was tiny, with a pink toilet and sink, decorated, rather entertainingly, with Benji's associate's degree in business over the toilet. It was unframed and held up by a rusty railroad spike driven crookedly into the drywall. Angie cackled as she examined it. The sound echoed around her, bouncing sharply off the ceramic tiles decorated with black roses that climbed halfway up the walls. She smiled at the motif, recognizing it from the kitchen. Someone bought in bulk.

The living room was cavernously empty with only a couch covered in a drop cloth attempting to fill it. It also featured a creepy, dusty door leading to an even creepier, dustier set of basement stairs. Angie stood on the landing, contemplating the probable state of the basement given the state of the backyard (overgrown and also somehow very trodden—had someone put a show on that stage back there recently?) when she heard Benji's voice, talking to their mother.

She looked up, realizing this was a back stairwell going to all floors of the house, probably for servants. How very Victorian.

"What kind of setbacks are we talking about?" They were asking.

Hanayu said something unintelligible. Benji's groan hit a note so low and full of dread, it seemed to trickle through the bones of the house to Angie.

It hit something primal in her brain that hissed: *Benji sad. Fix.*

Angie climbed the servant stairs, following their voice to the third floor, taking care to step softly like a ghost. She didn't have the right to fix anything for them but maybe if things just happened to get fixed... she could be their helpful little poltergeist. Just one of the ghosts probably dwelling here. It was the least she could do, really.

With that thought, she pressed herself against the door, careful to check the direction of the hinges first.

"I shouldn't have said anything about the lack of incidents. The ghosts have been restless," Hanayu was saying. "I've been leaving offerings in the attic, but they keep throwing them around so maybe I'm picking the wrong offerings?"

Benji exhaled so loudly through their nose Angie could hear it through the door.

"Don't look at me like that, I kept up the house altar too. Maybe it just missed you."

"Well, I'm here now," Benji said, loudly. Then at a normal volume, continued. "So only one bedroom's habitable, the kitchen is barely functional, and the patio stairs aren't going to get fixed for another few days?" There was a pause, then: "Okay. Who can we call in? Who needs work and won't destroy my house even more?"

Hanayu rattled off some names. All the names seemed to be people connected to bands or venues both Nakamuras knew. Angie didn't recognize any of them.

"Call everyone," Benji said. "We need this place somewhere near code as soon as possible."

Angie heard their steps heading for the other staircase and hurried to intercept them. But as she stepped off the landing, she slipped on something, dust maybe—or maybe this place *was* haunted—and landed flat on her ass with a clatter.

"Motherfucker," she hissed, clutching her hip, which had made unfortunate contact with the bannister on the way down. "What'd I do to you?" She snarled at the ceiling.

The house creaked ominously.

She glared. *This isn't over, House.*

The door above her opened. Benji's mom peered out at her. "Who the fu—Angela Alice?"

Angie patted her head, and yup, the wig was gone. She tipped her head back and smiled, putting a finger up to her lips. "Let's keep this between us, hm?"

Hanayu blinked and swayed, grabbing the doorway for support. The wood looked rough and she pulled away immediately with a quiet "Ow!" Unfortunately, for Angie, it also broke the effect of her smile. Hanayu glared at her. *Score two for the house.* "No. I've heard about you."

"Terrible things, I hope," Angie said. She pushed herself up experimentally. Nothing seemed broken but the bruises would compliment the ones healing under her make-up and on her stomach. It was one of those weeks.

"Are you stalking my kid?"

"Believe it or not, I have better things to do with my time." She brushed herself off and plucked the wig off the floor. "Now, if you'll excuse me, they're expecting me downstairs."

She strutted down the stairs as carefully as possible, taking off her wig cap with a flourish. Sure, her hair was still pinned and smashed against her skull but it was all about confidence, wasn't it?

"This isn't over, young lady," Hanayu yelled then groaned. "Oh my god, you're making me sound like a sitcom mom."

"I have that effect on people," Angie yelled back as she opened the ground floor door.

Benji was just stepping onto the landing as she walked in. They stared at her from across the room. Their gaze burned her despite the space between them. *Mmm.* You couldn't teach intensity like that.

She leaned against the doorway with her hip cocked and spun the wig around her finger. "Come here often?"

"What the hell is going on?"

"I met your mom. I think she likes me." She winked. That she'd technically met Hanayu before didn't matter. It hadn't been a real introduction.

Hanayu came racing down Benji's staircase. "Ben! Ben! Angela Alice is here—Oh, so you did know and you decided not to tell me?"

Benji sighed. "It was an emergency."

"Emergency? How?"

"I invoked the impotent wrath of a nasty little men's rights corner of the internet." Angie shrugged nonchalantly, though the fact those assholes found and camped out at both her houses gave her the creeps. She hoped if they broke in, they found the hex tablets she'd inlaid all through her grounds. Cheryl had talked her out of booby trapping and the tablets were her compromise.

"Oh no." Hanayu covered her mouth, reacting just as Angie expected she would. "Oh honey, you stay here as long as you need."

"Mom, this is my house," Benji reminded her.

"Of course, Benny-chan." Hanayu put her hand on their shoulder. "Now, do you need anything? Toothbrush? Food? Tampons? I'm guessing you left in a hurry."

Benji closed their eyes in a long, annoyed blink, looking for all the world, like a teenager.

Angie was delighted. She tamped down her smile. "Thank you, Hanayu. I'm good."

"Benny," Hanayu gasped. "Where is she going to sleep? There's only one—"

"We'll figure it out," Benji said, sounding short on patience.

Good Lucy, this was entertaining.

"Ohhh, okay." Hanayu glanced between the two of them with a grin. "I see. We'll talk about this later."

"Mo—" Benji tried.

"No, no, I've got contractors to call." She walked briskly towards the door. "I'll get you someone over here in a few hours."

"Bu—"

"Love you, Benny-chan! Bye!" Hanayu was out the door.

There was a pause while Angie and Benji processed what happened. Then she burst out laughing. "Oh Lucy, I *love* your mother!"

Benji glowered at her.

"Chill out," Angie said. "Come on, I want to see what I can do to fix your kitchen."

Who was she kidding? She didn't do anything quietly. Benji was going to have to look at everything she fixed in their house and know it had her fingerprints all over it. Oh yes, she liked that very much.

CHAPTER 17

UFObb: ok did anyone see that gay award thingy for martin mejia?? there's some tea

Omegaluvr92: I think Marty Mac is bi…

UFObb: using gay in the general term, as a queer person, not bi erasing. also who still calls him marty mac??

👍 reaction by Omegaluvr92

Emoisthenewblack: Be nice y'all. Whats the tea bb?

UFObb: these pix: [link] b is soooo pretty but also i cant decide if im shipping them with angela alice or steph infection (thats leo starr, omegaluvr92)

Omegaluvr92: I haven't been living under a rock, bb, but thanks. I thought everyone shipped leo and martin

UFObb: old news. they clearly broke up. word is they hate each other. maybe leos moving on with our b?

Emoisthenewblack: Look at this clip I found on a real housewife's gram: [link]. Sorry bb, I think our Benji is Angela Alice's next victim

😭 reaction by UFObb, 😶 by Omegaluvr92

"What now?" Benji demanded, following Angelica and her messily bobby-pinned hair into the kitchen. "Are you secretly an HGTV reality star or something?"

She scoffed. "Please, I don't like mid-century modern enough for that." She poked a tile on the backsplash, it was mortared onto the wall but missing the grout. "I did, however, learn a lot about basic remodeling and fixing shit during quarantine."

"From who? The school of YouTube?" They said, as if they hadn't spent a lot of time in scrolling through how-to videos.

"Hell yes!" She pointed a finger gun at him. "Where's the grout?"

Benji crossed their arms. "Why are you being helpful?"

"Why are you helping me?" She countered, tapping her knuckle against the tile. The tattoos on her fingers fit the black rose aesthetic of the kitchen. Hanayu had been right, the tiles worked in both the bathroom and the kitchen well.

"Good question," they grumbled, but went and found Angela a bucket of water, the bag of grout, and an applicator they'd seen in the garage.

She mixed the grout up, letting it set for a few minutes before applying.

They had to admit, after watching her work, Angelica grouted tiles like a pro. They considered helping her but the stream of musicians/contractors Hanayu promised started arriving.

Benji closed the kitchen door, hiding Angelica. Reordering the list of tasks their mother put together into most to least important, Benji directed folks upstairs to put the four bedrooms in habitable order. Hazards were mostly dealt with in that part of the house but they walked through each room, making sure anything that couldn't be fixed quickly was covered or inaccessible. The retreat wasn't sober living and they weren't taking any chances.

The backyard was a hazard in itself, but could wait until the deck stairs were dealt with by an expert. And the kitchen, well, they'd see what it looked like after Angelica was done with it.

They spent the rest of the day running around, answering questions about where things should go, supervising, and fielding NoN issues in-between.

The busyness was good. Though they loved Sacramento, it was mixed in with the memories of quarantining here to be in a bubble with their parents, of walking the streets worried that they or their family would be in the crosshairs of the pandemic's anti-East Asian hate surge, and of course, always, always Sly. Odds were he probably lived in some suburb and rarely came into Midtown but those odds also said Benji was going to run into him someday. They pushed that thought away, breathing through the knot in their stomach.

Angelica, when they checked on her periodically, seemed to have entered some kind of grouting flow state. She wore headphones, her lips moving but when they paused to listen, she seemed to be mumbling a running monologue to the house, not singing along. They had to minimize their check-ins because they found themself standing in the doorway longer and longer each time, curious about what she was saying to the house or amused by the way she headbanged while grouting.

Sometimes she caught them looking and gave them a nod in greeting but as the day went on, she noticed less and less. It felt like a small victory, like this woman who was always on high alert trusted them.

But did they trust her? Not long ago, they would've said no, but here she was, in their house. *Talking* to their house. And they kind of liked it.

On their final stop-by, she didn't notice them at all for a good five minutes. In fact, she looked dazed when they thrust a water bottle in her hand and commanded her to drink.

"You're done for the day. Everyone's gone home," they said.

She took a drink and stretched her arms over her head, arching her back. Her grout-stained sweatshirt rose just enough to give Benji a peek at the curve of her hip, the lengthening shadows in the kitchen underscoring the jut of her pelvis like an arrow down. They remembered the shape of it under their fingers, how they'd almost—

They jerked their gaze away but not before she caught them looking.

"Careful Omega," she purred, her voice like a caress. "You'll get a girl's hopes up."

They narrowed their eyes. Were they back to flirting? It was strange to admit that was what they'd been doing, even in their own head. Stranger to admit they wanted more. They took a step forward and lowered their voice to a rasp. "Is the game back on, Angelica?"

She shivered. Though Benji was just out of reach, they could practically feel the movement against their skin. Their fingers flexed involuntarily, wanting to touch her, but they held themself back. She'd had a shit night and was hiding here, they weren't going to push her into anything.

"Maybe," she said.

They stepped back. "It's your move, Coma White."

She bit her lip, teeth leaving a notch in the remains of her lip gloss. They wanted to kiss her until her lips were bare. "Sweet Lucy, you're dangerous."

"Lucy?" They cocked their head, the name jolting them out of their thoughts.

"Lucifer." She waved a hand vaguely at the inverted cross hidden under her clothes. "He shares, though." She winked.

Benji snorted. "How generous."

Her eyes dropped to their lips. "If I wasn't trying to be better, I'd do unspeakable things to you."

"Backslide," they said. "I can take it."

"This was supposed to be safe," she murmured to herself. "I thought you were immune. I thought you'd never fall."

"And now that I might?" Had she only been after the chase? Benji fought the urge to put their armor up.

She swallowed and met their eyes. "I'm scared you could be the one that breaks me."

Slowly, they reached out and gathered her to them. She twined her arms around them like a vine, holding them in place. The two of them were the same height and she rested her forehead against Benji's, their breath intermingling. "Has it occurred to you," Benji said. "That this might be mutually assured destruction?"

"That's the emoest shit anyone's ever said to me," she said. And kissed them.

Every nerve lit up. It was soft at first then they were devouring each other, the kind of messy, needy making out Benji hadn't done in years. Angelica pushed into them until their shoulders hit the door frame. Benji dug their fingers into her messy pinned hair, biting her lip. She gasped into their mouth, pressing her breasts against their chest and grinding their pelvises together. The friction was delicious, so good it—

The front door banged open.

The two of them sprang apart. Fuck, had Benji forgotten to lock the door?

"Benny?" Their mother called from the entryway.

Angelica swore under her breath and pulled a mirror out of her pocket, checking her make up. Most of it was in place, but her lip gloss was long gone.

"Oh hell," Benji muttered. "One second!" They yelled through the kitchen door.

They adjusted their clothes, hoping their shirt would cover the signs of their arousal.

Angelica snapped her compact closed, lip gloss restored. The sheen of it emphasized how thoroughly kissed she looked. Benji closed their eyes and thought about NoN's last P&L report to combat the urge to put their hands back on her.

When they opened them, Angelica raised an eyebrow. They expected her to look smug but there was something vulnerable in her expression. Like they might reject her now that the moment had passed.

"Benny?" Came another voice. Oh no, Hanayu brought their father?

Kenji lived down the street from Hanayu and drew a long running erotic comic with a main character who was modeled off of her. Anyone else might find it creepy but Hanayu found it a mix of flattering and hilarious—apparently that character got them from next door childhood friends to teen parents. And now, she'd brought him to meet Angelica.

Cool.

Benji covered their eyes for a moment then kissed Angelica's forehead and went out to face the inquisition.

Angie stood rooted in the kitchen. Oh Baphomet, what had she done? She'd crossed the line she swore she wouldn't. So much for being better. At least Benji seemed into it, if the way they'd kissed her had been any measure.

Fuck, the way they kissed... the way they grabbed her hair and bit her and...

She shook herself. *Focus, Angel.*

Nope, no weird Mama voices. Stop that.

Oh, but it was the last kiss, the one on her forehead that burned the best. The tenderness was heady. She resisted the urge to touch her fingers to the spot, instead putting her wig back on before stepping out of the kitchen.

Benji stood in the entryway with Hanayu and a person who looked so like them that Angie had to be looking at their other parent. Everyone turned to look at her.

"Angelica, this is my dad," Benji said. "Kenji Yorita."

"Known professionally as Ken Sins." Kenji winked. It was surprisingly rakish for a man who wore his overgrown hair tucked behind his ears messily in black barrettes. He dressed the part of a comics geek with a big black T-shirt clearly bought for the "It's over nine-thousand!" joke on it than for fit, beige cargo pants, and hemp flip flops. But somehow he was making it work with that confidence.

"Why does that sound familiar?" She asked.

"Have you read my comic?"

Benji covered their eyes with both palms, but under them she could see their face was bright red with mortification. Oh, she was following this thread until they melted from embarrassment. It was too fun.

"What's it called?"

Kenji pulled out his phone with a flourish and pulled up his website. The banner image at the top was—

Holy shit, was that Hanayu?

Angie looked at Benji's mom, who snickered behind her hand. Angie glanced back at the image. Yup. Wow. "Your tits look great," she told Hanayu. "Are you that flexible in real life?"

Hanayu doubled over laughing.

Kenji put his phone away with a chuckle.

Benji dragged their palms down their face and pointed at Angie. "Don't egg them on."

Angie pouted. "No fun."

Hanayu wheezed, standing up. "I like her. Mom stamp of approval."

"What are you doing here?" Benji grumbled.

"We're taking you out to dinner," Kenji said.

"We don't—"

"I've seen the state of the pantry here, you'll never get laid on ramen and Kraft noodles," Kenji said sagely. "Which reminds me…" He handed Benji a six pack of what looked like plain mochi.

Hanayu cackled as Benji tore it open and stuck one in their mouth. "He'd know. He cleans up at cons." She winked at Angie. "We're not together, it's cool."

Benji let out another teenage angst groan but offered Angie the pack of mochi.

Angie gave Hanayu a thumbs up, at a loss as to what to say to that. She took the mochi though, enjoying the chewy rice flavor.

"Fine," Benji said. "But I'm paying."

That's what they thought.

CHAPTER 18

@ThatBitchAngela: Not sure how many times I have to point out I'm not affiliated with the Church of Satan (or any group) but do you really think I'd be running an outreach center like the Foundation if I was a fucking social darwinist?

Benji could still taste the mochi Kenji brought as their group walked to their parent's favorite vegetarian place, the rice paste sticking to their lips. He always brought some from Osaka-ya, the Japanese market by his house as a welcome home present, a tradition that started when Benji was a teenager touring first with Hanayu and then UFO. The consistency of it was grounding, they always felt more at home after eating that mochi.

"You're a Satanist, aren't you?" Benji heard their father ask Angelica as the two of them walked behind Benji. It was all they could do not to turn around. She could handle herself.

"Oh, so, you've been on the internet lately," Angelica said.

"Only most of my waking hours."

"Sounds healthy."

Hanayu sidled up to Benji. "What exactly is going on here?"

"Dad is about to ask something really embarrassing." They glanced behind them. Angelica was back in her wig, her grout-covered sweatshirt swapped out for one of Benji's jackets. She looked good in their clothes, walking down their street.

"Give your father a break, he's getting better." Hanayu said, jerking them back to the conversation.

"You've been saying that for years."

"Would you say your relationship with the Devil is spiritual or sexual?" Kenji asked, his voice full of academic curiosity.

Benji sighed.

Angelica chuckled. It probably wasn't the first time she'd been asked something wildly inappropriate like that. "Can you name three different types of Satanism? I don't talk to anyone about it unless they can."

"LeVeyian, Setian, and The Satanic Temple," Kenji said immediately.

"Dammit," she said. "What was your question again?"

"Your relationship with the devil: spiritual or sexual?" Benji glanced back to see Kenji had his sketchbook out. How he could write while walking was beyond them.

"I want to know about this whole rescue thing," Hanayu persisted.

"I think we're going to miss this light." Benji stepped forward as the walk sign started its countdown.

Hanayu pulled them back. "No, no. I wanna hear this."

"I feel like her relationship with the Devil is none of our business," Benji said, pretending not to understand.

Hanayu shot them a look that said she didn't buy what they were selling.

"Somewhere between spiritual and metaphorical," Angelica answered Kenji.

"Hm, so not sexual?" Kenji asked.

Benji pinched the bridge of their nose and looked at their mother, silently begging her to reel him in.

"Honey, that's between me and him. You wanna fuck Satan, you go ahead but you gotta work that one out for yourself." Angelica's Southern accent was leaking out, making her words elongate like molasses as she exuded menace.

Benji got distracted, wondering if she sounded like that when she came minus the menace. They might not mind the menace, actually. Dammit, this attraction was moving fast. Or was it? The two of them had been dancing around each other for years now.

Kenji frowned. "Too far. Sorry, I'm bad at finding the line on these conversations. I'm writing a scene that includes summoning Satan for a sex ritual, do you think it would be more of an invisible incubus situation or a full corporeal manifestation?"

"Um," Angelica sounded baffled.

Hanayu sighed. "I see my doppelgänger screwing the devil in the near future."

Benji was done. They dropped back to walk along Angelica and Kenji. "Kenji, let it go. She doesn't want to answer your questions."

"Too far again?"

"Yep."

Kenji stowed the sketchbook in one of his numerous pockets. "I didn't mean to make you uncomfortable, Miss Alice. Hanayu tells me I get carried away."

"That was me, Dad."

Kenji shot them an annoyed look. "I was speaking generally."

"It's fine." Angelica looked like she was fighting a smile. "It's been a long while since I've been the prude in a conversation."

"I call it the Kenji effect," Hanayu said, cheerfully slinging an arm around him. Color appeared high on his cheeks.

"I like to think it's a compliment," he said.

Angelica chuckled, making Hanayu and several of the people walking by laugh. Even Benji couldn't help but smile. Kenji looked puzzled, watching them.

"Funnier than I thought," he muttered, clearly making a mental note.

No, Benji almost said, *that's the Angelica effect*. But it sounded corny so they didn't.

When they got to the restaurant, Angelica went to the bathroom to wash her hands.

Hanayu elbowed Benji in the ribs. "You liiiike her."

"Mom, you're acting like a nine year old."

"No, that's more like her when she was eleven through sixteen," said the man who'd lived next door to her since they were babies.

"Focus Kenji," Hanayu said. "Our kid has a crush."

Kenji frowned. "Judging by the way her lips were swollen and how flushed they were when we arrived, it's more than that."

Benji covered their face. Kenji was so damn observant.

"Oh, Ken, I don't think they thought it was that obvious."

"But the way they look at each other…"

"I know, I know."

Benji fervently wished they could melt into the floor.

"Hold on, is that—" Hanayu trailed off and her chair scraped back.

Benji looked up just in time to see her run across the room to greet the chef. Kenji trailed her.

"What'd I miss?" Angelica murmured, sliding into the chair next to them. "You're wearing your teenage angst face."

"My what?"

"Don't get me wrong, I'm a fan. It's beautifully tortured."

"You're such a smart ass." But they were stifling a smile.

"Stop trying to distract me with compliments. What happened?"

"You're nosy too."

"That's just good management. I like to know the shit that's getting stirred before it becomes a problem."

"They know." Benji nodded at their parents, who were off chatting with the chef who looked like another Gen X punk. Kenji gestured about something, making Hanayu and the chef laugh.

Angelica sipped her water. "You told them?"

"Nope."

She frowned. "We're that obvious?"

"Kenji is observant but only when it comes to a few things."

"And those are?"

"Sexual tension, art, and crows. He can tell apart every single crow in the flock near his house. He's named them." He sent Benji and Hanayu long detailed emails about them.

"Are you worried about him talking?"

They shook their head. "If Mom doesn't want him to, he won't."

Angelica raised her eyebrows, one side of her mouth tipping up. "What about your mom?"

"Mom keeps family business private."

"So we're safe?" Safe felt like such a loaded word coming out of her mouth.

"For now." They hadn't expected this to escalate so quickly or for anyone to find out, at least for a little while. Though they trusted their parents, the exposure made them feel vulnerable.

"Hmmm." She tapped her chin. Chewed her lip then stopped herself.

"You're taking this well."

"It only makes things worse if I freak out in public." She picked up her menu.

"Should I look forward to a delayed reaction?" Benji asked, somewhat sardonic, somewhat nervous. Was she freaking out about this? Because they were, just a little.

"Depends." She looked at them. "How attached are you to the junk in your backyard?"

"I told you, those stairs aren't safe—"

"Good, then we can be unsafe together." She bared her teeth in something hellishly unsmile-like.

"Oh, for fuck's sake," Benji muttered. "I can't tell if you're joking or not."

She leaned in close behind the cover of their menus. "Neither can I."

"Chaos creature," they hissed.

She snapped her teeth at Benji. The thought of those teeth on thier skin sent a shiver through them.

CHAPTER 19

"Everything's good
So I'm in a mood
Cuz it can't last
There's nothing I can trust
To tell me otherwise

I'm afraid of happiness
I dread joy
I won't stop so don't try
I'm afraid of happiness
I've seen too much
I've seen enough

Everything's fine
I'm walking the line
Of ecstasy and terror
But I'm prepared
Cuz its gonna go south
It's just waiting to pounce

I'm afraid of happiness
It's the only way to be
Rather look ahead
Than savor what'll turn to dread
I'm afraid of happiness
Why aren't you?"
— "Happiness" by User-Friendly Omega off of *Drown*
Them All

That night, after Angie paid for dinner over everyone's protests and Benji's parents went home, she and Benji surveyed the large backyard. It was dark out but strings of lights were hung all around the fencing and the gazebo. Also a small spotlight was tacked onto the back of the house. Benji had had some choice words about safety when they'd seen that.

They insisted the two of them circumvent the porch entirely and exit the house via a side door off the servant's stair.

"How does it feel to be a sellout punk who owns a house built for rich assholes with servants?" She'd asked when they showed her.

Benji'd given her a slightly feral grin. "I hope the dearly departed 1 percent is still hanging around to see the anarchist shows my mom puts on in the backyard."

"So it *is* haunted." She looked at the house with gleeful awe.

"It's not. But if I'm wrong, I hope I'm pissing off dead rich assholes."

Angie couldn't help but laugh at that. "As a living rich asshole, I accept these terms."

Now, the two of them stood on the scrubby remnants of the lawn. Night blooming jasmine scented the air, twining around the fence and the tall trees shielding the house from the alley behind the thick, elaborately carved wooden back gate.

Angie tapped the crowbar in her hand against her shoulder. Various crates and debris was strewn on one side of the yard, haphazardly fenced off by boards strung with more string lights and signs that said, "Black widow breeding ground."

That sign gave her pause, actually. Angie wasn't scared of most things but, spiders? Not her jam. Black widows were nocturnal too.

"Well?" Benji said. "I thought you were going to wreck my yard."

She looked at them, restored to their controlled goth glory like she had never mussed them up. "What if I want to wreck you instead?"

"We're talking about that right now?" Was that color in their cheeks?

She put down the crowbar. "Yeah, let's pretend we're mature adults."

"One of us is."

"Yeah, you." She poked their chest.

Benji glared at her. "Don't be so logical. It's annoying."

"Make me." She stuck her tongue out at them.

They took a step forward.

She put a hand on their clavicle, thumb and forefinger bracketing the base of their throat. Benji's breath hitched.

Angie smiled.

"Stop that," Benji rasped. "I can't think like this."

She pulled her hand away. "You're not pretending you're not attracted to me anymore. That's nice."

Benji huffed. "Don't be insufferable about it."

"Do what I want."

"You always do."

"Not true. I have self-restraint… somewhere."

Benji pinched the bridge of their nose. "*Anyway*. What are

we doing here?" They waved at the air between them. "Us, this, whatever."

"No idea."

Benji groaned. "Figures."

"Look, I wanted you. I flirted with you because I figured it wouldn't go anywhere. I'm as surprised as you. Maybe more."

"Do you want more?"

"Do I *want more*?" Angie grabbed them by the shirt and jerked them to her, crooning in their ear. "I want to devour you. I want to defile you in all the best ways. I want to ruin you for anyone else."

Benji shivered against her, setting her nerves on fire.

"But is it a good idea?" She shrugged. "Probably not."

"Fuck, you're a menace," they said, hoarsely.

"You're the sensible one." She let them go. "You get to set the limits."

"Oh, so I have to make the decisions and you get to just be a loose cannon?"

It was Angie's turn to huff. "Okay, when you put it that way…"

"We're deciding this together or not at all."

"How, exactly?"

Benji's eye twitched. "Very slowly and carefully."

"Ugh, stop it, I'm already horny."

Benji grinned at her, that same feral expression. Her thighs clenched. "No fair," she whined.

"Two can play at that game," they purred.

"I thought we were being mature adults."

Benji shrugged. "You're going to have to stand farther away from me if you're serious about that."

Which is how they ended up sitting across from each other in the gazebo. The structure was also lit by string lights, these ones purple, and covered by climbing ivy. It was, unfortunately, very romantic.

"So," Angie said. She fumbled for words, unsure.

Benji watched her, the fire in their gaze banked, waiting.

How the hell did you do this? She usually went full-throttle into relationships, following her feelings until something—often her—fell apart. Now, she had the possibility of something with *Benji*, of all people.

Angie was afraid of fucking up. It was an unfamiliar feeling. She didn't care for it.

"Do you know how to do this?" She asked, frustrated.

"What?"

She waved her hands. "Relationships. Intimacy. But, you know, healthy?"

They grimaced. "Theoretically. I mean, I have had situationships that were... fine. I'm pretty sure. From my end, anyway."

"We're groping around in the dark, aren't we?"

"We'd be having a lot more fun if we were," Benji said, with a chuckle. "But no, I know what you mean. We're sharp-edged people."

Angie snorted. "We're assholes."

"Yeah, well, like you don't tend towards the poetic."

Impatience lashed her suddenly. "Benji, would you even want to be with me, beyond sex? I know being anything together would upend your life and be a fucking pain in the ass, even without adding my personality to the mix. I'm cool if you say no, I get it."

Benji regarded her, the purple lights making sparks in their eyes, gliding along the shine of their dark hair. It made her ache, gazing at them, but she refused to speak first, to look away.

"I don't know," they said, finally.

Disappointment and hurt cut through her like a blunt knife. She nodded, keeping her mouth firmly shut and her emotions wrapped tight. She'd asked for honesty and she'd gotten it.

What a mood killer.

"As much as I want you, I'm not sure I can get past the things you've done to my friends. I watched what your relationship did to Rohan. I've lived through love that festers, I don't want to do it again. I was there for the shit you pulled at Endfest last summer. I would be a fool to believe you can't chew me up and spit me out the way you've done to so many other people." Their tone was horribly gentle, but to their credit, they weren't trying to manipulate her into feeling bad for them. That rarely worked anyway. Angie had hardened her heart to that years ago.

"What, I haven't convinced you I've turned over a new leaf?" She asked, her tone aiming for joking but coming out sharp, like a razorblade in an apple.

"Angelica," Benji said, their spine straightening and their tone cooling off. "I watched you fuck up that guy in a way I still don't understand—"

"Join the club."

"—Let me finish." They waited until she mimed zipping her lips to continue. "While I know you never did anything like that to Rohan, I know you have the capacity for it. You have been telling me and the world for years that you're dangerous. I believe you. Hell, you made a whole album to hurt him."

"Do I make you feel unsafe?" She asked, her stomach dropping.

They shook their head. "Unsettled, at worst."

She nodded, letting go of the breath she'd been holding. "Writing that album hurt me too. It was a bad idea in a string of them. He and I talked it out. We're as good as we're ever going to be. But you two hurt me as well." She tried to keep the anger and pain out of her voice, matching their careful logic. "*From the Ashes*? It was his album, but don't think I didn't feel how you sharpened his words until they shredded me." She'd listened to it once in a fit of something between self-flagellation and self-hatred.

Oh Lucy, what a taste of her own medicine.

Benji closed their eyes for a long moment, biting down on a knee-jerk defensive response. They hadn't been thinking about her as a full person when they'd helped Rohan write his response to her devastating break-up album. She'd been the force of nature that hurt their friend and they'd needed to keep Rohan's reputation from succumbing to her narrative.

Fuck, they had been an asshole, hadn't they? Falling back on the sharpest knife in their arsenal, exactly as they'd done to Sly. "I'm sorry," they said, opening their eyes.

She shrugged, not looking at them. "I deserved it. I was awful and I reveled in my awfulness."

"I reveled in it too," Benji admitted. "It was so fun to fight with you. I felt so righteous."

She exhaled a sharp almost-laugh. "So many people do."

"You know it was never about your religion, right? It was about Rohan."

"I never thought it was about religion," she said. "If I did, I'd have gotten bored of fighting with you years ago."

"So, where does that leave us?" Benji asked.

She stretched with a yawn and stood. "Not fucking, that's for sure."

"Fair." They couldn't fault her logic though their body hated it. They stood too. "Let's figure out where we can sleep."

Unfortunately, that proved more complicated than they

anticipated. While the bedrooms that had been uninhabitable were mostly fine now, they lacked a very important feature.

"Looks like bed shopping is on the agenda for tomorrow," Angelica observed after Benji left the last bedroom, defeated.

"You can have my bed." Benji gestured at the room they usually stayed in.

"Where are you sleeping?" She asked.

"The couch is a pull out." They'd slept there while they were finishing *From the Ashes* with Rohan here. It was lumpy but that felt like penance now.

Angelica frowned, not bothering to hide the discontent rolling off her. "Fine, but then I get to buy your bedrooms beds tomorrow."

Benji blinked. "I wasn't aware we were bargaining."

"Consider it an evolution." She winked and abandoned Benji for their bedroom.

Benji stood there for a long moment, dazed. Damn, that woman bounced back fast.

CHAPTER 20

Dear Susan,

You always taught me to respect myself above everyone else. Very left hand path of you. (You'd hate that, wouldn't you? You always projected such a god-fearing image. Not even sending me to Christian indoctrination school convinced me though.) Well, I'm sure I'd have made you proud. I refused to sleep with the hottest person I've ever met because they refused to destroy their life for me. Winning all around. I am trying to mature and have healthy relationships.

Would you even know a healthy relationship if it bit you in the ass? I'm not sure I would. That's why I'm still writing to you, not baby me. Maybe when I write a letter that isn't bitter. Maybe when I work up the nerve to read yours. Maybe.

I'm fragile, Susan. I'm all bad potential and I'm

*still more volatile than I should be with this much
power. You should see the things I've gotten away with.
Aaand now I sound like a serial killer. Great.*

The sounds of the porch stairs being demoed woke Angie up from her restless sleep. "Good morning to you too, House," she snarled at the ceiling.

Picking up her phone, she swore at the clock (it was 9 am). Hauling herself out of bed, she used the bathroom mirror to get her wig on and slap on enough make up to make her unrecognizable. The bedroom was sparse, barely lived in, clearly a crash pad for Benji. Did they ever plan to live here or had they just bought the place and let it sit?

Not her problem. She pulled on her grout-encrusted sweatshirt over the last of her clean clothes and the small tablet from her go bag. She had more than bed shopping to do today.

A text came in from Cheryl, making her stop dead on the stairs.

CHERYL

Don't buy anything with the LLC card. I think one of those assholes is tracking it. Maybe don't order anything delivered either, just in case.

ANGIE

Shit. Did they come to your office?

CHERYL

No, we got a contingent who found the tour bus, we think it's from an outfitting order.

Angie's stomach dropped for multiple reasons. She went back upstairs to check the amount of cash in her bag. Enough for clothes and food for a few weeks, if she was frugal but not enough for six beds. She made a mental note to pack more cash when she refilled her go bag.

It was fine. She'd use her emergency credit card, opened under a whole separate LLC that not even Cheryl knew about. Was she paranoid? Maybe. Was it paying off? In spades.

She shrugged off the anxiety with a deep breath, humming a Miyavi song as she resumed her trek downstairs.

Benji sat at a card table in the living room that hadn't been there yesterday, a cup of coffee and a pastry box next to them. They looked up when she hit the landing. "Coffee?"

"Me and caffeine? Bad idea." She shuddered. She was an absolute lightweight when it came to any kind of drug. Probably for the best, drinking had only made her Daddy more of an emotive menace. Her years of unstable housing after his murder had made her cling to sobriety harder and caffeine made her shaky, anxious. Not something people reacted well to.

Benji shrugged and pushed the pastry box towards her then paused. "Unless you're on some kind of pre-tour diet?"

If she was at home, she'd be eating some pre-made breakfast calculated to the calorie by her nutrition team—but mostly because she couldn't cook for shit. Her label had commented on her weight once.

Only once.

She dropped into the folding chair across from them and flipped the box open.

"I got a selection. I don't know what you like."

Ugh, how thoughtful. You'd think they'd have the decency to be a heinous bitch after rejecting her so she could get over them faster.

"Thanks," she mumbled before biting into a large cinnamon roll. Delicious cinnamon sugar flooded her mouth. She hummed happily.

Most of the time she regarded food as fuel to get her to the next song, tour stop, whatever. It had only been during lock-down that she'd had the time to slow down and enjoy it again —and then there had been a long stretch where all the restaurants had been closed and her premade meals company was caught up in that. She'd had to resort to her own cooking and boy did that make her miss Rohan. Not just his cooking but watching him learn to bake in her kitchen. It had been so… pleasant. Sweet, literally.

"Can you cook?" She asked Benji. They were pointedly not watching her devour the cinnamon roll.

They shrugged. "Enough. You?"

"If it comes out of a box. Otherwise, no. I order a mean take-out though." She finished the roll and picked up a croissant. Mmm buttery and oh so flakey. "Do you want input on the beds or can I just order them?"

Benji's gaze shot to her. "You were serious about that?"

"Darling, I'm serious about everything. It's part of my charm." She paused. "Or maybe my menace. Eye of the beholder, I guess."

They let out a put upon sigh. "Is it too much to ask that we shop online?"

"Look, you want six beds in less than a week. It's either something shitty and cheap off the 'Zon or something better and local. Also, I need clothes." She put her hand out. "Just give me the keys and trust me."

Benji regarded her hand with the eye twitching suspicion usually reserved for—well, her. Angie poked her finger into her cheek and tried for a cute, harmless smile.

"Frightening," Benji said drily.

She sighed and dropped the pose. "I'll rent a car." So, they didn't trust her, what else was new? She hummed to herself, masking her hurt as she pulled up a car rental site on the small tablet from her go-bag. She hesitated. Would renting a car possibly put her in danger? She'd have to show her driver's licence. What if someone leaked it? What if they used all the cameras and computers on the car to find and track her?

A set of car keys landed on the table in front of her. "Don't wreck it, okay?"

She grabbed the keys before they could change their mind. "Have faith, Omega."

Having faith in Angelica was exactly as hard as Benji thought it would be. She was gone for hours, communicating nothing but a single picture of a basic bed with the caption: "You're getting five of these and an extra long for big boi Steph."

They weren't sure how they felt about her buying things for their songwriting retreat, let alone their *house* but they had to admit it took some pressure off the budget. Though how they were going to explain that to Leo was a whole other story.

Maybe they could say the beds were donated? Eh, that sounded like it could get into weird tax territory, especially since Angela had been involved in the label before her relationship with Rohan imploded. They'd just tell him the truth. Later. When she wasn't hiding out here.

Whenever that was.

They stared sightlessly at their computer screen. They'd barely slept last night and they couldn't entirely blame the pullout bed. They hadn't slept well the night before either. Sharing space with Angelica wasn't exactly restful. Or maybe it was having her so close yet not in their bed.

Benji flopped back against the reassembled couch and groaned, the sound lost under the hammering as the contractors replaced the stairs they'd spent the morning demolishing. So far, it was progressing quickly, if loudly. You'd think it would drown out their thoughts but they'd been raised in clubs and had the hearing damage to prove it. They had plenty of practice having angsty thoughts at a hundred decibels.

They were twisted up about last night which was annoying. It wasn't like they hadn't meant everything they'd said. They shut the computer and went to work on the kitchen.

Angelica made grouting the tiles up look easy enough. Benji refused to wallow just because they wished it was less complicated to say yes to her. To let themself be carried away by her brand of chaos.

They mixed up some more grout, remembering the last time they'd denoted their life. The week where they'd run a dulled knife up and down their arm, a bottle of vodka at their elbow and a cigarette hanging from their lips. They'd been burnt out beyond recognition, dealing with an indecipherable wrongness they couldn't describe even to themself.

Then one day, the knife slipped. They'd watched the blood run down their arm and done the only thing they could think of—jammed some gauze in the wound and driven themself to the "rehab" Sly kept ending up at after UFO moved to LA.

They'd walked in and immediately wished they'd gone somewhere else, anywhere else but this was the place they'd known, the place they could've driven to without thinking.

They looked at the nurse at the front desk and held out their hands. "Please."

The gauze had fallen off with a wet splat. They swayed, the last of their cigarette burning their fingers.

It was always better to check yourself in voluntarily. Always better when you were famous and rich.

Locking themself up away from the world was both helpful and terrible. It was like jail but where people constantly asked how you were and then didn't believe you if you said you were anything but crazy. But it also put the whole overwhelming business of life on hold.

No fame, no social media, no calls, no wondering how much make-up they could get away with wearing today. It was painfully clarifying: all their wishes had been granted and they had no more dreams left. Benji woke up one day and realized they'd hated the life they fled. They hated the fame machine, the expectations, pretending they only wanted to be this genderbent on stage.

Was this how Sly felt every time he landed in this place? They had wondered, staring at the ceiling. They had talked about Sly for the first time in years, prying the shrapnel of the relationship they'd detonated in group therapy, laying it on the floor in painful chunks.

But there were highlights too. Like their roommate, Jo who, at the time, was an actor with a very dignified coke habit. They were the first person Benji told about their gender.

They'd pegged Benji as a baby queer the minute they'd seen them and decided to mother them. It'd been annoying at first, especially since they hadn't even told Hanayu they were here. They hadn't told anyone.

Jo connected Benji with other trans and gender non-conforming folks and stubbornly kept in touch after both of them left the facility. Benji was grateful. They needed Jo. After quitting the band, their whole way of life crumbled with it. They didn't want to go back on-stage. They couldn't be Benji Omega or the Suicide King and didn't want to show people who they were yet. It felt too new, too vulnerable.

They hid, went to therapy, sold the LA house, and bought a small condo that felt manageable. It was safe. It was suffocating. Benji didn't talk to anyone besides their therapist, Jo, Jo's friends, and their parents for nearly a year.

They'd only started venturing out again when they met Rohan at a small charity event where the organizer sat them together because they were the only two Asian musicians there. A silver lining to an otherwise shitty event. Becoming friends and starting the label together resurrected Benji's career and social circle in one go.

Now, Benji was considering jeopardizing that relationship, because of what? Sex? No. Something more than that. Angelica was the first person they'd met in a long time who could stand toe-to-toe with Benji and match their intensity.

Sly, as much as they'd loved him in their fucked up way, never could, and he'd never once looked back the way Benji looked at him.

Angelica did. The way she looked at them kept them up at night, twisting in the possibilities, sweating in the heat.

She inspired songs—for themself and Benji hadn't written for just them since the breakdown.

Why did it have to be her, of all people? Why couldn't Benji have a simple relationship?

Their hand slipped and the grout wand thing dropped out of their grasp, clattering to the ground. They stared at it, suddenly so, so tired. They were tired of complicated, of balancing everyone's emotional well-being around them. It wasn't like Benji was good at it. Their broken friendship with Rick was Exhibit A. You try to protect everyone and inevitably someone gets hurt.

A figure in black picked up the grout wand. Angelica met their gaze as she stood. The understanding in her eyes felt like the nail in the coffin.

She wasn't touching them and she said nothing but she radiated something that felt like tenderness.

Maybe that's why they kissed her. Maybe they wanted to see what it was like to kiss someone when they came home, like they were in some sort of domestic arrangement. It was gentle, chaste almost. As chaste as anything between the two of them could be.

Angelica's eyes were still closed when they pulled away.

Regret lanced through their haze. They hadn't asked and the two of them had just agreed they wouldn't—

"I'm so—"

"Don't apologize." Her voice was quiet but her words were steely. "I'm savoring this before you bring reality in."

"If we're ignoring reality, then…" Benji reached out and wrapped their arms around her, hiding their face in the curls of her wig, breathing in its hairspray scent mingling with Angelica's spicy, almost cinnamony smell.

Her breath hitched but her hands came to wrap around their lower back. It felt… nice? Comfortable even. She relaxed into them little by little and they relaxed too.

Benji wasn't sure how long the two of them stood together, intertwined. Eventually their neck complained and then Angelica's stomach rumbled so loudly they both laughed.

Benji stepped back. Angelica turned away, picking up her bag of purchases off the counter but not before they saw the tears in her eyes.

"Hey." They touched her shoulder. "Why the—?" They gestured at their own face. How had they not noticed her crying? Between the physical signs and her broadcasting it should've been obvious.

She wiped the tears away with the backs of her hands, smearing her make up. "Don't worry about it."

"Did I do something triggering?"

She shook her head, still not looking at them, no emotions rolling off of her. "I'm not going to tell you." She glared, crystalline tears darkened by her mascara caught in her lashes. Damn, she was lovely.

Stiffening, Benji forced a casual shrug. "Fine."

The air in the kitchen felt hot and aggressive. Her nostrils flared and her hands, streaked with make up, fisted over the bag handles.

Benji waited, refusing to buy into whatever this was.

Then as quickly as it came, she snuffed her anger out with a deep breath. Wrapping her arms around herself, she sang something Benji half-recognized under her breath.

Benji felt like they had whiplash as they watched her self-soothe. Should they leave? Should they do something?

Still holding herself, Angelica said, "It's just been a while for me."

"A while for what?"

"Since someone held me. I forgot how much I missed it. Or rather I had gotten used to the ache. Sometimes relief almost hurts when you're used to the pain, you know?"

Benji's eyes prickled, heat building behind them. "I do. I do know."

Finally, she met their eyes. "Fucking sucks, doesn't it?"

"Yeah," Benji said hoarsely. "It does."

CHAPTER 21

"You want them to see you
You spill your guts
Wreck your car
Offer up your insides
With all these little suicides

You're slumming it
Drumming it into your jag and
Their marble floor
You can't take it anymore
Again and again and again
And again and again and…

Little rich kid who cleaned you up
Who propped you up
Who tried to keep you from death?
Who felt your every last breath?

Who watches as you
You spilled your guts

Wrecked your car
Offered up your insides?
Who dies a little
With all these little suicides?
(The King, the king, the king)"
— "Every Last Breath" by User-Friendly Omega off of *Suicide*
King

After that, Angie hid in Benji's room, sorting through the wigs and clothes she'd picked up at the costume/thrift store on K Street. She'd have stayed in there forever but Benji had heard her stomach grumbling and they refused to let it go. Ten minutes later, they were knocking on the door, asking what she wanted to eat.

She considered being petulant and yelling "Nothing!" but it still made her giddy that Benji was being nice. Plus, she really was hungry.

After delicious Indian takeout, the two of them stood on the deck looking down at the unstained but fully built stairs. The wood was covered with plastic to protect it from the rain forecasted that night.

"Very sturdy-looking," Angie said. She didn't know much about stairs but these seemed pretty good.

Benji studied the stairs for a moment then jumped down from the deck to study them from the front. They caressed the railing under the plastic. Were their lips moving? Was Benji doing *spellwork*?

Angie watched them for a long moment, trying to gauge what exactly she was seeing. "You doing witchy shit?" She asked finally, too curious to be subtle.

Benji paused. "No. Not exactly."

"What exactly then?"

They looked up at her, eyes mapping her expression like they could read her mind. "I'm not really spiritual. I just… I picked up some animism stuff from my grandparents, they were Shinto and really into the idea that everything had a soul."

Angie nodded. She'd heard of this. She never would've pinned Benji for that kind of practitioner but it fit with their brusque brand of considerateness. She sat on the deck, dangling her legs next to the stairs. "Let me know when you're done." Deliberately looking elsewhere, she studied the camellia tree growing nearby.

After a pause, Benji continued, brushing their fingers under the plastic covering and resting their hand directly on the wood of the railing. Out of the corner of her eye, Angie could see them dip their head, eyes fluttering closed for a minute. Then they straightened, removing their hand and replacing the plastic. "Done."

"Cool." Angie stood and stepped onto the plastic.

"What are *you* doing?"

"You want to know if these things are going to hold, right?" It wasn't like she hadn't watched several workers impact testing the build an hour ago. Plus, the ghosts of the house hadn't pushed her down any more stairs. Maybe they'd liked the compliments and chatter she'd kept up while grouting.

"I—yes," Benji said, failing to suppress the frustrated snarl in their voice.

Angie chuckled to herself. Truely, there was nothing more fun than pushing their buttons. She descended with dramatic slowness, holding her head high like the Bitch Queen she was. When she reached the bottom she did a slow twirl. "Woman survives stairs—totally unharmed!" She said in her best old-timey newscaster voice. "Full story at eight. Don't touch that dial, folks!"

"Were you a theater kid?" Benji asked suspiciously.

Angie laughed. "I went to a Christian school. Can you see me being Mary in the nativity play?"

Benji still looked suspicious.

"Did I explore the drag scene and the weird theater scene in New York while I was there? Sure. Did I maybe go to musical theater camp one summer? Not telling."

"Ah, there it is! The truth comes out!" Benji said, gleefully pointing at her.

She put a wrist to her forehead with mock distress. "Oh! I am found out! But—" She straightened and pointed back at them. "Takes one to know one!"

Benji gasped. "How dare you," they hissed.

"Out with it!" She said, tapping their chest. A tremor of laughter vibrated under her finger. "I know there's a theater kid in here waiting to burst into song."

"I just did backstage work, I swear!" They cried.

"Liar!" She exclaimed.

"No, that's actually true," they said, breaking character. "I was in like, three bands and helping the Razors, I didn't have time to do any other rehearsals. The only reason I helped out at all was I had a crush on the lead actress."

"Classic." Angie pushed down a jagged flash of jealousy at a girl who Benji probably hadn't spoken to in fifteen years.

Benji grimaced. "She was also my bassist's girlfriend. He wasn't a great boyfriend and I took my shot."

"Ooh juicy!" *Now,* Angie was really interested. Then some old trivia poked her brain. "Wait, was this your bassist when—"

"Yes." Benji sighed. "After that, Sly crashed his car. Later, I realized it was deliberate."

"Holy shit," Angie murmured. Her memory supplied her with the lyrics to "Every Last Breath"—and she realized she had used that song to poke them casually last summer. Baphomet, she should've known better. "Oh hell, Benji, I—"

They waved her words away though their shoulders were

stiff and they clearly weren't okay. "He survived himself. He survived me too. I was such an asshole."

"You blame yourself for what? Being a teenager? His brain chemistry?"

"I blame myself for putting his pain on the page and profiting off of it."

Angie sucked a breath through her teeth. "What's done is done. What have you done to offset it?"

Benji brushed thier hair out of thier eyes, not looking at her. "I leave him alone and donate all of my portion of *Suicide King*'s profits to suicide prevention organizations."

"Plus, you take care of everyone at the label, sponsor and co-lead the Gender: Complicated support group at my Foundation, let your mom put on punk shows in your backyard… did I leave anything else?" Slowly, she took their hand, noting the tremor in their fingers. Her heart ached for them. She felt a little sick at the idea that she'd been rubbing salt into their wounds by singing their old pain back to them.

Benji frowned at her hand holding theirs but didn't pull away. "You know about the support group? I'm supposed to be an anonymous sponsor."

Angie raised her eyebrows at them. "I might be in disgrace but don't think I don't know exactly what goes on at my Foundation. That's my big good thing and I take it seriously."

Benji nodded. "Noted."

"Anyway," Angie said, "What's left to do for your retreat? Beds and bedding are coming tomorrow. The bedrooms are pretty spartan but done. Is it just staining the stairs and getting the kitchen in working order? Maybe some furniture for the living room?"

"Pretty much," Benji said. "Will it be safe for you to go back home in a few days?"

Angie shrugged.

They hesitated, thinking something over. Then: "You could stay, if you needed to, during the retreat."

Shock made her lightheaded but her snark was on autopilot. "Trying to guarantee some drama in your event so people have something to write about?"

They shook their head. "I think you could be an asset to my writers and maybe get some good songs out of the deal. Cross-pollinate ideas and all that."

Angelica stared at Benji like she was waiting for them to laugh and take their words back. They held her gaze steadily. They meant every word but, she was right, there was another shoe to drop. There was a shuddering, aching fear in their chest that they were making a mistake. Though whether the mistake was saying it or not, they weren't sure. "Also, I'd like to spend more time with you."

She cocked her head, studying them more intently. Her hand flexed around theirs. "This is a test."

They blinked. "A what?"

"Rohan and Leo will be here. You can ease them into the possibility of you trying something with me. It's clever. A planned explosion and if it goes badly, well, no skin off your nose."

How bloodless did she think Benji was? Okay, yes, that was part of it but they really did like her. Benji loosely interlaced their fingers with hers, tightening the clasp of their hands. She stared at their intertwined hands like she couldn't quite comprehend what she was looking at. "You and I dating is no one else's business, if that's what we decide to do. It'd be nice if this took the edge off the surprise but I... I like you."

The knot that had been in their stomach since they talked about Sly tightened at their words.

Angelica raised her gaze to theirs, her eyes wide. Like, really wide, the whites showing all around her greyscale irises. "Is it weird that hearing you say that made me wet and terrified at the same time?"

Benji's mouth went dry at the thought of her wet. Now, they were a whole different kind of tense. They licked their lips, her eyes devouring the motion. "Does that mean you'll stay?"

"Yeah." She grabbed them by the collar, pulling them towards her. "But you're staying in my bed tonight."

Benji cleared their throat and said primly, "I believe that's *my* bed."

"Believe what you want," she said, pressing her nose to theirs. "But you let me in and I may never leave."

Benji shouldn't have found that as hot as they did but what the hell. They were in it now. They caught her mouth in a bruising kiss, dragging her all the way flush against them. She gasped into their mouth, her knuckles pressed against their throat. Benji ran their nails up under her shirt against the smooth skin of her hip up to the underside of her breast.

She pressed even harder against them, her height making her pelvis grind against them in just the right spot. Fuck, they just wanted to strip her naked and make her scream right here on the deck.

Groaning, Benji said, "I think the bed is big enough for both of us."

She grinned against their lips, her elation unconstrained. It made Benji feel like the top of their head was a balloon, lighter than air.

"But," Benji said, regretting the words as they said them. "I think we should take it slow. Physically."

"Awww." Angelica pulled back just enough to look at them. "Are you afraid once we start fucking we won't want to stop?"

"Yes," Benji said, half to themself. "And I still have a lot to do."

"But we can still do stuff?"

"I mean, yes—"

"Excellent," she said with an evil smile. They could almost see the things she was imagining doing to them and, damn, *why* exactly were they not having sex right now?

Benji gave themself a mental slap. They could resist her. They could. "You know, now I know exactly what you mean by wet and terrified."

"Fun, isn't it?" Her fingers skimmed the edge of their waistband. "Can I see how wet? Just a peek?"

"Angelica." Benji crossed their arms, mostly so they didn't reach for her.

She backed off immediately, holding her hands up in surrender. "Give me concrete boundaries, please. Or I'm going to keep pushing to see how far you'll let me go."

"Okay, um." Benji focused on getting the blood back to their brain. "Nothing below the waist. Not tonight, at least. It's too new. I need to adjust to new partners before we get to that. Though, I have been tested since my last partner."

"Same." She nodded. "Nipples, yes or no?"

"Yes."

"Hickeys?"

"No."

"Got it."

"What about you?"

"I'll match you for now but don't you fucking tickle me or I will punch you. It's reflexive."

"Not really my kink but noted."

"We'll have a more in-depth talk about kinks later."

Angelica paused. "Though… breath play, do you like it? Cuz I like being a little rough."

"I've noticed," Benji said drily. "Light contact on my throat is fine."

She nodded. "Cool. I wouldn't mind light choking either."

"Like this?" Benji circled her throat with their fingers.

Her breathing hitched, her eyes going half-lidded. "Uh-huh."

Heat flooded Benji. They tightened their grip, drawing her back against them. She smiled slowly. Never had they seen someone look so in control with another person's hands around their neck. Holding her like this was like cradling the most beautiful bomb in their hands. After years of overcompensating for the shrapnel in their personality, it was freeing to not be the most jagged person in the relationship.

The trick would be not destroying each other.

CHAPTER 22

Host: *How did you come to Satanism?*
Angela Alice: *The way most of us do: through a banged up copy of the* Satanic Bible *in high school. I went to Christian school so it was a very exciting, taboo thing to find in a used bookstore.*
Host: *You famously say you aren't part of the Church of Satan though, how did things evolve?*
Angela Alice: *Yeah, no fuck that. I'm not down with that* Might is Right *stuff, especially when it's plagiarized by an abusive asshole. Of course, I didn't know that for a long time but even when I read it and some of his other books, the eugenics and misogyny didn't sit right with me so I did more research. No one organization really fit me and my semi-theistic view so I just made my own shit up as it felt right.*
Host: *Would you consider yourself a lone practitioner?*
Angela Alice: *Depends on your definition of lone.*
—from the *Morningstar in the Morning* podcast

While Benji worked on label business, Angie talked to the Devil in their bedroom. She stared at the tiny folding paper triptych altar she'd taken from her go bag and set up on the windowsill. These days she preferred Lucifer with his intellectual rebellion aspect or Baphomet with their queer, occult duality but when she was really worried, she sometimes fell back on old habits: chewing the lipstick off her bottom lip, getting real Southern sounding when she didn't mean to, or talking to Satan.

"This is going to end badly, isn't it? There's no way it won't," she murmured. The Devil was a warm presence at her back, listening. "We're going to go down in flames and they'll never speak to me again. No pun intended."

Soft laughter crackled behind her, just barely loud enough to hear. She didn't look back. There was never anything to see. It was all in her head or it wasn't. It didn't matter. The Devil was the only man who'd ever been constant in her life. The only protector she could count on.

"I know, I know, not exactly your wheelhouse. I'm not asking for anything." Always best to make that clear. "I'm just trying not to fool myself."

She sighed, watching the way the flickering lights of the old ceiling bulbs illuminated the images of Satan, Lucifer, and Baphomet she'd printed out and folded together. She had a bigger, more intricate triptych she took on tour but this would have to do. She stood there for a while, listening to the house creak around her, trying to empty the worry from her mind. Not kneeling, never kneeling.

Her deities did not like to see her on her knees.

Finally, she gave up emptying her mind. "Bless me, bless my people, bless this relationship. Protect us from harm and assholes. Thank you oh lightbringers, oh Morning Star, and Sabbat Goat, and Prince of Hell." She touched each image in turn, pressing a bit of the buzz of power around her into each painted figure.

The warmth smiled at her back. She smiled at Satan, sitting before her. "Thank you for listening." She felt the barest touch of fingers running down her spine before the warmth faded. No one ever listened to her as well as her gods did. It was hard to beat an entity who never talked.

She heard Benji on the stairs and debated putting her makeshift altar away. But no, this whole thing was a test, wasn't it?

Benji's footsteps approached the door then paused. After a moment, they knocked.

"Come in," she called.

They paused on the threshold again, taking in the scene. In the beat of silence, Angie shut down a million memories of people rejecting her, protesting her, screaming at her because of her beliefs.

"Do you need candles for that?" They asked finally, nodding at the paper altar on the sill.

Angie shook her head, head ringing with relief. "Only if you have electronic ones. I'd rather not set my altar on fire."

"We can pick some up tomorrow," they said.

Angie smiled. "Thank you. Are you finished working?"

"Unless someone has a late-night emergency." Benji chuckled wryly. "But Leo is at home for a rest day so we should be okay." They crossed the room and stood next to her, looking out the window, past her altar. "How do you want to handle the Rohan aspect of this?"

"Directly." Angie grimaced. "You want to tell him or should I?"

Benji sighed. "Honestly? None of the above. But I don't want to be an asshole and ambush him."

"We don't have to do it tonight." She brushed her fingers against theirs.

They kissed her cheek, so fast she barely registered the press of their lips before it was gone. "I'd rather get this over with." They pulled their phone out, navigating to the call icon.

"Calling? You *are* old."

They chuckled. "Do you want to wait around for him to text back?"

"Ugh, don't make sense. It's rude."

They shook their head. "Kids these days." Their finger hovered over Rohan's contact. It was in their favorites, which surprised Angie more than it should've. "Ready?"

"Always and never."

"Video or audio?"

"Audio." She patted her ponytail, which was fine but not camera-worthy.

Their gaze lingered on her face. "You look good," they said, as if reading her mind.

She smiled and cupped their cheek. "You do too." She kissed their nose, their cheek, their mouth... and lingered. They kissed her back, their lips soft then demanding then, unfortunately, gone.

She made a whiny, needy sound in protest.

"Let's get this over with and then we can have fun." They hit Call and put it on speakerphone.

"Hey Benji." Rohan picked up after only a couple rings. "What's with the call?"

"Hey Rohan, you're on speakerphone," Benji said.

"Hi Ro!" Angie said, with a slightly manic chipperness. This needed to go well. She wasn't about to let her ex torpedo this.

Rohan was silent for a solid minute. "It happened, didn't it?"

Angie raised an eyebrow at Benji. The two of them really should've discussed strategy first. Oh well.

Benji sighed. "We don't want to ambush you when you

come up but…" They pressed their lips together, seemingly at a loss.

Angie waited until they gave her an imploring glance to say, "We're trying out dating. It's all very new. Experimental, you might say."

Rohan exhaled audibly. "Okay, okay." She could picture him raking his fingers through his curls and squeezing his eyes shut as he searched for something nice to say. "That's um… thanks for telling me."

"Don't worry Ro, Benji still loves you very much and I'm still deeply ambivalent about you. You'll adjust, buddy," Angie said, doing her best 'dad about to divorce mom' fake joviality. Maybe it was self-sabotaging but, Lucy, it was getting so *serious* in here.

Benji glared at her. "Not helping."

She batted her eyelashes at them. "Aw, I was trying so hard."

"Try harder," Benji said drily.

Rohan snorted. It was weak but it was there.

Angie pointed at the phone with her best *See? I'm helping* expression.

"Angelica will be at the retreat too," Benj said. "She's agreed to help our songwriters."

"Are you going to pull your support again, Angie?" Rohan asked, his voice tight. No doubt he was remembering their break-up when she'd tried to sabotage his album and the label. Fair enough.

"Do you want me to give you the 'I've turned over a new leaf' speech or do you want to get a few jabs in just for old times' sake?" Angie gave the phone a feral grin.

Benji made a warning noise.

"Angie—" Rohan started, his tone that same placating one that used to hit all her buttons when they were fighting.

Her anger flared, but she punched back at her first reaction, her desire to escalate. Forcing a breath out, she relaxed her tense abdomen. "No. I'm not starting this again. Did I do some shitty things? Yes. Can I guarantee I won't be shitty again? No. Neither can you. But we can try and I will. Nothing hinges on me. The risk is minimal. If you have a problem with me being at the retreat, tell me now. I will disappear."

Benji's eyes widened at that last bit.

Angie blew them a kiss.

After an eternity, Rohan sighed. "It never gets less annoying when you back me into a corner."

"I know," Angie said, sweetly. "We good?"

"Take the phone off speaker. I need to say something for your ears only."

"Ooh are you going to give me the 'if you hurt my friend' threat?"

"Yes," Rohan said, sounding like he pushed the word through his teeth.

"I'm a grown up," Benji said drily. "And you're not my real dad."

"Humor me," Rohan replied.

Angie raised an eyebrow at Benji. They shrugged and handed her the phone. She took it off speakerphone. "Okay, it's just you, me, and the NSA."

"Are they still wiretapping you?"

"Probably." She shrugged.

"Right. Okay. *Not* my problem. Listen, Benji is not as hard and prickly as they look. They care and they're kind and if you destroy that, so help me, Ang—"

"Save it. If they weren't so kind and caring, I wouldn't be here. I *like* them. They like me. Nobody's chaining our ankles together." She looked at Benji. "Unless you're into that, booboo."

They looked at the ceiling and heaved an overdramatic sigh.

"Ugh, don't put that imagery in my head," Rohan said. "You *know* what I mean."

"I do," she said, more seriously. "I'll do my best to take care of them. I am trying."

"I know you are. Just…" Was he reliving all the fights they'd had too? All the bad things they'd screamed at each other? "Don't do what you did to me to them, okay?"

"I wouldn't. Not again." All the fight, all the humor dropped out of her. She felt limp. Only Rohan could make her feel this much regret this fast.

"Yeah, well. Give Benji the phone, will you? I need to confirm logistics while…" She didn't hear the rest, just handed the phone over. When they were distracted, she walked out of the room, each step heavy, her body something she actively carried. She had to get this feeling out or it'd take root and spread.

Lucy, it was so much *work* to shield people from her fucking moods.

She trudged down the stairs, pausing at the landing. Thinking anything productive was a struggle but a familiar one. She couldn't leave the house like this. She needed a place where she could just vent.

Her gaze lit on the door to the servant stairs, the ones that went all the way down to the basement. Good enough. Here's hoping it was soundproof and she didn't break her neck getting down there.

It took forever, dragging herself across the room, down the barely lit stairs into the half-finished basement. There was a string hanging from the ceiling, presumably for a light but what did she care? She wasn't here to look at it.

She felt her way a few feet away from the base of the landing to minimize echoes and opened her mouth.

CHAPTER 23

"All my compulsions twitch
(twitch twitch twitch)
Every whim is an itch
(itch itch itch)
Every scratch bleeds
To hold back my needs
(need need need)

I am your blood-slicked queen
Your favorite murder scene
Don't look
Don't touch
Once you have me
I'm too much

Love me, love me
You'll always love me
Miss me, miss me
You'll never miss me
Once you're free, free, free"

— "Always Love Me" by Angela Alice off of *Romance Inverted*

Benji had just finished reassuring Rohan they actually did know what they were doing when they heard it. At first, it sounded like someone having a mental health episode in the alley behind their house, something which happened with distressing frequency as the city failed to help its unhomed population. But as they craned their head out the window to see if anyone needed help, the cry took on a familiar melody.

Angelica was singing. At the top of her lungs, her voice cracking with exquisite distress which would sound great at a show but was downright disturbing coming from... Benji's basement. Oh hell.

"I gotta go." Benji hung up.

They ran down the stairs, bounced off the couch in the living room and nearly threw themself down the basement stairs. She stood in the dark, singing bits and pieces of songs all sewn together with no order, dramatic and loud and oh god, with so much emotion.

This, they realized, was her without the restraints, the blast walls she kept herself confined in. This was why she was so good on stage. Why there were tears streaking down their cheeks.

How often did this happen? Was this a relapse? Normal? The worst it got? They remembered her holding that man up as he went limp in her hands. No, definitely not the worst.

They stood there, letting her voice wash over them as their mind whirled. Eventually, she seemed to wind down, her voice going hoarse and her words faltering until she fell quiet. Then she turned to them. "Next time, join in, if you like."

She sounded so normal, nothing but a scratchiness to her words to indicate her... singing tantrum? Emotional drainage?

"I'll keep that in mind," they said, keeping their tone casual as they wiped the moisture from their cheeks. They blew out a breath, consciously pushing out all the tension knotting up in their body—hers, theirs, even Rohan's. They refused to take it on. "When should I expect the next one?"

She cocked her head. "I've unsettled you."

Benji shrugged, though she was right. "Just trying to make sense of it."

She laughed. "There's no sense. No, that's not true. If I'm stressed enough and haven't been on stage recently enough then I need to find a release or it festers."

"Is that what happened to that guy?"

She pursed her lips in thought. "Mmm… that's a more extreme option."

"Are those your only emotional outlets?"

"Well, writing too. And therapy. Exercise, maybe?" She considered it. "Sex, but it's been a while." She winked.

Benji sighed, they should've expected this. They knew what they were signing up for and it wasn't anything especially stable. "Okay, next time, so you don't freak out my musicians…" They pulled on the lamp cord, turning on the bare bulb above them and revealing the large basement. It was mostly empty aside from a stage at the far end and a few old couches along one wall.

"Oh shit! I thought the sound was surprisingly good," Angelica said, wandering into the space. "Let me guess, your mom puts on shows here."

"Yes, and more importantly—" They pointed at the thick door they stood next to. "Use it. It cuts the sound. I don't want Leo to think this place is haunted. He already won't shut up about doing a seance here."

"Too bad, I'm lots of fun at a seance." She patted the wall. "You would be too, wouldn't you, House?"

"Did you really name my house… House?"

"House doesn't mind," she said, like that made any sense.

Angie got on stage and spun in a slow circle with a smile. "I like this. I like this a lot."

"I'm glad you approve," Benji said, trying for their usual dryness. But the truth was, there was something heady about her approval.

"And you." She prowled across the basement towards them, surprisingly fast until she was in front of them, grabbing their collar. "I like you a lot."

Benji found themselves smiling. "The feeling's mutual."

"Good," she said, dragging them to the nearest couch. "Show me."

Benji checked with themself as she pushed them into the cushions. Were they even horny anymore? They found their answer as she straddled their thighs.

"Good?" She asked.

"Yes, but I can't shift gears that fast," they said. "I might just be good for a bit of making out and then making you some tea for your voice."

She considered this then shrugged. "Works for me."

They bit down on the urge to double check that she was sure. If nothing else, Angelica didn't say shit she didn't mean. So they took her at face value and kissed her.

She hummed her approval and licked into their mouth. They sucked on her tongue and her hips bucked, rubbing against their thigh. Their hand came up to rest on her collarbone as they imagined her getting off on their thigh. Fuck, that'd be hot.

No, they were holding on to the boundaries they'd set for dear life. For… reasons. Their hand was sliding down to cup her breast through her shirt and they were forgetting why.

Their phone rang. Leo's ringtone, his song "Better," in fact.

Benji swore against Angelica's lips.

She paused. "That has to be Leo. Also, having your phone on sound?" She laughed. "Old timer."

"Are you *trying* to start an age-play thing?" Benji said, grabbing for their phone.

"Oooh, I haven't done that before." Angelica considered it. "Maybe later."

Benji chuckled, finally finding their phone. "I'm taking this, okay?"

"Yeah, yeah." She waved their words away and got up, much to their chagrin. But then she sat next to them and flopped down so her head was in their lap. "I'm gonna nap."

Benji gave her a stern look. "Behave."

She yawned and flipped them off, closing her eyes.

Shaking their head, Benji answered the phone. "Something better be on fire."

"Like your sex life?" Leo replied. "No, wait, that sounds like you have an STI. Anyway, I heard you're sleeping with the enemy." He sounded downright cheerful.

Benji covered their eyes. "Is there an actual problem you're calling about?"

"Oh no, I just called for tea."

Angelica laughed, the sound vibrating in Benji's lap and reminding them that they'd been trying to exercise their sex life not a minute ago. They hung up the phone, silenced it, and tossed it on the couch.

"Uh-oh," Angelica said, eyes full of mirth. "Benji baby's maaad."

"Only if you're not in my bed in the next three minutes."

She raised her eyebrows. "That sounds like more than making out and sipping tea."

"And if it is?"

She rolled off them and landed on her feet, light like a cat. "Race you." Then she was gone. Benji scrambled to run after the pale ribbon of her hair.

She was fast, nimble, and she was cackling. Benji found themself panting by the time they hit the bedroom door as it swung back after she barrelled through it. She laughed at them from the bed, barely breathing hard as they leaned against the doorframe, heaving air into their achy lungs. "Fucking smoker's lung," they grumbled even though they'd smoked maybe one cigarette in the last few years.

"Let me help." She grabbed them by the shoulders and pushed them onto the bed, straddling them but, they noticed, careful not to put pressure on their torso.

Then she bit their neck and they lost their breath all over again.

Mmm Benji tasted salty and delicious. The sound they made when Angie sunk her teeth in was even better. And the pull of their fingers in her hair...

Lucy, she could get addicted to this. Especially the neediness in their haste as they stripped her shirt and sweatshirt off in one go. She returned the favor then dragged her nails around the sports bra they wore as they unhooked her own bra.

Their mouth went to her nipple and her head dropped back, trying her best not to grind her pelvis into theirs even though it was *right there* and felt *so good*. She respected boundaries, dammit. Also, she'd already lost her grasp on that and rubbed against them in the basement.

"Your hips are so rigid," Benji observed, letting go of her nipple.

"I'm trying to be good," she said.

"You want it so bad, don't you?" Benji's voice dipped into an obscene whisper.

She moaned in response.

They rolled her nipple, still wet from their spit, in their fingers. "And you're such a bad, bad girl."

"Takes one to know one," she ground out.

Their fingers fell away from her nipple, tracing downwards over her bare skin, leaving tingles in their wake. "You wish I was bad enough to say we shouldn't and do it anyway." Their fingers stopped right above the waistband of her pants. "But I'm a different kind of bad."

"Oh yeah?" Angie held herself rigidly still, waiting. "What's that?"

They traced the edge of her waistband then looked up at her. "The kind that'll torture you by sticking to their guns until I decide you've earned more."

Then they flipped her on her back and proceeded to do things to her that made her almost forget neither of them orgasmed.

CHAPTER 24

"Told you who I was
Didn't believe me
But now you see

I am not nice
I am not clean
I have done the things
I said I mean

Whisper your reality to life
Breathe it in my ear
Everyone told you
But you couldn't listen
Couldn't loosen
Your fingers
Clutching your dream
Of me"
— "Who I am" by Angela Alice off of *Bitch Queen Cometh*

enji woke up on the edge of the bed, Angelica all around them. Like, *all* around them. Her arms and one leg were wrapped around their torso, her face was buried in their neck, and that white blonde hair was trying to smother them. They brushed her hair off their face and lay there for a moment. She smelled like supposedly energizing green tea shampoo they'd picked up the last time they were in town, and that spicy-sweet scent they'd always know was her. They felt steeped in her. Her smell, her taste, the sounds she made when they brought her pleasure, the softness of her skin, the calluses on her knuckles, the sharp edges of her teeth.

Here and now, in this bubble the two of them were in, Benji was just fine with that. But soon when reality came crashing in with Benji's business partners in tow, everything would change.

She stirred against them, her lips brushing their neck. Benji shivered. They could almost feel her brain wake up, like rising pressure before a storm. Her eyelashes fluttered against their skin. "You're still here." Her voice was even raspier than normal, low and intimate.

"Did you expect me to sneak away in the night?" Benji turned to face her, barely managing to not fall off the side of the bed in the process.

She paused like maybe she had expected that. "I figured you'd be up early being productive."

"Rest is productive."

"I've heard that." She pulled back to look at them. "What do we have left to do for the retreat?"

They frowned. "Don't you have things to do too? Tour prep?"

She grimaced and the room seemed to dim.

"What?"

She screwed up her face, forcing the words out like they physically hurt. "I don't want to tour."

The implications rolled over Benji. "Oh. Ever?"

"Maybe. Yes. I don't know!" She pulled her limbs in, curling in on herself. "Ugh. I know I'm being selfish but last time broke me."

Something clicked in Benji's head. "Your new leaf…"

"You didn't think I changed spontaneously out of the goodness of my heart, did you?"

Benji mulled this over. "I didn't think too hard about it," they admitted. At first they hadn't believed her and then when they had… well, they'd been thinking about other things instead of the why. "I take it you haven't told your manager you don't want to tour?"

"You're the first person besides my therapist I've said anything to."

That shouldn't feel like a victory, but it did. "Do you want help or are you going to try to tour anyway?"

"I haven't decided. Nothing's set in stone yet but my gig with that festival up here."

"You're playing MetalQuake?" It was one of the biggest festivals in Sacramento, filling Discovery Park every year for four days in October. This year's would start in a few weeks. Benji had played it with UFO years ago but hadn't been back since they'd come out as non-binary. The festival drew all kinds of rock fans and wasn't too picky about what their performers got up to or said on stage. For the most part, it was fine but they'd heard things over the years that didn't make them eager to go back.

"Headlining," she said. "Guess they decided they finally wanted someone who wasn't a man closing a night. Though they tried to offer me Thursday." She snorted. "Cheryl got them to give me Saturday but…" She shrugged.

Benji could guess the expectations of failure implied. Metal wasn't exactly known for being super welcoming to any type of femininity.

"I'm hungry." Angelica sat up, grabbing her phone. She glanced at the screen. "Oh hell, speak of the Devil and he shall provide. I have to make a call." She kissed the side of Benji's head and rolled off the other side of the bed, landing lightly on her feet.

Benji blinked and she was gone. Well then. They moved to the middle of the bed and picked up their phone. Leo had sent them some very NSFW gifs. There was a text from Jo, checking in on them, and about a hundred emails.

Benji let Jo know they were fine but might need to talk later. They reminded Leo they were, in fact, HR at NoN, such as it was. The emails, they skimmed and mostly ignored.

Angelica stuck her head back in the room. "So, change of plans. My band is apparently enroute and will be here in ten minutes. How do we want to play this?" Agitation rolled off her.

Benji inhaled deeply. "Why is your band coming here?"

"Cheryl thinks we need to practice for the show." She shrugged. "She gets this way sometimes."

"Are they staying here?"

"Nah, Cheryl's got them booked somewhere fancy. It's in their contract."

Benji nodded, recalibrating their expectations for the day. "And they're coming here, because?"

"To kidnap me."

"Aren't you the boss here?"

"Most days, but it's good for morale if I let them push me around a bit." She grinned.

Benji chuckled.

"So you wanna tell them we're fucking around or what?"

Benji's humor died. "They're your people. It's up to you."

She considered it. "No point in hiding. I'm not exactly subtle."

"Not in any sense of the word."

She winked. "You say the nicest things, babe."

"Only the best for my sweet lil lady," Benji replied, deadpan.

She guffawed. "Touche, pumpkin."

Benji narrowed their eyes. "Baby girl."

"Love button."

"Sunshine."

"Muffin."

The doorbell rang. Well, it boomed, echoing through the house. Benji suspected the last owner had been hard of hearing.

Angelica jumped, her eyes widening. "What was that, snugglebutt?"

Benji bit the inside of their cheek so they wouldn't laugh. "The doorbell, pudding. Your people, I suspect, snookums."

"No fair, getting a twofer, hot stuff."

The doorbell shook the house again.

"Oh Lucy." She rolled her eyes and went to the hall window that looked over the front stoop. Benji rolled to the foot of the bed to watch her. Wrenching it open, she yelled down. "Patience is a fucking virtue!"

"And you ain't got it!" Yelled back someone from the lawn.

Angelica made a gesture Benji couldn't see but could guess at the content of.

They chuckled.

The way she talked to her band reminded themself of when they were in UFO, being loud and abrasive with José, Keith, Sly, and then Grace who'd replaced Sly on the bass, after. It was just how they'd communicated, happy, sad, pissed, whatever. Benji barely talked to José, Keith, or Grace since the break-up though it had been cordial enough.

Sly, they hadn't spoken to since *Suicide King* came out. Guilt prickled through them. Maybe they should just reach out. Break the unbearable silence and apologize.

Angelica ran by, bringing Benji back to the present.

Getting up, they pulled on a robe and followed her at a more sedate pace.

Angelica threw the door open and ushered her band in. Benji leaned on the living room wall to watch the show. The Sirens of Scream congregated in the hall wearing what looked like the most normal clothes they could dredge up from their respective closets topped off with the classic celebrity incognito baseball cap-sunglasses combo.

A white girl with dead black hair and a too small pink tracksuit that said "Evil" on the ass threw herself at Angelica. "Bitch, I thought you were dead!"

Angelica sidestepped her which didn't seem to faze the other women at all. Tracksuit hit the wall instead, bouncing back with a grin.

The small butch Black woman next to her crossed her arms over what looked like an early 2000s interview outfit complete with plaid short sleeve button up and baggy khakis. "She wouldn't shut up about it, either."

"Well, what if they were lying to us?" Tracksuit demanded.

"Cheryl was very secretive," noted the third woman, the tallest of the quartet. She wore a floaty sundress with a cardigan like a church lady, which clashed with her backwards baseball cap.

"Don't you encourage her, Daniella." Early 2000s butch poked Sundress's arm.

"Yes, dear."

"Ladies, ladies, ladiessss." Angelica made a placating gesture, her accent shifting to that of a Southern preacher. "I stand before you, alive as I've ever been. Safe and whole in the grace of our good lord Lucifer."

Daniella peered at her. "You're being silly. Did you get laid?"

Benji made the mistake of shifting then, the old house betraying them by creaking loudly. They glared at the wall. *Not appreciated.*

As one, the band turned to look at them.

Angelica cackled.

Benji kept a straight face and gave the group a brief wave.

The band looked at Angelica. Then back at Benji.

Angelica grinned, somewhat manically, though no emotions rolled off of her.

Benji kept their face blank.

She winked at them over the heads of most of her band and Daniella's shoulder.

Daniella broke first. "Pay up, Marsha. I fucking told you."

Marsha grumbled, pulling out her phone. "You had inside information." Daniella's phone pinged.

"You should've listened to me," said the third woman, primly.

"Shut up, Gemma," Marsha grumbled.

"Be nice to my girlfriend," Daniella said mildly.

"I *am* nice, Dani."

That made the whole band laugh, Angelica included. Then again, she'd been barely keeping it together during the whole exchange. It was nice that she was enjoying herself. Not that Benji was particularly suffering.

The laughter died down. Gemma eyed Angelica. "You look like you just rolled out of bed."

"I did," Angelica said. "I only got Cheryl's message a few minutes before you arrived." Her posture straightened. "I'll get ready." She headed for the stairs, pausing to squeeze Benji's arm as she passed. "You good?" She murmured.

"I'll be fine," they assured her.

Her gaze searched theirs then she nodded, taking the stairs two at a time.

Benji headed to the kitchen and rummaged through the pastry box they'd bought yesterday. Most of the ones left were okay enough. They offered them to the Sirens, reserving the custard-filled donut for Angelica. She'd eaten the other one with such relish they figured she'd like another. Benji very studiously did not think about what watching her eat that donut had done to them.

"Now," Dani said. Benji looked up to see her brush powdered sugar off her hands and cross her arms. The gesture showed off the ropey muscles of her biceps. Benji was betting she was the drummer. "Who the hell are you and what do you want with Angie?"

Benji blinked. "Do you really not...?"

At the same time Gemma said, "Dani, that's Benji Omega."

"Benji Omega!" Marsha squinted at them. "I *knew* you looked familiar."

"I know who they are," Dani said, exasperated. "I was trying to be intimidating."

Marsha leaned towards Benji. "Did you get work done? You look great for your age."

Benji leaned away. "How old do you think—?"

"Come on, Marsha," Gemma said. "Seriously? Are you stoned again?"

"Pshhh," Marsha said. "No. We're not on tour." Then her eyes got big. "Ohhhhh wait. Oh shit. Are you dating Angie?"

"Yeah," Dani said, glowering. "What's going on here? We're concerned."

"For me or her?"

"Both." Gemma leaned back to glare over her sunglasses.

"But mostly Angie," Dani said. "Are you trying to nail her?"

"Dani!" Gemma snapped.

Dani ignored her girlfriend. "Well?"

Benji stared at Dani until she shifted uncomfortably. "Would Angelica want you to pry into her private life like this?"

All three musicians got shifty and quiet. "We worry about her," Gemma said, after a minute. "You've been an asshole before. We don't know that you'll be any different now."

This was familiar territory. It reminded Benji of the conversations they used to have with people their mother dated.

They didn't know what to say. How could they claim they'd never hurt her when they'd been happy to cut her with words for years? How could they say they'd keep her safe when it seemed like nothing was safe these days?

"But I do." Angelica stood on the landing, hands on her hips. "I know them and you'll trust my damn judgment."

Benji expected the Sirens to bow to that. They were hired guns after all, not her sisters.

Gemma took her sunglasses off. She said nothing but the look she and Angelica exchanged was potent.

"I'm being careful," Angelica said, her voice less hard-edged. "It's not like last time."

"I hope not," Marsha said, going still, her gaze unfocused. "I've never cried that hard in my life."

The room went dead quiet, the kind of mortified silence that wells up in the wake of a secret slipping out. Benji kept themself still and blank, watching Angelica.

Her expression froze. Guilt radiated in a heavy, sick cloud filling up the space until it was almost hard to breathe. Around them, Benji could hear the Sirens' breathing change until it was shallow, fast.

Gemma pinched herself. Dani muttered under her breath,

tapping a beat on her collarbone. Marsha rocked on her heels, closing her eyes.

Benji's stomach twisted. Making their way to Angelica, they stopped with their face just inches from hers. She met their gaze, her gray eyes anguished.

"Angelica. Come back." When she didn't move, they considered touching her. Then again, sometimes people didn't want to be touched in moments like this. So instead they took a page out of her book. Somewhat literally. They sang:

> "Dress me in pretty lies
> Drown between my thighs
> When you surface
> Don't be surprised"

She blinked and focused on Benji. The heaviness in the air lightened, fading. The band behind them sighed, loud in the quiet space. Benji sang the pre-chorus anyway, just to be safe.

> "Told you who I was
> Didn't believe me
> But now you see"

Her mouth curved into a rueful half-smile. As Benji launched into the chorus, she joined in. Her voice sounded rusty at first but warmed up quickly.

> "I am not nice
> I am not clean
> I have done the things
> I said I mean
>
> Take me at my word
> Isn't it absurd

To listen when I talk
When we have this spark?"

Her gaze was fixed on them as the two of them sang together, feeling out the harmonies and not quite blending until the last line when they hit a sweet spot in both their voices. The resulting harmony gave Benji goosebumps and tingles.

"See why I want to do a duet?" She said as they trailed off.

"You would see this as an opportunity to push that." At least she wasn't teasing them about Benji knowing such a deep cut off of her third album.

"Did you not hear us singing together? Was I the only one who got chills?" She looked at her band.

"No, it was good." Dani cocked her head. "But that reminds me, didn't this asshole write on *From the Ashes*?" She looked like she'd happily murder Benji. "Have they apologized?"

"Yes," Benji said.

"Oh." Dani blinked, surprised. "Don't you hate her though?"

"No." Benji looked at Angelica. "I don't."

"You say the nicest things," she purred. Benji found themself leaning closer…

"Sounds like a low bar to me," Marsha muttered loudly.

"Since when do you have standards?" said Gemma.

"I've been reading. Self-improving and shit."

"I'm considering them on probation," Dani declared. "Approval pending."

"Can we leave the prison system out of my love life?" Angelica said, still looking at Benji. There was a mildness to her tone but a wisp of something complicated and unhappy emanated from her.

Benji had been able to read between the lines on the last

incident, they suspected the band had been present for her breakdown on tour, but this, they weren't too sure of. They made a mental note.

"Shit, sorry, Angie." Dani's tone was also casual but her face, behind Angelica's back, was stricken. Her girlfriend put a hand on Dani's arm.

"No worries." Again the wisp of her emotions disappeared like they'd never existed. "Let's go."

The other women nodded and filed out. When they were gone (and Marsha had made the apparently requisite "I'm watching you" gesture), Angelica kissed Benji hard enough that they lost coherent thought.

"Sorry about this," she said. "I'll be back in the evening but I'll try to keep you posted."

"I get it if you need to go late."

"I'm trying to be better about that though. It was an issue with Ro."

"I'm not him but, appreciated."

"Darling, trust me. I'm not mixing the two of you up." She grabbed them by the hips and kissed them again, lingering so long there was a pointed knocking on the door.

Benji had just enough mind left to hand her the donut they'd saved for her as she left. She looked at the donut with surprised delight. "My favorite."

"I'll keep that in mind."

"Put it in your Angie file." She winked and left.

When she was gone, Benji shoved a pastry in their mouth and ate whatever it was. They were pretty sure it was stale but they didn't care. Their mental gears spun.

How weird would it be to do some deep Googling on the woman they were sort of, maybe dating?

CHAPTER 25

Dear Susan,

Life has come to call. I had a reprieve but the job I fought and half-killed myself for found me and is dragging me back. Dramatic, I know. Maybe it's true what they say that you get frozen at the age you get famous.

Ugh, 19 year old me. Not someone I'd like to be ever again. I guess that's maturity or some shit.

I have someone who's something to me. For now. I don't know. I'll probably scare them off. Track record is a pretty good indicator.

Then again, I do like beating the odds. Could've been just another statistic years ago. I climbed over the body, the addict, the victim, the small-timer I could've been to get here. I survived myself and the white lighter club. Our family. The road. The men who tried me. The industry. The trauma I've defined myself with.

Sometimes I think if I found a healthy way to deal, to let it go, I'd lose the outlines of myself. Who I am, if not what has been done to me? What I've done in response?

Yours is the deepest mark. Guess the state has forgiven you though.

Have you served enough time? Has the system done you any good along with all the harm? Am I being selfish by wanting to keep you in there? Is what Daddy's life could've been worth whatever you've endured?

Who am I without the pain you gave me?

The day of the retreat was hectic before the sun came up. A dream about Mama making her pancakes woke Angie up with a moment of intense nostalgia then a mindless, heaving panic. Her half-awake brain registered she was sharing a bed, propelling her out into the hallway and up the stairs with her fist in her teeth before she reined herself in.

That nonsense, of course, woke Benji who found her sitting between the second and third floor, trying to catch her breath. They rubbed their eyes and sat on the stair below her wordlessly.

"Nightmare," she said, after she'd unscrambled her thoughts.

They nodded. "I get them too. Not as spectacularly though."

That surprised a laugh out of her. "Be honest, can you see me doing anything without dramatics?"

"I have to assume it happens sometimes."

"Only when no one's looking." She leaned her head against

the wall, old wallpaper crackling under her hair. "It was about Mama."

"Want to talk about it?"

She shrugged. "She's getting out of prison soon. I'm sure you know the story, everyone does." At Benji's nod, she continued. "It's... freaking me out."

They put a hand on her calf, rubbing their thumb up and down her shin. "Do you think she's going to try to hurt you?"

Angie shook her head. "Supposedly she feels remorse."

"That doesn't mean you have to forgive her." Benji's voice was firm.

"I don't know if that's even on the table," Angie said. "But sometimes I have these dreams..." She covered her mouth as her eyes prickled. She refused to cry over Mama, not anymore. Focusing on the rhythmic stroke of Benji's thumb, she sucked in a breath. "Of when things were good. These memories I totally forgot about bubble up and they feel so *real* and in that moment, I miss that time so much. Then I wake up." She groaned. "And I feel so naive. So soft. It scares me."

Benji scooted up to the stair next to her and slowly wrapped their arm around her shoulder, giving her space to pull away. She leaned into them, nestling her head in their shoulder. They pressed a kiss to the top of her head. "You're not naive for reliving your good memories or missing that time—"

"But," she broke in. "They're all a lie. There was so much under the surface, lurking."

"No child understands everything about their family dynamics. Hell, I still don't understand mine some days. But that doesn't mean you can't have fondness for the times you were happy."

She opened her mouth to protest but they held up a finger. "I'm not done."

She grumbled but gestured for them to continue.

"Thank you." There was a smile in their voice. "Last thing: I'm afraid of being soft too."

She looked up at them in surprise.

"The last time I was soft, I was young and I had to carry Sly's burdens as well as mine. It broke me. When he left I wrapped myself in armor. I thought it would protect me but I was still broken inside and I kept crumbling. I had to break down so much armor to get back to the pain to even begin to heal."

"Are you better now?" Benji's face when at the private health facility flashed through her memory, closely followed by their expression when they told her the story about Sly.

"Yes but not completely," they said, confirming her suspicions. "It's a process."

"That's what everyone says," Angie grumbled.

"True, but look at it this way." They smiled wryly. "If either of us had been any less soft, I don't think we'd be here, like this." They tapped her knee with their free hand. "So that's a point to being soft, in my book."

Angie huffed a laugh. "That's hard to argue with."

"So don't." Benji stood and offered her a hand. "Have a highly dramatic breakfast with me instead."

Maybe because it was so early, breakfast was the least dramatic part of the morning. The fridge was fully stocked, possibly overstocked even. The two of them had gone grocery shopping after rehearsal yesterday and Angie had way too much fun running around Costco buying ridiculously large portions of things.

Benji made some pretty decent scrambled eggs and Angie loaded berries and yogurt in a mug and called it a parfait. The dishwasher was half-installed and the dishes were half-packed in boxes in the garage so they were eating off of whatever was clean. The kitchen was looking mostly functional though. Angie grouted the last of the tiles last night, though there had been some delightful interruptions that slowed her down and meant she'd finished sometime after midnight.

It made her yawn just thinking about it. Hopefully, lusty endorphins would keep her going or she was going to have to steal a nap somewhere.

Her phone buzzed.

DANI

We got a problem. Marsha has food poisoning. Gem's not feeling great either. Think it was lunch. Did you have the salad?

Oh shit. Angie tried to remember what she'd eaten during their really late lunch yesterday. She'd treated the meal like fuel and shovelled it down so she could get back to rehearsing. Dani refused to eat any salads that contained iceberg lettuce. Apparently, the firefighting school she'd dropped out of to pursue drumming and living as her authentic gender had only served sad iceberg salads put her off the vegetable for life.

ANGIE

I don't think so. Y'all need supplies?

DANI

Aren't you supposed to be laying low?

ANGIE

Who's looking for Angela Alice at the pharmacy in Sacramento?

DANI

Point. Yeah, we could use the usual.

Angie squinted at her phone, trying to remember what the usual was. Generally, the tour manager took care of supplies for things like this. Angie wasn't exactly a caretaker.

"Babycakes, what do people with food poisoning need?"

Benji glared at her over their own phone. "Who the fuck is puking?"

"Half my band. I'm heading out for a quick supply run."

Benji made an unintelligible grumble. A text with a list of groceries popped up on her phone.

"Thanks, cutiepie!" She kissed the top of their head, dumped her dishes in the sink and hurried upstairs. "I'm taking the car."

Benji grumbled into their coffee cup. They really weren't human until they'd had a cup or two.

She hadn't eaten the salad so the slight cramping of her stomach just must be stress. *Do not get sick,* she instructed her body.

Benji had already fielded calls from Leo, Rohan, Hanayu, and the dishwasher guy who was supposed to *be here two hours ago* by the time noon rolled around. They were stress-washing the breakfast dishes when they realized they hadn't heard from Angelica in hours.

Drying off their hands, they checked their texts. Nothing since she'd proudly informed them she'd found most of the list at one of the few pharmacies still left in Midtown. That had been over three hours ago. Maybe she was busy taking care of her band?

Benji tried to picture Angelica nursing someone and came up blank. Patience wasn't exactly her strong suit.

Worry curdled in their stomach. They called her, braced for her to make fun of them for calling without a text.

The call rang and rang and went to voicemail. Instead of leaving a message, they called again.

"Leave me alone!" She screeched. "Oh fucking Lucy, not agai—" There was the familar hacking, choking sound of someone retching.

"Angeli—"

Dani came on the line. "Hi new lover, how are you at nursing feral singers?"

Benji squeezed their eyes shut. "She has food poisoning too."

"Yup. I have my hands full with two other patients and Angie's not regulating her emotional shit."

"Oh hell."

"Get ready to test that relationship, buddy." Dani cackled but it sounded forced, tired. "But for real, if you can't take care of her, please send me someone who can."

Benji checked the time. A tour bus full of their most promising talent was due in less than two hours. Angelica had their car. "Which hotel are you at?"

Dani told them the name of the closest nice hotel.

"I'll figure it out," they promised and hung up. Tapping the phone against their forehead, they swore under their breath.

The garage door next to them opened and their mother stepped into the kitchen. She took one look at them and said, "That bad, huh?"

"Angelica has food poisoning at her band's hotel, everybody else is due soon, the dishwasher still isn't working and I need to go get her but she has my car," Benji snarled.

"Whoa, there." Hanayu raised her hands, palms out. "Deep breaths, Benny-chan. You been drinking?"

"What? No!"

"Destroyed anything?"

"No!"

"Anyone die?"

"What!"

Her shoulders relaxed. "Eh, it's not that bad yet."

Benji stared at her. "Goddamn, mother. Your standards are *skewed.*"

She grinned and playfully punched their shoulder. "Explains a lot, doesn't it?" She chuckled. "Gave you some perspective, though, didn't I?"

"Yeah, sure." Benji shook their head but they couldn't help but smile.

"Good. Now, what do you need me to handle? You want me to pick up your girl or hold down the fort and hound the dishwasher people?"

"I'll go get her but I don't know where to put her. She's—" They waved their hands, not sure how to describe it. "Doing that broadcasting thing she does."

"Well, you've got a working shitter in the attic. *Jane Eyre* it. The ghosts won't mind."

Benji refused to dignify the ghost comment with an answer. "You, of all people, are telling me to pull a wife in the attic?"

"Wifing up already? I get to walk you down the aisle, right? I'll fight your father for it."

"I'm not—argh." Benji covered their face, shutting her out for a second. "Look, best case scenario, everyone's going to freak out and think the house is haunted."

"It is."

"No. It's just old and neglected, *which I'm working on.*" They said as the house creaked ominously as if in agreement.

"I know I taught you some half-assed Shinto but I don't think yelling at the spirit of your house endears you to it."

"*Anyway.* I will figure this out. Please hold down the fort and scavenge anything that might help a sick person."

Hanayu saluted. "You got it. I've got a stash of Pedialyte and crackers in my trunk."

"Thank you for digging into your hangover kit." Benji slipped on their shoes and shoved a mask and ballcap on.

A ten minute walk later, they were slightly less stressed as they rode the elevator up to the penthouse suite of a rather nice chain hotel. They were frankly surprised the Sirens were able to get the label to cover a room this fancy without their singer.

The elevator opened to one door. The entryway before the door seemed relatively calm, no loud noises or bad feelings.

The minute Dani opened the door though, everything flooded out. Stomach twisting misery, the sound of Marsha groaning, the sour smell of three people's bodies rejecting food.

"Jesus." Benji jerked their mask back up.

"Tell me about it," Dani said. "Not even a goddamn window I can open."

"Where is she?"

Dani pointed to a half-open bathroom door. Benji could just make out the figure curled into the corner closest to the toilet. "Is she movable?"

Dani shrugged. "I can get you a bag."

Benji gave her a hard look. "What was all that shit about looking after her yesterday?"

Angelica groaned, the sound bouncing around the tiled space. A fresh wave of misery cascaded off of her, making Benji's muscles, especially their stomach, tighten. Dani hugged herself while Gemma groaned too and from another bathroom, Benji heard what was probably Marsha retching.

"You get it now?" Dani asked. "I would kill for Angie, I would be her friend if she let me in. But I'm not idealist and I have a girlfriend and another bandmate to take care of. Gem's not gonna get better like this. Marsha either."

Benji nodded, heading for the bathroom. They could respect her logic even if it pissed them off that it meant Angelica became the sacrifice.

"But that doesn't mean I won't fuck you up if you hurt her," Dani said, cracking her knuckles and using her height to loom over Benji.

"Noted," Benji said, pushing the bathroom door open.

Angelica's head jerked up at the creak of the door and she full-on hissed, her fear and aggression making Benji's hackles rise. Her face was pale and blotchy, her lipstick gone but for a few remnants around her mouth, and her hair in a hasty ponytail that was half falling out.

They pushed the feeling away, along with a stab of sympathy the sight of her elicited and crouched in front of her. "Hi baby."

She narrowed her eyes at them and slapped the toilet lid closed. "I told you to leave me alone."

"I'm here to take you home."

She paled. "In a car? Are you sadistic?"

"Here's that bag," Dani said, setting what looked like a takeout bag by the door.

Angelica slapped a hand over her mouth as the smell of old grease wafted from it.

"Take that away," Benji snapped. "*Now.*"

"That's all I've got," Dani protested but she removed the bag.

Benji looked at her drooping shoulders and reigned in the urge to snap again. They should've thought to bring one themself. "Call the front desk please."

Dani nodded and left.

"Aw big scary enby," Angelica said in a mocking baby talk voice. "My savior."

"Are you going to fight me the whole way?"

She considered this. "Maybe." Then she doubled over and moaned. "Ughhh, this is really ruining my sex appeal."

"Being a dick while I'm trying to take care of you would be even less sexy."

She glared at them from her fetal position. "Fuck off. I can stay here."

"Not while you're projecting and making everyone worse."

"Uggghhh." She dropped her head. "Fine. I don't want you to see me puke though."

"Might be unavoidable," Benji said.

Another wave of misery wafted off of her as she curled deeper into herself.

"Hey." Benji touched her chin softly with their fingertip. She looked up. "I still like you though. Even though you're a jerk when you're sick. Even if my poor innocent eyes see you puke."

She smirked. "Yeah, you do. It's part of my appeal."

"Sure, we'll call it that." But Benji couldn't help but smile.

"Fresh bag." Dani thrust a paper bag through the open door.

Benji thanked her, handing it to Angelica. "You ready?"

"Lucy, no."

They stood and offered their hand. She glared again but took it, standing hunched, hands protectively around her middle but somehow defiant. *Like a cornered honey badger,* they thought and suppressed the urge to laugh.

Instead, they draped the oversized hoodie they'd worn in over her and wrapped a guiding arm around her shoulders. She made an indecipherable grumble and tucked herself against their side. They wanted to cradle her in their arms until she felt better. They settled for giving her arm a brief rub and steering her out of the bathroom.

"Feel better, Angie," Dani called as Benji navigated the two of them out of the front door.

She made a pitbull growl deep in her chest. Benji gave her a look. She glared back then said to Dani, "Thank you."

Benji glanced back to catch Dani's surprised look as the door closed behind them.

The drive was touch and go but thankfully short. Climbing the stairs to the attic nearly resulted in a meltdown. Angelica ran the last few steps to the bathroom, slamming the door behind her.

"She's going to be such a good patient," said Hanayu, her hands on her hips as she and Benji stood awkwardly trying not to listen to the retching sounds echoing in the bathroom. The house moaned as if in sympathy. "Reminds me of you when you were a kid."

"I grew out of it."

"Eh." She wiggled her hand back and forth, clearly saying *sort of.*

Benji chose to ignore this. "Thank you for babysitting her."

"No problem, it'll give me a chance to revisit all the magazines I stored up here." Hanayu fussed with the offering plate on one of the windowsills. Fresh oranges and a bottle of sake sat next to a couple of cigarettes and a small bowl of coins. Hanayu added a few pennies to the bowl, humming to herself.

Benji glanced around at the battered cardboard boxes with Hanayu's scrawl on them taking up the one wall without a window or door in the attic. The sight stirred memories of her sitting on their childhood bed when they were sick, reading them the latest *Spin, Maximum Rocknroll,* or a zine she'd bought at a show.

As if she'd picked up their line of thought, Hanayu shrugged. "Figure she'd appreciate the distraction."

"If she's too much of an asshole, let me know and I'll take over."

The bathroom door swung open. Angelica leaned against the frame, bent in half but glaring balefully at them. "You say the sweetest things."

Benji walked over and kissed the top of her head. "You know what you are. Be nice to my mom and text me if you need anything. I'll be downstairs dealing with the talent."

She dropped her head against their chest. "You're lucky I like you. And you have such a comfy chest."

With a chuckle, Benji put their arms around her. "Yeah, okay. I'll take your word for it."

"You better," she said into their shirt.

They could've stayed that way for longer but their phone buzzed with a five minute warning from Rohan and they had to pry themself away. But as they left, they heard Angelica say, "So, what's this about you reading me old magazines?"

"Drink some water and I'll pick something out," Hanayu replied as Benji closed the door behind them.

CHAPTER 26

Chuck: *Your real name is Angelica, isn't it?*
Angela Alice: *Congrats on your wikipedia reading skills.*
Chuck: *[clears throat] Thank you. Why change your name for the stage?*
Or, I guess, why not change it more?
Angela Alice: *[shrugs] No one really calls me Angelica, not even my*
parents did. And… it's so delicate sounding. I can't afford to be delicate.
I'm not sure I ever could. Angela is harder: An-Je-La. You use your teeth
when you say it.
Chuck: *Thus the song "Angela Dentata"?*
Angela Alice: *[giggles and sings] Watch your… fingers. [winks]*
— The Heavy Metal Hour with Chuck

Angie spent the rest of the day in a haze, trying to keep down liquids. She and Hanayu had a fight about drinking Pedialyte, which Benji's mom won by refusing to read aloud anymore until Angie tried it. It didn't taste as bad as Angie thought.

"That's cuz I only get the good flavor," Hanayu said smugly and went back to reading aloud from some local zine called *TUBE. Magazine.*

Hanayu's collection had a local bent so Angie didn't know half the bands but the sound of her reading voice was soothing. A real contrast to her aggressive singing voice.

It had been a very long time since someone had read aloud to Angie. She had vague memories of Daddy reading to her when she was young. *Winnie the Pooh, The Very Hungry Caterpillar, Charlotte's Web*, kid stuff like that.

It was a little surreal to instead be listening to stories about Dog Party, Fat Wreck Records, Spitboy, local clubs, burlesque, art, anarchy, and old political issues, most, unfortunately, still relevant. Also Benji. Hanayu had a whole box of publications which had covered her kid.

"I have a box of my coverage too but I think you'll be more interested in these," she said, grinning.

Benji's band had appeared in much more mainstream places: *Alternative Press, Rolling Stone*, Benji's infamous post-band break-up coming out photo shoot in *PAPER*, even newspaper clippings carefully cut out and put in those plastic sleeves teachers used to try make everyone put their homework in before everything went electronic.

"Stole these from Benji's old school binders," Hanayu said. "Not that they did half their homework assignments anyway. Too busy being a punk." The pride in her voice made Angie ache.

She'd called Mama once after her second album *Pheno-Barbie Doll* went platinum. (It had seemed too touchy to call after *Murder Baby* went gold.) Susan had called her "Satan's whore" and berated her for putting her family's business in the streets. Given Mama had made local news all by herself, Angie thought this was rich.

She pushed the ache away when Hanayu's voice faltered and tears sheened the other woman's eyes. Benji's mom looked up from an article about User-Friendly Omega's third album release party. "What's wrong, hun? You look sad."

Maybe it was because she'd puked up everything inside her and then some or just the kindness in Hanayu's eyes but Angie blurted, "Thinking about my mom."

"Oh." Hanayu closed the magazine and put her full attention on Angie. "Want to talk about it?"

Angie grimaced, hunching into herself as she suppressed the emotions bubbling up inside her. Her stomach twisted. "No," she said, scraping the word out between her teeth. "It would make us both miserable if I did."

Hanayu cocked her head, the gesture so like Benji it was discombobulating. "This thing where you project your emotions, it's hereditary?"

"On my dad's side."

"Ahhh," Hanayu said.

"You know the story," Angie guessed.

"Your wikipedia page is very in-depth."

Angie squeezed her eyes shut. She hadn't googled herself in years out of self-defense. "I can imagine."

"Yeah, well it was very illuminating to learn about the woman my kid wouldn't shut up about when they came back from tour."

Angie's eyes flew open. "From the Endfest tour?" *Since last year?*

"Oh yeah. Not nice things, mind you. But you came up enough that I was curious." Hanayu gave her a wry smile. "Your fangirling really got on their nerves." She laughed. "But I guess it worked."

Angie snorted. "What can I say? I'm charming."

Hanayu leaned forward. "Angela, I like you. You give just enough fucks and you're clearly gone over my kid. But, I know what you've done to your exes. Benji tells me you're turning over a new leaf. I know you're both adults, but allow me a mother's prerogative here, one scary bitch to another, you might have your emotional lightshow but there's a reason we call ourselves Razor Bitches." She patted her pocket.

Angie sighed, tamping down the automatic aggression pulling her shoulders back and making her lip want to curl. "I know y'all were bouncers at all-women punk shows and all that. Very badass. Love it. But if you think you're the only one with a sharp in this room or the only one who's used one, you're wrong." Flashbacks from her years on the road, running from supposed home to home until she landed in LA and was promptly abandoned by the only person she knew in the city flickered at the corners of her vision. She ignored them. Her fingers felt sticky and she was loosing the battle but fuck, she hadn't started this. "The blood on my hands is old, maybe like the blood on yours. I'd like to think you've grown beyond it. Because I have."

Probably.

Hanayu's eyes were wide, her breathing shallow. One of the oranges on the offering plate by the window rolled off and hit the floor with a much louder smack than seemed possible, making both women jump.

Hanayu patted the wall absently.

Angie closed her eyes, taking as deep a breath as her cramped position and tender stomach would allow. "I do my best not to hurt the people around me. That goes doubly for Benji. I appreciate your concern. I understand it." She opened her eyes and smiled at Benji's mother. "But don't threaten me again."

Hanayu's shoulders relaxed and she blinked, glancing at her hands. "Damn," she muttered, then looked back at Angie. "That was intense. You'd use that on people who threaten Benji?"

Angie blinked, taken aback. "If they asked me to. They're very capable though."

Hanayu nodded. "It never hurts to have a partner who can

back you up." She reopened the magazine. "Where was I? Oh, here we go: 'UFO's afterparty was held at—"

"Wait, you're not freaking out?"

Hanayu looked her in the eye. "No, you rose to my bait beautifully." She smiled. "I wanted to see what you were capable of even as weak as you are now."

Cold-blooded but she could respect that. "And? Did I pass?"

"Your restraint could use work but I appreciate that you're trying. Don't stress too much about it. You need rest."

Angie laid her head back against the peeling wallpaper of the wall behind her. It seemed better not to point out Hanayu had riled Angie when the other woman was supposed to be taking care of her.

The tour bus of NoN songwriters pulled up into the driveway just as Benji reached the ground floor. They threw open the door and straightened to their full height as they strode down the path to the sidewalk. The bus door folded into itself. Leo bounded out, wearing his usual summer outfit of tiny shorts and half a shirt. He was lucky they were having a warm September.

"Hello darling!" He kissed Benji's cheeks. Was that liquor on his breath? "How is your queen of darkness?"

"Puking her guts out." Guilt prickled them but Benji knew she was in good hands.

"You knocked her up already?"

"Food poisoning." Benji said with a quelling glance.

Rohan descended more sedately. "Is it… safe inside?"

"She's fine. Mom's tending to her up in the attic."

Leo laughed. "Angela always gave me 'most likely to haunt an attic' vibes. Please tell me its echoey up there." Then he shut up because the other songwriters descended. Even Leo occasionally had a sense of propriety.

NoN was still a small label so most of the songwriters were members of Patrick's sister Sabrina's band Doc Conjure (she gave Benji a dirty look, still not over their falling out with her brother). There was also Leo's writing partner, a reserved man named Sam, and a one person electronica act Rohan had recently signed. Oh and—

A baby blue mom van screeched to a halt across the driveway, effectively parking in the tour bus. Nancy rolled down the passenger side window. "This okay, sweetie?"

Benji gave her a thumbs up. Jean and Pauline piled out of the back, unloading the van with the bickering efficiency of old bandmates. In less than a minute, Nancy introduced herself to everyone and recruited most of the other artists to help carry her drum kit into the house.

"This is chaotic," the electronica artist proclaimed with a grin. Benji searched their memory for their name.

"Get in here, Gus," Rohan called, carrying Jean's bass case as Sam trudged up the driveway, his arms full of mike stands. Benji had told Hanayu to stock the house with all the stuff the band needed but apparently the Razors decided it wasn't enough.

Gus, the electronica artist, who Benji now remembered used the stage name Frank's Laboratory, giggled and jogged down the sparse lawn to the van.

Benji checked to see if the Razors needed any more help but Leo managed to carry half the equipment, flexing his muscles to the enjoyment of most of the retreat members.

Once everyone was inside and mostly settled in the living room, Benji handed out room assignments. Rohan did his whole inspirational speech about how they were all going to blossom creatively and cross-pollinate and other flower metaphors Benji quickly tuned out. It seemed to work for the group of artists though and that was all that mattered. There were lots of nods and smiles.

Leo looked a bit glazed but perked up once introductions started.

Though Benji knew everyone there for the most part, they paid close attention, noting the dynamics of the group. They were in charge of assigning who would work with who in each session and though creative sparks couldn't be predicted, personalities were much easier to gauge.

Sam seemed to have taken to Nancy. He examined her knitting intently and complimented her skill when she brought it out to demonstrate what she did in her spare time. Jean and Pauline thought Gus and Leo were hilarious, cracking up when the two of them were the least bit funny. Sabrina, leaning against Leo, went out of her way to tell the Razors how much they inspired her but was still cool towards Rohan and downright frosty to Benji. Kevon, Doc Conjure's drummer and Flo, the band's new bassist were in their own little world, giggling at inside jokes and nudging each other.

Soon enough, introductions were over and everyone scattered to put their stuff away before the first session. Ignoring Rohan's concerned expression and Leo's waggling eyebrows, Benji climbed the stairs to check on Angelica.

They found Hanayu still sitting in the armchair, reading an old feminist punk zine while Angelica sat, jammed into the shallow corner of the bathroom door frame, asleep. Benji froze at the top of the stairs, not wanting to wake her. Angelica looked somewhat better, though there were purple hollows under her eyes and she frowned in her sleep. It ached to look at her. They wanted to scoop her up and feed her broth until she was back to being the chaos creature they were used to.

"She hasn't puked since you left," Hanayu said quietly.

Benji wrenched their attention away from Angelica. "Glad to hear it. I can take it from here."

Hanayu checked her watch. "Is it time for the sessions already?"

Benji nodded.

"You're not going to join us?"

"I will, tomorrow."

She rose, stretching with a groan. "She's all yours, kid." She gave them a brief hug and left.

Benji took her place in the armchair, picking up the zine. Angelica stirred but seemed to stay asleep. After watching her for a long moment, Benji started reading aloud from where their mother left off.

Angie slowly surfaced to the low, slightly frayed sound of Benji's voice reading an interview with My Chemical Romance. They were doing what sounded like impressions of each member and the interviewer. It was… not good.

She muffled a laugh as they said something in what was supposed to be Mikey Way's voice but mostly sounded like some sort of terrible sad boy Jersey accent. UFO and MCR had had some overlap, surely they must've met? But given she could barely remember what year it was right now, maybe she was making things up.

"Entertaining yourself?" she croaked. Lucy, she was going to have to do some serious vocal chord maintenance before her performance.

Benji paused. Was that red on their cheeks? "Maybe."

She couldn't help laughing this time.

"It wasn't that bad." They closed the magazine. Their cheeks were definitely red now.

"Honey, it was soooo bad. Have you even met My Chem?" She'd come up after the band broke up but was hoping to catch them when they played MetalQuake.

"Not officially."

"What does that mean? You yelled at them at an awards show or something?"

"I saw them at an event and hid."

"No!" She straightened then winced as her neck and shoulders twanged. "Tell me everything."

They shrugged. "I don't remember which event. I think it was one of those hotel room afterparties for some award show or something. They were getting in the elevator on our floor. I hid behind an ice machine because I was hyperventilating so hard." They chuckled. "I think I was twenty, tops. The rest of UFO made fun of me for months afterwards."

"Awww wee baby Benji."

"You sound like you're feeling better," they said drily.

"Let's find out." She hauled herself upright. Everything ached and her stomach swooped. She went still with a grimace, letting it settle.

"Promising."

She shrugged, gingerly bending over to rinse her mouth out in the sink. Her tongue tasted like something died in there. "Getting there."

"Want to try eating?"

Her stomach didn't try to escape at the mere mention of food so she nodded, accepting the single cracker they offered her. She took the tiniest bite, washed down with a sip of Pedialyte.

Her stomach accepted it so she took another nibble, meandering towards Benji as she did. "Lap," she said, when she stood in front of them.

They looked up at her from the chair, one leg crossed over the other. "Have you tried full sentences? I hear they're all the rage."

"You *are* out of touch."

"Use your words." Their expression was bored but there was a mischievous crinkle in their eyes.

Her face flushed hot. Did she have a fever? Maybe she was just reacting to how hot they were, sitting in that beat up velvet armchair like they owned the place. She was too worn out to feel horny, but nothing could stop her from *appreciating*. "I was to sit in your fucking lap."

They uncrossed their legs and opened their arms. She crawled into their lap, the process more awkward than she remembered. After accidentally putting too much pressure on their leg and then almost slipping as she overcorrected, she settled. They cradled her in their arms, her head tucked against their jaw. She sighed, melting into their embrace.

"I'm glad you're feeling better," they said, after a long moment.

"Worried about me?" She said it teasingly but she held her breath, waiting for their response.

"No," they said. "I knew you'd be fine in time."

Oh. That was true, she guessed. Disappointing but—

"But," they continued. "I hated seeing you in pain and I hated not being able to be there for you while you were sick. I trust my mother with my life, but it was hard to leave you with her."

Oh, there it is. She nuzzled against their neck. "You *like* me," she purred.

"I like-like you."

The words made her ridiculously giddy.

She pulled back to look at them. "Are we going steady now? Should I give you my letterman jacket?"

They smiled. "I don't think either of us have class rings, so how else will people know?"

She grinned. "Too bad I lost it."

"Wait, did you actually have a letter jacket?"

"Are you shocked I was athletic?"

"I can't imagine you doing a team sport."

"What do you call a band?"

"Point."

She chewed her lip, debating telling them. They watched her, a fond smile on their face like they could tell exactly how ridiculous this tidbit from her past was.

"So my mom made me join a team…"

"The suspense is killing me."

"I didn't like any of them so I just closed my eyes and picked one." She chuckled at the memory. "I ended up with golf."

"That's barely a sport!"

"I'll have you know there's a lot of walking involved."

"How long did you play?"

"Oh, I got kicked out right after we got our jackets for threatening the boys team with my clubs. We had to wear these short skorts and those assholes couldn't take a hint unless it had a nine iron attached to it." She shrugged. "What I learned came in handy later when I had to schmooze with execs. It's amazing what risks they'll take if you pitch it to them over a green."

The sound of footsteps creaking up the stairs made them both freeze. She waited for Benji to push her out of their lap but if anything, their grip tightened. She nestled into their embrace, feeling smug.

After what seemed like an eternity, a strawberry blonde head emerged from the stairs. Leo grinned as he paused a few steps down from the landing. "Isn't this cozy?"

"Is there a problem with your session?" Benji asked.

"Session's over. I was sent up to see if either of you crazy kids want lunch." Leo put his hands on his hips. "This is cute. Like, troublingly cute—"

"Phones were invented for a reason," Benji said coldly.

"They only work if you answer them," Leo replied cheerfully. "Thus you are graced with my illustrious presence."

"How lucky we are," Angie said with poisonous sweetness.

"You are, aren't you?" Leo said, winking. "Think how awkward it would've been to send literally anyone else up."

Well, she couldn't argue that one.

Neither could Benji. They sighed. "I'll be down shortly." They turned to her. "Want me to bring you anything?"

"Lucy, no. Just leave the crackers."

"Are you sure you two haven't been possessed? This is *un*canny." Leo squinted like he was looking for signs of possession. "I know a really good exorcist, just say the word—"

"You can go now," Benji told him.

"Oh! I've been dismissed!" Leo pressed a hand to his chest. "The audacity! The nerve!" He turned and went back down the stairs, still exclaiming. "Dismissing me! Of all people…"

"Wow, he's annoying," Angie said.

Benji chuckled. "He grows on you."

He must, she thought. *Or Martin wouldn't still be obsessed with him.* Out loud, she made a disbelieving noise.

They kissed her temple. "Trust me. Now, get up."

"If you insist." She huffed and climbed off of them, trying to be careful but still almost jabbing them with her elbow.

"We'll have to work on that." Benji unfolded themself from the chair. They stretched their arms over their head, giving her a delicious peek at the taut skin of their abdomen. She wanted to run her fingernails over the skin, to lick it—

She really was feeling better. *Excellent.*

"Do you want to stay up here or are you feeling well enough to go to our room? There might be folks around."

Mmm she liked it when they said "our."

"Angelica?"

"I'll go down." Her mother screamed in her head, reminding her *people* might *see* her, making her check her reflection, fix her hair, and swipe on some of the emergency lip gloss from her pocket. The voice of her mother calmed, grumbling as it realized Benji had seen her looking like an unkempt ghost.

They hadn't seemed to mind though and she held on to that warm feeling as she followed them down the stairs.

Unfortunately, she checked her phone when she hit the landing.

CHAPTER 27

Sirens Group Chat

Angie swore under her breath, feeling her blood pressure spike. Reckoning was upon her and she was in a house full of people.

Benji glanced back at her, the hall too narrow for the two of them to walk side by side. "Problem?"

"I'll handle it," she said, not caring that their step stuttered at her 'don't ask questions' tone. She had to think and the very thought of touring unleashed a wailing torrent of *Noooo* from every instinct. But she hadn't told Cheryl that, fuck, she hadn't even told the band.

She was on autopilot, only realizing she was in Benji's room when they put the crackers with her bottles of water and Pedialyte on the nightstand. They watched her pace, frowning loudly.

"What?" She snapped.

"You're worrying me."

She bit down on the nasty retort coiled under her tongue. Instead, she shoved a cracker in her mouth and chugged some Pedialyte. She needed to be sharp for this. Business sharp, not knife sharp. "I think the tour thing is coming to a head. I need to have my shit together. I need to figure this out."

"Don't they know you're sick?" Their lips twisted. "Never mind. Money doesn't care."

"Cheryl knows and she's stalling them but I'm better now and I—" Her stomach cramped, protesting. She pressed her hand against it.

Benji's eyes tracked the movement. "Is anyone going to die if you don't handle this today?"

"Melodramatic, much? No."

"Then rest. You're not better."

"I can't! Even if I did, it wouldn't be fair to the band."

"Have you talked to them about not wanting to tour?"

She dropped onto the bed, head in her hands, elbows digging into her thighs. "No."

"Are they in any state to have that conversation?" They crouched, balancing on their toes to meet her eyes.

She glared. "Shut up with your logic."

Benji rolled their eyes. "I'm just saying, you have a chance to strategize. Use it."

"You've met me, right?"

"You can't tell me you've never strategized before. Not with your level of success."

"I can plan an album and, like, what I want my tour to look like. The rest?" Angie shrugged.

"Right, so what do you want your life to look like?"

She stared at them, mind blank. What *did* she want her life to look like? She'd been chasing the idea of being a rock star for so long she hadn't stopped to think that the pace she'd been running at was destroying her. Destruction seemed like the point. But was it?

Benji's expression softened. "That's what I thought."

"Is this what it felt like for you?"

They shook their head. "There was a lot more going on than just burnout and mental health—not that I'm trying to minimize everything you've got going on."

She nodded. "Gender stuff."

"Yeah," they said quietly.

Silence stretched between them, the sounds of people talking and eating drifting up through the floorboards. Leo's booming laugh set off a fainter cascade of mirth. Benji could be down there with their friends and fellow artists but instead they were up here, metaphorically holding her hand through what was probably her Saturn return.

Her gaze tracked over their face, noting the shadows mostly hidden by make-up, their wrist resting on one knee, hand dangling to show off nails she'd painted black and purple for them last night. She stored the details in her mind, squirreling away the joy their sheer presence brought her.

Oh shit, this could be—

She cut the thought off. Of course it could be, but not right now.

"Go." She made a shooing motion with her hands. "Eat. I need to think."

They nodded but instead of heading for the door, their knees hit the floor in front of her. They reached up, cupping her cheeks. Their lips touched on hers, making her thoughts black out and her entire body tilt down towards them. It took all her strength not to drag them to her and—

"If you need me..." they murmured against her lips.

She widened her knees until they bracketed Benji's shoulders. "Tempt me, I dare you."

They stood with a chuckle. "Rest. Figure your shit out. I'll see you later."

"Tease!" She yelled as they left, earning herself a middle finger salute as they closed the door.

Ugh, now she actually had to be an adult and figure her shit out. She flopped back, staring up at the ceiling.

"Lucifer, help me," she muttered. "Am I about to burn down what I've built?"

Over the rest of the afternoon, Benji mulled over Angelica's dilemma. They hadn't realized how much she bought into her own myth of being a spontaneous force of nature. They'd seen evidence of her ability to scheme both for good and bad but, in hindsight, those had been relatively short-term projects.

Then again, as Hanayu liked to tease them, they sometimes forgot not everyone had 5-, 10-, 15-year plans. Their mother could laugh all she wanted, she was the reason Benji felt the need to be so organized. They'd never told her that, but hopefully she was self-aware enough to remember the chaotic days when she was working, playing gigs, and trying to raise Benji at the same time. Benji had been her assistant by the time they could write, scrawling dates in the calendar for her and helping her plan meals for the week. By high school, she let them basically tour manage the Razors for a couple summers, before UFO took off.

Kenji had been the one to teach Benji how to plan, though even he didn't take it to the level his kid did. He had comics planned out a year in advance and he used to show Benji his storyboards and timelines, laid out along the walls of his various rooms over the years like the connections map of a very artistic conspiracy nut. As a child, Benji loved seeing what they assumed their father's thoughts looked like spread out from ceiling to floor. They would always make a beeline straight for those walls when they stayed with him.

Now, they wanted to run upstairs and beg Angelica to let them bring out their planning templates and goal documents to help her reroute her life. They'd had so many planning sessions with past lovers, friends, bandmates, even Sly after his second, third, fourth "rehab" stints. As far as Benji could tell, the plans rarely stuck.

Finally, after a long talk with Jo some years back, they'd accepted they couldn't fix anyone's life. There was no plan that could help someone that didn't want to be helped. Which hurt but what could they do?

But still, the compulsion pulsed under their skin.

Maybe I want to make sure she writes me into her plans. Maybe I want to write her into mine.

The thought stopped them dead in the middle of checking the stage set-up in the basement. They put down the amp they'd been repositioning and sat on it, staring into space. They'd never written any of their partners into their long-term planning. None of their relationships seemed to be destined for the long-haul.

She could be different. She is different.

Could she? That she was different wasn't a surprise but could the two of them actually work for longer than a few months? Admittedly, they worked together better than Benji had expected. Rohan had taken it better than they expected too. It wasn't public yet but still…

It was too soon to tell, they decided, standing. The two of them certainly hadn't burned through the honeymoon period yet, let alone even scratched the surface of their sexual possibilities. Benji's cheeks were hot as they went back to moving the amp and checking the cords.

Once Angelica felt better and the retreat was over, they would be very amenable to diving deeper into exploring those possibilities.

"Is this a bad time?" Rohan stood at the bottom of the basement stairs. They couldn't make out his expression from across the long room but something about the way he was holding himself made Benji brace themself.

Benji straightened and swiped sweaty hair out of their eyes, cursing the nostalgic impulse that had made them get long bangs again. "What's up?"

If this is about Angelica, I swear—

Rohan crossed the basement until he was close enough to say, quietly, "I'm worried about Leo."

"Is he drunk?" Benji looked up before realizing they couldn't see through the ceiling.

Rohan shook his head. "Not that I can tell, but he's been drinking at every meal."

"Even breakfast?"

"He had mimosas for the group when he picked us up."

Benji squeezed their eyes shut, trying to remember if that was illegal or not. Surely if limos did it, tour buses were okay? They had certainly gotten shitfaced many times on various buses but they hadn't been worried about legality then.

"I wouldn't bring it up but it's been more than usual. I don't think he's an alcoholic or anything, it's just—" Rohan ran his fingers through his thick hair, which Benji noticed was getting long enough that it too was falling into his eyes, elongating his curls into more of a wave. A silly thing to focus on but 'friend in trouble' conversations pulled them out of their body into a mildly dissociative space.

"He goes through these phases, you know?" Rohan continued. "Where he gets a hair trigger and then he drinks to mellow out and yeah, it's not good."

"What does Cazzi say about this?"

He sighed. "She said it sounded like a trauma cycle and he probably needed therapy."

"A what?"

He frowned in concentration as if trying to summon up her exact words. "It's where you get triggered by something then your body is like 'whoa stop' and if you listen to it then you can figure out what you need and do that. But if you don't, you go into this deep rooted belief you have about yourself like 'I can't be loved' or 'I'm the only one I can trust.'"

That last one hit Benji between the eyes, making them a little light-headed.

Rohan didn't seem to notice. "So, then you do something you regret like eating way too much ice cream or being mean or drinking or whatever but here's the kicker: if you stop there you can get off the ride and figure out what you need. If you don't, it's all cyclical shame until your brain feels like you've punished yourself enough."

Benji blew out a breath, seeing how this cycle could fit the things they'd done, Sly's attempts, hell, Angelica's worst behavior. "You think Leo's in this cycle?"

"I think the drinking is the thing he regrets and I'm afraid if he doesn't stop and figure his shit out soon he's going to hit that shame spiral hard and it's going to blow up bad. It has before."

Benji nodded. "You know him best, what do we need to do?"

Angie wanted toast. This proved to be a taller order than she expected. First, getting to the kitchen. Could she have texted Benji and gotten them to get her some? Sure, but they were busy and she was better, dammit. So she put a baseball cap backwards over her hair, still wet from her shower, dug out her black lipstick, and put on her best 'don't fucking talk to me' face.

It worked, mostly. She got stares from some people jamming together on the back porch but nobody was bold enough to make a move.

In the kitchen, she shut the curtains, turned on the light and rummaged around for the toaster and the bread.

She'd been talking things through with herself, with her Unholy Trinity, with her notebook for hours. The circles she'd dragged her thoughts in were enough to drive her up the wall.

So instead she was here, the skin on her back tingling

because there were three doors to the kitchen. It was impossible not to put her back to one of them and only the one to the garage locked. As she fought to make the new plug of the toaster fit into the narrow old socket, she hoped she'd get out of here before someone decided to pluck up the courage to see if that was really Angela Alice in the kitchen.

The floorboard by the door leading to the living room creaked. Angie stiffened, fingers dipping into the pocket with her knife. Benji would be pissed if she threatened one of their people, she reminded herself, forcing her hand to relax away from her sharps.

The door swung open, admitting Leo, holding a margarita and an empty plate just as she forced the plug in with a thump. "Oh darling, don't force it in. Haven't you ever heard of foreplay?"

"Put away the drag persona," Angie snapped. "I'm not in the mood."

He put the plate in the dishwasher. "Rude. That was just me being friendly."

"You don't like me enough to be friendly." She shoved her bread in the toaster and faced him.

"Insecure, much?"

Angie snorted. "I'm a lot of things, but I burned insecurity out long ago. I don't care if you like me. I'm stating a fact."

Leo took a sip of his margarita and gave her a long look. "You should teach motivational classes. 'I burned insecurity out of me and YOU CAN TOO.'" He threw out an arm, his voice echoing around the closed kitchen.

"I'll consider it for my next career phase."

"I always thought you had it in you to be a cult leader or run a MLM."

"Careful, you're making me blush."

"I mean it, cross my heart." He made a little X over his heart with a finger.

"You know, I told Benji you were annoying but I think you might be growing on me. Like mold."

Leo winked. "Hey, mold gets a bad rap. I like wine, cheese, and penicillin as much as the next girl."

"Maybe more on the wine."

"Excuse me?" He went still.

She shrugged. "You've been drunk every time I've seen you." Probably. It had been hard to tell when she and Leo had been cheering Rohan on for that cooking competition he won all those years ago. Then again, there had been champagne. Not that she was judging. She had her own vices.

The toast popped and she fished it out, hissing as she burned her finger in the process. The bread was toasted right to her perfect range of crunchy but not too burnt. Excellent.

When she turned to get the butter, he was still staring at her. "Mm. Too far. Are we at the angry yelling part now?"

She was inured to angry yelling but if he went after her toast she'd be hard pressed not to do something she'd feel bad about later.

He gulped half his marg. "I'm thinking about it."

"What's there to think about?" She really should stop baiting him but going upstairs meant going back to trying to plan for the future. She took a bite of her buttered toast, propped her hip on the counter, and watched him. He was big but emotionally fragile. She could take him.

"You're Benji's girlfriend. I'm *trying* to be nice to you."

"Don't bother. I'm never nice." She took another bite of toast. Her stomach was holding up, thank Lucy.

"Also, I don't want you to do that freaky Vulcan mind meld on me."

"Smart. I probably wouldn't though. Benji would be mad or whatever."

"You haven't fully brainwashed them yet?"

Asshole. She hadn't done anything like that to Rohan, why

would she do it to Benji? "You've been in the industry too long if you think brainwashing is hot," she snapped.

He slugged back more of his drink. "Touché."

Maybe she should make a peace offering. "Want some toast?"

His eyes narrowed. "Are you trying to sober me up?"

"You mistake me for one of those pushy caring people who try to sneakily 'help' you. Do I seem passive aggressive?"

Leo dumped the rest of his marg down his throat. "No, you're actively aggressive." But he didn't leave.

She put another piece of toast in the toaster. "Why are you still here? You avoiding something out there?"

"Why? Are you?"

"You first."

Leo sighed. "Rohan's one of those pushy helpful people."

Angie rolled her eyes. "Oh, I *know*. Is he doing that worried puppy eyes thing? Like he wants to say something but is trying to figure out how to put it delicately?"

"Yes! I know it's out of love but I hate it!"

"Shit, same. So, what, you weren't sneaky enough drinking?"

Leo frowned. "I'm not Mrs. Robinson."

"Who?"

"You know, the Simon & Garfunkel song from *The Graduate*?"

She stared at him blankly.

"It's about an alcoholic wife hiding booze everywhere. *Anyway*, I'm not like that."

Angie shrugged. "Okay."

"I can't tell if you're being judgy or really don't care."

Angie grabbed her toast without burning herself this time. One edge was blackened though. She frowned, pulling the burnt bits off over the sink. Toast was one of the few things she could make and she reserved the right to be picky about it. Plus, ignoring Leo seemed to annoy him.

Sure enough, after a few minutes of silence, he said, "Is this you telling me you don't care?"

"I feel like I've answered this question. Is it that hard for you to believe someone doesn't care about you?"

His face shut down. "No." Leo pulled a pitcher of margarita mix from the fridge. His shoulders hunched and his downcast eyes meant his golden lashes caught the yellow kitchen light.

Angie felt a twinge of guilt until she noticed he flicked his gaze up to gauge her reaction. Rage heated her core. Guilt trips had been used to control her growing up. *Don't you want to make Mama look good? You don't want Daddy to lose business, do you?* She sank her teeth into her toast with all the venom she didn't want to unleash. She had no room to talk, she used all the emotional manipulation she'd been taught.

Leo drew back. "Damn, what'd I do?"

"Reminded me of something I'm trying to change about myself."

"Depression and maybe a little too much drinking?"

"Very self aware. You want a round of applause? No, that choreographed 'You mean bitch, you drove me to drink' routine you just did."

"Screw you, I di—"

Angie yanked his shirt until he bent to eye level. "Don't bother, I am the queen of emotional manipulation—"

"Among other things."

Angie bared her teeth at him.

"Motherfucker!" He jerked back. She let him go, marveling as he didn't spill a drop of his drink. "How long until Benji is recruiting you to keep me in line, huh?"

She cocked her head, studying him. "Benji doesn't want you to drink?"

"Oh no." Leo backed up further.

Angie stalked closer, feral glee lighting her up. Something about big men being afraid of her—

"I thought you were trying to change!"

Angie froze. Damn drunk boy band drag queens who somehow know exactly what to say. With a growl, she stomped back to her toast, abandoned on her plate. Lucy, it was cold already. Ugh.

"That worked?" Leo unfolded from his defensive stance and sipped his drink.

Angie glared at him. "Lucky for you." She shoved the rest of her sad toast in her mouth and chewed with all her anger.

"I'm just going to leave now." Leo edged towards the door.

"No, you're not. I listened to your problems, now, you listen to mine."

Leo deflated. "Ugh, fine."

Benji and Rohan found Leo when he stormed out of the kitchen, yelling, "Call your damn band, Angela!"

Benji let him barrel past them out into the backyard. Rohan went after him. Benji poked their head into the kitchen. Angelica stood by the counter, dusting crumbs off her fingers. She rolled her eyes when she saw them.

Benji stepped into the room. "Pushing buttons already?"

"I forgot about the whole Martin breaking up the Beatboyz thing, so sue me." Her voice still held an extra rasp in it.

"Still stuck on what to do, huh?"

"No, he's right. I need to talk to my band. And I will, in the morning."

Benji nodded. "Let me know if you need anything."

"A soundproof room for the screaming."

Benji paused, thinking. Hanayu might know a—

"Kidding. But I could use a cup of tea. My throat is *rough*."

Benji smiled. "That, I can do."

Half an hour later, Angelica sat next to them on the couch as they watched the showcase of songs that came together during the sessions today. She sipped her second cup of tea with honey and lemon, watching the performances with an intensity that caused more than one musician to clam.

Benji tried to keep their focus on the stage but it was hard when she leaned into them, casually but not obviously affectionate—unless you knew how little Angelica touched people. The contact warmed Benji but the glances from the other musicians made it impossible to relax.

"Who do I have to fight to get you to chill?" She asked as Sam and Sabrina handed the stage off to Leo, Gus, and Kevon.

Benji shrugged, glancing around.

She followed their gaze. "I can't tell you how hard it is not to jump up and say something territorial, right now."

Benji shivered both from mortification at the thought but also from arousal. "Appreciate the restraint."

"Should I be more discreet?" She pulled back, putting space between them. Her question sounded casual but the extra stiffness in her spine and the faint whiff of hurt coming off of her gave lie to that.

Benji snaked a hand around her waist and dragged her back against them. "Not unless you're afraid to be seen with me," they said into her hair.

She dragged her eye teeth against their neck. "Never," she rasped against their pulse. For a moment, Benji forgot they were in a room full of people—

"Hey! Save the gross couple stuff until after the sexy song," Leo yelled from the stage.

"Maybe our song is so sexy they're feeling it already," Gus said.

"Damn, we're good," Kevon said. "I heard those two were trying to kill each other last summer."

"How about you play the song before you start congratulating yourselves?" Benji snapped. Out of the corner of their eye, they could see Angelica's feral smile.

Kevon gave them a hasty salute, Gus dropped their gaze to their keyboard, Leo huffed and picked up the mic. "Girls, gays, and theys, this is our yet untitled, sexy song."

Gus tapped out a luxuriously slow, full beat on the keyboard. Kevon came in a bar later, picking out atmospheric chords on the low end of his guitar. Leo crooned nonsense syllables, placeholders to be filled in on a later session. Then he hit the chorus:

> I need a quick fix
> A night so good
> I can forget his tricks
>
> I need a man
> Forget his name
> I need it fast
> White out my brain
>
> Baby, got too many thoughts
> Don't ask my number
> Just get me off

The band petered out and Leo shrugged. "That's what we got so far." The song was rough but Benji thought it had potential. The rest of the evening went by in a pleasant blur of half songs and suggestions. Then Benji climbed the stairs with Angelica and they collapsed together in bed.

After a few tired kisses, Benji fell asleep in her arms. It was becoming easier and easier to imagine this as domestic, as permanent.

It's been barely over a week, they reminded themself. *Don't get your hopes up.*

It was unfortunate, really, that they were so out of practice at lying to themself.

CHAPTER 28

"Draw a card for me
I'm out of luck
Out of fucks
Draw draw
For me

Cards for sorrow
(hold out for tomorrow)
Cards for pain
(it's not in vain)
I've got the whole deck

Shuffle shuffle
Deal them again
Hope for a better hand

They tell me it gets better
All the time"
— "Reading" by User-Friendly Omega off of *Drown Them All*

I n the morning after a tentative breakfast that happily stayed put, Angie was getting ready to go to talk to her band when Cheryl called. She considered ignoring it but something told her to answer. She always listened to those instincts.

"Oh, thank god you finally picked up."

"Hello to you too."

"The suits are talking about delaying the tour," Cheryl said without preamble. "How hard do we want to push back on this?"

"I—what do you mean?" Had Cheryl guessed Angie didn't want to tour anymore?

"I take it you're still on a social media hiatus."

"I had food poisoning."

"Angie, you tweeted deliriously while the anesthesia was wearing off from dental surgery. I had to take your phone away from you."

Angie had vague memories of that. "That was pre-breakdown though. Pre-flip phone." Destroying her old smartphone had been deeply satisfying and a cry for help—especially when she'd awkwardly used her computer to take a picture of the wreckage so she could post it, her hand still bleeding from breaking the screen. She'd looked at red drops on the keyboard and realized everyone had been right to tell her to go to therapy.

"While I appreciate you're establishing healthy boundaries with your socials, we have a situation brewing: those men's rights creeps are teaming up with the evangelicals and they're pressuring their reps to try to ban you from various parts of the country."

"What does that even mean?"

"Taking your music out of libraries, banning your merch in schools—"

Angie scoffed. "Let them, that's only fueled sales in the past."

"And banning you from playing venues in certain towns."

"Isn't that a First Amendment violation?"

Cheryl sighed. "That's what our lawyers are countering with but these assholes are calling your music hate speech."

"Hate? Against who?"

"Christians, traditional families, men, straight people. You name it."

Angie barked a laugh at the bedroom ceiling. It was so enraging it almost made her want to tour just to spite them. She'd heard all this before but this sounded extra coordinated. "Any idea who is behind all this?"

"No. The label wants to lay low and battle this out with lawyers. I put out some feelers but so far nothing."

"Be careful," Angie said. "I don't want you getting doxxed or anything."

"Oh trust me, I am."

"Good. I'll talk to the band." And put out some feelers of her own. She knew at least one hacker who owed her a favor.

"Don't do anything reckless," Cheryl said. "We'll get this sorted out and you all on the road in less than a year, mark my words."

"Less than a year," Angie repeated. Maybe in less than a year she'd be over whatever this was and be ready to tour. Who needed to plan when she could just do what she'd been doing for most of her career?

"Maybe less," Cheryl said, misinterpreting her tone.

"Keep me posted," Angie said and hung up. Maybe she just needed to wait and see, try to be cautious for once in her life and not alienate her band by telling them what was probably just a passing feeling. One she'd been having for the better part of a year but what was that in the grand scheme of things? Barely a blip.

Instead of dwelling on it, she opened up a message thread to NosiNetscraper, a hacker who had been an early fan of hers. The two of them traded information and favors from time to time.

ANGIE

I need a favor...

The day passed in a blur for Benji. Rohan talked to Leo and seemed satisfied he'd gotten his friend to step off the trauma cycle. Benji hoped he was right, but they were too distracted to make sure of it.

Angelica floated in and out as they ran sessions or wrote with people. Something was up. She was on the phone more than she wasn't. Even so, it was tantalizing to have her so close but not able to spend time with her. But they had an idea to remedy that tonight. It was a bit cheesy but they thought she might enjoy it. Well, they hoped.

When they caught her between sessions and calls, they tried to couch it casually. "Want to go to a show that's not in my basement tonight?"

She chuckled. "What do you have in mind?"

"How do you feel about surprises?" They said, like a challenge.

She puffed up her chest, crowding into their space. "I can roll with whatever you throw at me."

They grinned. "Good. Get ready to sweat and scream."

Her cheeks went red but she smoldered at them. "Darling, what about the children? They might hear."

"Not where we're going."

That evening, dressed in their emo best—or at least the best their Sacramento closet could support, Benji handed the retreat off to Rohan and Leo for the night. Well, and also to Hanayu, who had strict instructions to text Benji if something went awry. She'd rolled her eyes, reminding them, "Everyone's an adult here. Let them live and fuck up."

She was right. Probably. But it didn't hurt to plan ahead. They were trying to have a casual conversation with Nancy and Hanayu when Angelica finally strutted down the stairs, ready to go. Hanayu wolf-whistled.

Nancy said, "Oh my."

Benji just stared.

Angelica looked amazing. Her wig was black, her eyes were set off by stark black liner, her lipstick was deep purple. She wore tight black jeans, an off the shoulder In This Moment shirt, and an unzipped striped hoodie. She looked like some of the dangerously cool goth girls they'd crushed on in high school. An old sweet spot of attraction.

She took in their outfit and smiled.

"We match." Benji looked down at their black jeans, Nova Twins tank, My Chemical Romance hoodie, and Converse. Their eyeliner was silver and black, their lipstick a bit more subdued, and a beanie low over their hair for an attempt at anonymity.

Her smile widened. "I had help." She winked at Hanayu.

Hanayu winked back and threaded her arm through Nancy's. "I think that's our cue."

Nancy chuckled as they disappeared into the basement.

"Did she tell you where we're going?" Benji asked.

Angelica shook her head. "Just what you were wearing."

"Good." They offered her their hand. She took it and they led her across the grid of Midtown streets to Harlow's, a small club with good sound on J street. The show had already started and there was a short line. Not that they waited in it. Benji took her to the back entrance and texted an old acquaintance who was working the show.

The two of them were ushered in through the patio and taken to the table Benji reserved by the sound booth in the back. Benji popped their ear plugs in and pulled their mask on. Angelica did the same as she sat next to them on the bench. On stage, a man was aggressively DJing a Coheed and Cambria song while the crowd moshed and sang along.

Angelica leaned in, yelling to be heard. "I've never seen people mosh for a DJ."

"Welcome to Emo Night." The tour had a cult following among millennials of a certain bent but it had originated here in Sacramento.

She laughed. "I've always wanted to go to one of these."

Suddenly, the DJ was joined by three other guys. They moved the DJ table and pulled out instruments, setting up.

The crowd roared.

Angelica cackled. "Bet they play one of yours."

Benji groaned. "Our music is too young for nostalgia. Give it another five years." UFO had broken up less than a decade ago.

"Still could happen."

"Fine. I bet they won't." If they did, Benji would feel really old.

"I bet they will and if I win, you have to dance with me."

"I'd dance with you either way."

Her expression softened for a moment. Then her eyes gleamed with trouble. "Then you have to mosh with me."

Benji hadn't moshed in a good ten years, but what the hell. "And if I win?"

"What do you want, darling?" She leaned in, her neckline dipping to give them a great view of her breasts and the lacy bra they were nestled in.

"Everything," they said. "But I could get that without a bet."

"Oh, probably," she agreed. Smug like a cat who'd eaten the cream. How did smug look so good on her?

"I want to expand my boundaries," they said suddenly.

"If you win the bet?" Angelica asked, frowning.

"Either way."

She smiled, squeezing in closer to them. "Tell me more."

The singer yelled, "Emo Night, are you ready?"

The crowd roared again.

Benji put their mouth to her ear. "I want to be in you. Tonight. If you think you can be quiet."

Her breath hitched. "Back at you, baby."

The band started their first song: "Ocean Avenue" by Yellowcard. At the sound of the crunching guitars, Angelica whooped and then they were both singing along. By the second song, the two of them were standing.

By the third, Angelica was wrapped around Benji's back, her chin on their shoulder and her chest vibrating against their spine as she yelled along to "Stacy's Mom" by Fountains of Wayne. Benji knew the song but they couldn't help but laugh at Angelica knowing all the words to a song about a teenager crushing on a MILF. She was unabashedly into these songs too, singing with her whole body, gesturing and acting out the lyrics like she was the one on stage. Pure joy radiated off of her, infectious and free.

The crowd was similarly jubilant, screaming all the words so loud it was impossible to hear the singer. Benji soaked in the energy as they lent their voice to the chorus. This is why they went to concerts. The release and rejuvenation they couldn't get anywhere else.

Then it happened. The band launched into their next song and the minute the crowd heard the slick bassline, they roared —exactly the same way they would when Benji was standing on stage, their bassist showboating in front of them as she fingerpicked the chords to the User-Friendly Omega's biggest hit.

Angelica laughed maniacally against their back. The singer and crowd started singing but it was her voice they heard as she crooned Benji's words in their ear.

> "Looking like I'm the life of the party
> Sit in the corner drinking Bacardi
> Don't know how to talk to anyone
> Don't know how to get in on the fun"

"What do you think? Ready to mosh?" She asked.

In answer, Benji grabbed her hand and towed her into the mosh pit. She laughed again, the sound an undercurrent to their words as the crowd sang:

> "Overthinker, overdrinker,
> Can't make up your mind
> Said, I know your kind"

Benji dove into the pit, knocking into people who were slam dancing their way around the edges of the circle. Angelica danced into the middle with a twirl, arms outstretched, touching everyone crashing around and somehow not breaking her wrists in the process. Then she ran around the pit, high-fiving everyone. It was her pit now. Benji cackled as she caught them by the arm and spun them around with her.

> "Cute but you'll never be fine
> Let me make this simpler,
> And she said,"

Here, everyone who didn't quite know the words to the pre chorus or verse came in strong.

"Fuck me, I'm beautiful
This tie ain't suitable
This dress is removable"

Angelica dipped Benji like the two of them were in a ball-room not on a dance floor and if not for their masks, they would've kissed her. Instead when they came back up, they wrapped their arms around her neck, pressing their forehead against hers and sang the final lines of the chorus, backed by the crowd.

"And you're so doable
So fuck me,
Beautiful"

"Gladly," she yelled.

This time, she grabbed their hand, dragging them past the crowd and the band and the bar, out into the cool night. They were around the corner when she ripped off her mask and Benji's and kissed them.

Benji's nerves lit up like a blindingly bright lighting rig. They dragged her closer and she pushed them up against some nearby wall. Her hands roamed up under their top and they cupped her face, holding her to them.

When their kiss broke for air, Benji was dizzy, hazy with want.

"Home," Angelica gasped. Benji pushed aside the strange hope that word on her tongue generated. "Now. Or I'm going to do something reckless."

It was too far to run but the two of them still made record time. To avoid everyone else, Benji took her up the servant stairs and frankly, it was a miracle they only stopped twice to make out. A bigger miracle no one came to investigate all the creaking noises. Perks of having a possibly haunted house.

Back in Benji's room, they had the door locked and Angelica naked in two minutes flat. She grinned at them, make-up smeared, hair a mess, eyes feral—utterly gorgeous.

Benji took their time stripping. They still sometimes got a bit shy when first undressing before a new partner. Any insecurities were burned away by the hunger in her eyes—and the way she pounced, knocking them bodily onto the bed.

"Boundaries," she rasped, straddling them. Nothing below the waist touched but her knees around their hips. It was torturous. "Now."

"Why? Are you in a hurry?" They grinned.

She pressed her palm lightly against their throat. Benji arched into the contact, breath hitching. "Not at all. I can go slow. I can stay here all night."

"As much as I'd like to see that, I guess we can do other things."

"Oh, you guess?" She smiled and leaned down to brush her teeth against their shoulder.

"If you insist," Benji said primly though the effect was ruined by how fast they were talking. "I'm good with fucking and being fucked. Fingers, tongues, whatever as long as it's, *you know,* meant for it."

She chuckled against their shoulder. "There's a story."

"Later," they admonished her. "No spanking, no baby talk, no role play unless we've discussed the scene before."

"Got it."

"You?"

She hummed. "First, what words are okay for...?" She palmed their hip bone, thumb sliding too slowly to their thigh.

That she thought to ask made them smile. "Dick and clit are fine but it depends on my mood."

"Right now?"

They considered it. "Clit."

She nodded. "I'm good with most things but they don't always work the same every time, if that makes sense?" Though her face was still against their shoulder, Benji could feel her unease.

"Same," they said, stroking her side. "That's what talking's for."

"Yup," she said, but with more relief than Benji expected. Like this conversation had gone badly for her before.

They pulled her to them, pressing her skin against theirs. "I want this to be good for you, but if things aren't amazing we'll just have to try again."

"I think it's terrible already," she joked. "How many times do you think we have to try to make it right?"

"As many as it takes."

"And if we never get it?"

"We may just have to keep fucking forever."

She laughed and ground her pussy against their clit. They lost their mind a bit at how good it felt. "Oh, also I'm not peeing on you."

"Not my kink, so not a problem," Benji said, flipping her onto her back. They pinched her nipples in the way that she'd liked before. By her moan, it was still good. They licked their way down, enjoying her taste, but she stopped them.

"Don't be delicate with me. Make me feel it."

With a grin, Benji flicked her clit with a finger. She dropped back onto the pillows with a loud moan.

"Tsk tsk," they said, lips hovering over her pussy. "You're going to wake everyone up."

"Oh, you're going to make me be quiet?"

"If you're quiet, you get rewards." They licked her clit, circling her entrance with a finger to demonstrate.

"You're going to pay for this," Angelica gritted out, biting into the meat of her palm.

"Counting on it," they said and that finger slid into Angie, their tongue dragging along her clit at the same time. She arched, losing her mind to the sensation, her free hand finding Benji's thick hair and latching on.

They seemed to take that as an urging to go harder. They slid another finger into her, fucking her in rythmic strokes that complimented whatever their tongue was doing. She couldn't distinguish much through the lightning spikes of pleasure building, building, building…

Her whole body went rigid, convulsing to bring them flush against her as her orgasm hit, drowning her for an endless moment.

She collapsed as the force of it wrung her out and let her go. They bit her thigh, sucking a hickey into her skin before crawling up to lie next to her. They grinned down at her, propped on their elbow.

She grinned back. "You're pretty good at that."

"Please, I'm *excellent* at head."

"I'll show you excellent." She pushed them down and straddled them. Dragging herself down their body, she trailed her nails over their clit.

They groaned.

She licked them, enjoying their earthy, salty taste.

"Tease," they rasped.

"Quiet, I'm working." She flicked them with just the tip of

her tongue in punishment. Their breath stuttered, they made an impatient, needy sound.

Angie chuckled. Then she took them in her mouth, sucking and licking and using her fingers until they begged.

When they came, she swallowed it all and kissed them. "See?"

"Hmmm?" They looked blissed out and she reveled in the languid pleasure in their expression.

"*That's* excellent." She thumped her chest.

"Give me five minutes." They pulled her against them. "I'm not done with you yet."

They stroked her hair. She slung her leg over their pelvis, nestling her thigh over their clit.

"Mmm, maybe less than five minutes." Then they were kissing her, she was grinding against their hip and they produced a condom from the bedside table after a bit of awkward finagling.

She rolled it on, torturously slow until they growled at her. Then she slid down over them. The way they filled her felt so good and when she was fully seated, they both paused, making intertwined moans.

Then she rocked into them and they pushed up into her and she almost lost her balance. They caught her before she went off the bed but they were both laughing so hard it took them a moment to restart. Until she ground down, leaning forward to cup their throat. "I bet you can't make me cum again."

"I bet you can't make me cum first." They strummed their fingers over her clit.

She tightened her grip. "Let's find out."

It felt so damn delicious to have them in her that she happily lost the bet a few minutes later but Benji came so quickly after she called it a tie.

"Not even," Benji scoffed after they detangled their limbs, lying next to each other, panting. "I very clearly won that."

"I would argue we both won." She draped herself on them after they got rid of the condom. They wrapped their arms around her, kissing the top of her head.

"If you have to be reasonable, then yes, we definitely did."

She smiled against their chest. "I'm always reasonable."

They laughed. "Fuck, I like you so much."

She squeezed them to her, words getting caught in her chest. *I love you. I'm so fucking in love with you. I never want to let you go.* Instead, she said the lesser truth: "I like you so much too."

CHAPTER 29

Dear baby little past Angie,

Ugh, okay here goes. Hi. It's your future self. I'm older than you might expect. We didn't die with a white lighter in our hands at twenty-seven, believe it or not. And we freaked out about that, which I'm betting you can believe. Anyway, I'm not good with children so let's start with 19 year old Angie.

Hey bitch. So, funny story, you're about to get really famous. You're in no way prepared for it but that'll make people money so they'll indulge you. I wish I could go back in time, tell you that you don't have to do all the things you did to shoot your shot. Those rich dates you manipulated, who used you back? Most of them will amount to nothing but lyrics fodder and messiness. You're a scrapper though and you'll survive your mistakes (so far).

And baby, where I am, right now, you got something really worth surviving for.

Benji woke up buzzing with a song. Pieces of lyrics sang in their mind, vague but too promising to pass up. Sung in their voice but also in Angelica's. They turned to look at her, wearing an Otep shirt and soft pants, half under the covers, her foot touching theirs though she was facing her side of the bed. It *was* her side, wasn't it?

Benji was fucking smitten. It was a done deal. Maybe it wasn't love yet but it would be if they let it and they didn't care who knew.

They cuddled up behind her. "Still want to do a duet with me?"

She turned around, immediately awake the way they'd noticed she often was. No wonder she didn't need coffee. She grinned. "I knew you'd come around."

"This was all a plot to get my voice on your record, wasn't it?"

She wrapped herself around them. "Mm-hmm with some perks." She kissed Benji, pressing her pelvis against theirs.

Between exploring those perks in bed and in the shower afterwards, it was another hour and a half before the two of them left the room.

The rest of the retreat was halfway through breakfast when they descended. Everyone paused, stared at Benji and Angelica before pointedly resuming eating. Well, almost everyone. Rohan was presumably still on his way in from Clementine and Leo whooped. Benji belatedly realized they were holding Angelica's hand.

Angelica bowed in response to Leo's outburst and did a princess wave like she was on the back of some mayor's car in a hometown parade. There was no trace of redness in her cheeks, though Benji's face heated at the scrutiny and implications. She really didn't have any shame.

They were both amazed and slightly envious.

Somehow, they made it through breakfast without Leo saying anything immature. Possibly because Hanayu and the Razors were sitting all around him. Jean cracked her knuckles ominously every time Leo opened his mouth and Hanayu had that too-casual posture she adopted when she had her foot on top of someone else's under the table. In fact, Leo made more than one strangled yelp during the course of the meal. Paulina kept pouring him coffee refills. Nancy asked him rapid fire questions like he was in a job interview.

Angelica sipped her tea with a smile like Morticia Addams in that gif from the first 90s movie.

After breakfast, Benji finagled the schedule to give them and Angelica time to write. Unfortunately, that meant going out to the gazebo since even the attic was full of groups jamming and going back to their bedroom meant no writing would happen.

So, after Angelica donned a huge hat and lathered on sunscreen, the two of them settled on the uncushioned seats. Shading her eyes, Angelica surveyed the house windows, the setback of Benji's neighbors and finally, her hat almost falling off, the sky.

"Don't worry, I don't think anyone will recognize you in that hat."

"Things have been blowing up with the assholes online," she said. "The only reason Cheryl isn't here with a couple of eight packs wearing Kevlar vests and earpieces is because I promised to be careful. You're my witness. I checked."

"You want me to sign and timestamp something?" They could tell she didn't want to talk about it.

"Yeah, my people will call your people."

Benji frowned, unable to stop themself from asking, "Is it getting that bad?"

She grimaced. "Hard to tell, it being the internet and all. All it takes is one keyboard warrior to crawl out of the metaphorical basement though."

"How often does this happen?"

"Reconsidering being associated with me?"

"No." If a little online hate scared them, they would have hidden in a bunker years ago.

Her shoulders dropped.

"I've had my own shit over the years," they continued. "I just need to know if we need to upgrade my security systems."

"How much of your security system is Nazi-stomping punks?"

"About sixty percent but I can always host a house show," they joked. The extensiveness of their security system already felt like it was reaching panopticon levels but they'd dial it up to keep her safe.

She huffed a laugh. "Let's write. You said you had an idea."

"I want to hear yours first."

She went silent, pressing her lips together for a long moment. "I'm not sure I'm so in love with the idea I had. I still want to duet with you but my idea—I think it's time passed."

"I only have a few scraps of phrases." They showed her their notes app where they'd written:

- *Vicious and dreaming*
- *Emo night/being at a concert w/ her*
- *I want more*

"So maybe we can use some of what you had and put them together," they said, feeling more raw than they'd expected. It felt like she was playing the role they usually did, taking a half-formed idea and polishing it.

"We can try." She sounded dubious but pulled out her phone. "It's really rough." She pressed play, lips in a thin line again. "And these speakers suck."

She wasn't wrong, her flip phone's speakers were tinny as shit. They ignored that and focused on the music itself. It was bare as most demos were, starting with just a piano track.

No, not a piano, the notes shifted and bent into what almost sounded like flutes. A mellotron, maybe even a real one and not a digital facsimile. They hadn't heard one of those in a long time. Not many people fucked with those strange precursors of a keyboard when they could do stuff digitally. It lent a creepy, surreal carnival feel to the track. Benji could picture her in soft focus, playing with gauzy curtains blowing behind her and a candelabra on the mellotron.

Through the speakers, Angelica hummed along with music, as if she was picking out the melody by ear. It lent the track a musing air Benji liked. Then the humming became words:

> *"I am an empty casket*
> *Every vein torn open*
> *Thought I was clever*
> *Thought I was smart*
> *As I sold my pain"*

"Another voice," murmured Angelica on the track. "A duet maybe?" Then she took another breath and kept singing:

> *"I am a spider in my web*
> *Sick with hope*
> *Sick with dread*
> *Trying to reel you in"*

"Chorus?" her recording muttered. "Maybe."

"What's the fun in being clear?
When I'm alive in
In the moments you hate me
Why make this healthy
When we can buuuuurn?"

Ahh, they could see why she thought the moment had passed for this.

"Fill my casket
Crawl into my web
If there's a way to keep my head
I haven't found it yet"

She sang the chorus again, taking the mellotron riff up the scale and sort of resolving it on a tritone. The tone faded away and she breathed a fragile half-laugh so unlike her, Benji almost replayed the track just to hear it again.

They emerged from the track, their thoughts buzzing with possibilities. "We could work with this if you wanted."

She shook her head. "I don't think I want to be in that headspace. I want to see if we can bottle that joy from last night." She looked at them, quirking a smile. "I've never danced with anyone in a pit like that before."

They smiled back. "Me either. Screaming songs along with the crowd, made me feel like I was back at my first MCR show watching them do *The Black Parade*."

"Feeling the bass in my chest took me back to my first Rise Against concert, it was so loud I couldn't tell what song was playing, the mix was shit but they hijacked my heartbeat anyway." She scribbled a few things in the notebook she always seemed to carry with her. "I like this. Nostalgia and new love— relationships, whatever." Her hair and hat shielded her face but a flash of something unsure still ricocheted through the space.

Guess Benji wasn't the only one afraid to use that word. They cleared their throat and sipped their water. "Yeah and um, nostalgia, especially millennial nostalgia and emo is big right now."

She gave them a sardonic look. "Planning a comeback?"

They made a face. "Maybe in five to ten years. They haven't had enough time to miss us and I need to write a really cool dance song."

"If that's a Bowling for Soup reference, you're ridiculous."

"I can only aspire to their levels of ridiculousness," they said solemnly. They tapped the keyboard they'd brought out and plugged into the least sketchy extension cord outlet in the gazebo. "But at least I have my own keyboard." They played a random three chord progression.

She shook her head, writing something down. "Okay, how's this," she read,

"Vicious and dreaming
Keep me screaming
I want more than
Four on the floor"

"Verse or chorus?" They hummed and tapped out an upbeat melody. It was poppy on the keyboard but they could imagine it with horns without getting to ska. Sort of like "Broken Hearts Parade" by Good Charlotte.

"Chorus but what if we had a slightly different chorus every time?" She sang it again, lining up with the chords they were noodling on.

"Neither pop or punk but sure, we can try that."

"What can I say? I'm difficult."

They ducked under her hat to kiss her cheek. "Yeah, you are." They remembered her singing over the crowd, serenading them. "Oh, how about this as a verse?"

"Sing my favorite song
Scream it back to me
Like they were your words
All along"

"Yessss." She turned on her recording app and sang her chorus then had them sing it again.

"You want to start with the chorus?"

"Yeah, hook 'em before they know what hit them."

"Mercenary, I like it."

She winked.

They stole her notebook and wrote down another chorus:

"Vicious and dreaming
I had meaning
I wanted more
Than keeping score"

She sang it to them. "What if we changed 'I had meaning' to 'I was scheming'?"

They nodded. "More accurate. I like it."

They went back and forth until the song was done, then recorded a very rough demo that was interrupted by the light rail rushing by, warning sirens blaring, a usual occurrence but still made Benji start.

Angelica tensed next to them.

Benji squeezed her hand. She exhaled hard, visibly relaxing. A tension they hadn't noticed leaked out of Benji. Would they ever get used to how much her emotions affected theirs?

Maybe someday, if they were lucky.

It was surreal how hopeful that thought was.

The rest of the retreat was a blur. Angie hung around being helpful where she could when she wasn't practicing with her Sirens.

On Saturday, Benji took the group to Porchfest, a festival where nearby old houses turned their large porches into stages and bands played all day. Angie invited her band to join them as they picnicked on grassy street dividers, sitting on the lawn of a house decorated like a pirate ship for Halloween to watch Dropkick Murphy covers, and overflowed into the street in front of an artist co-op house. Marsha showed up for a set before wandering off to reorganize a nearby Little Free Library. She had her head in a book for the rest of the time, bobbing her head to the music as Gemma steered her from set to set.

Gemma and Dani spent most of the sets with their arms slung around each other in that comfortable affection of a long relationship. Angie caught glimpses of them like that a lot over the years and it always hit her with a mixture of warmth and longing. She wanted that but it never seemed to be in the cards. She knew they fought too but their fights seemed to resolve quickly without any of the lasting damage her fights always seemed to have.

She glanced at Benji, beside her. They were leaning against a tree, watching a punk band sing in Spanish with avid concentration. They seemed to handle her fine but had the two of them been in a real fight yet? She was tempted to pick one just to get it out of the way but she quelled that instinct. Why couldn't she just enjoy what they had right now? Pain would come if she hastened it along or not.

Benji seemed to feel her gaze and they turned their focus to her. "Everything all right?"

She nodded and for a while, she wasn't lying.

Finally, the NoN folks packed up their stuff and got out of the house. When even the Razors were gone, Angie had her way—as loudly as she damn well wanted—with Benji on the couch. Oh, the sounds Benji made when they weren't trying to be quiet were delicious.

But the next day, she was reminded her world would have to expand again past the borders of Benji's neighborhood. Preparations for the MetalQuake show ramped up with security preparations more intricate than the props and costume changes—which, given the theatricality of her shows, was saying something. The show was in less than two weeks.

Most of the choreography and sets were recycled from past shows but she planned to include a few unreleased songs and reorder the setlist to keep it fresh. Set pieces wouldn't arrive until a couple days before to minimize storage costs so she and the Sirens practiced in Benji's basement.

Though there was now a security guard detail on her LA house and her vacation home was pretty much abandoned by protesters, there didn't seem to be a point to going back with the show so soon. Plus, Benji didn't seem to mind. They claimed they could work just fine remotely.

The Sirens seemed fine too. Dani took to cooking in Benji's kitchen because the penthouse kitchen "wasn't homey enough." Angie found Marsha asleep in the gazebo during breaks more than once, a book on her chest. Gemma interrogated Benji on the state of their home repairs and offered Hanayu advice on how to better utilize the backyard for shows. Some of her suggestions made Benji look like they wanted to tear out their hair but, overall, they took it in stride.

It was… homey. She couldn't remember the last time she'd felt at home with other people like this. Her parents' house had been too chaotic for her to relax for more than a few hours at a time. Sometimes, when she hunted for them, she unearthed a few good memories from that time: Mama baking or Daddy making her laugh, times when they went out in public and her parents put on a good front.

Now that she had the real thing in her grasp, she held on with both hands, afraid it would soon end.

CHAPTER 30

"Somewhere out there
Sits a girl like a scar
Waiting for someone far away
Hoping they're coming to stay

I'll meet you out there
For that expensive dinner
At the end of the galaxy
We'll watch it all end
Hand in hand

Somewhere far away
Is someone like me
Waiting for that scar on my heart
Cut me deep, and we'll never be apart"
—"At the End of the Galaxy" by User-Friendly Omega off of
And Down We Go

The day of the show dawned—well, who knew how it dawned, Angie certainly wasn't awake for it. She woke up midmorning and did her show day routine: ate well, stayed hydrated, babied her voice, the usual. It felt normal until she got to the venue and Cheryl showed up. Cheryl rarely came to shows anymore unless they were a big deal. Angie had been happily fooling her nerves into forgetting this would be one of the bigger, if not biggest crowd of her career.

"You're gonna kill it," Cheryl told her in the tour bus they'd rented since the park didn't have any amenities. It wasn't Angie's bad ass yet stealthy and environmentally friendly bus but it was fine for tonight.

"Of course we are," Angie said as her usual glam team bustled around her. If she was a guy she could turn up in last night's clothes and last week's eyeliner and it'd be *rock and roll* but whatever. At least she'd stopped wearing the white contacts that were part of her music videos and promo pictures. They were just too damn hard to see through, especially on stage.

"You're staying off socials?"

Dani, who was sharing Angie's mirror, squinted at Cheryl's reflection as her make-up artist worked on her foundation. "Are you trying to psych her up or psych her out?"

"Yeah," Marsha said, applying fake blood to her neck. She preferred to do the finishing touches to her gore herself. "You're usually subtler than this."

Cheryl sighed. "It's under control. We're still having some threats—"

"When haven't we?" Gemma muttered.

"But MetalQuake says they have security handled," Cheryl said.

Angie raised her eyebrows, earning a frown from the make-up artist trying to dust powder on her face.

"I told them to double it," Cheryl continued. "We should be fine."

"But you're here, just in case," Angie finished her thought. "Appreciated." She took a breath and told herself she was calm, she was okay, everything would be fine. Then she hummed "A Really Cool Dance Song" by Bowling for Soup.

Cheryl nodded, tapping the table by Angie's hand. Angie caught her manager's hand in hers and squeezed it briefly. Cheryl's eyes widened at the rare touch but as she turned away, Angie caught the edges of a smile.

Angie stood on the wings of the stage with the band. There was no curtain, just the dark night shrouding the stage. She hummed tunelessly while the crew put the finishing touches on the set up.

Benji had gone rigid when she repeated what Cheryl told her. "Where do you need me?"

"Somewhere safe," she'd replied. "I'm gonna need bail if I do something reckless."

They hadn't laughed at her joke but they hadn't argued either. Her lips still tingled from the force of their kiss, like they could press safety into her mouth.

Now, she held her hands out to her Sirens, palms cupped together.

Marsha and Gemma slung their instruments around to the back. Dani stuck her sticks in her bra strap. The band came together, forming a tight circle. Each woman placed her fingertips on Angie's palms. Angie concentrated on the three sets of warm callused fingers in her hands.

She waited a beat before saying, "Baphomet, bless this show." She closed her eyes. Tingles crawled up her back, tracing the lines of her shoulders until they relaxed. She could do this. "Protect my people from my excess and all external threats. Especially tonight. Lucifer, shine your spotlight on us and show us any danger before it comes." The tingles reached out beyond her bones, spreading like wings. "May our music sound damn good and our show be badass. Amen."

She dropped her hands. The Sirens exhaled in shaky unison and took their places. A crew guy put a mike in Angie's hand. She flicked it on with her thumb and ran out on stage.

Benji stood with Hanayu off to the side of the moat of security dividing the stage from the crowd.

"Look at all this muscle," Hanayu said. "No one's getting through it."

Benji's response was cut off by the sound of their own voice. Angelica had switched her intro track. Instead of "So It Begins," UFO's sweetest track "At the End of the Galaxy" piped through the speakers.

"Awww." Hanayu elbowed them. "That's fucking cute."

It was. A sweet thing just for them. Benji glowed.

The song ended. Angelica and her Sirens ran on stage. The lights went on, blinding in the dark. The crowd went wild. Benji was entranced. They hoped they could sink into her performance the way they'd never let themself before but knowing those internet creeps might be lurking about kept their head on a swivel.

They noticed Hanayu kept glancing at the crowd too.

"So I'm working on a new album…" Angelica said after four back-to-back songs. She paused, letting the cheers die down. "I have some new material I'm trying out. You wanna hear it?" The crowd roared louder.

She nodded at Gemma. The guitarist stepped forward and picked a sparse chord progression.

> *"Oh, I've been opened up*
> *Veins and voice spilled*
> *On the ground*
> *Oh, I'm opened up*
> *Dissected and splayed*
> *Heart passed around"*

Benji remembered when she'd shown them the demo for the song a few days ago. She'd shown them a few demos she'd recorded with the band a while back before getting blocked on the album. This song was Benji's pick for the show. It had sounded good practiced in their basement, but now? Holy shit.

Even the crew stopped to listen. One of the people handling the ropes for moving the set pieces around stared, transfixed.

The drums rolled in, Marsha's bass line underlining the chord progression. Angelica dropped her voice to a growl for the pre-chorus.

> *"Am I fucked up?*
> *Was I hateful?*
> *Am I fatal?"*

They hated that she used to think that about herself. They hoped it was past tense, at least.

The stagehand had abandoned his ropes and was openly filming her now.

She let the questions hang in the air before repeating them, closer to a scream. Then she belted out the chorus:

> *"My pain is for sale*

Actions beyond the pale
I'm alone and disowned
Rising from my own grave
I'm alone and disowned
Nothing left to save

"Oh lord I've been opened up," she moaned.
Hands rooting around in my chest
Knives slicing up my breasts
Oh gods, I'm so opened up
Naked but not ashamed
Stripped but untamed"

She sang the pre-chorus and chorus again then paused, filling her lungs, and delivered the kicker, her voice somewhere between a scream and a chant, repeated three times:

"I'm alone, unowned, and free
Reveling in the dirt on me"

Not anymore, Benji thought fiercely. *You're not alone anymore.* Then: *What the fuck is that stagehand doing?*
Benji ran towards the stage.

Angie finished the song, buoyant and floating as the crowd's roar made her feel light as air.
The commotion by the security line punctured it. Benji struggled against three guys in black polo shirts. She couldn't hear what they were saying but they were pointing—

She spun around and ducked. There was no pain so the knife coming for her missed—probably.

A man stumbled past her, close, too close to Gemma.

Instinct and adrenaline kicked in, shredding her self-control. She screamed. The crowd screamed back and she was moving.

He took a swipe at Gemma but the guitarist swung her instrument, knocking him back.

Right into Angie.

She grabbed for him but he elbowed her back, knocking the breath out of her. She closed her arms on thin air.

He ran for the crowd, despite the line of security and—

One of them stepped back for him, creating a hole. Benji broke away from the guards restraining them and ran for him.

He sliced at them. He drew blood. Benji stumbled back.

Hanayu caught them as the man ran through the hole in security, knocking aside audience members. She looked up at Angie, her eyes scared and angry.

Angie threw herself off stage with a shriek, dropping into the dust and dead grass.

He hurt Benji. *He hurt Benji.*

"Satan, guide my hand," she hissed.

Security tried to stop her but she just snarled and climbed over the barricade. The audience was a confused, angry mass. A mob in the making.

"Trap him!" she yelled, her voice a guttural roar.

But he had a knife. He brandished it, creating a circle around him. He was trapped but armed and trapped animals got desperate, she knew that well.

The crowd parted as she barreled through. Whispers and fingers and cameras trailed her, she ignored them.

Eyes on the prize, Angel.

"Yes, Mama," she murmured.

Then she was on the edge of the crowd surrounding her attacker. He brandished his knife at her. She caught his wrist and squeezed until the tendons creaked under her grip. His hand opened, the knife falling to the ground. She stamped it into the dirt.

Angie was rage. Angie was vengeance. Angie was lost.

She dragged him to her by his shirt. "You hurt Benji," she rasped.

"You're an abomination." He shook in her hands. Maybe she was shaking too.

"Tell me not to hurt you." She wanted to hurt him. She didn't know how bad anyone was hurt but she wanted him to feel it a thousand-fold.

"I'm ready to die." His eyes were wide. His voice wobbled. His beard was patchy, showing acne through the hair.

He was young.

Things slowly came into focus. Someone was crying behind her. Someone was calling her name. Her real name.

"Angelica!"

She turned. Benji stood onstage with her microphone, holding their arm but okay. Her band stood with them. "Please."

She looked at them then back at the boy—he was a boy, wasn't he?—in her hands. He came alive in that moment, lashing out with his fists, catching her in the shoulder, in the ribs.

She hugged him to her, squeezing until his arms flailed, and he gasped for air. "You're very lucky," she hissed in his ear. She pulled his head back by his hair, forcing him to look at her.

Angie took a deep, shaky breath and let her feelings crystal-ize. The fear, the shock, the anger, the pain, she tried to channel them until that was all she could feel, until his face was all she could see.

"Be my mirror," she told him, his heart beating frantically against hers. "Feel what you inflicted. It is not power. It is sickness, it is infectious. It is a maze with no exit. Trust me. I have harmed. I will harm. I am harming you." Tears dripped off her chin. Her words were thick. "I am giving back your pain. I am giving back your hate. This is our chance to change."

His eyes shone with tears. He swallowed hard, wilting into her. Limp, pliant.

Perfect.

She let him go. He swayed in place. Picking up his knife, she plucked the sheath off his belt and tucked it into her bra. She pulled out the stiletto she kept strapped to her ankle though, just in case.

"Come on." She pushed him in front of her, stiletto hidden in her palm, the other hand keeping a firm grasp on his shirt.

All around her, the crowd shifted, bringing them back into her focus.

They were crying. *Shit.* Not that it stopped some people from holding their cameras up.

"You all did great," she told the closest lens. "Really great."

The person behind it sobbed.

Mmm, she needed to work on this whole comforting thing.

It was eerily quiet as everyone watched her escort her own assailant to security. When she got close enough, someone tried to take him from her.

She hissed. "What happened to the guard who helped him out?"

The guard pointed at the ground where Hanayu stood over a man in a fetal ball. The other guards gave her a wide berth. Hanayu caught sight of Angie and waved. Planting her foot on the man's hip, she called, "Whatcha want to do with him?"

"The police have been called, ma'am." A man strode over, wearing a special embroidered polo proclaiming he was the head of security.

Hanayu huffed and muttered something Angie could only guess was not pro-cops.

"Where the hell were you twenty minutes ago?" Benji demanded from the edge of the stage, towering over the head of security, their eyes cold.

Cheryl stood next to them. "My question exactly. I want a full explanation, *now*."

He started saying something official sounding but Angie didn't care. She shoved her attacker at him until they both stumbled. "Take care of him. Keep my manager informed. I want to know exactly how this is handled."

Then she pulled herself up onto the stage, not especially gracefully, but she didn't care. Halfway through her attempt, strong hands reached down and Benji helped her up.

"You're okay?" She asked.

In answer they dragged her into their arms and kissed her and—

She pulled back and looked at the crowd. Most of them were still here, watching avidly. She turned back to Benji. "Well, I guess we're public."

"Good." They kissed her again, wrapping their arms harder around her and—

"Ow! Fuck." She inspected her arm. It was sticky, her formerly white sleeve red with drying blood. "That little shit got me."

Unfortunately, that put Benji in overdrive and she found herself propelled towards the medic tent.

She dug her heels in. "One last song."

"What? You're bleeding."

She gestured out at the sobbing crowd, milling aimlessly around the stage. "I take care of my fans. We're all bleeding—"

They shot her bloody arm a sardonic look.

"Metaphorically. Anyway. If I haven't bled out or gotten tetanus or whatever, one song isn't going to make me worse."

Benji sighed. "You're not asking, are you?"

She kissed their cheek. "You learn fast."

They sighed and let her go, shaking their head as they headed backstage. She called the crew over. "We're doing 'Lightbringer.' Me and the piano, nothing fancy. No one's doing any hard work after that. Just set me up and take care of yourselves."

Then she grabbed the mike. "Hey denizens, I know we went a little off the rails there, but can you stick with me for one more song? I want to end on a better note."

The crowd roared, rushing back to the stage. A grand piano was wheeled out and a bench was placed for her to sit on. Before she could sit though, Benji returned, brandishing a roll of gauze and some tape.

"No point in getting blood on the keys," they said, bandaging her with the efficiency of someone well acquainted with a first aid kit.

"Don't get mushy on me, now."

They paused in placing the final piece of tape on her. "Angelica," they murmured, pushing the hair out of her eyes. "You are certifiable and I'm barely holding it together. Play the damn song so I can get someone with actual medical experience to tell me you're okay." They kissed her temple.

"I'm okay," she said, though she was suddenly feeling a bit mushy herself. "You're sure, you're okay?" She gestured at the slash on thier arm, hidden under a bandana.

"I'm fine for now and I'll be right off stage in case you aren't." They finished their patch job and went to stand just out of the crowd's view, watching her.

Angie didn't bother to hide her smile as she sat, placing her fingers on the keys. They really did get it. They knew the fans needed this, hell, she needed this.

She played the opening piano riff, slow and solemn. Quiet rippled through the crowd like a relieved sigh. Angie felt her shoulders drop as she gathered air into her lungs to sing.

"A star burns in my heart
The morning come again
Knowledge and spark
My burning denizen"

Warmth bloomed along her spine, burning and tender. With one hand, she ripped open the bodice of her shirt, exposing the inverted cross on her chest. She could play this one handed, she always did. She threw her head back, raising her arm. She barely felt the sharp sting of her wound.

"Oh Lightbringer
Deep beneath my feet
Oh Lightbringer
Fallen angel of my night
To thee I will never kneel
It is never your will"

The warmth traced the sigil on her back, the tattoos on her arms, the cross on her chest. She smiled at the sky and finished the hymn. Voices joined hers.

She glanced back to see the Sirens backing her vocals until they became a choir. Angie blew them a kiss, hoping they couldn't see how her fingers were shaking.

She turned the mike to the crowd and they joined in, their voices swelling until she and the Sirens fell silent. The park echoed with the final chorus.

"Walk with me Lightbringer,
All together,
Daughter, child, and son,
Walk with us,
Together as one"

As the chanting stopped and the echoes died, Angie stood, slowly. Black holes ate through the corners of her vision. "Take care of each other!" She told the crowd. Then she mouthed a thank you to her band and sauntered carefully off stage.

Benji hooked an arm around her the minute she was out of sight. "How bad is it?" They handed her a bottle of water.

She downed it in one long swallow, leaning against them. "I could use a nap."

They made a grumbly sound that managed to sound both concerned and like 'I told you so' without saying a word.

"Yeah, yeah." She handed the bottle back.

"Can you walk?"

"What? Ye—"

"I can feel you shaking."

Angie glowered at them. "I can walk. Slowly."

Benji nodded and the two of them headed for the medic tent.

The festival owner sidled up. "Is there anyway you can fini—"

"No," Benji snapped.

Angie chuckled. "Normally, I don't like people speaking for me but they're right."

He was going to say something more but Benji gestured. Cheryl appeared, bristling. It was all over after that.

"It really doesn't hurt that bad," she told the medic when the two of them reached the tent.

He shook his head. "I saw what happened. You were in shock. You're only feeling it now because the adrenaline is wearing off." He pointed at her shaking hands.

"Exactly," Benji said, from the chair next to her.

Angie shoved down the biting words on her tongue. She'd pushed it too far and she knew.

Well, at least I didn't kill anyone. Or get killed. And Benji's okay.

It seemed better not to remind anyone how much worse this could've been. Instead she got nosy about Benji's wound.

Apparently, they hadn't gotten their own flesh wound looked at after staunching it and helping Hanayu kick the rogue security guard into submission. The medic called backup and made them sit down.

"Hypocrite," she said, affectionately. Then hissed as the medic applied disinfectant to the slice across her forearm.

They squeezed her other hand.

She smiled at them. They smiled back.

Another man stepped into the tent, wearing the bright yellow medic polo shirt. Ah, backup had arrived.

Benji's hand went limp in hers.

CHAPTER 31

"*I was a man*
Desperate and damned
Full of pills and fans
Trying to make amends
With shaky hands

Fade to black
They brought you back
Let you go 72 hours ago

All Hail the Suicide King
Wind him up, make him sing
All Hail the Suicide King
He is the void
You cry for"
—"Suicide King" off of *Suicide King* by User-Friendly Omega

"Benny?"

Benji froze. Very few people called them by that name anymore and no one in that voice. They turned slowly, Angelica's hand falling from their numb fingers.

There he was. Benji's very own Suicide King.

Sly looked better than Benji had seen him, well ever. Older sure, but who wasn't these days? He stood there in all his ridiculously gorgeous glory: his broad shoulders, barrel chest, his cheeks no longer gaunt and his soul patch gone, replaced by a well-cultivated reddish beard. His hair was one color, his natural color, a red-brown Benji wasn't sure they'd ever seen, and fell in long waves around his face. "Sly," Benji breathed his name.

Sly grimaced, like he wished he hadn't said anything. Benji was frankly shocked he had. Sly hadn't spoken to them in over a decade. "Yeah."

Silence fell, muffling the sounds of the festival trying to get everyone to leave. Or maybe Benji's ears were ringing, they weren't quite sure.

"Hi, I'm Angie." She stuck her hand out to Sly. Benji marveled at how they had managed to forget she was there.

"Sly." He cleared his throat and shook her hand. "Sorry, this is awkward." He glanced at the other medic who was focused on Angelica's wound with the intensity of someone eavesdropping.

Angelica cocked her head. "Sylvan Alpha?"

Sly choked out a startled laugh at his stage name. "Wow, it's been a long time since anyone called me that."

Angelica shrugged. "Being a fangirl has its perks."

"Really." Sly raised his eyebrows at Benji, just like he would've all those years ago.

Benji shook off the surrealness of the moment. "What are you doing here?"

"I'm working the event," Sly said. "So, I think that's my question."

Angelica glanced at Benji, assessing their expression before speaking for both of them. "Putting on shows, getting stabbed, you know. Usual stuff," she said, like she was joking.

Benji felt like a raw nerve, like everything rubbed them the wrong way. "What, you're a doctor now?" They sneered at him.

There were flickers at the corners of their vision. Parking garages where they'd gather themselves for the inevitable visit to watch him recover from the latest "accident." Where they'd cry and scream and put their emotions away so he'd never know how much he wrecked them every time, how much hurting himself hurt Benji. The smell of the cigarettes they'd chain smoked, their hands shaking, burned in their nose.

Sly shifted uncomfortably. "Resident actually." He gathered himself, looking Benji in the eye for the first time. "I'm training to be a psychiatrist. But I have a med degree and this pays better."

"Admirable." Angelica flicking her gaze at Benji as if gauging their reaction.

Sly shrugged.

More awkward silence. Benji's brain screamed a thousand different things. They wanted to apologize, to rage, to scream, to run away, be anywhere but here. They hated him.

No, that wasn't right.

They were angry. They were thrown. They were looking at a Sly they didn't know: cleaned up, respectable, mentally healthy. It made them happy to see him better and it made them feel poisonous, like they had been the problem all along.

Angelica gazed at them then at Sly. "I can go if you want to talk—"

Sly and Benji talked over each other. "No—"

"Sure—"

Sly rubbed the back of his head with his signature rueful smile. The one that used to make everyone, Benji included, want to climb him to kiss it off. It did nothing but make them grit their teeth in frustration now. "You're being treated."

"We're done." Benji picked imaginary lint off their jeans.

Angelica rolled her eyes, irritation rippling around her. "You haven't even gotten yours looked at. Talk to each other, you dipshits." She looked at her medic. "Stop dawdling, I know you're listening in."

The other medic made a strangled sound and had her bandaged up so quickly, Benji's head spun.

Angelica stood and kissed Benji's cheek. "Apologize. I hear good things about it."

"Don't," Benji hissed at her.

She shrugged. "Your life, your shit, baby." Then she sauntered out, towing the other medic with her.

"Your girlfriend seems nice," Sly said, after she'd turned the corner. "Can you show me your wound?"

"She's not." Benji pulled aside the ruins of their sleeve. The fucking fanatic had slashed their bicep. Hanayu had bandaged it with a bandana. They were still pissed they hadn't gotten him back but Angelica had taken care of that. As much as it had terrified them to watch her go after him, she had been magnificent.

"Not your girlfriend or nice?" Sly carefully removed the bandana. It was stuck to Benji's skin and he had to douse it in alcohol to get it off.

Benji glared, gritting their teeth against the sting. They'd lost track of the conversation. Their stomach was one big knotted mass and they felt light-headed. Were they breathing? "You hate psychiatrists."

Sly blinked. "That was over a decade ago. Things change."

"They failed you. For years." Benji nodded at the long sleeves Sly wore under his polo.

Sly moved to cover his wrists and stopped halfway. "That experience will better allow me to help my patients." The words sounded rote.

"Spare me your admissions essay," Benji said, through their teeth, clenching their fists.

Sly's composure broke. Finally. "What do you want from me, Benny?" He snapped, glaring at them. "Do you even know?"

"Of course I do." Benji forced in a breath as they lied. They weren't sure if they wanted to apologize or relive all the pain they'd felt coping with Sly's mental health problems, give in to the sadistic impulse to make him know what he'd put them through. The thought of it felt good, in a sickening way. Vindictive and vindicated. The lights of the tent seemed fuzzy, haloed and diffuse.

Benji needed air.

They exhaled hard, forcing their fists to unclench. *Inhale. Exhale. Inhale...* This was not who they wanted to be. Benji wasn't blameless in all of this.

Sly inhaled sharply as he inspected their wound. "She wasn't kidding about the stabbing, was she? Shit, you were at the Angela—Oh that was... oh." He looked behind him like Angelica was still there.

"You don't have to treat me," Benji said, finding their compassion at last. They wouldn't want to take care of someone who'd hurt them the way they'd hurt Sly.

Inhale. Exhale.

Sly's nostrils flared and his jaw flexed though his touch was gentle he meticulously cleaned Benji's wound.

Benji waited for the explosion. *Inhale. Exhale.*

Sly shook his head. "You hurt me so much with that album."

Benji lost track of their breath. "Every time you killed yourself, you killed me too. Every time I had to pick you up, clean you up, keep you breathing, staunch the bleeding…" It was their turn to shake their head, realizing they sounded too much like a song. They closed their eyes, the world wobbling from too much adrenaline and not enough oxygen.

Inhale. Exhale. Start again. "I know. I'm sorry. I fucked up. I never expected it to get that big." Benji opened their eyes. "I loved you so much and it got toxic."

Sly looked away. "We hurt each other. We were young. We didn't know better."

Benji exhaled. Some of the knots in their stomach loosened. If this was the closest they got to forgiveness, they'd take it. They'd known Sly hadn't loved them the way they'd loved him. The sting was a cut reopened. Old and familiar, one they'd thought they'd come to terms with years ago.

Apparently, old wounds died hard.

"We weren't that young," they said, feeling like they were sticking their finger in the cut.

"Young enough that our brains weren't fully grown." Sly sighed. "Everyone does harm, there's no undoing it. All you can do is make amends and do better."

"Is that why you're still talking to me?"

"I guess so."

"You're the shrink, shouldn't you know?" Benji couldn't resist the jab.

"I'm still human, Benny," he said gently. "Do you really want to keep fighting about something that happened over a decade ago?"

Benji bit down on the acid words filling their mouth. They had rehearsed this so many times over the years, readying themself for all the things Sly could throw at them and this was… anticlimactic. But then, their friendship with him had always been dramatic. Maybe the fireworks they'd expected were more familiar than needed.

"I'm sorry," they said again. It was all they'd wanted to say, when you really got down to it.

Sly nodded and finished dressing thier wound in silence. When he was gone, Benji sat in the tent alone. Was this closure? They weren't sure but at least the dreaded encounter with Sly was over.

Maybe now they could move on.

CHAPTER 32

"Don't talk to me
Don't touch me
I'm a raw nerve
Biting harder than you deserve

My skin's peeled back
Slick and sliced
Muscle and fat on display
Look away look away

I'm sensitive like a trigger
Every sound is a twitch of my finger
(Run away run away)
Can't take this
(Run away run away)
Can't fake this
(Run away run away)

I hate you (hate you, hate you)
I hate me (hate me, hate me)

It's all too much
Stop this ride I'm gonna go off"
— "Raw Nerve (Run Away) by User-Friendly Omega off of
And Down We Go

Angie's insides felt unsteady, delicate as she loitered out of earshot of the tent. Benji was talking to the one that got away. The person they'd hurt and loved the most. Was it fucked up that she was jealous?

And yes, someone had just tried to hurt her in a much more physical way but somehow this felt like a more existential threat.

But that's love for you, isn't it?

And she did love Benji. The knowledge had crystallized in her when they'd try to warn her about the attacker. She just hadn't had time to process it and now it hit her like a wall of sound, drowning out her senses.

Don't just stand there! You were attacked, there could be more, Mama's voice cried in her head, snapping her out of her fugue. Glancing around the fairly deserted backstage area, she tracked all the crew members around her.

There was the medic who treated her, smoking with a roadie. Several members of the security team stood watching her and the tent. She sized them all up, watching the way they watched her.

"There are more if you want them." Cheryl stepped out from behind a stack of speakers. Angie hadn't seen her at all.

You're slipping, Angel, Mama murmured.

"Or I can call one of my contacts," Cheryl continued. "Get someone on our payroll."

Angie had long wanted to scroll through her manager's contact list. It sounded like quite the collection—some of which she didn't even keep on digital records.

"It's fine," Angie said.

"It's really not," Cheryl said. "We've had some close calls but that was by far the closest."

"I handled it."

"This time. When we tour—"

"I don't want to tour." The words snapped out of her.

Cheryl barely acknowledged her sharpness. "We don't have to discuss it tonight. After what you've been through—"

"No. I've felt like this for a while. I can't do this anymore—"

"Can't do what?"

Angie spun around. Her band stood behind her.

Forgetting all my lessons—

Shut up Mama!

Angie scrunched her face up, forced herself to unlock her jaw. She took a deep breath. "Yeah. Okay. So."

Burn it down. A different voice, a warm touch traced her spine until she straightened it. Her hesitancy fell away. "I don't want to tour anymore. I can't take another breakdown and I don't want to put anyone else through it."

Her band and Cheryl stared at her, absorbing her words.

"Are we breaking up?" Marsha asked.

Angie shook her head. "I still want to make music, maybe do the occasional shows—"

"Tours are our main source of income," Gemma cut in. "Royalties are shit and you know it. Especially split four ways. We're not getting the deals you are." Her gaze said what her words didn't: *you get paid more than all of us combined.*

"I know. I can talk to Cheryl about renegotiating the royalty rates, get you more of a cut of the merch—"

Cheryl grimaced but nodded.

"I like touring," Dani said.

Angie said, "If you want to tour with other people—"

Dani shook her head. "It's not about—"

"I thought we were a team!" Marsha cried, tears in her eyes.

"We are," Angie said. "But I've been doing this for a decade and I can't keep this up anymore. These are my songs, my trauma I pour out every night, my mental health—"

"So what, you get a pretty partner and you want to be healthy?" Marsha demanded.

"What's so wrong with that?"

"I thought you were going to let what you love kill you!" Angie's words from a particularly depressive moment in her breakdown period thrown back at her. She hadn't realized anyone was taking those to heart.

"Marsha!" Dani and Gemma cried in censorious unison.

"I want to live!" Angie snarled.

Cheryl put her hand on Angie's shoulder. "We want you to live too."

But Angie wasn't done. "I built this. I did. I got myself to LA despite everything. I survived on no money and no friends. I dragged myself to every bar and club and coffee shop and open mike for years. I went on dates with creepy old guys and grit my teeth and twisted them until they gave me a contract. I fought the paps, the critics, the protestors, the shit in my head. This is my fucking act, my fucking band and it ends when I say it does."

The band drew back, their expressions various flavors of betrayed. Angie felt like she'd punched herself in the stomach.

Cheryl clapped her hands, drawing all their eyes to her. "We've all had a rough night. Let's decompress and talk this over in the morning, okay? After a nice big brunch." She hustled the band back towards the tour bus.

Before she disappeared around the corner, Angie caught her arm. "I meant what I said about touring."

"Of course, you did." Cheryl smiled her placating smile.

Suddenly, Angie's future seemed to unspool before her:

tomorrow Cheryl would play mediator. Angie would find herself touring to make amends, trapped back into the cycle of her own making.

This is what happens when you let people in, Mama whispered.

Angie let Cheryl go, turning away without saying anything. She didn't have a ride out of here but if she changed out of her concert gear and walked far enough…

Benji stepped out of the medical tent. Their gaze, though a bit unfocused, found her immediately. If she started running now, she'd be lost in the dregs of the crowd before they could find her and—

She dug her heels into the dirt and stayed still.

Benji stopped in front of her. They looked as fucked up as she felt, which probably meant she looked worse. But they opened their arms and she fell into them.

"I heard you all fighting," they murmured into her ear. "Sounds like it went well."

"About as well as your reunion went, by the look on your face."

They pressed their face into her hair. "There was closure at least."

She squeezed them tighter, feeling the tremors running through them, the raggedness of their breath. Were they crying? Rage heated her face but she knew better than to act on it. This was Benji's battle. "I hear good things about closure."

"I'll give you a full review once my anxiety calms the fuck down." They sighed. "Did you tell them? About the touring?"

"Thus the fighting. To be continued tomorrow."

"Fun."

"So fun. Being an emotionally mature adult sucks."

"And we're doing great at it." Benji groaned.

"So great. But hey!" She leaned back and bopped them on the nose. "We said our piece and no one died, so that's a win."

Benji smiled half-heartedly, swiping thier eyes. "I could stand to see that asshole who attacked you get closer to dead though. When he attacked you—When you went after him—" They shook their head and stroked her cheek. "You were amazing but I thought you'd do more damage."

"Are you mad I didn't?"

They shook their head again. "Just surprised."

She shrugged. "He was a child. If he's hit twenty *I'll* be surprised. I was so lost at that age. I don't know what they told him to get him ready to die for such shit but I'd like to think now he has a chance to live. Not," she added, "that I was planning to kill him."

"Ready to die?" Benji blew out a breath. "That's *terrifying*."

She patted their arm. "It's over. For now."

Cheryl rounded the corner. "Good, you're still here. We have to talk."

Benji's arms tightened around Angie. "Can this wait?"

"No," Cheryl said. "It's one of those nights."

CHAPTER 33

Angie gave Benji a squeeze. "I got this."

They sighed. "I know you do." They kissed the top of her head. "I'll go make sure Mom didn't knock down any more security guards."

"I like their mom," Cheryl said. "She doesn't fuck around."

"It runs in the family," Angie said, watching Benji's retreating back with a smile. When they were out of sight, she turned to Cheryl. "How bad is it?"

Cheryl turned so her back was to the guards and said quietly, "Your mom's release date got moved up."

"On a Saturday night?" Angie asked, her lips numb, and her brain whirling. The guards around them shifted around, fidgeting and frowning.

"Yesterday, right before close of business, I didn't want to distract you."

"And now is better because…?"

"I figured you weren't going to sleep anyway."

"Eh, there was a chance." Maybe. If Benji really tired her out with some life-affirming sex. "When's the new date?"

"Monday."

"Fuck. Any reason why?"

"Bureaucratic jargon. There's more though."

Angie closed her eyes and exhaled hard. "Spit it out."

"You got an encrypted text." Angie opened her eyes to see Cheryl holding up Angie's phone. She'd forgotten she'd left it with her for safekeeping. Given it had been glued to Angie's hand this time last year, that felt like progress. Then Cheryl's words hit.

Only one person sent her encrypted texts.

Angie took her phone back and opened the text.

It was a huge data file of information, compressed so it could fit on her phone, along with a note from the hacker she'd contacted:

NOSEYNETSCRAPER

TL;DR: They're conservative funded, usual suspects. Sorry I didn't get through this fast enough to warn you about the attack tonight but it was their crown jewel plan, buried pretty deep. Glad you handled it. They're monitoring your mom though, if that's anything to you.

Angie swore and showed it to Cheryl, who grimaced. "If this was obtained any way legally we could show this to a judge and have her kept in for her own safety."

"And if they have people in there?" Angie felt trapped. She'd been writing letters to Mama but she couldn't even send them. Was Angie ready to face her? To be responsible for her well-being? Could she abandon her own mother?

Pull yourself together, Mama sneered from her memory, her skin ghastly green in the lights of the jail visitation room.

Angie's fists clenched. Heat prickled behind her eyes. That

memory was her second worst memory of Mama. The jail let Angie see her in a private room, one that turned out to have a two-way mirror.

Her hands had shaken and she'd felt like she was gonna throw up or cry or worse. Her hands shook now, her stomach twisting to reclaim that feeling as the memory swallowed her:

"You don't have to go in." The lawyer who'd gotten her the visitation looks surprised at his own words.

"Thank you." Angie gives him a brave smile until his expression eases. She can't give him any reason to call this off. She hasn't seen Mama in days, they won't post her bail. Angie hasn't got the money to get her out even if they did. This is her chance. "But I gotta see my Mama."

"Of course." He opens the door.

She walks in and the sight of Mama in chains and orange and not a lick of make-up is like a slap in the face. She's never seen Mama out of the house without being put together. Hell, Mama wouldn't let her out of the house since she was thirteen without at least some gloss on.

Mama turns to look at her, her eyes flicking to the lawyer behind Angie. Her lip curls then she smiles.

Angie sits at the table. "You okay, Mama?"

"Be careful with that one," she murmurs, tilting her head at the lawyer.

"It's fine," Angie says, like she can't guess exactly why they'd let this happen. Like she can't figure the lawyer's slim protection at best.

Mama's expression hardens, her smile going brittle and fake. It's probably the expression she's worn since they took her in. Her party smile, her being seen with Daddy smile.

The thought of Daddy socks Angie in the throat and she chokes. The inside of her head is red and sticky and sick-smelling. Breathing is suddenly hard, her vision getting dark at the edges.

"Angelica Marie Alice you snap out of it this instance," hisses Mama. "Don't you do this to me."

Angie blinks back to reality. Mama's sweating, her knuckles white.

Angie sees the lawyer out of the corner of her eye, panting hard and looking bewildered. He pulls himself together fast, pretending nothing happened.

"What happened, Mama?" Angie asks. Her hands clasp and unclasp, sticking to each other almost like—almost like—

"Pull yourself together," Mama snaps. "You are so like your father."

Angie's heard that before, a thousand different ways depending on the speaker's feelings about Daddy, but never said with the amount of disgust and venom Mama sinks into them.

"What?" Angie's mind scrambles, falling though she doesn't move at all. Last week in the Before Mama said the same words like it was such a lovely thing, like she was so lucky to have the two of them.

"With your big feelings, twisting the rest of us around your fingers like puppets," Mama snarls.

Angie leans away. Mama's got a temper, she can be cruel but she's never like this. Not to Angie.

Then again, nothing's like it was Before. "I-I don't understand."

"You're going to take his side, aren't you? This one last time." Mama sobs a laugh. "Of course you are. You were always more an Alice than a Warner."

"But-but you didn't do it." She can't have done it. If she did it then Angie's an orphan. She'll have to live with the uncle Mama never let her be alone with—Mama wouldn't do that to her—to Daddy. No matter how much they fought and no matter how many times he came home late and stank like rose perfume.

She gives Angie a look that makes her feel thicker than a brick and half as big. "Don't be naive. I did what I had to do." She says it quiet, without moving her lips.

"Why?" Angie barely has the air to breathe the question.

"Because Little Angel." Mama softens, whispering her baby name like Angie's still a child. So low, Angie doubts the lawyer can even hear. "He was leaving me. He was leaving us. And he didn't get to do that."

Angie can't breathe. Everything's red and sticky and tastes copper. In her memory, Mama stands in the kitchen, Daddy at her feet, washing a knife in the sink.

She turns to Angie and says, Angel, you're not supposed to be home yet.

Angie's fear is too big. It swallows everything and the cops are there and the paramedics and Angie's in the ambulance with the body cuz they'd only brought one and there had been a pulse and—

A spike of pain lances her hand. Mama's pinching the back of Angie's hand with her nails. Angie gasps, surfacing.

"Don't make me go back there," Mama rasps. Tears run down her face but her expression is wooden. She lets go, pulling back like she can't stand to touch Angie. It hurts more than the pinch. "You're an Alice through and through. I pity the men you'll snare."

"Get her out of here."

A guard hauls her up but Mama's eyes never leave Angie's.

"Miss, are you okay?"

Angie nods but it's a lie. She looks into the mirror in front of her. She'd done exactly what she'd been trying not to do and no doubt someone caught it on tape. She gives the mirror the most broken look she can manage, letting her mask fall. They might use her but she won't let them feel okay about it, won't let them lie to themselves about it.

"Angie?" Benji stood in front of her. Cheryl is a few paces back with Hanayu and the guards are even farther back, watching wide-eyed.

"I'm afraid," Angie whispered. "Mama's getting out and they might hurt her. She's going to be out. In the world. With me. I'm afraid of it all."

Benji traced their fingers down her sleeves, a barely felt touch. Their hands hovered over hers. After a moment, she raised hers to meet them. The clasp of their fingers against hers was grounding, pushing back the tide of memories and old pain.

"We'll figure this out," they promised. "But first, let's go home."

CHAPTER 34

By the time Benji shooed away Angelica's manager and their own mother, drove Angelica back home, and helped her out of her concert costume, they were exhausted. Well, their body was, their brain was wired. They lay in bed next to her, mind whirling. First the stabbing, then Sly, then this. What a night.

She rolled over and poked them. "You're still awake."

"Am I keeping you up?"

"No more than freaking out about my Mama and the men's rights group who hates me enough to possibly go after her."

"Talking might help." It would certainly distract them from

reliving what an asshole they'd been to Sly. Hopefully, despite that, the two of them both had closure now or whatever.

"You learn that in therapy or something?" She chuckled then launched into everything she knew about the situation, which was deeply not funny. When she was done, Benji spent thirty minutes reading the documents her investigator dug up. They'd been very thorough and the results were not likely to help anyone sleep well. They read snippets to her anyway because she wanted to know and hadn't gotten a chance to read any of it.

She groaned when they were done. "I asked em to fuck up the Bitch Hunt's stuff wherever e could but e warned me those assholes had a tech team that would probably get things running within a few days."

Benji noted the pronouns and wondered who this mysterious badass was. "Is it worth leaking any of this, maybe after we get your mom somewhere safe?" Benji rubbed their eyes under their glasses.

"And inspire more people to join them?" Angelica covered her eyes. "I haven't checked socials yet but I'm betting there are people cheering them on and wishing that kid finished the job."

"Social media isn't everyone." Benji pushed back her despair so it didn't cloud what brain capacity they had left.

"I *know*, but given these fuckers found each other on socials, forgive me for feeling personally attacked."

Benji wrapped their good arm around her shoulders and dragged her to them. "I get it. I do."

She sighed into their chest. "I know. I just... I feel helpless."

They rubbed her back. The despair in her voice, in the curled hunch of her shoulders made them feel feral, violence simmering in their chest. They channeled the spite towards finding a solution. "You know what stood out to me in all that shit your friend dug up?"

"Not a friend. E owed me a favor."

"Not the point."

"What then?"

"Those fascist fundies are scared. Shitting themselves scared."

"Of me?" They could feel her grin through their shirt.

"You, people like me, people with different gods, the list goes on. Hell, they barely trust each other."

"Yeah, so?"

"So, they've got a major crack in their armor. We've just got to figure out how to tear it wide open." Then Benji would revel in watching them run around like chickens with their heads cut off.

She looked up at them and grinned. "You're hot when you're devious."

"You just like it when I'm using my powers for you and not against you."

She shrugged. "It was hot then too." Before they could remark on that, she yawned. "Plotting makes my brain tired."

"Sleep then," they said.

She snuggled into their side. "You too."

Benji turned out the light. They lay in the dark as Angelica fell into a restless sleep curled into their side. It wasn't the most comfortable position but it was comforting to feel her safe beside them.

They loved her. There was no escaping, no explaining away the warmth in their chest as they held her, the knowledge that they'd happily burn down the world of her enemies.

They'd known they were lost when she'd screamed their name and leapt after the attacker. She'd seemed suspended in midair, her hair and the panels of her deconstructed skirt streaming behind her like a cape. She'd landed like a superhero and stalked after him like a predator. Hell, if she had actually done serious damage to that brainwashed dick they'd be at the jail posting bail. Which might be the far side of devotion but they'd worry about that later.

They turned and buried their nose in her hair, breathing in her spicy-sweet smell. For now, they'd do their best to protect her and figure out how to take a crowbar to the fractures in the Bitch Hunt. Those close-minded fanatics wouldn't know what hit them.

Smiling, Benji fell asleep.

In the morning, Benji had a half-formed idea. It wasn't pretty and annoyingly, it required some help. "I need to call a council of war," they told Angelica when she woke up.

She squinted at them. "Something tells me I'm not going to like this."

"You can invite whoever you like," they said. "But if we're going to move this fast we'll need extra hands."

She grumbled but grabbed her phone.

A few hours later, a motley crew of conspirators gathered around the dining room table. Cheryl and the Sirens sat next to Angelica. From Benji's understanding, there was a pin put in the whole touring discussion. Uneasy energy hovered in that corner.

Across from them, sat Rohan and Cazzi. Benji had been worried there'd be more animosity there but the two women exchanged awkward greetings and mostly ignored each other. Well, Angelica ignored Cazzi. Rohan's fiancé subjected her to the same analytical inspection she used on everyone. Luckily, she kept her assessment to herself, for now.

Next to Benji, on Angelica's other side, sat Hanayu and Kenji. Hanayu wore boots that said 'for Nazi kicking' on the side and showed them off by propping her crossed ankles on the table. Kenji sketched her shoes as the meeting got going.

Finally, on screen Leo and Martin tactically ignored each other. Well, mostly. Martin had tried to greet Rohan, got a polite yet lukewarm response, asked about Rick which elicited an awkward pause since Rick and Benji weren't on speaking terms, and finally got the message to shut up for a while. Leo texted Benji to let them know he'd muted the other man. It was a more mature response than Benji had hoped for when Angelica said Martin was invited.

After everyone arrived and settled in, Benji clapped their hands, commanding attention. "Thank you all for coming," they said, standing. "We're on a time crunch so let's get into it. Tomorrow morning, Angelica's mom is getting released from prison about a hundred and forty miles from here in Chowchilla. This timeline was suddenly moved up and has special interest from the dicks that attacked her last night, a misogynist asshole group called Bitch Hunt."

Cazzi raised her hand. Benji bit back a sigh as she spoke without waiting to be called on. "Is the group's focus just Angela or do they have a broader statement of purpose?"

"Statement of purpose?" Marsha said. "They're insecure entitled incels not a non-profit."

Benji cleared their throat. "They do, in fact, have an 'about' page."

As if she'd been waiting, Angelica rose, holding her tablet, and read in a saccharine baby voice, "For too long, men have been subjected to witch hunts by conniving women looking to victimize males through false allegations, 'diversity' initiatives, wrong religions, and other lies. Bitch Hunt will take back the God-given place of biological men as the head of households, industry, and churches by taking down the false idols who spread impure thoughts and dangerous ideology." She poked a finger into her cheek and pouted. "Uh-oh, I'm a bad role model."

The Sirens, Hanayu, and Martin laughed. Everyone else was trying to hold onto a somewhat business-like demeanor.

Benji sighed. "Thank you. Was the voice really necessary?"

"Too scary?" She batted her eyelashes at them.

"It took away from the severity of the message, yes," Benji said, smothering a laugh.

"Eh, let the girl have fun," Hanayu said. "You wouldn't even let her do grievous bodily harm last night."

Kenji shook his head and tsked.

"*I* didn't do anything," Benji said. "She makes her own decisions."

Angelica nodded like a bobble head, her smile as doll-like as it was in the music video for "PhenoBarbie Doll." "It's true! I think my own impure thoughts all by myself!"

Benji covered their face with a hand, partially out of frustration and partially so no one would notice how hard they were laughing. If Angelica knew she was getting to them she'd derail the whole meeting just to make them laugh more.

Through their fingers they saw Cazzi clasp her hands on the table. "Angelica," she said, gently. "Do you want to keep deflecting or do you want to get through this so you can have a plan in place and less anxiety?"

Benji dropped their hand, bracing themself as Angelica said, "Good Lucy, you're annoying."

Benji privately agreed with her but was about to say something placating when Cazzi replied, "Doubly so when I'm right." She smiled.

Angelica huffed. "Therapy witch."

"Not a th—" Cazzi started.

Angelica ignored her, pushing back into her chair, and crossing her arms. "Yeah, okay. Let's do this. I appreciate everyone dropping their shit and being here."

Benji brushed her shoulder with their knuckles. "We have some inside intel on this group and, while they've got some backers with deep pockets, they're on the verge of serious in-fighting. One faction is obsessed with Angelica and the other thinks there are other targets they should be focusing on."

"We've already warned the people on their list," Angelica put in.

Benji nodded. The list was extensive and surprising in who the Bitch Hunt thought was "threatening." Reaching out took Angelica and her people all morning while Benji refined their plan and coordinated the meeting.

"The question is," Benji continued. "How do we leverage these cracks and incapacitate the organization while getting Susan Alice to a safe place while we do it?"

"Awkward question," Leo said. Benji braced themself again. "Your mom murdered your dad, right? So, do we need to keep you two separated or what?"

Angelica pressed her lips together. "Good question," she gritted out. "I don't want to see her and I don't know if she'll come with us if I'm there, but it's our best bet."

The room absorbed this.

Martin spoke first. With a crisp nod, he said, "Understandable. You need someone who she will listen to." He tapped something on his phone. "I'm coming up. Moms love me and you need a car they won't expect. I'll text the details."

"Well—" Benji started.

"Wear your biggest crucifix," Angelica said. "Mama desperately wanted to be a good Christian girl, you know, before prison."

"Of course," Martin said. "Gotta go, my personal trainer's here. My assistant will text you the details."

"You're the best." Angelica blew him a kiss as his screen disappeared.

"Moms love me too, for the record," Rohan said.

"Yes, we do, sweetie." Hanayu smiled fondly at him.

"I thought this was top secret," Leo grumbled. "What if his personal trainer or assistant or whatever leaks the plan?"

I thought you muted him, Benji thought.

Angelica shook her head. "Martin's NDAs and lawyers are legendary. His people know the drill."

"I bet," Leo muttered.

"That's the pick-up plan taken care of," Benji said. "Where are we taking her?"

Rohan and Cazzi exchanged one of those looks long-term couples use to talk without words. "We just bought a place not too far from there in Santa Cruz," Rohan said.

"I can come along," Cazzi said. "If you think you need a mediator. I've done work with women in prison."

Angelica groaned and dropped her head back.

Benji raised an eyebrow at her. It wasn't a bad idea as long as she and Cazzi didn't sharpen their claws on each other.

Still upside down, Angelica glared at them. She straightened with a huff. "Fine. Yeah, you can come."

"The world's most awkward road trip," Dani muttered to Gemma, who snorted.

"As for your Bitch Hunt men," Cazzi said. "You're thinking of them as a group. These are individuals who all joined for their own reasons."

Angelica's eyes sparked. "We need to carve them off one by one."

Cazzi made a non-committal motion with her hand. "You need to find shared humanity."

Something clicked in Benji's head. "We need to find common ground."

"With those assholes?" Hanayu said, outraged.

Benji held up a hand. "Just enough to sow doubt."

"Doubt," Angelica repeated, tapping her lip thoughtfully.

"But we can't come at this directly," Rohan said. "They

won't listen to anything you say if they think you're trying to persuade them. We need to slip it in, like how we used to undermine haters by making them laugh." He nodded at Leo.

"Laughter is a pop star's and a drag queen's biggest weapon," Leo agreed. "That and catchy hooks."

"I'm not pandering," Angelica said.

"You couldn't pander if your life depended on it," Cheryl said.

"Exactly," Angelica replied.

"Maybe," Rohan said, thoughtfully. "You just need to convert them to *your* cult."

That prompted an explosion Benji didn't expect. Angelica yelled, "For the hundredth time, Ro I don't have a cult!" While her band yelled various iterations of "We are not!"

Cheryl looked up at the ceiling with a sigh.

Rohan held up his hands in surrender and repeated, "Metaphor, it was a metaphor...." until finally the outburst died down. "What I meant is you're the most persuasive person I know."

"Face-to-face," Angelica said. "I'm not doing a fucking basement tour to beg these little shits to stop being afraid of losing their privilege and not attack the rest of us."

"Just curse them," Gemma said.

"A curse for compassion," Dani said.

Angelica went still. "I curse you with compassion, with empathy, with all the things you're scared to feel." She turned to high five Dani and Gemma. "Hell yes."

Cazzi grinned.

Benji smiled too. "And we have *so* much information on these people."

Angelica turned excited eyes on them. "We can personalize them."

"No names," Cazzi put in. "Names will make them feel attacked, and be attacked when your fans go after them.

Uncertainty will allow them to attribute more to the curse. Like how fake psychics will use very general information to fish for specifics they can drill down on."

"Give it a hook," Leo said. "Make it a series and make a jingle that people can sing so they're amplifying the energy and the effect."

"This is diabolical," Hanayu said, wiping an imaginary tear from her eye. "Warms a mother's heart."

Kenji chuckled. "We could turn it into merch too. Patches and stickers, small things."

"I'll make a sigil," Cazzi said, running a hand along one of the lines of sigils tattooed on each of her arms.

"Would it help to share across our accounts or duet the videos?" Rohan asked. "Like, especially as men?"

The women around the table and Benji nodded.

"Duh," Leo said.

After that, the meeting focused on logistics, winding down. Then Cheryl stood, nodding to Angelica and her band. They all retreated to the basement, presumably to hash things out.

Benji did their best to shut out the anxiety from their brain. They couldn't help whatever was going on down there.

The meeting drifted apart. Leo logged out to get to a gig at Hot Dog Marg's. Benji's parents headed out with hugs and a reminder that if Angelica's mom needed anything, both of them had connections to help her transition back into society. Rohan and Cazzi seconded the sentiment.

At the door, Benji hugged thier parents and whispered, "I saw Sly last night."

Hanayu jerked back. "Where? What happened?"

Kenji squeezed Benji's bicep in wordless support, his eyes sympathetic.

"At the medic's tent. He bandaged me up." Benji felt raw all over again talking about it.

"And?" Hanayu prodded.

"We talked some things out. It was... I don't know. Good, maybe. I'm still processing." They shook thier head.

"Oh Benny-chan." Hanayu hugged them again. "I'm glad you two finally talked."

Kenji patted thier back. "These things are always messier and more mundane than they look on TV. Shikata ga nai."

Benji wasn't sure they agreed that it couldn't be helped but they appreciated thier parents' support. Also that Kenji dragged Hanayu away before she could start interrogating them for every detail of the conversation.

After they left, Cazzi handed Benji a piece of paper with a phone number. "Mine for Angelica—and you." She smiled. "I know you and I don't especially get along but I'm always happy to chat. And if you need tips for talking to Patrick..." She tapped the paper.

It took Benji a second to remember she called Rick by his legal name not his stage name. Cazzi and Rick were old friends —and old, not quite, flames. It had been a whole thing. But they'd sorted it out, which probably meant there was hope for him and Benji.

One crisis at a time, they told themself. They'd figure out if that bridge was too burnt to cross again another day. But they nodded and took the paper, tucking it carefully into their pocket.

"Thank you for helping out tomorrow," they said.

Cazzi shrugged. "I have my reasons."

Rohan put an arm around her and kissed the top of her head. "After this though, we have to talk about wedding stuff. Maybe next week?"

Benji squinted at the pair of them. "I thought I made it clear I was not involved in planning at all. Just tell me the date and I'll be there." If they got involved, they would take over.

Rohan waved this away. "It's nothing like that. We just wanted to know if you wanted to be part of my groom's party too. Leo and Rick are my joint best men and well, you're one of my best friends but I figured you didn't want to deal with the bachelor party planning. Also Leo would kill me if I let anyone else plan it."

"Oh." Benji blinked, more touched than they expected. "Yeah, of course."

"Great!" Rohan let Cazzi go to hug Benji.

Benji grinned. "Are you prepared for how raunchy your party is gonna be with Leo planning it?"

Rohan laughed. "Not even remotely."

own in the basement, Angie and her band sat in the circle of sofas and chairs they'd dragged together to lounge in during practice breaks. Cheryl sat on the arm of Angie's armchair, face placid and spine rigid.

"I don't want to break-up," Angie said. "Just to be clear."

"We got that," Dani said. "We talked a lot last night."

Angie braced herself, ready to take whatever they said. The Sirens had the right to walk away if they wanted. She wouldn't do anything to stop them.

"We want to be our own band," Gemma said.

Angie blinked but kept her shock in check. She hadn't actually expected them to straight up leave.

"We like playing together," Dani said. "We like playing with you too but if that's not an option—"

"I still want to play occasional shows," Angie blurted. "If you'd be willing to come back for that," she continued, catching herself.

The Sirens shared a glance and a shrug. "We'll talk about it," Gemma said finally. "But probably."

"We want you to help us launch our band," Marsha said, arms crossed. Out of the three of them, she was clearly taking this the hardest. Angie wasn't shocked. Marsha was younger and handled change badly. She had a minor meltdown any time her dad even hinted at changing their holiday plans.

"What kind of band—" Cheryl started.

"Done. I'll help however you need."

Cheryl glared down at Angie.

Angie shrugged back at her. It was the least she could do.

Dani and Gemma smiled at her. Marsha's glare softened.

"We're not sure exactly what we'll be yet but we're noodling on some ideas," Dani said.

"Something different enough," Gemma said. "Brand differentiation and all."

"Also, none of us are Satanists," Marsha said, with another shrug.

"Fair enough." Angie laughed. "So… we're good?"

The band nodded.

"Thank Lucy, though, I'll miss you." Her voice caught on the words but she wrapped her emotions under her skin. "But I'm so happy for y'all. You're already a great band and I bet now that you're doing your own thing, you'll be amazing."

"We'll miss you too." Dani stood and gestured for Angie to come closer.

Standing, Angie found herself caught in a bone-crushing hug.

"Don't be a stranger, okay? Just cuz we're not working together doesn't mean we can't be friends," Dani said.

Friends. Tears sprang to her eyes, unbidden.

"I'd like that," she said, her voice hoarse.

"Shit, you're making me cry!" Marsha yelled, slamming into them.

"This is so much better than the last time we did this." Gemma threw her arms around the three of them.

Only their manager stayed out of the fray, sitting fully on the armchair now, watching them and shaking her head.

"Cheryl?" Angie asked. "Do you want to join this mess?"

Cheryl laughed. "Yeah, okay." She wrapped her arms lightly over the knot of women.

Happiness and hope despite everything bubbled up in Angie, making tears slip down her cheeks. She let the feeling expand out, cradling them all.

CHAPTER 35

Dear baby Angie,

I wish we had learned how to make friends, to trust them, to keep them. I feel like I'm only learning now and only because the people around me refused to give up. I know it's hard to feel, let alone be, vulnerable. I'm still figuring it out but I think it might be worth it.

Hang in there, little one.

The next day, Angie resurrected herself at a hellish hour. It was earlier than she'd needed to get up but she had to do something before she faced Mama.

Kissing Benji, she told them to sleep a bit longer and went to sit in an armchair in the basement.

Digging through her inbox, she found the email from the Office of Victim and Survivor Rights and Services. The email itself was nondescript, serviceable, with brisk compassion. It was the attachment that filled her with dread.

An apology letter from Mama. Supposedly, they'd reviewed

it and wouldn't send it to her if it was "inappropriate" but what did that even mean?

Her finger hovered over the attachment, shaking.

What if it was as bad as she feared?

But...

What if it was better? What if it was everything she hoped for?

Then again, what did she even hope for? She knew her mother had done it. Nothing would undo the past. She wasn't sure she'd want that even if it was an option.

"Enough dithering," she muttered, pressing the button before she could talk herself out of it. She had to know what she was walking into.

Angel—

I have no magic words to fix this. I said some terrible things and what I did was worse. When I killed him, I took both of us from you. I can't imagine what hell I left you in. I have no faith in either side of our family—having awful families was something me and your Daddy bonded over when we first met. I can see now why you felt like the Devil was your only option. I can see, though I can't approve. Not sure if I have the right to approve though.

Anyway, Angel, I've been watching your career. I always knew you were talented. You've put to use the things you inherited him to a scale that I think he'd be proud of—

Angie stuffed her fist in her mouth, scraping her knuckle against her teeth as she sobbed. Somehow the veiled criticism was more comforting than the bland written-for-the-censors first paragraph. Not everything had changed in the last fourteen years. Swiping tears out of her eyes and forcing a breath in, she read on.

You're a big deal now. I never expected my little Angel to be famous. I don't know if you'll read this—they tell me you may never—but I hope, maybe, you won't forget me.

Was this a ploy for sympathy? A prelude to asking for money? Over the years of being famous, Angie had had plenty of "family" come out of the woodwork looking for "help." People who'd abandoned her or abused her when she'd been passed around from so-called guardian to so-called guardian after Mama lost custody. Foolish of them. She'd been feral and cruel then, happily shredding them for asking. She was better about helping now, but like so many of her colleagues in fame, guarded and cautious about possible leeches.

Though I don't know if you'll ever forgive me, or if we'll ever speak again, let alone have a relationship, you'll always be my little miracle. I love you.
   Mama

Angie curled up and cried for probably too long before dragging herself back upstairs. Benji was on the phone, pacing the living room when she ascended. They looked at her face and held out an arm. She crashed into their chest.

Pulling the phone away from their mouth, they said, "Emergency, sorry."

From the phone, she could hear sobbing. Relatable. Her brain slowly emerged from the trauma soaked fog she'd been in for most of the morning. The sun hadn't even risen yet, which meant this really couldn't be good.

But still, Benji took a moment to press a kiss to her hair and hold her, in between saying, "Leo, Leo, slow down. Is anyone hurt?"

Angie shot them a questioning glance.

"Car accident," they mouthed. Then into the phone, "No

one else involved? Okay, are *you* hurt?" They squeezed their eyes shut. "Please tell me you called 911 before you called me."

"I can't call them! They'll test my blood alcohol," Leo yelled so loud Angie could hear it through the phone.

"Shit," Benji groaned. "Okay, I'm going to text you a number. Call it the minute you get it and turn on tracking on your phone. They'll take care of you. I will call you in an hour. Answer, okay?"

Leo mumbled something that seemed to satisfy Benji.

"Good. I'm calling Rick. He'll meet you there."

Leo said something snarky sounding.

"Yes, he will because unlike you, apparently, he cares about your ass." Benji hung up and texted a number from memory. Then they sighed, shoulders dropping.

"Is Leo okay?" Angie asked.

"Crashed into the back wall of Hot Dog Marg's trying to back out of his spot without putting his car in reverse. Probably has a concussion, definitely has a broken nose from the airbag. I don't even want to know what his BAC is." They pressed a knuckle into their forehead.

"You got him a private ambulance service?" Angie guessed. She'd called her fair share of numbers like that, for band members, strangers, and at least one country star. She never rode in the back with them, she freaked out just looking at an open ambulance, but at least she called.

"Yeah, we'll try to keep it out of the media. He better fucking take help this time." They glanced down at their phone as a notification popped up.

LEO IS SHARING HIS LOCATION WITH YOU.

They grimaced. "I have to call Rick now. We're on the outs."

"More of that ridiculous love triangle fallout?"

They nodded. "Long, not especially flattering story." As they dialed, Angie caught a glimpse of the time and swore.

She ran upstairs, threw on the cleanest, least witchy or Satanic clothes she could find, did a whirlwind version of her getting ready routine and ran downstairs again just as there was a knock on the door.

Benji got it, checking the peephole first as they always did. When they opened it, Cazzi stood on the porch, holding an honest-to-Lucy basket.

She held it up. "Rohan got nervous and baked."

"Thank Baphomet." Angie grabbed the basket. There was a selection of muffins and what looked like her favorite coffee cake. Damn, that man was terminally nice. Not that she could possibly eat with all the knots in her stomach.

"Call your damn ex," Benji told Cazzi. "He's ignoring my calls."

Cazzi frowned. "Which one?"

"Rick!"

Cazzi sighed. "Not my ex. Why am I calling him at the asscrack of dawn?"

"Leo's on the way to the hospital. He needs a friend." Benji showed her the tracker and gave her the address Leo was headed to.

"On it." Cazzi whipped out her phone immediately.

Angie elbowed Benji. "Go get dressed, Martin's gonna—"

A black electric SUV, windows tinted within an inch of legality pulled up in the driveway. The back window rolled down halfway. Martin leaned out and made a hurrying gesture. As requested, he was wearing a cross you could probably see from space. The morning light hitting the diamonds and gold on it was in danger of blinding her.

Benji swore and ran upstairs. Angie wasn't worried. She'd watched them agonize, laying out the perfect, "meeting your girlfriend's convicted murderer mom" outfit last night. She ambled over and offered Martin a muffin as Cazzi explained the Leo thing behind her.

"What's the calorie count?" Martin asked, eyeing them suspiciously.

"Who knows?" Angie held the basket up so he could see them. "Rohan baked them."

"I've got to try this." Martin rolled the window down and grabbed two. He handed one to his driver and took a big, savoring bite out of his. "Mmm pistachio. He really has gotten better since we were in the band."

"His Nānī made him practice so much for that celebrity cooking show," Angie said. "He fed half the neighborhood. The other half was on keto." She laughed.

"No, Leo will be fine." Cazzi paced by, grabbing a muffin from the basket. She made a circuit of the lawn. "Probably, I mean, I'm not a doctor."

Martin stiffened. "What—is Leo okay?"

Angie patted his hand. "He's probably fine. Don't go rushing down there. You're here for me, remember? Also, he'd definitely blow a gasket."

Martin's hand was a fist under her fingers. "Did someone hurt him?"

"Only if you define substance abuse and a brick wall as people." Angie squeezed his hand. "Hey."

He looked at her. There was a shit ton of torment in his eyes.

She gave him a soft smile until the torment dialed down to acceptable levels of emoness. "You really love him, huh?"

He shrugged. "I'm not sure I deserve to, after what I've done."

What had he done? Angie was *dying* to know. Leo didn't seem afraid or in any way cowed by Martin, but who knew? What she did know was the way his gaze lingered on Martin and despite whatever happened, Leo showed up when Martin invited him.

She tsked. "Where's that ego I know and tolerate? Who gets to decide what you deserve?"

He shook his head. "You don't get it."

"Probably not. In payment for helping me today, I will listen to you pour out whatever sad history you two have. We can devise a plan."

"For what?"

"Making amends and maybe—" She waggled her eyebrows. "More."

He groaned. "I know you finally hooked yourself that cute bit of ass you've been obsessed with—"

"Thank you."

"Which I totally called, by the way—"

Angie rolled her eyes.

"—But that doesn't make you a relationship expert."

Angie rolled her eyes again, harder. "Just think about it. I'm on the inside now. I can get the scoop from all the other boys in the band *and* Benji's deliciously devious mind."

"What about my mind?" Benji asked, striding up. They checked their phone. "Don't we have to leave?"

"Yep," Angie said, opening Martin's door. "Move over." She hip checked him.

"No way." Martin pushed her back and got out. "I'm not sharing a back seat with *a couple.*"

"You act like it's contagious," Benji mutters.

"You wish you could catch this shit!" Angie called after him as Martin rounded the car to the front seat. He ignored her. Laughing, she got in the car, Benji at her heels.

Putting her phone away, Cazzi climbed into the very back.

"What?" Angie asked, "Are you also afraid we're contagious?"

"If you keep being annoying I'm taking the basket back,"

Cazzi warned. She pulled a book out of her tote and opened it pointedly between them.

Angie flopped back into her seat, looking at Benji. "This is a two-plus-hour trip and I'm expected not to sow chaos?"

"What do you usually do on tour?" They asked, checking on Leo's location.

Cazzi popped her head back over the seat. "Patrick's on his way, by the way."

Benji thanked her and returned their attention to Angie.

She thought about their question. "Read, write songs, nap, fight people on social media, the usual."

"How about we start with breakfast?" Benji held up the basket.

Angie frowned, considering if eating would make her feel sick as Martin's driver backed up smoothly into the street.

"Food can be grounding," Cazzi chimed in.

"I thought you were reading," Angie shot back.

Unperturbed, Cazzi said, "I asked him to make some plain popover things if your stomach isn't doing well. I know this is stressful for you."

The urge to lash out made Angie dig her nails into her palms. Instead, as Benji rummaged through the selection for a popover, she grated out, "Thanks."

Cazzi gave her a thumbs up. "Here to talk if you need it."

Angie's eye twitched.

Benji offered her the popover with an amused expression and grabbed a muffin for themself, coming perilously close to her coffee cake.

Angie thanked them but pointed at the cake. "That's mine. No touch."

"California is a common property state," Martin said, from the front.

"So?" Angie said, through a mouthful of popover. It was delicious, dammit.

Benji frowned. "We're not married, yet."

Angie's heart leaped at the last word.

"*Yet*," Martin said ominously.

"Jealous!" Angie crowed.

"Who says I want to be married?" Martin shot back.

Angie didn't expect that to start a discussion on the merits, legal benefits, and issues with the institution of marriage but then again Cazzi was in the car and Benji had strong, rather fascinating opinions on the matter. Mainly, that it was a problematic institution but they weren't opposed to commitment.

Angie grinned at that. She wasn't sold on marriage either but the way they'd looked at her when they said "commitment" made her very happy.

The discussion carried on around them as Benji made extended and heat-inducing eye contact.

"Get a room!" Martin yelled. "Ugh, I hate new couples." But he smiled.

Cazzi said something about new relationships acting on the brain the same way hard drugs did and the conversation was off and running again.

It passed the time. Angie almost forgot they were getting closer and closer to seeing her mother for the first time in her adult life.

CHAPTER 36

The pick up spot by the prison was fucking bleak, all concrete and chainlink. Flat land as far as the eye could see, for an easy shot, Angie guessed.

Benji squeezed her knee as if they could hear the awful turn of her thoughts. She was probably broadcasting. She hummed along to the quiet music the driver was playing. She could barely hear it but it sounded like trip hop. The driver's name was Novia, as they'd found out when Cazzi asked, ten minutes into the trip, making the rest of them look like stuck up elites.

Novia got them there early and without incident so now Angie had time to kill. She wanted desperately to get out and stretch her legs but who knew if there was a BH asshole watching? She couldn't see everyone in the cars around them and she wasn't willing to risk it.

The prison doors opened. Angie went rigid. There had

been a couple false alarms, other parolees released to waiting cars or, depressingly, to a long walk to the bus stop.

But no—Angie would recognize that gait anywhere. The defiant grace and stiff carriage of a woman who looked like she wanted to hold her hands in fists but didn't because it wasn't what ladies did. She walked into the sun, wearing the clothes Angie had brought her to wear in court all those years ago. She'd never worn them because she'd taken the plea deal but somehow she'd kept them. The blue pantsuit was a bit too small for her and the shoes with their sensible heels looked painful but Mama still held her head high, sun glinting off her blonde hair. She wore a shade of lipstick that wasn't quite right for her now tanner, more weathered skin, but that she wore it felt like a good sign.

Before she could overthink it, Angie wrenched the door open and got out. She'd imagined saying something pithy, maybe a riff on that *Mean Girls* line, something like, "Get in bitch, we're getting you out of here."

Instead, she just stood there.

Mama's step faltered when she saw her.

Angie's heart was in her throat. Would she turn away? Was someone else waiting for her? Maybe she'd snared a man from inside using only the power of her penmanship and ability to play damsel-in-distress. Angie wouldn't put it past her, hell, she'd applaud.

Then Mama's steps sped up, far past propriety and the comfort level of those heels. She barely slowed herself in time to stop in front of Angie, inches from touching her.

"Angel," she breathed, her eyes shining. "You came."

"I read your letter," Angie blurted out.

"You did?" Mama covered her mouth.

Angie took a deep breath. "I-I don't know if I forgive you," she admitted, voice wavering. "I'm not sure I'm that big of a person but I need you to be safe and you need to come with me."

"I don't understand."

Angie gestured her into the open car. "Get in, and I'll explain everything."

Mama peered in. "Who are all these people?"

Angie scanned the waiting cars around them, the sun making the windshields near-impossible to see through. Was that an engine starting up?

"We're friends of Angelica's." Benji took off their seat belt to hold out a hand to Mama. "I'm Benji Nakamura."

Mama regarded them suspiciously but shook their hand out of politeness. "Susan Warner."

"Benji's my—" Mama's name gave her a delayed double take. She tore her eyes away from the cars. "You're using your maiden name again."

"Is that a problem?" Mama asked stiffly.

"Nope," Angie said, as a crunch of tires brought her attention back to the cars around them. Had anyone come out of the prison? She didn't think so. Then why was this beige car with the tinted windows pulling out?

"Good," Mama said. "Now back to what you were saying—"

"Get in the car!" Angie sank all her paranoia into the words. The car rolled towards them too slowly and there were too many shapes moving behind the tinted windows.

Mama jumped, scrambling into the car. Angie threw herself in after her and slammed the door shut. "Go!" She snarled.

Novia stayed calm, to her credit, but pulled them out of the lot with a squeal of tires, barreling past the beige sedan. It accelerated to catch up. Angie snarled, wanting to climb out of the car and pull some action movie bullshit that would land her on the other car and she could—

A hand landed on her knee. "Angelica," Benji said. "You're freaking Susan out."

Angie blinked, turning to look at her mother next to her.

Mama panted, gripping her seatbelt like a lifeline even though it wasn't buckled.

Taking a deep breath, Angie hummed to herself, buckling Mama's seatbelt. "Sorry. I'm trying to work on that." She smiled at her.

Mama's eyes snapped to her face. "Don't you pull that on me," she hissed.

You're just like your father.

Angie's smile dropped. "Fair enough."

"Looks like we lost them," Novia said, from the front.

"Nice work," Martin told her.

"I got the plate number," volunteered Cazzi.

"Don't know what we'll do with it but, great," Angie said.

"Displace your tension elsewhere," Cazzi replied. Then she turned to Mama. "Hi Susan, I'm Cazzi. I'm not a therapist but I have some background in psychology and counseling people who have been incarcerated. My fiancé and I do a lot of work with the Foundation in LA—"

"Which he founded with me," Angie interjected. "Back when we were together."

Mama's eyes widened in understanding then narrowed.

Uh-oh. Angie kept her evil grin on the inside but it was a close thing. Benji shot her a look from around Mama like they knew exactly what she was doing. But they didn't say anything.

"So you're the reason RK and my daughter broke up?" Mama asked sweetly.

Cazzi's face took on a pleasant blankness, like a creepy doll. Angie was impressed, she couldn't hit that level of uncanny valley without serious make-up. "I'm not the reason. It was a messy situation but more importantly, we all moved past it."

She paused, then delivered the clincher. "And Angie has apologized for all the trouble she caused."

That turned Mama's attention back to Angie. *Damn.* "What trouble?"

Angie huffed. "Not important. Don't you want to know why we were being followed by the world's most boring sedan?"

"Is it those…" Her mouth worked like she was working herself up to swearing. "Rhymes with 'witch' hunt men? The ones who took credit for the attack on you?"

"Wow, you have been keeping up on things," Martin said.

"The prison system provides tablets with limited, monitored internet access," Mama replied. She put out her hand. "Susan."

He shook it. "Martin."

"I know who you are." She smiled. "You're one of those Beatboyz. The one who left."

"Wow, Angie," Martin said. "I know where you got your meanness."

Mama's smile didn't budge. "Her father was worse." She wasn't wrong.

"What's that?" Angie said. "Could it be the elephant in the room?"

Benji stifled a laugh with their fist. Unfortunately, not well enough.

Mama turned her attention to them. "You, young m—"

"Benji uses they/them pronouns," Angie interrupted. "They're non-binary."

"Oh," Mama said, temporarily at a loss. She furrowed her brow but didn't bother to hastily smooth her forehead like she used to. "Well, whatever your gender, you're important to Angel. You're dating?"

"Yes." Benji glanced at Angie.

From behind Mama, Angie shrugged. This version of

Mama was different and the same all at once, it was hard to gauge her.

Mama studied them. "You're some kind of emo? Punk? Anarchist?"

"Something like that," Benji said, their body language going casual, non-threatening. "My mother knows a lot of people who have reintegrated after prison, if you need resources."

"How kind," Mama said, sounding deeply suspicious. She turned to Angie. "Where are we going?"

"Ro and I have a place in Santa Cruz," Cazzi piped up. "We thought it might be a good place for you to land while this blows over."

"How kind," Mama repeated, still sounding suspicious. "Where are you going to be?" She asked Angie.

Angie shrugged. She figured she'd go back to Sacramento but she hadn't actually planned that far ahead.

Mama tsked. "What do we say about planning? Those who plan ahead keep their heads."

"How about 'Thanks for not letting me get kidnapped by incels'?" Angie snapped, face getting hot. "How about 'good plan, surviving all those years'? Or even 'nice work, not getting stabbed on Saturday'?"

"That *was* nice work," muttered Martin.

Mama opened her mouth then stopped herself. She nodded and pressed her lips together, looking down at her hands. "You're right. I'm not one to talk about planning ahead."

"No shit," Angie said. "I mean, Lucy, the fucking irony."

"Lucy?" Mama asked.

"Lucifer."

"Oh." She visibly swallowed her thoughts on that. "Yes, very ironic." She moved fast, grabbing Angie's hands like she might pull away. Angie clamped down on the reflex to jerk back. It was unreal, feeling her mother's cool, slightly clammy fingers around hers. There were calluses she didn't remember, brushing against Angie's calluses that definitely weren't there the last time Mama held her hands. "Angel," Mama said. "I am so sorry. You shouldn't have had to see that—"

Their fingers stuck together like, like—

"Pull over," Benji yelled. "Now!"

"It's okay, I can suppress it," Angie said, breathing as deep as she could.

"The only way out is through," Cazzi intoned.

Angie glared at her.

"Find a rest stop," Benji told Novia. "Please. I think we all need some air."

Ten minutes later, Angie stood behind a cinder block bathroom, hair hidden under a beanie and face buried in Benji's chest. "Do I have to do it?" She asked into their shirt.

They smoothed a hand down her back. "You don't have to do anything you don't want to."

"How diplomatic."

They chuckled. "You want the truth?"

"I can't handle the truth—or that movie, I've never seen it."

"Me either."

"That's why I love you, your taste in movies. And that you're honest even when I don't want to hear it." She almost hoped they hadn't noticed the truth she'd slipped in there.

Unfortunately, and against the odds, they still had pretty decent hearing for a former touring musician. "Oh you love me, do you?" Amusement curled through their words.

She looked up, heart in her throat. Their expression was

neutral except for the slight curl of their lips. "Yeah, I love you or whatever. Whatcha gonna do about it?"

"Call your bluff." They kissed her. "And love you back, or whatever."

She melted into them, the kiss making her forget even the smell of the rest stop bathroom besides the two of them. She was airy, full of light and giddiness. She was loved by the most delightfully headstrong, lovely, caring person she knew. Her obsession loved her back and she felt whole.

Reality chose that moment to come crashing back.

"Can we hurry this up?" Martin demanded, rounding the bathroom and crossing his arms. "This place doesn't even have a vending machine."

"Have a muffin," Cazzi said, thrusting one at him from the basket in her hands. "And let them have their moment, it's cute."

Angie gave them both the finger.

Benji sighed.

Cazzi held out the coffee cake to her. "Might be good to have a snack before you talk with your mom."

"Yeah, okay." Angie snatched the cake and the basket out of her hands.

Benji smoothed their hands over her shoulders. "I'll be here if you need me. Yell or wave or something."

"I'll be fine."

"But if you're not—"

"You'll be the first person I call. Stay back, okay? I don't want you having to deal with my projecting."

They smiled. "I'll be fine."

"Stubborn ass," she said fondly.

"Takes one to know one."

"The longer we stay here, the more likely we are to be found," Cazzi interjected.

"Yeah, stop stalling," Martin said.

"Fuck, fine." Angie stalked over to where Mama was staring at the flat vista of freeways around the stop and thrust the basket at her. "Want some?"

Mama turned, wiping her eyes before looking at the basket. She picked up the other small loaf of coffee cake. Angie shouldn't be surprised. Mama used to make coffee cake all the time when she was growing up, but Angie had forgotten that's why she loved it. Now, the memory of watching Mama bake hit her like one of the cars rushing on the freeway.

They munched on the cakes in silence. Angie tried to focus on the soft cinnamony goodness but it was hard to focus when Mama, the voice in her head for the last twelve years, stood next to her in the weirdly normal flesh. Not berating or commanding or insinuating, just tired-looking and watching all the cars going by with the fascination of someone who hadn't seen this much sky in nearly fifteen years.

Your fault. The voice didn't sound like Mama's so much as it sounded like a distortion of her own.

Cool. Great.

Mama finished her cake and carefully brushed her fingers off. Then she looked at Angie. "I'm sorry. I should've let him leave. I just—" She swallowed.

Just getting into this, awesome. Love it. Angie tightened her grip on the basket in her hands, bracing herself.

"I just suffered so much for that man and he was going to leave for a younger version, a younger victim. I thought if I had him, he was contained." Mama laughed harshly, the sound rusty.

"I was arrogant. He was never contained. He did what he wanted and when he got bored with us, I couldn't take it. I wish I could say I was saving the world from him but really I wasn't thinking. I was angry. I'd been pushing down years worth of anger, trampling my self-worth to fulfill someone else's vision of safety and I realized we were never safe. We were dependent on the least reliable man in town. I was the one who'd gotten us there. If I'd thought for a second, I'd have cleaned out the accounts and gotten us out of there. If I'd have thought—"

She reached out towards Angie's cheek but didn't complete the gesture. "I missed so much. I failed you so badly. Oh Angel." Mama choked down a sob.

Angie's eyes were already full, making Mama a watery image. She blinked them clear, letting the tears fall. "You did. You really did." She let the sob tear through her throat. She'd imagined having this conversation so many times and it rarely went this well. "But I've fucked up too. So many times. I shouldn't have come to visit, I shouldn't have given them the evidence to convict you, I shouldn't have freaked out when I saw—"

"No, no, Angel, no." Mama grabbed Angie's arms. "Sweetheart, no. You were a child—"

"I was sixteen—"

"A child," Mama said firmly despite the tears in her eyes. "Prison's not something I'd wish on anyone but it gave me time to think. I found people who helped me learn. Who helped me realize all the harm I did and was dealt. Angel, we warped you so bad. We gave you no tools but paranoia, manipulation, and violence. It was all we had to give but that doesn't make it right."

"I'm trying so hard to unlearn all that shit," Angie said. She was ugly crying now, tears and snot thickening her voice and sticking to her cheeks. "I would've killed that kid on Saturday, the one who attacked me. He cut Benji and I wanted him dead." She shook her head, wiping her face with the back of her hand. *Ugh, sticky.* "I'm not broken up about it either. Not wracked with guilt."

"Because you didn't do it," Mama said. "You stopped yourself."

Angie shook her head. "They stopped me. Benji did. Am I some kind of sociopath or something?"

Mama shook her head. "I've met plenty of sociopaths. Your father included. You always cared for people far more than he did. Angel, look at all these people who came with you to pick me up." She gestured at the group bickering by the car. "They don't like each other, heck, they don't all like you, but they came."

"The way I am, like Daddy—"

"I don't know if you remember, but Daddy never kept people. He didn't have friends for long or jobs. Heck, his family didn't even really like him."

"I thought that was cuz they thought he married down."

Mama shrugged, unfazed when she'd once screamed at Angie for asking what that meant twenty years ago. "That was the last straw. Even the girls who fawned over him had started whispering by the time we started dating. I should've known." She shook her head.

"All for a bit of respectability and what did that get us?" She chuckled drily. "Not that I have to lecture you on respectability. I'm getting distracted. Angel." She squeezed Angie's biceps. "I don't know if it helps but I don't feel bad about ending your father's life. What I feel bad about is the harm it caused you. You are what's important to me and I'll do whatever it takes to build some sort of relationship with you. I don't care who you worship or how close you came to murder. If anyone understands, it's me."

Angie considered this, letting the silence stretch between them. Did she want Mama in her life? What would happen if she turned out to be blowing smoke up her ass, telling Angie everything she wanted to hear?

Then she'd survive. She'd done it before. But now…

She looked back at Benji, watching them as they leaned against the bathroom building, ready to help if she needed it.

Martin stood by the car, telling a story with his whole body, charisma oozing off of him, Cazzi and Novia watching entranced.

Well, now, she wasn't alone.

She looked at her Mama, older, tireder, not quite softer but maybe kinder. Watching Angie with hope in her eyes.

Angie took a deep breath and decided to try trusting.

CURSE VIDEO #1—ANGELA ALICE
INTERIOR: Small room with dark curtains hiding the walls and an altar covered in lit candles. The camera is pointing down at ANGELA ALICE and her SIRENS, dressed in hooded white robes. ANGELA raises her eyes to the camera, she wears white contacts.
ANGELA: I have been hunted
SIRENS: [together] Hunted.
ANGELA: By those in fear.
SIRENS: Fear.
ANGELA: I have been merciful.
SIRENS: Merciful.
ANGELA: But no longer.
The Sirens smile.
ANGELA: I curse you with compassion.
SIRENS: Compassion.
ANGELA: With empathy.
SIRENS: Empathy.
ANGELA: With all the things you're scared to feel.
SIRENS: [singing] Feeeeel.
ANGELA: [sings] Your leaders are broken
Your compasses are spinning
You're lost
SIRENS: Lost.
ANGELA: [reaches to the camera] When your luck runs out
When nothing goes right

When you can't remember the fight
Remember me
SIRENS: Remember
ANGELA: You've dug your hole
Now crawl on out
The deeper you dig
The closer to me
Hunt me and I curse you
SIRENS: Curse.
Burn your list
Burn your manifesto
Burn your leaders
SIRENS: Burn, burn, burn.
Let them take your money
Let them take the fall
Your power is not theirs to take
SIRENS: Take, take, take.
ANGELA: I curse you
SIRENS: Curse, curse, curse.
ANGELA: I curse you
SIRENS: Curse, curse, curse.
ANGELA: You will never be free.
SIRENS: Free, free, free.
ANGELA: Until you let go—
[Cut to black]

COMMENTS

Murderbb4eva: Holy shiiiit!! Did you see the news? That asshole who tried to stab her narced on his whole org. Curses work y'all 😈

Omegaluvr92: I heard they were selling essential oils for men and laundering the money

Murderbb4eva: They also sold Manergy energy drinks and

a "wellness" box with "expert-chosen" ingredients like "all natural" horny goat pills and an ED paste someone said was just ginger and lotion

Omegaluvr92: Manergy was them?? My brother loves that shit

Emoisthenewblack: Ginger?? Down there? No thank you

UFObb: the whole thing was a multilevel marketing hate group? lol only on the internet

Omegaluvr92: yeah they're being charged with embezzlement, fraud, intimidation, harassment, stalking, and more. Got their assets frozen & leaders arrested (the ones they could find)

UFObb: looks like those pills were making dudes sick too

Emoisthenewblack: Serves them right for going after Benji Omega. Angela Alice let him off light.

Omegaluvr92: The videos of her running after that guy after he hurt Benji though? Relationship goals 💀

Murderbb4eva: I'm Benji + Angie stan

EPILOGUE

1 YEAR LATER...

DOUBLE TROUBLE: RAZOR BITCHES BACK ON THE ROAD
OG punk forces of nature Razor Bitches are back on tour for the first time in almost twenty years. Recently signed with indie label Now or Never Records, the ladies put out their new album Don't Misunderestimate the Menopausal Bitch *to critical acclaim and now are touring the states. Supporting them is Ladies Don't, made up of the members of Angela Alice's former backing band, the Sirens of Scream.*
Ladies Don't is also signed with Now or Never and are making waves with a succession of hit singles. The band, led by guitarist and singer Gemma Cole, is reminiscent of Against Me! *and* American Idiot *era Green Day. They're heavily promoted by Alice herself, in between her infamous series of curse videos aimed at the now tattered hate group Bitch Hunt. And yes, that's the LD girls in the robes behind Alice in those eerie videos.*
But enough about Alice, we all know better than to be on her bad side. Especially with Benji Omega glowering besides her. (Can we say that was the end of their social media feud we were all secretly hoping for? Because it was. Their duet "Four on the Floor" is our #1 emo nostalgia song.)

Back to the Razor Bitches, if you haven't heard of them, remedy that now. They're our pick for best comeback act of 2023 and the hottest tour of 2024. Between them and Ladies Don't, it's going to be a hard rocking show.
—Tour Tracker Blog

Benji adjusted the corset they'd custom made themself and yelled up the stairs, "We're going to be late!"

"Fashionably late!" Angelica yelled back from the bedroom they now shared.

"It's a sold out show, they're not reserving seats for us," Benji reminded her.

"I told you we should've pulled the celebrity card."

Benji shook thier head though she couldn't see them. "And I told you if you want to be successfully washed up you have to stop playing that card."

"Whatever," she said, strutting out to stand on the landing. "What do you think?" She winked and stuck out her tongue, dressed as Eddy from the *Rocky Horror Picture Show* in a vest and head wound.

"Eddy!" Benji shrieked in their best impression of Columbia, trying to match their outfit.

Angelica pretended to ride a motorcycle down the stairs, crashing into them and catching them about the waist to bend them back in a kiss. Benji tangled their arms around her neck and fell into the kiss with abandon.

When the two of them came up for air, she was wearing more of their lipstick than they were but that could be fixed in the car. Benji herded her to the garage and handed over a make-up wipe as she yelled, "Bye House!"

The house creaked as if in acknowledgement. Benji still wasn't convinced there were ghosts but at very least, the spirit of the house had taken to Angelica.

In the passenger seat of their car, she fixed their face and hers as the garage door rolled up.

They made it to the Colonial Theater less than ten minutes early and stood out in the October cold at the back of the line —halfway around the block. Being out and about in Sacramento still sometimes raised the hairs on the back of Benji's neck, like Sly might jump out at them, but so far they hadn't seen him since MetalQuake. If—when they ran into him again, well, it'd be awkward and they'd be anxious but maybe that would be the end of it.

"I haven't been in a line this long in a decade," Angelica grumbled, jerking their attention back to the present.

"You can't say I don't give you new experiences," Benji said.

She laughed. "No, I definitely can't."

Though it'd been touch and go for a while, she seemed to be settling into a slower lifestyle, making music on her own time, supporting the launch of the Siren's new band, working to create a chapter of the Foundation up in Sac, moving in with Benji, renovating the house together, boosting the Razor Bitch's comeback, overseeing the Bodily Autonomy Fund, cursing the Bitch Hunt and helping along their fragmentation, doing the occasional concert or event… yeah, slow was a relative term. Especially when it came to her relationship with her mother, which was rocky, the two of them still figuring out boundaries and how to talk to each other.

Benji had pulled back on their NoN responsibilities a bit, letting Rohan handle the Razor Bitches while they managed Ladies Don't, but still had their hands full helping Leo get a hold on his alcohol use and finishing up renovations. And with Angelica. She wasn't an easy partner, headstrong and dramatic but, she was worth it.

They smiled at her in that gooey way they caught themselves doing from time to time.

"Stop it," she said, catching them. "People will think you like me."

"So?"

She smiled. "Then I'll think you like me and that lipstick you reapplied won't stand a chance."

"Fuck the lipstick," they said, just to see if they could goad her into kissing them again.

"Later," she whispered in their ear.

They shivered.

L eo lay on the hammock strung across his balcony and contemplated the starry Halloween sky. Samhain, if you were pagan. Idly, he enumerated both names and pondered the significance.

It was all procrastination.

An offer burned a hole in the phone he'd tossed on the bed and left for the hammock. His agent called it "a huge opportunity" and his accounting software called it "the only way you're going to dig your way out drunkenly buying a gay bar, you twat." Yes, his software was British. It made his debt sound fancier.

But were his mind, hell his body, and his fledgling sobriety ready to go back on reality TV?

It'd be great material for your memoir, his agent had said. The thing she didn't say was if he took the gig he could probably wrangle an extension on the deadline that was looming over his blank word document.

But, reality TV had wrecked him last time. He'd barely left that drag show with his sanity and he'd left literal wreckage in his wake. They'd been right to kick him off.

Did he really want to go back to the manipulation, the backbiting, the constant drinking? And did he want to do it while trapped on an island with people who were just trying to fake a romance long enough to win a cash prize?

Damn, that did sound like juicy memoir material though. And the money was good. Even if he didn't win, it would keep him out of the red for a few months. Might be enough for him to come up with a miracle or two. And it wasn't as if he was in danger of losing his heart. He wasn't *naive*. Not anymore. Getting your heart broken on a grand scale had some advantages.

And if he did find someone? Well, then Leo could finally get the hell over *him*.

Plus, with the frequency he kept running into Martin, being on an island might just be the break Leo needed.

Fuck it. What could go wrong?

Loved No Love in LA? Leaving a review helps others who might also love it find it (and helps us indie authors keep writing). Thank you!

Katta

READY FOR BOOK 4?

Once upon a time there was a hugely successful boy band. All the singers were very straight, even bad boy Leo and heartthrob Martin. Even when they were secretly dating. Even when that secret broke them up and took the band with it.

Now the fairytale is over. Leo's a drag queen with a queer bar about to go under. Martin's a bi pop idol whose star is fading. Their relationship, such as it is, has never been worse. Too bad they're stuck on an island filming a reality dating show and the storm clouds are rolling in.

No Love is an Island coming 2026!

Acknowledgments

Oh wow, how wild to be here again, writing my thank yous a third time. Firstly, thank you, dear reader, for taking a chance on my most batshit book to date. Angie and Benji drove the boat on this one and while I love how it came out, I know they're not everyone's cup of tea. The two of them are all my sharp edges transfigured until they stood on their own (and then ran away with the book).

Anyways, on to the good stuff: the wonderful people who supported me and this book in its making. Everyone who loved and told me they loved the first two books in the series: you make my day every time and add an extra sparkle to my writing. Special thanks to my family, my uncles who read and tell people about my books, my parents who are excited about every release (my mom who loves them and my dad who bought me a bunch of Satanic research material for this one).

Next, thank you so so much to my amazing beta readers including ShanShan Guo, L Yeh, Shana, and C.A. Vargas. My deep appreciation to Noah Saint Jenkins, my sensitivity reader for Japanese-American and nonbinary representation. This book is a million times better thanks to everyone's suggestions, especially those who pointed out things outside my experience.

I did a lot of research to make sure I did my best to portray the characters outside my experience of being a cis white woman but please note no one character is meant to represent the whole range of experiences for any one group. All mistakes are mine and mine alone. To learn more about people like my characters, please read and consume media by creators in those identity groups.

For supporting my books, joining me in my Satanic research rabbit hole briefly to read a truly wild Anton LeVey title and recommending a better text (Magic at the Crossroads by Kate Freuler), Victoria Raschke and the Witchlit podcast has my undying devotion. Special shoutout for introducing us to Markus K. Ironwood aka Swamp Witch Stephanie, my favorite drag queen, who coined the name Steph Infection and allowed me to borrow it. It's about to get a lot more use ;]

My author discords keep me learning and growing my community. As always, my writing group To Be Named is the best cheering squad and support team a girl could ask for. I'm deeply lucky to have found you all.

And my darling enby, the chaos to my order and order to my chaos. You are my sanity check, you loved me at the height of my bitchdom (high school), and you love me still as the years mellowed me out (somewhat). All my iterations love all of yours.

ABOUT THE AUTHOR

Katta Kis' first job was playing a vampire baby in a student film, sealing her fate as a goth child for life. After a variety pack of jobs and apartments, she is currently settled in Northern California. She cohabitates with her two adorable demon babies masquerading as cats and her high school romance which never ended. When not writing, she can usually be found reading or at a concert.

Keep up with her through her newsletter!

ALSO BY KATTA KIS

Love in the Liner Notes

Book 1 of the Pagans & Pop Stars series

Two ex-boy band heartthrobs.

A witchy sex educator.

The love triangle no one expected.

Cazzi has been in love with her childhood best friend Patrick since, well, forever. He's the only one who gets her paganism, her passion for sex education, and knows what happened on the worst night of her life. But when she kissed him, it ruined their friendship. Now Patrick is back in her life—until his old bandmate throws a wrench in their relationship.

Rohan is an ex-boy band heartthrob on his last bid for a comeback career. But this is jeopardized when Cazzi inspires him to leave his tempestuous girlfriend, causing a rift between Cazzi and Patrick in the process.

Between the emotional fallout and work drama, Cazzi is duct-taping her mental health together with ritual, marijuana, and the brownies Rohan bakes for her. As Cazzi and Rohan grow unexpectedly close can their relationship survive when the machinations of his ex threaten to expose her biggest secret?

Out now!

Love at the Rock Show

A burnt-out former pop star